Yesterday's magic. Tomorrow's science.
In the ultimate battle, one must prevail. . . .

MINDSPELL

"A critique of those who, not satisfied with the Mystery of life, have to create special mysteries of their own—and work havoc on themselves and others through their lust for the extraordinary."

Andrew M. Greeley
Author of *Ascent into Hell*

"A FASCINATING AND UNUSUAL NOVEL."

Pittsburgh Press

"Both a suspenseful mystery and an unforgettable romance, as up-to-date as the latest headlines about genetic engineering, as classic as any Gothic tale of witchcraft . . . a compulsive page-turner, impossible to put down."

Indianapolis News

"Casts a spell over your mind which won't easily be forgotten . . . If you've an appetite for eerie entertainment! *Mindspell* offers a fascinating and frightening feast of fear."

Robert Bloch
Author of *Psycho*

MINDSPELL

Kay Nolte Smith

BALLANTINE BOOKS • NEW YORK

Library of Congress Catalog Card Number: 83-61050

ISBN 0-345-31766-1

This edition published by arrangement with William Morrow and Company

Manufactured in the United States of America

First Ballantine Books Edition: September 1984

TO THE MEMORY OF ALL THOSE WHO MET
"KELLA HAGAWARD'S" FATE

PROLOGUE

By the end few could remember any longer, but in fact she had once been beautiful.

Her hair, when they cut if off, fell to the dirt floor of the cell like lengths of blue-black silk. When they shaved her head, her skull was smooth and perfectly shaped, the skin gleaming as white as fresh milk. And when they took the pin and went over her body inch by inch, seeking the place where the Devil had left his mark, the moons of her breasts were high, white, and firm, even though she was known to be eight-and-thirty.

Some of the townsfolk thought Kella Hagaward might have made her pact with Satan for her beauty, but others believed she had done it to acquire her skill with herbs.

In either case the parish in southwestern Scotland had long suspected her of some kind of strangeness, if not sorcery, for she stayed too aloof from her fellow Christians. After her husband died she was invited to go live with his brother, Thomas Hagaward, who held the tenancy of a large farm, yet she stayed on alone in her cottage by the edge of the wood. True, she needed to be near the forest to gather herbs and other plants for her midwifing, but she was often away from her cottage all night. When she was not, anyone who ventured that far could hear her singing to herself in her strange, smoky voice or playing on her reed flute, while on her hearth stretched a large black cat that went everywhere with her and whose company she seemed to prefer over that of any man, woman, or child.

Still, no one in the village had been prepared for what happened. One spring day in 1643, at the midday meal, Thomas Hagaward's eldest daughter began to choke on her food until her face mottled with purple and her neck swelled. Then her body grew as hard as wood and bent like a bow so that no one could hold her down, not even her father. As he and his wife

1

watched helplessly, one part of the girl's body after another—a leg, an arm, another leg—began to shake as if with the palsy. Finally she fell into a trance lasting well over an hour. When she woke she could not move her left arm or leg. The strange fits came on her for three days following and always left her entire left side numb even when one of her sisters pinched the flesh of her arm so hard it later turned blue.

On the fourth day Kella Hagaward came to the door, offering to try to help the child, who was, after all, her dead husband's niece. She brought a special mixture of herbs wrapped in a piece of black silk. But after taking only three sips of the infusion, the girl began to choke worse than before. She vomited up a muddy stream and then cried out to her mother in a hoarse voice, "Take her away! 'Tis Aunt Kella that has made me sick in this fashion—she has put a spell upon me!"

At first her mother gave no credence to this charge, thinking it a child's foolishness. And Kella herself swore there had been nothing in the mixture but buckbean, nettles, and ribwort, although the proportion of each to the other she would not tell. But within a month the girl's two younger sisters also were stricken. Unable for hours at a time to walk or even to sit up, they would sometimes vomit up ungodly and amazing things—flocks of hair and many stones and once a great ball of hair in which were found pins and needles.

By fall the milk of four of the Hagawards' cows had turned thin and scarce. Although the family used the accepted cure for bewitched cattle—a sprig of rowan berries from the ash tree was nailed to the door of the byre—the cows died.

Soon thereafter the miller's son was taken with a great redness and paralysis in his right arm—with which he had been pitching stones at her black cat. And one of the deacons of the church, in great distress, confessed that after he passed Kella on the road one day, his sexual member would no longer function when he lay with his wife. The parson, who was learned in those matters, said the power had been given to witches many times to render the male organ powerless or even to steal it.

The parson finally went to Kella to exhort her to confess, but in the midst of his most earnest pleas he suddenly pitched forward, clutching at his throat. By nightfall he was dead.

Yet she denied all subsequent accusations, swearing she had

2

neither murdered the parson by sorcery nor bewitched anyone, including her nieces.

In the first week of her trial a Pricker was brought from Edinburg with his special case of brass pins. While Kella Hagaward stood blindfolded before the court he rubbed the palms of his long, thin hands over her naked body and then slipped his three-inch pins into her flesh, one after the other, causing threads of blood to unravel all along her skin. Finally, on her left breast, almost in her armpit, he found the mark: a tiny dark thing shaped like a spider, where the pin went in up to its head without making Kella moan or even flinch. When the Pricker told her to find the pin and take it out, her hands crawled blindly over her skin but she couldn't find where it lay.

No further proof was needed. Those who served Satan always bore his mark, in the shape of a spider or a toad or a bat, which was insensible of pain and would never bleed. Four times the Pricker pushed the pin into the spidery mark, but no blood came from it.

When Kella still would not confess that she belonged to Satan, the magistrates decided to send for the Witchfinder-General of Scotland.

He was a man as white and soft as rising dough but with a holy fire inside him. He put the magistrates to shame with his zeal, for he could question Kella for more than a day and a night without stopping, while his eyes burned as bright and hot as new coals.

It was his zeal that persuaded Thomas Hagaward's eldest daughter to confess, with much weeping, that she and her two sisters had followed their aunt into the woods one night. There they had seen her taking part in a witches' Sabbat, paying homage to Satan in ways too horrible to tell.

In the fourth week of the trial, when there were gray pits of exhaustion under Kella's dark eyes and she had responded to no question for several days, she astounded everyone by raising her voice in a strange song that no one understood and crying out that yes, she had made a pact with Satan.

Yes, she said, her voice hoarse, she had gone to many Sabbats in the woods. Yes, she had joined in the dances and had sung for the services. Yes, she had feasted of the Devil's food—beef and bacon and roasted mutton, and all without salt—for salt is the sign of eternity.

3

"Did you pay homage to Satan?" the Witchfinder-General asked. "Did you prostrate yourself and genuflect before him, in horrible mockery of the ceremonies of our church?"

"Yes, I did."

"And did you give Satan the kiss of infamy?"

"Yes," she answered, "I did kiss his fundament." She started to collapse but the Witchfinder-General pressed on, holding her up and never letting go of her body or his questions, until she said that yes, yes, she had had carnal knowledge of Satan, whose penis was immense and scaly and caused indescribable pain as well as pleasure, and whose semen was like ice.

Then Kella fell down as if no bones or blood were left within her, and never made another sound until she was in the square with all the townsfolk looking on as the fire was lit.

Then she raised her head, and her eyes, which had been like two dead birds, fluttered alive and aimed at the carriage where her nieces watched with their parents. To the astonishment of all, Kella laughed suddenly—a sound that was ugly and black. She shouted to the family, "You called me witch so take you my curse! In your family let there always be one who is just like me—among your children and your children's children and down to the end of time! In Satan's name I say this curse—always a Hagaward who is just like me!"

The Witchfinder-General decreed that because of Kella's final blasphemy she would not receive the mercy of strangulation before going into the fire.

When she finally did expire, some in the crowd swore that a huge bat escaped from her body and went shrieking up in the smoke. Others declared it to be her cat, who never was seen again.

I

INNER DEMONS

1

The rolling blue-green hills were visible through the window only in brief snatches when a gust blew aside the dark veils of rain.

The room was lit by two sources: white-hot flashes of lightning and a small candle on the table beside the woman's head. The candle flame was erased each time lightning struck. But it returned to cast a twin reflection in the eyes of the minister who sat beside the woman with an expression that slid between pity and fear.

"Can you tell me where you live?" he asked softly.

The woman did not open her eyes. "By the wood," she said. "My house . . . at the edge of the wood."

"Is your house near a town?"

There was a long pause, while tag ends of thunder played out in the distance. Finally she said, "Two days out from Dumfries, it is."

"And you live all alone?"

"Aye. Nay." The woman laughed, a harsh disembodied sound from a face that was otherwise as still as a death mask. "Have the cat."

"What's the cat's name?"

She laughed again. "Has many names. Makes me good company."

"You aren't married, then?"

"Was married. He died."

"And you had no children?"

Lightning leaped onto the woman's face, but her eyes remained closed. "Nae bairns that lived," she said. A look of pain rolled across her face.

The minister shook his head. He wanted to touch the woman's hand and comfort her, but he didn't dare. He glanced out the window, where the rain hissed like something cold and angry, and then back to the woman. "Tell me what year it is."

"Year of our Lord. Sixteen hundred and forty-three."

The minister leaned forward. "And this place you come from, is it—"

"Fire," the woman said. "I come from fire . . . All my body . . ." Her face convulsed, and the motion ran the length of her frame. "Eating me . . . fire eating me . . ." She began to make a highpitched, panting sound that reminded the minister of the way his wife had sounded in childbirth—or might have sounded if she had hated her child.

He shivered, astounded at his own thought. "Forget the fire," he said. "Can't you—"

"Nay, Nay! Never! They prick me, they put the turkas on me, they want me to burn because I love the Master!" Her voice went on, but thunder gave a loud whipcrack and then a massive rolling of hooves, so the minister couldn't hear what she said. He watched her lips move, and it didn't seem to him that they were shaping English sounds.

"Don't think of the fire!" he cried, over the noise from her and from the heavens. "The fire isn't going to hurt you now. Don't think of it!" Gradually, as the thunder subsided, so did her voice. "Put the fire away from you," he said quietly. "Will you? Can you put it away for a while?"

The woman twisted to one side. Then she sighed deeply and put her crossed hands on her chest.

"Tell me about when you were married," he said. "About the man you—"

"A mickle man. Black and cold."

The minister's eyebrows went up. "Your husband?"

"Nay. Nay. The Master. The Master! A mickle man. Cold. Gae cold."

The minister felt the word on the back of his neck. "Tell me about your *husband*. He's the one I'd like to hear about now."

"Him," the woman said, almost spitting out the word. "Gave me nae bairns. Only his family. His family!" Her lips pulled wide and expelled a sound that was neither a grunt nor a laugh. "Unhunhunhunh. Curse family!"

"Please," the minister said, "please, Polly, don't—"

"Not Polly!" the woman cried.

"All right. Everything's all right. Now, I want you to—"

8

"Did he do it? Did Master give us power, down to your time? Tell me. Tell me. Who has the power in your time?"

"Don't worry," the minister soothed. "Don't think about it. I want you just to rest and relax. Rest and relax. Let your mind become empty, quite empty. Let yourself come back to the present, to this place and time, slowly and comfortably. Relax, Polly, and be comfortable. In a few minutes you'll wake up, and you'll feel good. You'll feel fine and comfortable. I'll count to seven, and then you'll wake up and be fine."

At the count of seven the woman opened her eyes. She looked out the window, yawned, and said, "It rains every time, don't it, Reverend? Wonder if the creek's flooding yet. Because if it is, that old truck of ours ain't gonna get me home."

"Yes, you'd better go right away," the minister said. He turned off the tape recorder on the small table beside her.

She stood up—a tall, rawboned farm woman whose looks had rushed into middle age well before their time; the calendar was only now catching up with them. She pushed big hands into the pockets of her housedress and said, "It happened again, didn't it?"

"Yes, Polly, it did."

Her blue eyes were earnest in her wide, rather flat face. "What does it mean, Reverend? Why does this awful woman keep coming? What does she want with me?"

"I don't know, Polly. I wish I did. Perhaps we shouldn't go on with it."

The woman took a breath that crushed her breasts against the tiny flowers on her dress. "I feel like I got to go on, Reverend. If I don't let this woman out I'll be . . ." She frowned. "I don't know what I'll be."

"I'll tell you what you *are*," he said. "You're a good woman, Polly Whiting. So you just get on home now and don't think about all this. Go fix Bill his supper."

"He'll be hollering for it, all right." She grinned without mirth, picked an old cardigan from the arm of a chair, and went to the door. "I bless you every day of my life," she said. She opened the door, raised the cardigan over her head, and ran out into the deluge.

* * *

9

The Reverend Walter Bailey watched her go, thinking that nothing about the way she looked, talked, acted, or lived could account for what had been happening lately.

When he had come to the parish twenty years earlier, Polly was already part of the flock: the girl Bill Whiting had met and married somewhere up in Pennsylvania and brought back to his farm. Polly had always been one of the most devout. She even kept Bill from switching to tobacco farming, for the church was opposed to smoking as well as to drink. She had never missed a Sunday service except when her children were born, and had come to most of the night meetings, even when her ceaseless chores put owllike rings of weariness around her eyes.

As lightning flashed, the minister saw her yank open the door of the pickup truck and lurch up into the seat. The rain drummed so hard he couldn't hear the noise of the engine, but it must have caught, for she pulled out of the yard, the single red eye of a taillight glaring through the rain. The Whitings had driven the battered vehicle as long as Bailey could remember. None of his parish had much money, and Bill Whiting had less than most. No matter how hard he worked, the farm sucked in his energy and gave little back.

The candle the minister had used to hypnotize Polly was still burning. He blew it out and then licked two fingers and stopped the wick from smoking. There was a split second of pain. He thought of that pain multiplied a thousand times. Still, if the person had had commerce with Satan . . . He sat heavily on the couch where Polly had lain.

He had begun hypnotizing her simply to get rid of the headaches that had started to plague her. Hypnosis had attracted him when he saw a pastor in Louisville use it help a compulsive overeater. At first he had been leery, but as he trained for it, he learned it was a wonderful, though incompletely understood, tool for helping people. Some of his parishioners, he knew, objected to his practicing hypnotherapy—and not just the poorest and least-educated of them—but his calling was to help people, and he was not about to let anyone prevent him, provided the Bible didn't forbid the method. And it didn't.

The first session with Polly cured a headache, nothing more. She had come into the den cautiously, a little nervously, her face thick with pain but disciplined by the pull of the bun of her hair. Bailey soon saw that she was a fine subject, for her lids

10

started to sag the moment he told her to stare into the candle flame. Later, when he brought her out of it, she touched her eyes gingerly, then wonderingly, and for a moment pleasure commandeered her weathered face.

But on her third visit, just as he was about to bring her out, her voice changed, the twang replaced by a Scottish burr and the words sending invisible ants along the minister's spine.

Now she had spoken in that strange voice a total of six times. The third time the voice had given its name. The fourth time Bailey had been prepared with a tape recorder and had played the session back to Polly, whose face worked in disbelief and whose hands crept up to cover her ears. By the fifth time the Reverend found himself confronting two possibilities: Either Polly had somehow become a vehicle for a seventeenth-century Scottish witch, or she was playing some kind of trick on him. But neither possibility was possible.

If it was a trick, then Walter Bailey could no longer trust his judgment of any human being. Besides, Polly had lived her entire life in Pennsylvania and West Virginia. She had dropped out of school at fourteen—how could she know Scots words like *mickle* and *bairn* and speak in a burr that Bailey knew to be authentic? And how could she speak of Satan as her master— she who would do anything for the Lord and the Church of the Shepherd?

But if her behavior was not a hoax . . .

Bailey did not believe in reincarnation. He did believe in age regression under hypnosis and had even induced it several times, but the idea of someone's regressing into another life was not, as he understood things, possible. Or right.

He put his head in his hands. Many times he felt inadequate to his calling, aware that his shoulders were as thin as his hair.

He had followed his father into the Church of the Shepherd, a small sect scattered throughout the southeastern United States. Doubts and questions had never plagued him. Although he had an inquisitive nature, it rested on a bedrock of religious conviction. If the answer to his present questions was that Satan had invaded Polly Whiting's spirit and was using her to some hellish end, he knew he was neither wise enough nor strong enough to see it, let alone to fight it.

He crossed the room to his cluttered desk and finally located the name he wanted—a professor who headed a department of psychiatry and was also part of a department of parapsychology. As he reached for the telephone, the wind rose again outside his window, and the rain hissed with cold tongues.

The professor looked over his glasses at a reporter from a local paper.

In the donnish manner he had once been able to restrict to his classroom, he said, "There are only two people who can be *certain* whether or not there is a hoax going on—the Whiting woman herself and the Reverend Walter Bailey. The fact that people who know them swear that neither is capable of such a hoax is not, of course, proof that they are not perpetrating one. We deal here in probabilities only."

The reporter said, "Couldn't she have picked up the Scottish accent from TV?"

The professor nodded. "It certainly is true that there are models to emulate on the television and movie screens. And in real life, for that matter. As it happens, Bailey is of Scottish descent himself, and although he has no accent, it's quite possible that over the years he has used some or all of the Scottish words we now hear from the woman. However, we have to consider this fact: In a conscious state the woman seems quite unable to reproduce any other kind of accent, though she was willing to try. One of our linguists worked with her at some length, but the results were, at best, like bad amateur acting—nothing like the authentic Scottish sound she produces under hypnosis. So we have to consider that this case may in fact be a type or subcategory of responsive xenoglossy—that is, the ability to speak a foreign language without having learned it in any normal way."

"Is there anything to validate the content of what she says—the witch business?"

The professor smiled. "Ah. That part is the most interesting. According to one of my historian colleagues, witches were treated much more harshly in Scotland than in England, perhaps because King James, that very credulous man, unleashed a great wave of witch persecutions late in the sixteenth century. Over four thousand people died, tortured in the most revolting ways, and a number were burned at the stake. So in that regard the Whiting woman's 'voice' is accurate, although she almost certainly wouldn't know such relatively esoteric points."

"Why not?"

"Because she has no books in her home other than religious tracts and farm manuals."

Writing furiously, the reporter asked, "Does she say anything else historically accurate?"

"Yes, she does." The professor tented his hands. "She claims to have been put to death in 1643 and to have lived near Dumfries. The Scottish persecution of witches occurred in four separate epidemics. One took place in the 1640s, probably caused by the passage of various acts that urged people to seek out witches more intensively. The epidemics affected different parts of the country at different times, and whereas there was virtually no persecution in the Dumfries area prior to 1625, there was a good deal of it afterward, for nearly a hundred years."

The reporter grimaced. "Makes you glad you live in the twentieth century."

The professor looked mildly surprised by the thought.

"The time I saw her," the reporter went on, "she kept asking, 'Who has the power in your time?' What do you think she meant?"

"It's difficult to say. Reverend Bailey thinks the 'witch' could be trying to find out whether her powers were passed on to her descendants. On the other hand, she also says her family should be cursed—that is, her husband's family. So it's hard to be sure just what she means."

"Do you think it's worth trying to find out whether she has descendants alive today?"

The professor's smile was indulgent. "How on earth would you go about that?"

"I guess I'd start by trying to locate people named Hagaward."

"There's no reason to suppose the descendants would still carry that surname, is there, after three and a half centuries? And do you have any idea how many descendants there could be by now? Thousands and thousands of them. And what makes you think any of them live in America?"

"I guess you're right," the reporter said.

Still, he did give it a try, looking up the name in half a dozen of the library's collection of phone books. He couldn't find any

13

Hagawards at all, only names like Hagadorn, Hagman, Hagarty, and Haggar.

It occurred to him that the name Hagaward might have altered over the centuries. But if he checked for names similar to it, he'd be spending the summer hip-deep in phone books. And who would pay for the calls he'd have to make?

So he merely mentioned his idea about the names in the piece he wrote.

2

The company was located on the Thames River in Connecticut, in a spare, slate-gray building that sat incongruously among ornate nineteenth-century estates like a monk at a Regency ball.

On the wide glass entrance doors there were chrome letters declaring BIOLOGICONN, INC. A DIVISION OF HAYWARD INDUSTRIES. In the lobby, with its black leather chairs and chrome-and-glass tables, hung a sculpture that looked like hundreds of crystal and silver beads strung in an intricate, curving-stair design: an artist's interpretation of the DNA molecule with its long, thin double helix.

Several dozen press people were assembled in a conference room near the executive offices. Most of them were science reporters. Some had been covering the genetic-engineering field—also known as gene-splicing or recombinant DNA—since the beginning.

Early the previous week word had spread widely that a significant advance was taking place at Biologiconn. The company had been so besieged with requests for information that the president finally had scheduled a press conference.

The president was also the subject of considerable curiosity as the sole descendant of the founder of Hayward Industries still active in the huge pharmaceutical firm. Four months earlier the other two Haywards involved in the Industries had died when a company plane crashed, leaving the president of Biologiconn alone to carry on the tradition of the family business genius.

The tradition did not seem to be in danger: The president, who had been an exceptional student in school, earning an MBA by the age of twenty, not only had grasped the idea that genetic engineering was the wave of the future but had persuaded Hayward Industries to establish a division devoted to it exclusively, and had gone on to persuade several of academe's top cell biologists to work with that division. The president had been elevated to its head five years earlier, exhibiting an executive style that was said to be articulate and decisive, with an impressive command of financial and scientific matters.

The president appeared at precisely three o'clock along with the company's chief microbiologist and a publicity aide, and welcomed the press. They studied their subject, whom most of them had not seen before. All Haywards disliked personal publicity.

"Young, all right," a man from one of the national magazines said to his neighbor.

"Only thirty-five, I hear."

"Got the Hayward looks," said a man from a New York daily.

The president glanced around the room with dark, discerning eyes and said, "None of us at Biologiconn like to make announcements about our achievements until after they've been reported to the scientific journals. For reasons you'll understand in a minute, we were particularly anxious to hold this announcement for at least three more months, but there's been so much rumor circulating that we decided it would be better to go public."

There was an anticipatory rustle, which the president acknowledged with a nod. "From the beginning, as you know, one of the many hopes for recombinant DNA technology was that it would allow us to perform gene therapy someday—that is, to correct genetic disorders and defects by actually repairing the defective gene. I think most of you know the nature of the problems involved in turning that hope into a reality. Our chief microbiologist here will fill in the details on that—but suffice it to say that it was a long time before we could understand how even the simplest gene in a mammalian cell regulated and expressed itself. It was another big step, or series of steps, before we could correct a defective gene in the laboratory, in a culture. From there to working with living subjects, animal experimentation, posed another set of hurdles, and we faced still more in learning to use genetically engineered human cell lines to correct disorders. Of course when I say 'we' I'm referring to the scientific and industrial community as a whole. We all stand on one another's shoulders. But today's announcement is about the achievements of a group of our people here at Biologiconn, working with a group from the medical center of Westchester University.''

Into the president's manner, which, so far, had given the same impression of chrome-and-efficiency as did the building itself, there crept an unmistakable edge of excitement. ''The ovum of a Jewish woman who carries the gene for Tay-Sachs disease was fertilized *in vitro*—in glass—with the sperm of her husband, who also carries that gene. The genetic defect responsible for Tay-Sachs was detected in the very early stages of the development of the embryo. A gene that will correct that defect—a gene produced by the technique of recombinant DNA—was transplanted into the embryo. The embryo was then implanted in the mother, who is now in the sixth month of what shows every sign of being a successful pregnancy.''

There was a moment of silence, for nearly everyone in the room understood the magnitude of the achievement. The president went on to give further details of the process, which had been attempted many times before success was achieved. It involved removing one cell from the embryo at the four-cell stage, allowing it to grow in a culture while the rest were frozen, and analyzing the culture for the missing enzyme that caused Tay-Sachs. The embryo, which was by then several weeks old, was thawed and the missing gene transplanted into it—which presupposed the ability to integrate that gene into just the right place. The mother's body had been kept ready to receive the implanted embryo by means of hormone treatments.

There was silence momentarily. Then hands and voices rose eagerly.

For the next half hour the president and the microbiologist answered questions: The work had certainly been preceded by a great deal of animal experimentation, as well as the human experimentation involved in correcting disorders like diabetes;

the work *had* been done in accordance with the federal guidelines still in force; no, the identity of the mother would not be released now, under any circumstances, although it could and should be said that one of the parents was a scientist working in the field of gene-splicing.

When all but the obvious question had been asked, one of the female reporters asked it: "So now we've got the ability to make babies in test tubes and make them the way we want to. Brave new world—doesn't that scare you?"

The president answered calmly. "No. I find it awesome. The ability to modify nature, however slightly, is one that no scientist I know takes lightly. I don't take it lightly, either, be sure of that."

The microbiologist added, "You're wrong, you know, in saying that we can make babies in test tubes. We can develop an embryo in its early stages, but we're a long way from anything more than that. And believe me, we can't 'make them the way we want,' as you put it. All we've done is to repair *one* gene, which we were able to do because it's simple, relatively speaking. But when you talk about complex functions like intelligence, why, our understanding is primitive."

A man stood up, silencing other questioners. "I'd like to ask the president this. You're one of the youngest people in the country to have the kind of responsibility you do, and probably the only woman. How do you feel about that?"

The president regarded the questioner with no change of expression. "I hope," she said equably, "that that's not going to be the lead of your story."

"You mean you don't care to be seen as a symbol?"

"Of what—being young or being female?"

"Is either one a handicap?"

"I don't think of them that way," the president said.

She had the kind of beauty that consists not of harmonies but of contrasts: flawless, very white skin; a full, bright red mouth; and blue eyes so dark they seemed as black as her hair, which she wore short, cut in layers. It had the facets and the gloss of coal.

She lifted the cuff of her silk shirt and checked a gold bracelet-watch. "I think we should use the time we have left to talk about something more interesting and important than my age or sex."

Another man got to his feet. "How is all this going to affect the profit picture at Biologiconn and Hayward Industries?"

"Directly? Very little," she said. "This procedure represents a great advance in knowledge and techniques, but it's hardly the start of some kind of mass production. As far as I'm concerned, the profit potential of genetic engineering still lies with such things as bacterially produced insulin and vaccines."

"Is the Hayward family still among the ten wealthiest in the country?"

"I really don't know. You say 'the Hayward family' as if it's one entity with one bank account and one mind, but that's not the case, I assure you. By now the descendants of Duncan Hayward are scattered all over the country, even the world. I'm sure there are Haywards I've never even heard of, let alone met."

Another reporter asked, "Why did you urge your parent company to go into genetic engineering?"

"Because I think it's the most exciting frontier in the world." The president leaned over the lectern and clasped her hands. They were small, with blunt fingers, unpainted nails, and no rings. "Don't you often hear it said that this is the age of identity crises? People running to psychiatrists to find out who they really are? But there's a genuine search for identity, a healthy one, that's been going on since the nineteenth century. Ever since Mendel showed that our individual characteristics are caused by hereditary factors in the cell. To find out what and where those factors are—to identify the actual material of heredity, DNA, and figure out its structure and function—to me *that's* the kind of identity search that matters."

A man in the back row, who had not spoken before, said, "You're not interested in your family tree, then, Ms. Hayward?"

"Not particularly."

"Not even in your forebears in Scotland?"

The president raised one finely shaped black brow. "I don't see the reason for the question."

"I was wondering about your name—Cayla. It's pretty unusual. Where did it come from?"

"It's an old family name. May I ask where *you're* from—what publication?"

"*Profiles,*" the man said.

There were murmurs of surprise on all sides. Cayla looked away for a moment. The lines of her profile were a delicate contrast to the severe man-tailoring of her suit. She turned back and said, "I wouldn't think a magazine specializing in celebrity interviews would come to a conference like this one."

"We're interested in a lot of things, Ms. Hayward. From scientific breakthroughs to things like your name. It wouldn't originally have been something a little different, would it? Back in Scotland? Something like Kella?"

Her answer came so evenly that it seemed to negate the tiny, cold pause it followed. "I believe that's so. Why do you ask?"

"Your talking about identity searches brought to mind a piece I saw recently about a West Virginia farm woman. When she's hypnotized, she seems to be the reincarnation of a seventeenth-century witch named Kella. Kella Hagaward. Hayward-Hagaward. Pretty close, I'd say." He waited for a moment, oblivious of the stares from his colleagues. "This Kella claims she's a witch, and she keeps asking about some descendants of hers who's living today. I thought maybe you'd like the chance to comment."

The publicity aide moved to the president's side, but she shook her head. "Where did this story appear?"

The man shrugged. "County paper in West Virginia. I see it because I'm from the area."

All Cayla Hayward did was lift her hands from the lectern and put them at her sides. It only seemed as if she had clawed at the air. "I suspect that most of your colleagues are under the same impression I am—that this is the twentieth century and that we're here to discuss serious matters."

An assenting murmur rose from the crowd, but the man in the back persisted. "You have no comment, then?"

"How could I? What is there to say about such nonsense?"

"What about the names? You just told us that Kella is the original form of your—"

"If you want to discuss Biologiconn or Hayward Industries," the president said, "I have twenty minutes left. If not, this press conference is over."

The man shrugged again. "Back to business, by all means," he said, an old hand at masking his reactions. No one could tell he was congratulating himself.

19

But Cayla Hayward was an old hand, too, so no one could tell that she was trembling.

The news from Biologiconn hit the front pages everywhere, in stories ranging from a dignified GENE THERAPY ON HUMANS NOW A REALITY to a more lurid and less accurate GENE-FIXERS CURE BABY IN TEST TUBE. All of them pointed out that the breakthrough was exciting but hardly unexpected. Once the recombinant DNA process had been discovered in the early 1970s, providing scientists with the capacity to break apart and then remake or "splice" the genetic material, it was only a matter of time until they would be able to apply it in situations like the one involving Tay-Sachs.

There were of course comments and discussions about the ethical implications and the dangers that might conceivably lie ahead—several groups, some religious, issued statements of disapproval, but in general there was less public commotion than might once have been expected.

After all, the original fears about recombinant DNA—that a lethal strain of bacteria would escape from the labs and endanger the public health—had proved to be groundless, more the basis for a thriller plot than anything else. In fact many of the federal guidelines had been relaxed. Certainly the creation of "test-tube babies" who were implanted in wombs was not a new idea; it had already happened several times and had ended in pregnancies brought successfully to term.

So the story disappeared from the popular press within a week, and was alive only in the minds of victims of Tay-Sachs disease and in the scientific and religious communities.

During that week the *Profiles* reporter had been busy. He knew the "witch" discussion was too thin even for his publication. *Profiles* was really a glorified gossip magazine, but the glorification was important to its image. It camouflaged the gossip as news, printing it on the same quality stock as that used by the newsmagazines. The reporter tried to find some members of the Hayward family who would agree to be interviewed, but failed. He fared no better in locating talkative friends, so he gave up on that angle and, with a photographer, went down to see Polly Whiting and the Reverend Walter Bailey.

He came away with Polly's voice singing in his ears—

"Master, pass the power down, so you can be served always"—and returned to find that one of his sources had come through.

At the end of her day, around eight-thirty, Cayla Hayward ate dinner alone in the kitchen of her apartment.

She didn't in the least mind being alone. In fact, it was a welcome change after so many hours spent in meetings and conferences. She liked knowing that at the end of the day a private pool of silence was waiting for her, in which she could luxuriate for a few moments before surfacing to take up the night's work.

The stillness was particularly pleasing to her that night because, after leaving the office, she had had to stop by Rowan Hall, the ocean-front estate that once had been the main home of the Haywards. Although she had spent her early years in the huge gargoyle of a house, to go there cost her a special effort.

She changed into a high-necked white terry-cloth robe, went into the living room, and settled into one of the soft leather chairs. Except for their deep raisin color, they were like the chairs in her office, and the tables were of glass and pewter, worked in an unusual geometric design. Most of one wall was filled by a fireplace of light gray marble—a fogbank held in a prison of straight lines and lacquer.

She leaned her head back and closed her eyes. But in a moment, because she knew she was trying to avoid doing it, she sat up, reached to the coffee table for her briefcase, and snapped open the catches. Underneath a report was the current issue of *Profiles*. Her publicity director had brought it in just as she was leaving: "I just got this, Cayla. You won't like it, but you'd better look at it and tell me how you want it handled."

She didn't have to hunt for the article. A legend on the cover read HAYWARD WITCH-ANCESTRESS REINCARNATED?—SEE PAGE 14. She knew how the reporter had learned that particular piece of family history the moment she turned to the article and saw the photo of her ex-husband.

Tanned so deeply that his hair looked white, he was smiling from a cabin cruiser in some turquoise bay, one hand lifted as if in dismissal of any serious purpose or thought. None of the eleven years since their divorce had left a trace on his face. The caption read JOHNNY REDMUND, EX-HUSBAND OF CAYLA HAY-

Cayla wondered whether he had done it to hurt her after all this time. But malice had never been part of Johnny's makeup. Then she realized he would have made them pay him well for talking.

When they met in college he had been a serious business student and had one of the best minds in the class, with enthusiasm to match. He was from a very poor family, and at first she had enjoyed witnessing his pleasure in all the things Hayward money could buy. But by their first anniversary, she knew more was involved. Johnny's brilliance had not changed, but his enthusiasm had: Making the money—working in the Industries, as she was doing—had become an irksome duty, and all that mattered was spending it, lavishly. She didn't know what had changed him, or whether he had always been that way and she hadn't seen it. She knew only that she had wound up feeling used and stupid. The latter was worse by far.

Cayla looked at the rest of the article. There was a picture of a plain, middle-aged woman lying on a couch, eyes closed, and a minister seated beside her. There were a "witch" headline and mentions of "witch" throughout the text, which Cayla forced herself to read. Her publicity director had assured her there was no mention of either the press conference or any of Biologiconn's work; if there had been, Cayla knew, she would have wanted to ruin the reporter. But the article was bad enough without them: It resurrected the tale of a Hayward family curse, making much of the recent deaths of her two cousins, Joel and Kelvin, in the plane crash. The real curse, she thought, was the story itself, which had slithered beside the family for decades. The article's last sentence repeated its subhead: "Why is a West Virginia farm woman speaking with the voice of an actual, historical witch?"

She put the magazine down, thinking of the sophisticated technology that had been required to produce it—to set its type by computer, reproduce its glossy photos, print and bind its several million copies, and ship them within a day or two all across the country. Yet the magazine was promoting the existence of witchcraft, which could not execute or even conceive of one item of that technology. It was a kind of contradiction she had seen many times: technology used to advocate its own nemesis. She never had been able to see examples of it with equanimity.

How could the press cater so to people's gullibility? she wondered. And how could people themselves behave with simpleton credulity, which let them mentally abolish centuries of progress? She meant to put the magazine aside and get up, but memory pinned her to the chair, angry that she, of all people, should be asking such questions. Her nostrils began to pinch with the scents of Rowan Hall and her ears to flood with the reedy voice of her Gran.

She fought the mood away and stood up, pushing her hands through her short hair. The important thing was to decide what to do about the article. If anything could be done without fanning the publicity fires and, more important, without causing more family skeletons to come rattling out of their closets.

She started to pace rapidly and circled the room a dozen times before stopping in its center, her decision made. Even if the lawyers told her the *Profiles* piece was actionable, she would do nothing about it. Except to hire some discreet detectives to look into the past and present activities of Polly Whiting.

She put the decision and everything linked with it out of her mind, sat cross-legged on the rug, and read through the report on a proposed building extension. Doing it one way would cut into the existing parking lot; doing it the other would require a sacrifice of important storage room. She decided neither was acceptable and made notes of questions to ask at the staff meeting the next morning. Then she studied a memo from the lab director that projected the amount of insulin they could expect to produce bacterially by the end of the year. Finally she turned from Biologiconn's commercial concerns to its research functions: to a report on the progress of the Tay-Sachs case. The woman was still doing fine.

Around eleven-thirty she finished, put everything back into the briefcase, and went down the hall to her bathroom. There was no makeup to remove from her eyes—the lashes and brows were naturally thick and black. She had removed what was left of her lipstick and was brushing her hair when she found herself leaning closer and closer to the mirror, pulling back the hair at her left temple with three fingers.

She looked at the dark, velvety, irregular mark that had

crouched there, in the hairline, all her life. She dug her nail into it; there was no sensation. She pulled away from the mirror, snapped off the light, and went across the hall to bed.

The several million people who read the *Profiles* article in the next few days included a significant number of senators and representatives in Washington; some of them laughed, some shook their heads with the satisfaction of cynics, and some were upset. More than one clergyman also read the piece. None of the clergymen laughed, but some shook their heads in disbelief, and some were very upset.

3

"How have things been this past week?" the doctor asked.

"OK." The patient lifted her shoulders slightly. "Fine."

"No problems?"

"No. Oh well, you know, the usual. The client rejected some of the best copy ever written by man, woman, or beast."

"And how did you react?"

"I said the darling client was right, kiss kiss, and we'd try again. Then I went to my office and kicked hell out of my doll."

The doctor, who was wearing a yellow shirt and a beige sweatervest, leaned back in his chair and put his hands behind his head. He smiled at the patient. In her early thirties, she was nearly ten years younger than he. "Hyperbole is a great advertising tool," he said. "So what are you trying to sell me today?"

The patient stared out the window, at the rear windows of other Manhattan apartments. "Oh crap, I'm just trying to put off telling you." She put her head in her hands. "I did it again last night."

"OK. Then it'll be fresh in your mind."

The woman looked up. "Dr. Veere? I mean, Stefan— Don't you ever want to say get lost?—get lost, little whore who goes to bars and takes home anything with breath enough to ask her to spread her legs?"

Stefan Veere put his arms down on the desk. "Why do you need me to call you names when you're so good at doing it yourself?"

"Don't you care what I am?"

"I care that what you're doing makes you miserable. And I want you to keep on trying to understand why you do it."

"Understand? All I need to do is *stop.*"

Stefan Veere regarded her, his green eyes gentle. "There are two ways to make people stop doing something. Either you force them—threaten them with job loss or jail or whatever—or else you help them understand so they can stop by themselves. I'm not in the storm-trooper business, so why don't you just tell me about last night?"

The patient sighed. "Why not . . . Well, as one-night stands go, it wasn't bad. In fact it was pretty good. Of course, as dawn's rosy fingers began to streak the east, he just couldn't keep up with me. I was in one of my insatiable moods."

Stefan Veere shook his head. "Tell me what really happened."

"You don't believe me?" She began to cry. "You're right. It was ghastly. Worse than usual. He was *ignorant*—I mean, he said things like 'I done.' And he hurt me, and . . . oh crap."

Stefan Veere proffered a box of tissues and let her cry for a bit. Then he began the slow process of coaxing the self-loathing and pain from her eyes and restoring their intelligence. She and most of his other patients found in his manner not only a calm solid steadiness but also an easiness that made them feel they were talking to a person, not merely an aggregate of questions and suggestions.

Asked to categorize himself, Stefan Veere said he was a cognitive therapist—one who believes neurosis is the result of errors of cognition involving one's underlying judgments, values, and ideas. But what had brought him into psychiatry and still fascinated him was not the mind's ability to perceive, integrate, and reason but its dark side—its capacity to distort reality, to invent its own world, even to change the body it inhabited.

When his patient left, he made some notes and then went into the waiting room. He was a tall man with a look of wiry strength whose bearing suggested both scholar and athlete. His curly hair was the color of saddle leather, and his features were fine and regular, but his wide-set green eyes could blaze with an intensity he had learned to subdue when working with patients.

His new receptionist-secretary-bookkeeper looked up. "You're free this next hour. Want some coffee?"

"No thanks. Anyway, it's not part of your job to bring me food and drink."

"I don't mind." She had some questions about scheduling and billing. Then she said, "Oh, a Dr. Prentiss called. From the Society of . . . Parapsychologists?"

He smiled; tiny lines appeared in the corners of his mouth and eyes. "Yes. They sometimes call me if they think they might have a hoax on their hands—or, to be more accurate, when they want someone to say they haven't."

"Why you?"

"I know a lot about how to spot frauds," he said lightly. "In fact it gives me a lot of satisfaction to expose them. I don't know what it gives the Society of Parapsychologists—they've asked me to look into four cases, and I've shown all of them to be frauds. I thought they were getting tired of me. Still, a couple of weeks ago they did want me to go down to West Virginia and see some woman. But I don't have time to take outside trips for them."

The receptionist hesitated. "Do you think there are ever any cases that aren't frauds?"

"Let's say I think that some cases are harder than others to explain, and some people are more willing than others to believe. For instance, I recently read about an African whose witch doctor told him he would be crushed to death by a giant, invisible snake. Gradually the man became paralyzed, and finally was gasping for breath and unable to swallow, just as if a huge snake were crushing his ribs. If he hadn't been taken to a hospital—where, by the way, they discovered nothing organically wrong with him—he would have died. Now, what would you make of that?"

When the receptionist looked flustered, he laughed and said,

26

"Don't worry. It wasn't a test." He picked up the message slip. "Let me go see what they want today."

Back in his office, he cradled the phone between his chin and left shoulder and stretched out his long legs beside the desk drawers. When he reached Dr. Prentiss, he listened for a while, then said, "Certainly, if you're bringing the woman to New York. Wait a minute, haven't I read something about her in the popular press?" He listened again. "I thought so. Yes, I'll be glad to be part of the examining team on this one."

He hung up, made a note on his calendar, took out the folder on his next patient, then stayed motionless, realizing that he had gone to the outer office, talked with the woman there, even laughed, and never once felt the grinding awareness that she wasn't Barbara, that Barbara would never be there again.

Today, Stefan thought, he had gone for hours without thinking about her. He must really be getting over it, not just dealing with it.

He could hear her saying, "About time, my friend." He smiled.

Polly Whiting's husband came into their bedroom and looked at the empty suitcase lying open on the bed. "Well, girl," he said to his wife, "so you're really going."

Polly nodded. Wearing the long—and long-sleeved—night-gown that, in various incarnations, had covered her through the nights of their twenty-five years of marriage, she stared at the suitcase as if she had forgotten its use. "But if you tell me not to go," she said without looking up, "then I won't go."

"Now, Poll, we've talked it over a hundred times, with Reverend Bailey and everything. You got to find out what this business is all about. You got to see if those experts up there can figure it."

She reached toward the suitcase, then pulled her hand back. "Bill, you sure you don't think it's . . . like that old business? Because I promised you I'd never do anything like that again, and the Lord knows I never have, Bill. I swear it."

"Of course you haven't. You've been real sensible since the day we got married. I told you before—I don't think this business is anything like what you got involved in before."

Polly's sigh began in relief but returned to worry. "What if

27

it's all wrong, Bill? What if it's the Devil trying to work his way into my heart?"

Bill Whiting grinned. "The day you let the Devil within a mile of you, let alone inside you, that's the day I want to see."

"Bill!" She looked up at him for the first time.

"All right, all right. I didn't mean anything, Poll. I just know you're a real God-fearing woman, and if your own pastor tells you it's OK besides, then it's OK."

"Well . . ." She moved uncertainly to the wood cupboard where they hung their clothes. "I don't know what I should take. The pictures I've seen of New York City, it looks like what they wear up there is crazy."

"Or indecent," Bill said. "Better take your church dress, that's for sure."

"Yes." Polly pulled out a navy-blue rayon dress with a lace collar. "And my raincoat."

Bill sat on the bed watching while she folded garments neatly and packed them. She added a Bible and a pair of slippers. Then she went to the single dresser they shared and took out some undergarments. Screening them with her body, she slipped them in the case quickly, shut it and snapped the latches.

Bill picked it up and set it by the door. "Last night I'll see you for a while, I guess," he said, pulling off his shirt. His arms were tanned and thin, with knots of muscles.

"I know a wife is supposed to cleave to her husband, but I—"

"We can't afford to both of us leave the farm, you know that. I'm not complaining, Poll." He took off his undershirt and said, with emphasis, "I'm just saying I won't see you for a while."

She turned away, her cheeks as blotched with sudden color as if they had been slapped, and began to take the heavy pins from the bun of her hair and lay them side by side, like headless dolls, on the top of the dresser. When she turned back, Bill's overalls were on the chair, and he was in bed.

She snapped off the light and slid between the sheets. The bed creaked on her side; it always had. She lay on her back, eyes closed. When Bill's hand touched her thigh, she said quietly, "I'm saying my prayers."

"OK." In five minutes he said, "Are you done?"

"Yes."

Five minutes later, so was he.

Still lying on her back, she shut her legs like a scissors, pushed her nails into the mattress, and fought mightily with her soul.

"I know there are folks today, maybe even some of you hearing me right now, who wonder if it's really true that Satan lives."

The speaker pulled back and looked at his audience, which numbered close to three thousand along with a battery of television cameras. Although he was a small man, he had a superb weapon with which to command the crowd's attention and belief: a voice that could infuse meaning into anything. And although the voice was quite capable of working its spell in the presence of nothing but a microphone or a camera crew, the speaker preferred to do as many broadcasts as possible in front of live audiences, either in his home church or on the road.

He was launching another of his tours, starting in one of the largest auditoriums in the Southeast. On his previous tour he had crusaded for the teaching of creationism in the schools, and now he had another issue that he considered to be gravely important.

He had spoken at some length, in generalizations, on the prevalence of evil. Now he nodded, contemplating his words and their listeners. "Yes, friends," he said, "there still are people among us who deny that Satan lives." He leaned over the lectern, and the voice was suddenly a whisper. "There still are people who sneer at the thought, at the very idea, that Lucifer lives, that he walks on this earth, that he steals among us and spits his venom into our hearts."

The voice became a serpent, flowing like silk through the grass. "But nothing pleasures Lucifer, nothing pleases Satan like knowing people are denying his existence, like hearing they are claiming he is just a fairy tale."

The serpent lifted its flat head. "I tell you Satan lives and his power has never been greater. I tell you he lives in people's thoughts and words and actions. Today there are people who sit in the halls of government and refuse to honor the faith and the value of their fathers. Today there are people who sit on the benches of justice and refuse to honor the sacredness of human life. Today there are people who work in the laboratories of science and take unto themselves the work that belongs to God.''

The serpent reared, unleashing claws and wings and a dragon's roar. ''I tell you Satan lives and his power has never been greater! I tell you he can come among us to do his work directly!''

The audience seemed to have a single breath, which caught sharply when the speaker thrust an arm above his head and waved the newspaper he held. ''Have you read in your newspapers about a woman named Polly Whiting? A woman who has loved and feared the Lord all her life? A woman who is going through a terrible ordeal right now, because the voice that sometimes comes from her lips is the voice of one of Satan's creatures? Now, I don't know this Polly Whiting. I've never even met this Polly Whiting. I've never met her pastor. I don't know whether his church, the Church of the Shepherd, is joining with us in our great crusade to restore the faith and the values of our fathers. But I do know this, my friends—the Devil is growing bolder and bolder when he can put words right into the mouth of a woman who loves and fears the Lord!''

Slowly, as the roar echoed throughout the temple, the dragon retracted its wings and settled on its haunches. ''My friends, I think that poor woman is going through her ordeal for a reason. I think God is using her as His vehicle. I think He wants us to take a closer look at these people she talks about—this family that's known so much wealth and power. I think God wants us to take a closer look at their laboratories, and other laboratories like them, and ask what kind of work they do there. And when we do look, my friends, what do we find? That in those labs they are tampering with life itself! Oh, they can use the language of science—they can say that what they do is genetic engineering—but in the language of God's truth, they are trying to tamper with life as the Almighty created it!''

There was a mesmerizing pause. ''There is only one Genetic Engineer, my friends, and His name is the Lord! And to tamper with His handiwork—who would want to do that, my friends? Who would want to interfere with the sacred works that are God's alone to do? Well, I ask you, my friends—who was banished from the kingdom of Heaven and in hatred and envy has set himself up against God ever since?''

The voice had sunk almost to a susurrus again; the flat head pulled its limbless body through the grass. "Who, my friends, is old in the ways of wickedness yet eternally seeks new ways to disguise himself? And what better way in this twentieth century than to wrap himself in the cloak of science?"

The speaker pulled back and regarded the crowd, paralyzing them in the fixity of his gaze. Then, almost conversationally, he said, "Let us pray for our sister Polly Whiting in her ordeal. Let us never lose heart in our own ordeal. Let us never forget that Satan lives and that we must be vigilant eternally. Amen."

The crowd sent back an "Amen" that was like a wave breaking on a shore.

4

To the Reverend Walter Bailey's amazement, there were half a dozen press people waiting for him and Polly when they got off the train in New York.

He tried to shield her as she disembarked behind him, though she was taller than he and her limbs seemed to stick out around him like a handful of sore thumbs. He tried to explain to the journalists that there was nothing to be said at the moment and that there wouldn't be until a number of people at the Society of Parapsychologists had examined Polly, but the questions persisted. "Is this voice of yours trying to contact Cayla Hayward?" "Will you speak to Ms. Hayward if she wants to see you?" Polly put her hands in front of her face, palms outward.

Through the noise of their own voices, the journalists heard an increasingly loud hissing, which they took to be the train, releasing more steam. Suddenly a man stopped in mid-question, realizing that the hiss came from between Polly's hands. His colleagues' voices trailed to a halt, too, and they all stared, as if at a snake.

Somehow Walter Bailey got her moving through Penn Station, and the reporters followed. When the two of them stood on the street at last, both obviously bewildered, one of the photographers helped them catch a bus going uptown.

As the bus moved up Eighth Avenue, Polly kept her face to the window. When they reached the Times Square area, her back grew rigid against the seat, and her eyes acquired a fixed look of shock as they registered the combination of glitter and filth and the prostitutes, with their naked thighs below skimpy shorts and breasts that seemed not so much covered by tight sweaters as fondled by them.

It was not until Polly was left alone in the hotel room the Society of Parapsychologists had reserved for her that her gaze and posture started to relax. She examined the furnishings, which had the air of clean but mismatched clothes, and when the minister knocked on the door she had some questions. What had the reporters meant, and who was the Cayla Hayward they had spoken of?

Walter Bailey had thought it best not to show her the *Profiles* article when it first appeared, on the grounds that if she saw nothing about the Hayward connection, she could not be accused of being influenced in her trance-communications, but of course he couldn't lie to her when she asked the direct question.

"You've heard of Hayward Industries, I guess?" he said. "The big drug company?"

She looked startled for a moment, then nodded.

He decided not to mention anything about the Tay-Sachs experiment and to tell Polly as little as possible, in fact: "The Cayla Hayward they spoke of is a member of that family—of the drug-company people. And it seems that in the family history, way back in Scotland, there was an ancestor named Kella Hagaward. So you can see why those reporters were so interested in you."

"There really was a Kella, then," Polly said softly, working her hands in her lap. "There's been times, mostly in the middle of the night, when I figured I might be going crazy and making it all up without even knowing I was doing it."

Walter Bailey squeezed her arm. "You're not going crazy, Polly. There's no question of that, none at all."

She sighed and shook her head. "I need to pray for forgiveness. I didn't act nice to those people who were at the train. I hissed them away."

She got down on her knees.

Far from sending them away, of course, her hissing had guaranteed they would never let go of the story. One of them, a free lance who lived in Connecticut, decided to drive out to the Hayward estate to see what he could discover. He found huge grounds fringed by a fence as sharp as it was high and tall iron gates with a motto worked into each: VIVIMUS IN POSTERIS. On the far side of the house lay the sound, but no one had done any sailing from there in years, so the docks were virtually unusable.

The free lance had to content himself with pictures of the gates and some long shots of the house with its many turrets, each supporting a sharply conical roof.

Most of the reporters traveled only as far as the libraries of their respective publications. There, like their *Profiles* colleague before them, they discovered that although Hayward Industries had figured prominently in the business news for decades and was one of the corporate names known to most Americans, there was little in print about the Haywards as individuals. They seemed to have the almost pathological dread of publicity that was characteristic of the very rich.

The few available references to the family curse implied that it had been part of the family's history for several centuries. There was Isobel Hayward, one of the beauties of her day, who died in a freak accident at the Paris exposition of 1889: She fell from the Eiffel Tower. There were the recent plane crash in which the two male Haywards had died—its cause had not been discovered—and the invalidism of Cayla Hayward's grandmother, for which, rumor had it, no cause had ever been found either.

A reporter from the afternoon tabloid speculated that perhaps the tragic curse was the price the family had to pay for its decades of wealth and power, beauty and business acumen.

That same tabloid bought the shots from the free lance who had gone to Rowan Hall. The result was that two days after Polly Whiting and Walter Bailey arrived in New York, there was a story on the cursed Hayward family that included a brooding picture of Rowan Hall, a close-up of its iron gates, and a boldface translation of the gates' Latin motto: WE LIVE IN OUR POSTERITY.

* * *

"This really is the limit. They're writing about the damn family curse. They're taking pictures of Rowan Hall, so any burglar in the Northeast will know where it is. And now this—it's the limit!"

The man waved a day-old newspaper as if it were an enemy flag. It was a story, datelined Washington, that said several congressmen were reporting a surge of mail and phone calls protesting the "tampering with life" taking place in laboratories like those of Hayward Industries. "The damfool witch business got them all stirred up," he said. "Now they're going to make an issue out of gene-splicing. Which affects the Industries, damn it! Which supports all of us!"

He huffed and, along with the other eight people in the room, looked at Cayla. They were her immediate relatives, the clan: the descendants of her Gran's two male cousins, whom Cayla called aunts and uncles although they were actually her third and fourth cousins. At the behest of the speaker, Uncle Frank, they had gathered for a strategy session in a Hayward mansion on Park Avenue.

Since Kelvin's and Joel's deaths, the clan had looked to Cayla as its head. They had underscored that fact, perhaps unintentionally, by giving her the center seat in the richly paneled room, on a burgundy sofa with heavy carved claw feet. She had once thought of it as a sleeping animal with dark red fur.

"But who *are* these people?" asked Aunt Grace. "The ones writing their congressmen and making the fuss?"

Grace was Kelvin's widow. When Cayla was twelve, the couple had taken her out of Rowan Hall—on the day after a Christmas she would never forget—declaring Gran was no longer fit to raise a child. They were childless themselves, although Grace treated her horses as children who had arrived in an unusual form, and it couldn't have been easy for them to take in a youngster, especially one as confused and unhappy as Cayla had been at the time. But they had been good to her, and Kelvin had been more than that.

"Damn it, Grace," Frank said. "Don't you ever read anything but the racing pages? A lot of religious groups have gotten together to exercise political muscle. They can put pressure on Washington because, for one thing, they helped elect some of the damn politicians, and for another they've got a lot of money and they're organized as hell. And according to the

34

damn paper"—he slapped it with a large hand—"there's even a couple of Bible-belt senators saying genetic engineering is the Devil's work!"

Grace shook her head. "Is Frank right?"

"Yes, I'm afraid he is."

"It's the damn timing," Frank snapped. "That woman's nonsense about Kella, coming right on top of the Tay-Sachs breakthrough."

Cayla smiled at him. Even though he lived off his wife's money, traveling the world while maintaining homes in Boston, the Bahamas, and Greece, he was more in touch with political and financial realities than anyone else in the clan.

"It's really too bad," said Aunt Isobel, her dark eyes widening, "that you chose just this time to have your breakthrough."

"Breakthroughs aren't chosen, Aunt Isobel. They just come, and we're all thrilled when they do."

"Well, I just don't know . . ." Isobel said. Her words trailed off, and her gaze moved around the room as if she might have missed some object on her last visit. The house, built as a *pied-à-terre*, belonged to her. When Cayla had lived for two extended periods on her estate in Virginia, Isobel had tried without success to implant her own love of collecting. *"Mathematics?"* she would say. "What kind of thing is that for a young lady to be interested in?"

One of Aunt Sylvia's three daughters, all divorced, said irrelevantly, "For years now, Cayla, I haven't seen you in anything that isn't dreary and man-tailored. Whatever happened to your clothes sense?"

Cayla was wearing a suede skirt and silk shirt, both navy-blue. Her only jewelry was a thin gold bracelet, which she spun once with a finger. "Whatever happened to your manners?" she asked pleasantly.

Aunt Sylvia, Joel's widow, who had flown up from Boca Raton for the meeting, stopped halfway through lighting a cigarette. "Does the Sphinx know about all this?" she said.

Cayla said lightly, "If it does, it hasn't spoken."

The Sphinx was the family holding company her great-grandfather had set up. Officially named the Isobel Memorial Trust, after his mother, it became known as the Sphinx because it would never answer any questions. All the dozens of people who worked for it—accountants, lawyers, financial analysts—had the attitude that the money was *their* responsibility, as it legally was, and usually refused to tell family members what was being done with it. All the heirs received regular and very handsome checks but found it next to impossible to touch their principals.

Sylvia lit her cigarette and exhaled hugely. "The Sphinx won't like it, what with the Industries being involved."

"Damn right," Frank said. "So what are you going to do about it, Cayla?"

"The obvious things are being done," she said. "The Industries' people in Washington will use their influence to counter the effects of this letter and phone campaign. The publicity department at Biologiconn is feeding the media our views on the matter." She folded her hands. "Other than that, I don't know what to do."

Frank's eyebrows snapped up. "Congress is coming out against your own division of the Industries, and you don't know what to do? As brainy as you are, you don't know what to do?"

"No," she said. "I'm not good at dealing with craziness. I can deal with cost overruns and late deliveries and disappointing research results, but not with—" She put her hands beside her on the sofa, pressing into the hardness that was just below the velvet surface, reminding herself that the only way to confront the irrational was to keep oneself its cold, polar opposite. "If any of you have any idea how to stop a piece of lunacy, I'll be glad to consider it."

Isobel's son, looking maliciously innocent, asked, "Is anyone who objects to genetic engineering a lunatic? I thought a lot of scientists had doubts."

"Some, not a lot," she said levelly. "But you're right. No one who works with it takes it lightly, and some take it pretty darkly. And now every scientist who has any reservations at all about recombinant DNA will be brought out to air them for the press. Some of the doubters are very reputable indeed."

There was silence. They all looked at her as if she were an oracle who could and should solve all problems. It was a strange reversal of her adolescence, when she had often caught pity in their eyes and overheard them speak of her as "poor little thing."

They had given her a comfortable, if peripatetic, adolescence, and as she was passed around among them, she had been grateful for the scraps of their time and affection, which formed a patchwork to wrap around herself after Rowan Hall. But eventually she realized that most of them lived lives no more desirable than Gran's. They merely lived them in sunlight. Except for Joel and Kelvin, who had been active in the Industries, the men of the clan were nice but useless. The women were worse.

Once she realized that, she found herself questioning everything she had heard about the business genius of the men behind Hayward Industries. One weekend she had closeted herself in the University library to learn the truth.

A portrait had risen from old books and records: Fresh from Scotland in 1807, Duncan Hayward had begun putting herbs in his soap not only to make it fragrant but to give it healthful properties. By 1850 his son, a chemist, had led the growing business to specialize in medicinal preparations. By 1900 his grandsons had built the Hayward Company into the largest employer in the state of Connecticut. Their cousins made it into Hayward Industries, adding half a dozen major divisions, so that by 1950 it was a model studied in business schools both because of its efficient administration and because it financed growth largely through earnings instead of through debt. It consistently made huge outlays on research and development, and each year hundreds of the country's brightest new Ph.D.'s aspired to work for Hayward Industries.

As she read, the paper had swelled up in damp little spots, and she sat there amazed and a bit frightened by the intensity of her reaction.

That fall she had decided to major in business administration.

Cayla became aware that a voice was saying her name. She shook her head and asked patiently, "Yes, Aunt Isobel, what is it?"

In the precise and delicate way that had made Cayla imagine, when she was young, that her aunt's insides were made of watch parts, Isobel said, "You know how much I dislike publicity. It distresses me, it really does. Can't you issue some kind of statement or something?"

"Saying what, Aunt Isobel? That we're really not doing the

Devil's work at Biologiconn? I don't think I could force the words out of my mouth. I've told you all along, and I still say it—public silence is our best bet."

Isobel's son reminded her, "*We* didn't talk. The one who did was your ex-husband."

"Quite right. Don't worry, though—I've asked the lawyers to get in touch with him and see that he has no financial reason to say another word to a reporter. That should do it."

"Oh!" Isobel cried. "I just had a dreadful thought—what if some reporter finds out about Rachel?"

The nine expressions in the room congealed to a horrified sameness.

Frank said, "Isobel's right. Better make sure Rachel is out of bounds to the press."

"But look here," interrupted his wife, Aunt Dru. Of all the women, she had looked the most like the paintings of the legendary Hayward beauties, but every year she grew fatter, so that the beauty was a painting on slowly rising dough. "Nobody has said a word about the Whiting woman. How does she know those things she says, unless . . . ."

"Unless what?" Cayla asked evenly.

"Well, unless Kella Hagaward really does have some kind of power to come back. You know what your own Gran says. Why, old Cayla would tell you that—"

"For God's sake, Dru!" said Grace, almost shouting.

"Keep your foolishness to yourself," Frank snapped. "Be a hell of a thing if the press got on to *you*."

There was a silence as heavy as the room's furnishings. Everyone looked at Cayla. Then all the eyes turned away except Isobel's.

"I want you to see what I got in the mail two days ago," she said. "Anonymously. I never got an anonymous letter in my whole life. Someone clipped this . . . this cartoon and sent it to me. From a paper in Tennessee."

She held it out: a drawing of a white-coated female with a laboratory flask, inside of which was a blob, reproduced in red ink. Behind the woman was a smoky red haze, out of which grinned a dim shape that seemed to be part goat.

5

As soon as she came out of the house, her driver sighted her and pulled up the car. "Never mind, Carl," she called, to forestall his getting out to open her door. She slid in, and he headed for the Triborough Bridge and the thruway back to Connecticut and Biologiconn. The car moved like a cradle, taking the punishment of Manhattan's streets into its own body and transmitting none to its passengers'.

Cayla unlatched her briefcase, and though the top items in it all demanded her immediate attention, she took a folder labeled "Whiting" from one of the compartments.

It contained a report from the detectives she had hired several weeks earlier. Although she had read it twice, she did so again, intently, as if to make its contents expand. Of course it still told her only that the Whiting woman, now forty-eight, had been born and raised in Pennsylvania, the child of John and Esther Kendall; had been married to, and lived on the same farm with, Bill Whiting for twenty-five years; had raised two children, Harold and Susan, now grown; was a devout member of a fundamentalist church; had no traceable connection to any branch or member of the Hayward family; and had arrived in New York with her pastor-hypnotist four days earlier.

Cayla drummed her fingers on the report for a moment. Then she leaned forward, slid open the panel to the front seat, and told Carl to turn around and take her to an address on the west side.

Ten minutes later the car headed through Central Park. Cayla opened the folder again. On paper the Whiting woman's life was gray and mouselike. It seemed impossible to Cayla that her own life could be intersecting with it—as impossible as the joinings now taking place in her own labs had once seemed.

Who would have thought that a human gene could be spliced into the cell of a mouse? But it had.

She frowned, noting her assumption that in such a joining it would be Polly Whiting, not she, who represented the mouse.

The car slid to a stop in front of a brownstone in the West Nineties. According to the detectives' report it was where the experts were conducting their examinations of Polly Whiting, one of which would take place in a few minutes.

Cayla said the customary ''Never mind'' to Carl and got out. A sudden rumbling made her look at the sky, which had turned dark though half an hour before it had been beaming with an early April sun. Carl extended an umbrella through the window. As she took it, it occurred to her that she was not trying in any way to disguise herself. She looked down at the navy shirt and suede skirt and shrugged. As she went up the steps, there was a sharp cracking of thunder.

A small plaque on the building declared that its occupants were ''parapsychologists.'' A pseudo-word, Cayla thought, for pseudoscientists. On the wall behind the reception desk was a large sign: POSITIVELY NO PRESS PERSONS ALLOWED TODAY. When the man at the desk looked up, Cayla said, ''Where is the Polly Whiting session? Oh, never mind, I see one of my colleagues just catching the elevator.'' She was gone before the man could open his mouth.

There were three people in the small elevator. One of them was holding forth: ''Historically there was a lot of confusion on the subject of 'possession.' Was the witch a victim whom the Devil inhabited, or was she obsessed by him, having invited him in, so to speak? It's the difference between innocence and guilt, you'd think, but the fascinating point is that no matter which view was accepted, the witch was usually tortured and killed anyway . . .''

They all got out on the third floor and Cayla followed them to a room that held about twenty chairs. She stayed in the hall, waiting to slip in at the last moment. No one paid any attention to her. She thought of the careful procedures for checking all visitors to Biologiconn.

When a voice inside the room announced that the session would begin, she slid in and took a seat close to the door. A man standing against the wall—a tall, wiry man with reddish-brown hair—looked at her and raised an eyebrow. She nodded curtly and glanced away, to the front of the room.

The woman who stood there bore no resemblance to a mouse. She seemed to Cayla more like an ungainly member of the bird family whose size, violating its nature, forced it to walk instead of fly. She wore a matronly navy-blue dress, and one hand kept lifting to her mouth and then lowering to her side. Cayla was certain she had never seen her before, and when the woman looked out at the audience, she gave no sign of recognizing Cayla either.

Someone from the parapsychologists' organization announced that Ms. Whiting had agreed to be tested by several hypnotists who were unknown to her and that the present session would be conducted by a man who often used hypnotherapy in his practice.

The lights were turned down. The woman settled on an upright chair. The hypnotist went up to sit beside her and said, "Ms. Whiting, have you and I ever met before?"

"No, sir. I never laid eyes on you in my life." Her voice twanged like a bowstring.

"Nor I you," he said. "Are you quite willing to allow me to hypnotize you?"

"Yes, sir."

"You have no reservations about it at all?"

"No, sir. Since the Lord is willing."

"Fine. Would you mind slipping off your shoes?" She did so. "Good. Are you comfortable on that chair? Wouldn't you prefer to lie down?"

It seemed to Cayla that a touch of color suffused the woman's face, which was plain as a soup plate. "I'll sit," she said stiffly.

The hypnotist nodded. He took a shiny cylinder from his pocket—a pen—and told her to take several deep breaths, emptying her mind as well as her lungs with each, and then to stare at the pen, which he held only a foot or so from her eyes. "I'm going to start counting, Polly, and each time I say a number, I want you to close your eyes and then open them again to look at the pen, to look at the way it shines. Each time it will be harder to open your eyes, and when I get to the count of three, you won't be able to lift your lids at all because you'll be so sleepy . . ." He did as he said, his voice flowing pleasantly

41

and regularly. On "three" Polly Whiting's head sagged to the left, and one hand slid from her lap and hung at her side.

The hypnotist told her she was falling deeper and deeper asleep, and then he began to take her back in time, to her fifteenth birthday. Her voice, somewhat lighter in tone, described going to ninth grade on the school bus and being sleepy in English class. He told her then to go back to her tenth birthday—she said she was in bed with a cold—and finally to her fifth.

Cayla glanced around quickly and saw that the listeners' expressions were intent. The man still standing against the wall had cocked his head to one side, and his eyelids were narrowed.

Her voice distinctly higher, its twang even more pronounced, Polly Whiting began to talk of a kitchen in which she was sitting. "Ma's bakin' bread," she said. "Flour all over the table."

The hypnotist asked, "Is she baking you a cake for your birthday?"

"Cake? I dunno. She got to bake bread today." The child-voice was incongruous, coming from the graceless adult body.

"Who else is in the kitchen, Polly?"

"Just me and Ma. And the cat."

"What's the cat's name?"

"Ummm. Mitzi."

"Do you play with Mitzi?"

"Uh-huh." A childish giggle. "Pull her tail."

"Look around the kitchen and tell me what you see."

She answered slowly, with long pauses before naming each object. "Pa's boots. Muddy. Cupboards. Lotsa cupboards I cain't reach. There's the sink. It's got a handle for pumpin' water. And the blue stove."

"What are you wearing for your birthday?"

"Red. Red thing. Nice red—" She stopped. The sound she made seemed almost like panting. Then she shook her head. "Red thing. I—" She stopped again and was motionless except for the slow rise and fall of her breasts.

"All right, Polly," the hypnotist said soothingly. Carefully he lifted one of her large, stockinged feet and placed her leg across his knee. From his pocket he took a pair of scissors and drew its tip down the sole of her feet, from the ball to the arch. Her toes, studded with corns and bunions, curled downward.

"Now," said the hypnotist, "I'd like you to go back even

farther, to a time before you could talk.'' He asked her to return to the age of two months.

She seemed gradually to sink into herself. Her plain face became a double exposure; the worn adult features simultaneously looked smooth and formless. Her head fell back.

Once again the hypnotist drew the scissors down the sole of her foot. Her big toe extended and curled upward.

There was an excited rustling in the audience.

The hypnotist put her foot back down gently. "OK, Polly. Now we're going to come forward in time again, but we'll come quickly. I'll count to five, and by the time I get to five, you'll be in the present again, and when I snap my fingers, you'll open your eyes, and you'll feel very good. All right, Polly, here we go. One . . .''

Slowly the woman's body returned to its original sitting position, with one hand hanging loose. When the hypnotist got to three, she said, ''Birthday. Cake? Dress.''

The hypnotist frowned but said pleasantly, ''Are you at your fifth birthday again, Polly?''

''Yes. Five.''

''Well, that's good, but I'd like you to come forward in time and —''

''Red dress. Red. Wearing red.'' She made the strange panting sound again. ''Mitzi?'' she said. Her mouth opened in a yawn and closed slowly.

Then it yanked wide in a scream no one could have taken to be a child's.

Cayla felt her skin crawl against the cloth of her blouse. The cause, she thought, was the incredible contrast between the slack face and body and the agonized intensity of the sound.

In a moment the scream became words. ''Fire . . . eating me . . . all my body . . .''

Polly Whiting's pastor rose in his chair in the audience but sank back when the hypnotist held up a hand. ''Polly,'' the hypnotist said, ''can you hear me?''

''NOT Polly!''

''Who are you, then?''

''Kella! Kella Hagaward!'' The voice was low, powerful, husky.

''Yes, all right. Kella. That's fine. Kella, I'd like you to come away from the fire. Will you do that?''

"Nay! Tied to the fire! Hands tied! Feet tied! Fire eating . . ."

The voice, Cayla noted, had changed its accent with the first mention of fire. The twang had become a burr. So the woman knew enough to be consistent. "They want to burn me," she was saying, "because I love the Master."

"What Master is that?"

"Lord of the Dark! Beelzebub!"

The hypnotist said soothingly, "All right, Kella. Kella, what year is it?"

"Sixteen hundred and forty-three."

"How old are you?"

"Thirty and eight."

"All right. Now, try to see yourself when you are younger, much younger. Try to see yourself when you are fifteen, Kella. Do you see yourself when you are fifteen?"

Cayla leaned forward, clasping her hands. If the woman made certain references to the actual Kella's adolescence . . .

After a long pause she said, "Yes."

"Where are you now, Kella?"

"Kirk."

That was safe enough, Cayla thought. Of course every schoolchild knew that the Scottish word for church was *kirk*.

"What do you do there?" the hypnotist asked.

"Listen. Pray. Sing sometimes. Like to sing."

Hardly an act of clairvoyance, Cayla thought, to guess that a young girl might like to sing, especially in those bleak Calvinist times. But if the woman talked about playing a flute . . .

In fact she made another safe choice; she began to speak of the sermon she was hearing: "Preacher says we must be vigilant. Says we must look deep inside us for the smallest sign of sin, for the Devil can put his evil through the most wee crack . . ."

There was cleverness in that, Cayla thought—to pose as a good Christian when young and save the witch business for adulthood. Still, it was all so transparent. For one thing, if the voice was Kella Hagaward's, why did she speak in a modern Scottish accent? Why did no one raise that issue and point out that the speech of over three centuries ago was vastly different from today's? Cayla glanced around the room again, hoping to see skepticism on at least some of the faces, but even the man leaning against the wall, who seemed intelligent, had no expression other than concentration.

44

It was because she was looking away that Cayla missed seeing the change take place. She only heard the voice, which went from its not unpleasant low tone to something much harsher, and from the recital of Christian orthodoxy to its antithesis.

"Now comes the Sabbat," it cried. "Cursed be Jesu! Praised be our Master, Satan, who sits on his throne! We worship him as he commands. We go to his throne with our backs turned to him, as he commands. And then to show our love, we kiss! But not his ring—nay, not like a Papist. Nay! The Master turns his back to us and bends over, and that is what we kiss!" The voice burst into laughter that sounded like metal twisting. "And then we dance before him and play music, and we eat his feast, and he comes to us, to all of us . . . comes to me, and oh, he is cold, and hairy, as cold as ice, and big, so big, and deep inside me goes his huge and icy part, burning, burning, burning . . . Oh, my Master, oh, my Lord of Darkness, they burn me for your sake, they tie me to the fire because I am your servant! But you give me the power—yes, Master, the power! And you will pass the power down, so we can serve you always. Now and forever, down all the generations of the family, so all will do your will!"

The hypnotist, who had not tried to stop the torrent of words, leaned closer and called, "Kella! Kella, can you hear me?"

"Who has the power in your time?" she cried. "Yes, the power goes down all the generations, down to all the women who love the Master as I do and will bear his mark! Down to the girl-child far in the future who will be born with six toes on one foot, as the sign and symbol that she is his! Down the centuries, down . . ."

The voice went on, but Cayla ceased to hear it, aware only of the void that opened within her like ice cracking on a river.

She felt a hand grip her arm and pull her up. Not until it had guided her into the hall did she realize it belonged to the man who had been leaning against the wall. When she could, she said to him, "Please let go of me."

He hesitated. "All right." His eyes were green, and so intense that she wanted to pull away, but already she was standing with the wall against her back. "You looked as if you felt ill," he said. "I thought maybe you needed some air."

"Not air. Common sense." But she took a deep breath.

The man said, his casual manner contradicting the look in his eyes, "I had the impression it was the mention of a six-toed child that got to you. Do you mind telling me whether I'm right?"

"I don't want to be rude, since you helped me, but as a matter of fact I do mind." She straightened her shoulders. "Why were you watching my reactions instead of Ms. Whiting's performance?"

The man smiled. "You're much easier to look at than she is."

Cayla said nothing, but her silence didn't seem to disconcert him.

"Besides," he went on, "I've seen Ms. Whiting before."

"Have you? Where?"

"This is the third session I've attended. I was the hypnotist for one of them, in fact. I got a response very similar to the one you just watched."

"I see. You're one of the experts who are going to tell us whether she's a fake."

"You don't sound as if you approve."

"I'm afraid I don't."

"Why not?"

She hesitated. "Do you consider yourself a scientist?"

He seemed surprised, one dark eyebrow rising toward his lighter, curly hair. "You know, I never think in those terms. I just think of myself as trying to understand, I guess."

"By means of accepting the supernatural?"

He glanced down at his brown shirt and tweed jacket. "Where's the sign that says I do?"

"Aren't you a parapsychologist—whatever that means?"

He regarded her for a moment, as if taking mental notes. "If you don't know what a word means, should you be saying it with such disdain, Ms. Hayward?"

"Fair enough," she said. "But if you know who I am, you should know why I feel disdain."

"I think I do."

"How did you recognize me?"

He smiled again; his teeth were even and white. "You're dressed much too expensively to be somebody who belongs here. Besides, your picture's been in the papers lately." She grimaced, and he added, "I saw it in conjunction with the Tay-Sachs story. Congratulations on the work your company is doing."

"Thank you." After a moment, realizing she was watching the way the green in his eyes had deepened, she said crisply, "No one else in the room seems to have recognized me."

"I imagine you're the last person they'd expect to find walking in here."

"Why? When I'm the object of the whole performance? And incidentally, if Polly Whiting is such a clairvoyant, shouldn't she have identified me right away?"

"She's not claiming to be clairvoyant. Maybe you don't understand that term."

"Do I need to? As long as I understand the term *fraud?*"

He studied her carefully. "I've examined the woman, you know. You may not like to hear it, but she's not faking. Whatever is happening, I don't think she's doing it consciously."

"Sorry, but to me that sounds very gullible."

The man answered calmly. "I'm interested in finding the truth about this case, Ms. Hayward. The next thing to do, as I see it, would be to check out Polly Whiting's background, to see whether she ever had access to any kind of information about the historical Kella Hagaward. You don't dispute that there was such a person?"

"No."

"You know, if I had the time and money, I'd do the checking myself."

"Why?"

"Several reasons. One of them is her mention of a child with six toes." His green eyes pinned Cayla to the wall. "You still won't answer my question?" he said. "You won't tell me why the mention of a six-toed child made you look as if you'd been hit in the solar plexus?"

She managed to get away from his eyes, but didn't answer.

She heard him say, "OK," as if she were a child being soothed. She turned back to him, but he was checking his watch. "Since you seem to be feeling all right now, I'll leave you. I have a patient in half an hour and have to get across town."

As he went to the elevator, his walk made her think of both military discipline and barefoot ease.

Behind her she heard sounds from the room; the session was breaking up. Polly Whiting must have been calmed down and brought out of her trance.

Several people came out. She heard one man say, "But the positive Babinski reflex, I can't explain that. No one can *fake* it."

"Excuse me," Cayla said to him. "I was just discussing the case with a gentleman who had to leave but whose name I didn't get. Wearing a tweed sport coat? Tall, with auburn hair?"

"I think you must mean Stefan Veere."

"Do you know why he was asked to join the examining team?"

The man raised an eyebrow. "The son and grandson of mediums? I'd call that a pretty good qualification."

"Ah," Cayla said. "I guess you're right." When the speaker looked as if he might question her identity and credentials, she added, "I mustn't keep my patients waiting," and went to the elevator.

She frowned as she waited for it. He was someone, then, who believed in spirits and ectoplasm. It seemed she hadn't yet learned how to judge men.

6

By the time the car crossed the Connecticut line, the storm had cleared but Cayla's thoughts had not.

No matter which of the day's events she considered, it led her to the last place she wanted to go: the past. To think of the clan was to confront the contradictory things she had always felt about belonging to the Hayward family. But to think of the parapsychologists' sessions was worse.

She turned to look out the window. A sign for the next parkway exit loomed up. While she stared at it, the sound of singing came into her mind, echoing down the years.

"Carl, take this exit. I'll stop at the hospital." She leaned back, her dark hair and clothes disappearing against the leather. When she closed her eyes, the sound of singing drifted into her mind again, although she couldn't remember the very young child who had heard it. Were the first five years of life lost to everyone, she wondered, or only to her? She thought of how the Whiting woman had regressed to her fifth birthday, even her sixth month, or pretended to. Could one really pull one's mind back down the ladder of concepts and experiences, to a place where only the simplest existed? The adult personality, it had always seemed to her, was like a lab compound that, once synthesized, could never break down into its components. At least one wouldn't want it to. Not if one had struggled to break away from childhood and the obsessed and helpless women who had been its guardians.

They had frightened her. Often. Because she had hated the feeling, she had discovered an antidote for it: the schoolroom, where the work gave her a quickening sense of adventure, the tutors were pleased to let her advance as fast as she wanted, and the rest of Rowan Hall had neither influence nor relevance.

When Grace and Kelvin took her away, she wanted to bury everything about the girl who had lived there except the part that had come alive in the second-floor schoolroom. And she had succeeded, flinging herself as eagerly into the lives of the aunts and uncles as into the continuation of her schooling. She learned to ride, sail, ski, play tennis, and to laugh. Everything was so blessedly bright compared to Rowan Hall that sometimes even the nights seemed drenched in sun. She hadn't seen the pitfall until, when she was eighteen, her cousins introduced her to a man who seemed the apotheosis of their life: a superb athlete who made her laugh and treated her with an oddly touching tenderness. The affair began immediately. It was as searing as sunburn.

It took her two months to see that he was rather shallow, two more weeks to admit that he was anti-intellectual, and one night more to know she had to end things immediately. At dinner she deliberately talked at length about some of the issues being raised in her philosophy class. And he began, subtly at first, to undercut everything with a joke and then to mock her interest in the subject. Later he took her to bed and tried to make her beg for satisfaction, his mouth and hands as alien as a stranger's.

Only then, while realizing that the affair had betrayed it, did she understand how deeply she valued intelligence and its exercise. Over the weeks that followed, she painfully accepted what had made the betrayal possible: a blind surrender to feelings.

It seemed ironic that, five years later, she believed she was marrying a man who valued intelligence, only to watch him turn into someone too much like her first lover, and to realize that once again she had been blinded by the intensity of her response.

Fortunately she had the Industries, where she could spend days that left no time for regrets or lonely nights. She suspected that Kelvin deliberately added to her responsibilities as the marriage soured, but he never admitted it. "I like you to take big bites," he would say, "so I can watch you chew them."

At the beginning he had been skeptical, of course. When she graduated and came into the Industries with her new husband, Kelvin expected only one of them to last. He was right, except that she was the survivor. Soon Kelvin became her active mentor. He saw that she got experience not only in her area, finance, but in production, sales and research as well. "You've got to be twice as good as any man from the outside," he said. "Once because you're a woman, and once again because you're a Hayward."

Although she knew he was grooming her to head the textile-fibers division, she kept in close touch with some microbiologists she had met at the university and their vision of the future. After months of planning she presented Kelvin with a proposal that the Industries start a genetic-engineering division. It was complete even to site selection.

He called her to his office; he told her that the plan was brilliant and that he would recommend it to the board. "But you're not going to run it. Not at first, anyway. It's too big a bite, Cayla. Now, don't look like I just kicked you. My job is to see that your future turns out to be what it should, not to make it happen too soon. You need to work under a more experienced hand."

He was right, of course. She had had many things to learn about management: to be a good delegator, to make people see how to do things by asking them questions that sparked their own ideas, to fill the more boring jobs with less-qualified people, who would not be bored, and then to make them stretch. After a few years the president of Biologiconn was moved elsewhere and Kelvin told her it was hers. "Maybe it should have been all along." He started to shake her hand but wound up crushing her in a hug.

Cayia smiled, opened her eyes and looked out her limousine window. The car was turning into the drive of a secluded private hospital that was supported almost entirely by Hayward money. Normally she visited it only twice a year, and she regretted her decision to do so now. It had been the whim of a bad mood, but the mood had passed, she realized, because she had been thinking of Biologiconn.

Five minutes later she was in the hospital's reception area. She had barely taken a seat when the director came through the heavy inner doors, almost running, a hand outstretched in welcome. "I had no idea you were coming!" he said.

"I didn't either, Dr. Patrick. It was an impulse."

"I see. I do have a staff meeting at four o'clock, but I can delay it. No problem. Is there something you wanted to discuss?"

"I just want to make sure there's been no change in your procedures for protecting her identity."

"But of course not, Ms. Hayward!"

"Good. It's especially important at the moment that no one find out who she is."

"Ah, yes," he said, and she could read in his eyes that he knew why. "But I assure you, she's known only as Rachel Brown. Remember, we've been protecting her for thirty years." He rubbed his hands. "Well, now! As long as you're here, you'll want to see her, of course. I don't know how she is today," he added, "but I'll go and check. Let's hope you can have a nice visit."

"Dr. Patrick." She stopped him. "Do you happen to know what a 'positive Babinski reflex' is?"

"Why yes. It's a reflex of the toes, found in infants. When you stroke the sole of an infant's foot, its toes extend rather than flex—that is, they curl up, not under. With anyone older, the toes would curl under. Try it on yourself."

"What would it mean if an adult's toes curled up?"

"They couldn't, not unless there was a neurological lesion. It's an involuntary reflex, you see."

"What if the adult was under hypnosis?"

"And regressed to infancy, you mean? Then I'd say the person was an extraordinary hypnotic subject and there could be

51

no question that he or she really had regressed. The reflex couldn't be faked, you see.''

"Yes, I do. Thank you."

He smiled at her brightly and went away.

Outside, the lawn stretched for what seemed like miles. On Cayla's previous visit, Christmas Day, the grass had been frozen and brown, but now, under the late afternoon sun, it seemed ready to ignite into green at any moment. Nature's perennial symbol of hope, she thought. It seemed like a mockery in such a place.

When she was young, the adults had always spoken as if there were hope. Rachel was only gone ''for a while.'' Later there had been talk of new treatments for schizophrenia: of the insulin-induced comas; of the drugs, a number of them actually developed by Hayward Industries, that had revolutionized the treatment of mental disorders in the 1960s; and of the experimentation with dialysis. But none of them had been able to reach Rachel's mind for more than very brief periods.

The director's secretary appeared and led the way through the heavy doors, down a rubber-tiled hall, to a visiting room. A window gave onto the hopeful lawn, its glass reinforced with wire.

Cayla sat down to wait, but when the door to the visiting room began to open, she stood up quickly, pushing her hands deep into the pockets of her skirt.

''Now come along, Rachel, don't keep your visitor waiting,'' said a voice whose kindliness only underscored that it seemed to be addressing a child, and an attendant brought Rachel into the room.

For a moment Cayla seemed to be looking up, way up, at a presence that was dim but vibrant, warm but frightening. The feeling was over before it could be grasped, and she was left with nothing but the customary sense of slight shock that Rachel was only of average height.

The attendant said, ''Would you like me to stay with you today?''

''No, I don't think so. Thank you.''

The door closed. Rachel stood just inside it. Her hair, which Gran said had been a beautiful brown when she entered the hospital, was gray. It lay over her left shoulder in a single thick braid like a tail and stood out against her bright red sweater. Her pink dress was freshly pressed. The colors, Cayla knew, were Rachel's preference, but no doubt the cleanliness had been hurriedly imposed for the visit. Rachel was not neat.

Cayla said, "Hello." She had to clear her throat to continue; she never could make the word come out naturally. "Hello, Mother."

On some visits it elicited a response, but not this time. Rachel remained against the door, motionless, her expression as frozen as the grounds at Christmas.

On the evidence of old family pictures, she had never had the legendary Hayward beauty. Her nose was too short and her mouth too wide. But in those pictures her features communicated something Cayla never recalled seeing in them: vitality.

On Cayla's first visit to the hospital, Gran's nurse-companion, Hester, held her hand in a grip like metal and said, "Oh, here she is, your darling mother, now give her a kiss." She had thought Rachel must be wearing a mask, her face was so motionless. When she kissed it, the skin was so flaccid she had felt as if she were putting her lips against the drapes in Gran's bedroom.

She had wanted to cry then, and she wanted to do so again, to let go of the reins of control she had been gripping more tightly every day for over a week—to run from the dark things she couldn't understand, which seemed to be rising against her—to run to someone who would hold and comfort her. But the woman who might have done so was part of the dark things.

"Mother," she said, "why can't you ever—" She stopped. "Why can't you . . ." Rachel looked at her with no change of expression.

Cayla put her fingertips under her eyes and pressed hard. In a moment she said, "Wouldn't you like to come and sit over here?" She gestured to the tweed chair beside her own.

Rachel stayed at the door. Suddenly, as if they didn't belong to her, her hands flew to her temples like a pair of birds, poised there with outstretched fingers, then slid down her cheeks and closed over her mouth. She repeated the series of movements several times, as she often had. No one knew what it meant to her; the doctors could say only that the repetition of certain gestures or phrases, or both, meaningless to anyone but the patient, was characteristic of some mental disorders, particularly of schizophrenia. It was communication turned against itself, used not to reach the world outside but to secure the borders of the world within.

When Cayla had been old enough to be told of Rachel's condition, she had thought of the motto on the Rowan Hall gates. *Vivimus in posteris.* Was it, as her tutor said, just a Latin phrase expressing hope for the future? Or was it what Gran had always claimed—what now seemed more possible than ever?

After a while one of Rachel's hands left her mouth, crept into her sweater pocket, and pulled out a cigarette. "They try to steal them," she said. "They know how I sing, you see—just like Viardot and Malibran. They're jealous, so they poison the soup and try to steal the cigarettes. But I don't let them."

Cayla took out the matches she had placed in her skirt pocket, went over to Rachel, and held out a light. Rachel fastened one hand on Cayla's as she inhaled deeply. It was very thin and almost cold, like a bird's claw gripping a perch.

She looked up into Cayla's face, her eyes as dark and hard as two pebbles, the smoke curling out of her mouth. "I know you," she said. "I know you, I know you, I know what you want."

"I just wanted to see how you are."

"Why? Why? Who are you?"

"Cayla."

"Ah! Kella! Yes! I thought you'd come, Kella, I was expecting you."

"No, I'm *Cayla.*"

Rachel laughed. At least Cayla had always assumed that sound was laughter. Then Rachel began striding around the small room, puffing on the cigarette, muttering. "Kella gets in my head, you know, she makes me do it. She's after my voice, of course, just the way she was after my baby, the baby I had with Satan. She knows how beautifully I sing, that's why she comes in. She waits for me to have a cigarette and then she comes in with the smoke and sits there on the epiglottis along with the legato passages that triumvirate the coordination of my state of articulation and codification . . ."

As Rachel's words deteriorated from delusion into word salad, Cayla wondered what she could possibly have hoped to achieve by her visit—unless it was to mock the very concept of wanting comfort from one's mother. The way a witches' Sabbat mocked the Christian mass.

Suddenly Rachel stopped talking. She looked at the cigarette as if seeing it for the first time and ground it out in an ashtray. Then she walked slowly to the wall, placed her back against it, and slid down until she was sitting on the floor. Several times her hands flew to her temples. She kicked off her bright red slippers and pushed her bare feet into the shag carpet. "Ah," she said, wiggling her toes. "A-a-a-ah, that feels good."

As if they were being dragged, Cayla's eyes went to the left foot.

Perhaps that was why she had come, she thought—in the ridiculous hope that somehow things had changed and there would be only five toes.

She got to bed later than usual that night, the day's events swirling through her mind.

Her eyes finally closed around one-thirty, and her breathing became regular within twenty minutes. But an hour or so later she began to toss from one side of the bed to the other, her hands clutching at the heavy silk spread while her feet kicked out from beneath it.

She was struggling to get away from eyes, amber eyes, and a body that was black and furry. And claws. They were holding the creature next to her, trying to make her kiss it, and she was choking, fighting to push it away and choking while the amber eyes glowed at her and the sharp teeth shone . . . They were beating her because she pushed it away, they were telling her to sing, to sing, to sing . . . But when she opened her mouth, no sound would come because her tongue was swollen in her throat, and she was choking, and the creature with amber eyes was huge now, its mouth opening like a red cavern and each of its claws a scimitar, and they were telling her to kiss its face and fondle it . . .

Her eyes jerked wide on the darkness of the bedroom and the dial of her bedside clock: three forty-five. She sat up, one hand over the racing of her heart and the other feeling her hair, which clung to her scalp wetly.

At length she got up and went into the bathroom. It was many years since she had had the nightmare. As a child she had had it often, but when she was taken away from Rowan Hall, the nightmare had receded, and Biologiconn, she thought, had dispelled it forever.

She lifted one unsteady hand and touched the mark in her hairline. For the first time in her life she wished she did possess the power that had been prophesied for her, so she could use it to destroy Polly Whiting.

The thought was gone in a moment, but the fact that it had existed at all, and with such violence, made her whole body tremble.

She gripped the cool, smooth rim of the lavatory tightly and tried to think of the next day at Biologiconn.

7

Stefan Veere walked to his office and, as usual, reached it before eight, carrying the morning papers and a bakery bag with a cinnamon bun.

He liked to arrive early, while the city still had a patina of freshness and most of the faces looked as if they thought a good day was at least a possibility. He was definitely a morning person, although whether that was in spite of his upbringing or because of it, he could never decide. The fact that most people had a time of day, or night, when they seemed to feel and function best was one of the small mysteries of human behavior he liked to ponder. Such thoughts were a relief from the larger mysteries—why, for instance, some people lived contentedly in the real world whereas others held only distorted perceptions of it.

His office was empty. It was Saturday, so his receptionist would arrive at eight-thirty and his first patient at nine. In the tiny kitchenette he made himself instant coffee and carried it to the outer office, smiling.

He had never expected to be a professional man. Psychology had drawn him slowly, without his realizing where his queries were leading. Then, suddenly, he had had to decide whether to become a psychologist or a psychiatrist. It was the difference between a Ph.D. in psychology and an M.D. with three years of psychiatric residency. The decision had been tough. Medical training was expensive and long—but he wanted to be as familiar as possible with the organic causes of mental illness and to have the best clinical training. He became Dr. Veere and turned thirty on the same day, and four years later knew he wanted to work with people who were functioning in the world rather than those who had to be institutionalized. He had just decided to make the break when one of his former professors wrote to say he'd had a heart attack and wanted to cut back on his workload. He offered to recommend Stefan to a number of his patients if Stefan would consider coming to New York to start a practice.

In psychic circles, Stefan had thought wryly, that would have been regarded as a sign from the spirit world.

He had certainly never intended to start debunking psychics, but in his first year of practice, an Australian "seer" had taken the New York media by storm, and Stefan had been unable to resist challenging the man on a local TV show. He had duplicated one of the Australian's chief feats, bending a spoon by what seemed to be sheer mental power. The majority of the man's admirers went right on believing in his psychic powers— just as Stefan had learned, in the crisis of his adolescence, that people always would—but he had felt better for trying. The result was that in certain circles he acquired a reputation for being willing and able to expose psychic frauds. Some of his colleagues voiced disapproval—especially when they heard that he considered certain schools of psychiatry to be as fraudulent as the psychics.

At his desk he took out the cinnamon bun, broke it into pieces, and ate one before he thought of Barbara, who had always unrolled her cinnamon bun in one long strip and then eaten it in tiny bites.

He spread out the newspapers and scanned the tabloid. There was a Polly Whiting story on page 6. The last hard news about her had been the examining team's announcement that in its judgment she was not deliberately attempting a hoax. But recent stories about the fundamentalist coalition's attack on genetic engineering—which apparently involved bombarding both Congress and the gene-splicing industry with letters—had kept Polly in the news.

Two days earlier, when she left New York to return to West Virginia, the press had seen her off as if she were departing royalty—except that they showed little respect. Polly had turned on a particularly insistent reporter and hissed at him, her eyes and lips spreading wide to spit out the fear and hostility that Stefan knew were there, hidden beneath her placid, almost bovine manner.

He wondered whether the reporter, and the TV audience, perceived the fear and hostility or just the hissing. To him they were an indivisible package.

The door of his outer office opened; Abby had arrived. She said good morning and settled to work at her desk.

He turned to the other paper, which contained nothing on Polly Whiting but had a story about an *ad hoc* group of scientists who had issued a statement on genetic engineering. "For several years now," the statement was quoted, "the public's attention has been diverted from potential problems to the significant achievements in agriculture: the creation of new plant species or the addition of new characteristics to existing species. Now it is time for the public's attention to return to the subject of human genetic engineering and the ethical problems it raises. Although we deplore the recent sensationalist attacks, we believe there are reasonable grounds for concern." And later: "No one questions the desirability of cures for genetic disorders, such as the Tay-Sachs syndrome. But what provisions exist to keep such work from leading to the alteration of a healthy fetus in the name of 'improving' it?"

The fear of a "master race" mentality would have seemed absurd, Stefan thought, if some twentieth-century madmen hadn't shown it could exist. But madmen could abuse any technology. Should the fear that some monster might try to create "superbeings" keep one from trying to help those who were desperate to be normal? Like poor Annie, for instance . . . a patient he'd seen in his years at the psychiatric hospital. In her thirties she had begun to change from an attractive, well-adjusted woman into a slovenly, hostile creature who couldn't walk by herself and constantly grimaced, blinked, and twitched her fingers. Like many others in her mother's family, Annie was a victim of Huntington's chorea, a degenerative disease of the central nervous system. It was in the genes and had been traced as far back as the sixteenth centruy.

Wasn't the possibility of helping the world's poor Annies worth the risk it might entail?

Sighing, Stefan reached for his patient files. He was reviewing them when Abby buzzed and said, "You remember that Mr. Durham canceled his four o'clock? Now I've got a woman on the line who says she absolutely must see you today, so I'd like to give her Mr. Durham's spot. It's a Cayla Hayward. She must be the one in the news, don't you think?"

Stefan often said that after his first year of practice nothing ever surprised him, but his eyebrows lifted. And the real surprise, he noted after he had said yes, was what he felt besides surprise.

All day long, although he gave his patients no less concentration than ever, the face hovered disconcertingly at the edges of his mind—ivory skin, aristocratic bones, and the gypsy contrast of mouth and hair.

When his three o'clock patient left, Abby appeared at the office door to make introductions: "Dr. Veere, this is Cayla Hayward. Ms. Hayward, Dr. Stefan Veere."

He stood up and said, "Hello again."

"Hello." She was carrying a briefcase and wearing a gray suit as severe as a lecture. His memory hadn't done full justice to her face.

"Won't you come in and sit down?"

She glanced around the room, walked briskly to the desk, and took the chair across from it. "I wanted to talk to you. Your secretary said this was the first available time you had, so I took it. But that may have been misleading. I do want to buy your services, but I'm not here as a patient."

"That's good," Stefan said.

It stopped her for only half a beat. "What do you mean?"

He smiled. "It means I was hoping to see you again, but not as a patient." She started to speak, then closed her lips firmly. "So what can I do for you?" he said. "I'm afraid I don't have any services to sell, except as a psychiatrist."

"I think you do." She sat erect, on the edge of the chair. "I want to hire you to investigate Polly Whiting's background."

Stefan let almost a minute go by. Her glance communicated nothing. "Why?" he said.

"Because I want her exposed as a fraud."

"It seems to me," he said mildly, "that one should investigate first and then decide whether she's a fraud."

Her nostrils flared. "All right, if you're referring to the positive Babinski reflex, I'll concede that she's not consciously a fraud. Let's just say that I want her investigated. If you've been keeping up with the news, you'll know why."

Stefan nodded and leaned back, pushing his chair away from the desk. "Why do you want *me* to do it?"

"Last week you said if you had the time and money, you'd like to see whether she ever had access to information about the historical Kella Hagaward. I'm offering you as much money as you need, so you can make the time."

"That doesn't quite answer my question. Last week you called me gullible. So why would you want to hire me to investigate?"

There was another pause. Above the collar of Cayla's jacket Stefan could see her pulse beating rapidly, in defiance of her calm. "I spoke too quickly last week," she said. "I'm sorry. I've made some inquiries about you. You're not a parapsychologist. You're a cognitive therapist. I'm told you regard the reasoning faculty as the essential means of solving psychological problems. You've been in practice for six years, and you've occasionally helped expose people who claim to have psychic powers. It seems you have the ideal background for an examination of this situation. And of course you've already seen and worked with the Whiting woman."

Stefan knew she wasn't revealing all her reasons. Her tension wasn't the kind that released itself in aimless gestures and edges in the voice, but a deeper kind, which the body tried to conquer by holding itself as rigid as a shield. But a shield against what? he wondered. Of course she would be upset, as anybody would, by finding herself and her company in the eye of a storm, especially the kind that was now gathering. But why so tense with him?

"I wouldn't mind investigating," he said. "But I can't abandon my patients." He gestured at his desk calendar. "It's full. Besides, it's hard to believe you haven't already had Polly's background looked into. If you even made some inquiries about me."

"You're right," she said. "I did." She took the briefcase from beside her chair and unlatched it. The snap echoed in her voice. "I've had private detectives working for two weeks. They haven't found anything helpful. No connection or point of contact between Polly Whiting and my family." She handed him a folder.

Stefan read it through, feeling her eyes on his face the entire time. When he finished he said, "It looks pretty complete. I don't know what I could do that would be much different."

"I see." She put a hand flat on the edge of the desk. "You're not exactly what I imagined a cognitive therapist would be like," she said.

"In my last dream about the president of a genetic-engineering firm, he didn't look anything like you, either."

For the first time she smiled, though faintly. "I should confess that I don't have much faith in psychiatrists. The ones I've known haven't impressed me. Of course I've never met a cognitive therapist before. I thought there were only two basic schools of psychology—behaviorism and Freudianism. Conditioned reflexes versus unconscious feelings. I didn't know there was a school that believed in the importance of the mind."

"It's relatively new."

She moved her head as if to shake it, but instead it dropped into the cradle made by her hands and she whispered, "I don't know what else to do, who else to ask."

Stefan looked at the crown of blue-black hair, which caught the light from the desk lamp. Part of him reached for something professionally soothing to say. Part of him just wanted to reach.

Before either occurred, her head snapped up. "I'm sorry," she said. "Please forget that happened. It was inexcusable."

"Hey," he said. "It wasn't a felony."

"This is a business meeting. Displays of personal feeling are out of place."

"Really? When you're in the middle of something that deeply affects your personal life as well as your business?"

"I don't expect my staff at Biologiconn to produce results just because I want them so badly." He started to speak, but she shook her head. "No, please. Just give me a moment." She looked down, smoothing her skirt. Then she lifted her head. "There's something the detectives didn't know about. No one outside of my immediate family knows about it. If I tell you, if I trust you, it should make the investigation easier by giving it a specific focus.''

Stefan leaned forward, expecting to hear the real reason she had come to him, hoping his eyes wouldn't betray the extent of his interest. ''Does it have something to do with a six-toed child?''

She seemed startled. ''No. It doesn't.''

Covering his own surprise, he said lightly, ''You still won't tell me why you reacted so strongly to what Polly said?''

''I'd rather not discuss it.''

''Why not?''

''Why does it interest you?''

He considered. ''If you don't want to talk about it, I guess I won't either. It's just a personal thing, anyway.''

They regarded each other. It seemed to Stefan that they were both as wary as boxers. ''Look,'' he said, ''If you want to tell me whatever it is your detectives didn't know, I'll try to free up some times and look into it. Not a lot, though—just what I can get by juggling my appointments.''

She closed her eyes, and he saw a blue lace of veins on the lids.

''But you can't hire me,'' he said. ''It's not the kind of thing I care to take money for.''

The lids flew open. ''That's ridiculous. I want a business arrangement.''

''Sorry, you can't have it.'' He laughed at her look of bewilderment; she was losing the masklike calm. ''There are still a few things money can't buy. Or doesn't someone named Hayward know that?''

''I'd be in your debt.''

''No, you wouldn't.'' With the tip of a loafer Stefan pulled open one of the bottom desk drawers and stretched his legs to rest on it. ''Let me tell you what I'll get out of doing this. When people claim to be clairvoyant—or to communicate with the dead or to use psychic powers to bend spoons or lift chairs or whatever—most of them are frauds, easy to spot once you know the tricks. But then there are people who appear not to be frauds, who aren't trying to hoax anybody. They often believe deeply in their alleged powers, and sometimes they can do very strange things. Whatever's happening seems to be coming from the subconscious, bypassing conscious awareness. People like that have interested me all my life." He gestured at the room. "In fact they're what got me into this business."

"To me," she said, "the subconscious seems like too easy an explanation. It's the great opiate of the twentieth century, absolving all our sins by telling us we couldn't help committing them."

"You wouldn't think the subconscious was so easy if you had to try to understand it every day—to decide, in any given patient, whether certain behavior was volitional. To me the subconscious is one of the larger mysteries in psychology. And Polly Whiting is an interesting case in point. So I'd find it professionally interesting to learn more about the nature and cause of her behavior under hypnosis." That was the truth, Stefan thought. It just wasn't the whole truth.

"And if it's all outside her awareness and control, then she's not responsible for the trouble she's causing?"

Stefan sat erect and said gently, "Do you want her punished?"

She looked away. In the light from the desk lamp, her hair was a dark velvet cap. "I want her investigated." She turned back to him. "This is the connection: My family has a letter, an actual letter, written by Kella Hagaward in 1643, just before she died. Before they burned her as a witch."

"Ah."

"The letter was discovered sometime in the 1920s, at Rowan Hall. That's the main family estate in Connecticut. It would have been of great value to scholars, of course, but my family decided to keep it secret."

"Why?"

"I don't know all the details or reasons, but there was a vow of silence about it. It's been locked away at Rowan Hall ever since. There are strong family reasons why I don't want to make its existence public, but if it would stop all this . . ." She breathed deeply and clenched her hands. "I've realized, though, that the letter is a two-edged sword. I have to be able to show that the Whiting woman could have learned about its contents. Because if the letter became public knowledge and I *couldn't* demonstrate that she had access to it, then it could be taken as proof of what she says—proof that her trance-voice really is Kella Hagaward."

Stefan said, "It would be taken that way. Count on it."

"I know. But somehow Polly Whiting must have learned about the letter. That's why I went to that meeting last week, to find out whether she was using specific details from the letter."

"Was she?"

"I don't know!" She seemed startled by her own vehemence. Her hands, still clenched, came up to rest beneath her chin. "The cat she spoke of—according to the letter Kella had one. But that's really bromidic. Every Halloween picture shows a witch with a cat and a broomstick. The woman also talked of how Kella liked to sing, and the Kella letter does refer to singing. But that could also be purely coincidental. Maybe Polly Whiting is clever enough not to be specific. But she has to have read the letter, or at least heard about it. Otherwise how could she . . . How else could she know that Kella Hagaward died in 1643? Or that there *was* such a person as Kella Hagaward? How else?"

Another explanation leaped into her dark eyes, and for a moment Stefan felt an empathy so strong it turned her eyes into mirrors.

"There is no other way," she said. "It has to be the letter."

"May I see it?" he asked after a moment. "I think I must."

She put her hands in her lap and sighed. "Yes. But you'll have to swear to keep it confidential."

"Of course." He leaned back in his chair and stared at the ceiling, hands locked behind his head. "Does everybody in the Hayward family know about the letter?"

"No. It was found by my grandmother's branch of the family, and they're the ones who decided to keep it secret. Oh, the other descendants—my third and fourth cousins—do know there's some kind of record showing that Kella Hagaward really did exist and was burned as a witch, but they don't know there was actually a letter from her."

"Are any of the people still alive who were there when the letter was found?"

"Only my grandmother."

"And where is she?"

"At Rowan Hall. She's lived there all her life."

He looked across the desk again. "Perfect! Can you arrange for me to talk to her?"

"I'd have to take you. Gran is . . . peculiar."

"In what way?" When she didn't answer, he said, "I'm a

64

psychiatrist, remember? I've heard just about everything in the peculiarity department. Whatever the issue is, I guarantee it's not going to shock me, so don't let it embarrass you, OK?"

"My Gran," she said slowly, "is eighty-seven, a widow since long before I was born. She's been bedridden for much of her adult life—paralyzed. I've never known her any other way."

"That's not so bad. My grandmother was Dame Dorcas Veere, spiritualist and psychic adviser."

"It's true, then—you really did grow up with mediums?"

"Yes. Your investigators must have told you that. So how could your grandmother be any worse than mine?"

She smiled, broadly this time, and he smiled with her, part of him noting clinically how much her tensions had receded, and part simply seeing the lines of her mouth. Finally he said, "When can you take me to see her? I'm done for the day, and tomorrow's Sunday, so how about right now?"

"But it's at least a two-and-a-half-hour drive."

"So? We'd get there around eight. We can take my car. Of course if you have other plans . . . ."

"No." She sighed. "Let me call ahead and tell them."

Stefan watched her take the phone and dial, and it was as if the smile hadn't happened. Impersonality fitted back over her face like a mask. In a moment she said, "John, please get Hester for me." She waited, her eyes circling the room until they returned to Stefan's, and looked away. "I thought all psychiatrists had couches."

"Psychoanalysts do—Freudians. I prefer to look people in the eyes."

She took the challenge.

He knew people couldn't look directly at one another for long without some kind of communication taking place on a personal level—encounter groups were practically founded on that fact—but just as he could feel her gaze opening to his, it returned to the phone.

"Hester? Has she been doing all right today?" She listened. "Fine. I'm coming out tonight to see her, and I'm bringing someone with me, someone I want her to meet." She listened again, eyes narrowing. "I'll be there in less than three hours, Hester. Please make sure she's ready." She put down the phone with a finality that must have been heard at the other end. "We can go."

"Wait a minute," Stefan said. "You haven't told me why you're embarrassed about your grandmother, why you think she's peculiar."

Cayla lifted her head. Her eyes were large and bright, like black glass in candlelight. "In my family, Dr. Veere, as you will see, the women are either lazy or crazy."

"You're not," he said gently. "You seem very hard-working, perfectly sane, and pretty upset."

She stood. "Should we go?"

He rose, too. "Yes, I think we should."

8

The light faded as they drove; the car's passage seemed to pull the color from the sky.

Cayla glanced only occasionally at Stefan, answering his questions about Biologiconn, talking about the science series she wanted the Industries to underwrite for television. But the closer they came to Rowan Hall, the quieter she grew. She could sense the house from miles away: its musty cellars, the carved gryphons' heads on the fireplace in her room, Gran's eyes flickering in their strange way . . .

When the car stopped at the iron gates, two things had risen, a wind and a moon, so that a cold white glow illuminated the motto.

Stefan studied it. "We live in our posterity?"

"That's right." As he turned to look at her, she got out, pressed the button in one of the gateposts, opened a small door, and took out the phone kept inside. "It's young Cayla, John. Please open up."

Soon the gates swung inward like giant cell doors, and Stefan drove through. "Quite a system," he said.

"If the gates are opened without authorization, an alarm rings in the police station. They installed it in the 1920s."

"How many people live at Rowan Hall now?"

"Five. Gran and Hester, John and his wife—that's the butler and the cook—and a security guard. And there's some daytime help."

"How big is it?"

"Five hundred acres and forty-one rooms."

"Good God." She watched Stefan's eyes widen as the house appeared at the end of the winding drive: a stone monolith, capped by turrets with pointed roofs and studded with dozens of windows that the moon turned into blank stares.

On the ground level was an immense porte cochere, which suddenly flooded with light. Cayla led Stefan to the oak entry doors. One of them heaved open as they approached, and old John, his face as impassive as the doors, said, "Good evening, Miss."

She nodded. "John, I think we'll go right up and see her. Unless Dr. Veere would like something to eat or drink first?"

"No, thanks," Stefan said. His eyes were sweeping the central hall, sixty feet wide and three floors high, and the massive marble staircase that led up from it.

Cayla hesitated. "I haven't brought anyone here in years. It's hard to imagine how it seems to . . . someone else."

"Pretty gloomy so far. Does it get better?"

"Oh, no. Worse."

He laughed and then said, "Sorry," as the sound rolled around them and up into space. "It was the way you said it. I forgot that you grew up here. Isn't that what you told me?"

"I was born upstairs. My earliest memories are of a suite on the second floor, close to Gran's." She wanted to tell him about it, but she tucked her hair behind her ears and said, "Let's go up and see Cayla Hayward Randall."

"You didn't tell me you were named after her."

"There's always a Cayla in the Hayward family."

They started up the immense staircase, each step fifteen feet wide, the bronze banisters as ornate as candlesticks. High overhead was the stained-glass ceiling that had given to sunny days the colors of strange nights. When the chandelier that hung from it on a fifty-foot chain was lowered and cleaned, the crystal pieces had tinkled. Gran said it was like birds singing Bach.

Stefan stopped partway up. A prism of the chandelier reflected in his eyes. "It's extraordinary," he said, almost to himself. "The scale of things reduces people to dolls. What could it make you feel to be dwarfed by your possessions? Dear God, what a life you must have had."

He gave her a look she wanted to lean on, but she broke the contact and said lightly, "Oh yes, poor little rich girl."

Stefan turned away. On the landing was the gallery of portraits in heavy, ornate frames. "Haywards?" he asked.

"Yes. In the center, that's Duncan, the founder of Hayward Industries. I don't remember who a lot of the others are . . . ." Cayla stopped as the litany of their names began in her mind as clearly as if she were sitting on Gran's bed, listening. "That's not true. I do know. I've been told dozens of times. There in the corner, that's Isobel Hayward, who is supposed to have had a voice like Jenny Lind's. She fell from the Eiffel Tower at the Paris Exposition when she was in her late thirties. This one is Margaret Hayward, the queen of Edinburgh society in the 1780s or so. She suddenly went mad and had to be locked up. She was only thirty-seven. And here's Duncan's daughter, Cayla Hayward, who was said to know more about chemistry than her brothers. She had three children quite easily, but when she was giving birth to the fourth, at age thirty-eight, she died mysteriously."

She put her hands in the pockets of her slim gray skirt. "I guess if you're going to see Gran and read the letter, you have to know about the famous family curse." She couldn't look at the green eyes; she looked at Margaret Hayward, who had gone mad. "The press didn't get the whole story. It seems there's always been a family legend about a witch burned at the stake in Scotland when she was in her late thirties, who uttered some kind of curse on her descendants." She stopped. "I can't tell you how embarrassing all this nonsense is."

"You don't have to. I can see it."

She gestured to the gallery. "Six female Haywards have died or suffered some disaster when they were in their late thirties, and since they were all quite beautiful and most of them were also quite accomplished, it began to seem that a female Hayward is likely to be cursed if she's beautiful and gifted."

"Like you?"

She let herself look directly at him for a moment. "Like Gran. Gran was beautiful, she was talented and her paralysis became permanent in her late thirties."

The long, red room smelled of contradictory things—the dustiness of age and the salty freshness of the ocean.

A deep red carpet spanned its length, as did a bank of leaded windows. Several were open, admitting the ocean's scent and sound and a breeze that billowed their red damask hangings. At the far end of the room near the marble fireplace was the red velvet chaise. On it lay a figure in a claret-colored dressing gown.

Cayla moved toward it, breathing in all the room's contradictions. "Hello, Gran."

The old woman was looking out to the ocean but staring into inner space. Her hair was as white and fine as sea spray. When Cayla touched one of her hands, she stirred and turned her head. In the bones of her face was the memory of great beauty, over which spiders seemed to have laid their webs.

"Ah, young Cayla," she said. Cayla felt the gaze moving over her face like a blind woman's hand. Finally it went beyond her. "You've brought a man. Not that husband of yours, I hope?"

"I was divorced a long time ago, Gran, remember? This is Dr. Stefan Veere." As she said it, she realized how much she regretted having him meet Gran, or knowing about any of them.

"How do you do, Mrs. Randall?" he said. "It's a pleasure to meet you."

"Is it? Why are you bringing me a doctor, young Cayla? Doctors can't do anything for me. Not at my age."

"He's not here to treat you. He came because I asked him to help me, and in order to do it he has to talk to you."

The two women looked at each other. A childhood plea echoed in Cayla's mind—"I won't be like Gran, ever"—but she saw that in one respect she was; Gran's face held the caution she knew was in her own, born of rejection and regret. "You haven't kissed me," the old woman said finally.

Cayla bent to do so. Her lips left a faint print on one papery cheek.

The old woman told them to sit in the brocade chairs that

faced the chaise, across the fire. Then she tucked her thin hands inside the sleeves of her robe. "What's wrong?"

"I think someone may have found out about the letter."

Gran's eyes flared like coals in the grate. "What letter?"

"Dr. Veere knows about it, Gran. I had to tell him."

"You shouldn't have! You had no right!" The raspy voice came not from the chaise but from the shadows behind it.

Cayla knew her whole face had tightened.

There was a rustling, but only a sharp tip of nose, a long black skirt, and two knotted hands were visible at the far side of the fireplace.

"Hello, Hester," said Cayla. She turned to Stefan. "Hester is Gran's nurse-companion and has been for—how long is it now, Gran?"

The answer came from the shadows. "Sixty-two years."

"Hester is right," Gran said. "You had no business telling this man about the letter." She looked at Stefan, studying the curly hair and green eyes, the wiry frame and the gray fisherman's sweater.

He said easily, "Mrs. Randall, she told me about it because she's hired me as a kind of detective, to find out whether someone's been talking about the letter, and if so, who it is. I can promise you absolute confidentiality."

"You don't look like a doctor," she said. "Or a detective, for that matter. It used to be that doctors dressed properly, a nice suit and a good hat."

"Times have changed, Gran." Cayla held her voice on a tight rein. "If you had a TV or ever looked at a paper, you'd know that."

"The world can go to ruin without my listening to the sounds." The old woman turned away to the windows and the distant bass-drumming of the ocean. A gust of wind sent the fire rearing up in the grate. "So, young Cayla, you betrayed the secret of the letter. You've disobeyed me so many times."

"That's right. And usually with good cause." A heap of embers crumbled with a sigh. Cayla went on. "I've never asked you for anything, but I want you to answer Dr. Veere's questions and show him the letter."

"Don't do it," came the voice from the shadows. "Why should you talk to a man we don't know anything about?"

Ignoring the words, Cayla said, "Gran, listen to *me* for once."

There was no answer. The old woman's head was still turned away, so that nothing was visible but the white ball of her hair.

"All right," Cayla said. "I'll accept your refusal to talk to Dr. Veere, but then I'll never come here again. This will be my last visit to Rowan Hall, and to you. If that's what you want, Gran, well, all right. I'll ask Dr. Veere to leave with me now. But you've got to turn around and look at me and tell me you want it."

There was rustling from the corner but no motion from the chaise. The sound of the breakers grew louder, as if to cover the old woman's silence. When a log popped on the grate, both Cayla and Stefan started, but theirs was the only movement.

Gran's head rolled slowly back toward them. "What do you want to know, Doctor?"

He got up and walked to the chaise, hands deep in his sweater pockets, eyes holding the firelight. "I'd like to know about the time when the letter was found. Do you remember what year it was?"

"Certainly. What do I have to do besides lie here and remember everything? They found the letter the year I got sick for the first time: 1926. In fact it was the very month, June, just a few weeks after the paralysis began. I could tell there was some kind of commotion going on downstairs. Father and Gary—that was your grandfather, young Cayla, but of course you never knew him—they tried to keep it from me, the way they tried to keep everything, but Hester told me."

"That's right," said the raspy voice from the shadows.

Stefan looked toward it. "Wouldn't you like to come out and join us, Hester?"

"Why should I?"

"Maybe you could help. It seems you were already here at Rowan Hall when the letter was discovered."

"I came when the Lady took sick."

"Then you could tell us how the letter was found, and by whom."

"I could. But why should I?"

"Tell him," Gran said, with the simplicity of one who knows she will be obeyed.

When Hester leaned forward, the fire lit her face, whose sharpness came not only from its bones. "One of the handymen was cleaning out a loft. He found an old chest with leather straps and a name and address from Scotland on it. He brought it into the kitchen and they were all looking at it, the cook and the gardeners and everyone. I went down because no one had brought up the Lady's tea, and I found them all there, scratching their heads over some record books and letters, so old nobody could read the words. I told them to take the chest up to Mr. Kelvin—that was the Lady's father—and the next day he brought home a very old gentleman to look the things over. I heard them say that Duncan Hayward must have brought the things when he came over from Scotland and they'd been forgotten over the decades. They were the most excited about a letter they found, from Kella Hagaward. The old gentleman's eyes shone like shoe buttons, and he kept saying, 'It's authentic, I'll swear to that.' So when I told the Lady what I'd heard, she made Mr. Gary and Mr. Kelvin tell her all about it." Hester moved back, shrinking again to a tip of nose and a clench of hands.

Stefan moved away from them, to the windows, the bulky sweater accentuating the span of his shoulders. Then he stopped. "So, Mrs. Randall, except for Hester, the people who worked for you knew nothing about the letter's contents?"

"That's so."

"And the gentleman your father brought out to examine it?"

She frowned. "Goodness, I don't know. I can't even recall his name. I do know Father made him promise not to discuss the letter. In those days if a professional man gave his word, he kept it."

"Your father didn't tell anyone else?"

"I believe he did tell my uncles. But they wouldn't talk about it, any more than Father and Gary would."

"And why was that?"

The old woman shook her head impatiently. "They were the leaders of science and industry, the great research pioneers. They thought the family legend was silly. If we asked about it, we got a lecture on superstition and a reminder that we were living in the twentieth century, 'a time of unparalleled scientific progress.' When they heard what I thought about the letter, they decided to keep it a secret, just within the immediate family, so as not to embarrass the Hayward name and the Industries. They made me swear not to speak of it. That suited me—I didn't want a lot of curiosity-mongers coming around.''

"Did you think the letter proved the family legend was true?''

"Of course. And the very first time I read it, I knew it had been meant for me to see.''

"Why?''

"So many things. Our names . . . and she had a flute, the way I did before I . . .'' Gran stopped, her eyes lost in the distance.

Cayla touched one of her hands. "May we look at the letter? I'd like Dr. Veere to see it. And it's been years since I saw it.''

Hester rustled in the shadows and stood up. "You never liked to look at it. The last time, you ran out of the room. You said you wanted to forget all about it.''

"Circumstances are now forcing me to think about it, Hester. So will you please go and get it?''

"Not unless the Lady tells me to. And I don't think she'll let a strange man and a disbelieving granddaughter look at it.''

"I think she will.'' Cayla looked at Gran calmly. For a moment all other memories drained from the room and she saw only an old woman whose cheeks were cool and frail to kiss and whose robes always smelled faintly of lily of the valley.

"Oh, go get it, Hester,'' Gran said at last. "What does it matter? The letter will be hers when I'm gone, anyway.''

Hester's back, though bent, suggested rigid disapproval as she shuffled into the adjoining bedroom. She left the door ajar. There were sounds of objects being moved and of the safe opening. At length she returned with an oblong case of red velvet, which she put on the dining table at the other end of the room. She retreated to her corner.

The letter was written in dark ink on vellum, a heavy, pale-brown material made from animal skin, probably calf or kid. A faint odor of salt and must rose up from it. The writing was uneven yet seemed to be struggling for discipline, like an exhausted soldier.

Cayla had first seen the letter when she was ten. Gran had brought it out, eyes glittering in the strange way Cayla came to dread—as if they were staring into candles, except there never were any candles. It had seemed as if Rachel were in the room, too, instead of in the hospital, and so were the women from the portrait gallery.

Someone said, "It's terribly hard to read."

The voice was Stefan's. He was frowning, bent over the letter.

Cayla put her hands on the table, anchoring herself in the present, and said, "Kella was writing from her jail cell, to her sister, who apparently lived in a neighboring town. We don't know whether the sister ever got the letter or, if she did, how it got back into the hands of the Hagaward family—Kella was a Hagaward by marriage."

"The archaic spellings . . ." Stefan murmured. After a few sentences he began to grope with the words aloud: " 'They found' . . . no, 'they bound . . . my hands'? Is that 'hands'?"

"Yes." Cayla read softly:

They bound my hands together and put the thumb-screws on me, until the blood came leaping from my nails and everywhere. Only now can I start to use my hands again, and if their writing be hard to decipher, you have the reason.

She saw Stefan's eyes darken. He read on. "She was a midwife, then," he said. "Polly Whiting never made any reference to that."

"No. But there in the next paragraph she talks about her cat."

"Yes, I see it."

"And about her singing."

Stefan nodded. "Is that word 'flute'?"

"Yes. 'I do greatly miss its bird-voice which sang to me so many an eve.' "

"I presume it's true they had flutes in those days?"

"Gran says they're one of the world's oldest instruments. And she knows all about the flute."

Stefan read further. "Witchfinder? Is that the word? Was there such a thing?"

"The Witchfinder-General. 'I pray to my lord for power to make the Witchfinder-General suffer like to what I have endured till now, and shall endure on the morrow . . .' "

Stefan read on. "My God," he said. His eyes went for a moment to the dark patches of stains on the vellum, and then returned to the text. "I see. She wants her nieces to suffer, and all her husband's family, down to the end of time. Is that the passage everybody thought corroborated the legend of the curse?"

"Don't you think it does?"

"You could take it that way," Stefan said. He was staring at the last lines and the date beneath them—"1643 yeare."

From behind them Gran called, "Bring it to me. It's mine. She wrote it for me to read."

Stefan carried the velvet case to her and put it on the chaise.

"What do you think of it?" she asked.

"It's an extraordinary document. Why do you think it was written for you, Mrs. Randall?"

"Ah, God." She gestured at her body. "Haven't I been cursed? And haven't I passed the curse on to Rachel and to—" Cayla stopped her with a look.

"Do you think Kella Hagaward actually was a witch?"

"Don't you think so? Didn't you read what she says about the Sabbats in the woods?"

She began to describe them, her eyes fixed on nonexistent candles—the look that finally had made Cayla realize she was tied not only to her bed but to her obsession. Rachel, she had decided, must have been like Gran: helpless and obsessed, only so much worse that they had to put her in a hospital.

"Gran," she asked sharply, "who else might have known about the letter's existence? Have you and Hester mentioned everyone?"

"Yes, yes."

Stefan enumerated them. "Yourself, Hester, your father, your husband, your uncles and the gentleman who examined it for authenticity?" Gran nodded. Stefan looked into the fireplace shadows. "Hester, do you happen to remember the name of that gentleman?"

"No. It was a long name, that's all I can tell you."

"Did he come out here from New York?"

"Maybe. I think so."

"And you yourself never mentioned the letter to anyone?"

"Of course," Gran interrupted, "one other person knew. I told him myself."

"Who was that?" Stefan asked.

"Dr. Freud."

"Freud? You don't mean Sigmund Freud?"

"The one in Vienna. They sent me to see if he could cure me."

"My God." Stefan's eyes were almost comically wide. "You were a patient of Freud's?"

Cayla said, "Is that important to you? You're not a Freudian."

"No, no, but . . . to talk to someone who . . ." He pulled a chair next to the chaise. "How did you come to go to him, Mrs. Randall?"

"Father and Gary sent me." She raised herself, took the red-velvet letter case in her lap, and put her hands on it, like little piles of bones lying atop a reliquary rather than inside it. "Father found me reading one of my books. Oh my, he was angry. He got Gary, and the two of them grilled me like schoolmasters."

Cayla, standing by the fire, said, "You mean you were reading books on witchcraft?"

"I had to learn about Kella and her time. Hester got just the books I needed."

Cayla looked at Stefan, spread her hands in a hopeless gesture, and turned her back to the room, to stare down into the fire.

"What did you learn from the books?" he asked.

"Ah, many things. How they cast their spells, how they fed their familiars—who weren't always cats, they were dogs or toads or even birds, and the witch would feed them milk and bread mixed with drops of her own blood. I learned about the Sabbats and how they worshiped Satan, and how he put his mark on them with his teeth or his claw, a dark little mark that would never feel pain, and how—"

"Gran, for God's sake!" Cayla heard her words scream into the room. Her hands fought to call them back, and then locked. She made herself turn and face Stefan, who was looking at her in surprise. "Gran, it's not necessary to repeat that mumbo-jumbo."

"You told me to answer this young man's questions, and that's what he asked me about."

76

Stefan said, "So your father and your husband lectured you?"

"Oh, yes. Finally Father asked me straight out whether I thought my illness was connected with the family curse. I told them the truth—though I could have lied easily enough, and maybe I should have. That was it. Oh, my. Father's face went as red as the carpet. He tore the book right out of my hands. They took all the books and burned them. Fitting . . . Fire was always the end." Her fingers moved on the velvet case. "A week or so later Father told me he had taken the trouble to find out the latest, most scientific means of dealing with a problem like mine—psychoanalysis. He wanted me to go to Dr. Freud himself, so when word came that I was accepted as his patient, Hester and I sailed for Europe."

"Just the two of you? No servants?"

"I could take care of the Lady myself," Hester said.

"Ah, Dr. Freud." Gran smiled faintly. "I haven't thought of him in years. That's odd because I talked to him more than I ever talked to anyone except Hester."

"About the letter?" Stefan asked.

"Yes, and so many things. About Mother and Father. And Rachel, the dear sweet child." A sigh lifted the red robe. "I talked and talked and talked."

9

The old woman saw her granddaughter and the young man, and everything else, in a slight blur, partially because of her failing eyesight and partially because she didn't like to focus on the present, which contained only the fact of her great age. The clearest things were those in the inner distance of memory, where her strength and her legs were still alive, although of course her guilts and fears were too.

Somehow, the young man's eyes were like signals through a

mist, urging her to recall her past—just the way Dr. Freud had done, now that she thought about him. Of course, Dr. Freud didn't look at her. He sat directly behind her head, on a plush chair with a footstool. Yet his mere presence—for sometimes he said very little—the intensity of his listening, compelled her to say whatever came into her mind. "Never be afraid to say something because it is unpleasant," he had told her.

She smiled as she began to tell the young man how she had gone every afternoon for a session with Dr. Freud. He lived in such a solidly middle-class building, and they had had to hire a workingman to carry her up to the mezzanine, where his office was, and then Hester would come behind, with the wheelchair. There was a profusion of objects everywhere—pictures and books almost filling the walls, rugs covering the floors and couch, sculptures not only filling the glass cases but marching across the tables and desks, for Dr. Freud was a great collector of antiquities.

Yet it was orderly and strangely reassuring, like being in the crowded rooms of one's own mind.

Dr. Freud spoke beautiful English, although sometimes he had recourse to a German phrase to animate his explanations. In some ways he reminded her of her father—the thin, strong mouth framed by moustache and beard, the high cheekbones with deep concavities, and the odor of cigar smoke—although of course her father never would have allowed into discussion most of the things she told Dr. Freud.

She recited the Kella Hagaward letter to him and described the dreams she had been having since it was discovered. And as she spoke, the recollection of them had the power to wipe out the reality of the consulting room, with its welter of antiquities and the fire burning in the tile stove and the pillows propping her high on the couch, and to replace them with the sensation of flying free under a chill white Sabbat moon, hearing the chants and crooked laughter rise up from a field below, swooping down to join them, and putting one's mouth upon the cold, sweet flute and playing it for the revels.

The way the dreams came was difficult to explain. Normally one just fell asleep and had a dream, and that was all. But the dreams of Kella signaled their coming by making her edgy all evening—pushing her heart into her throat. Then when she finally went to sleep, the dreams seemed to possess her physically. She woke exhausted, with the bedclothes as disheveled as if she had kicked and thrashed about, although of course her left side was always immobile.

"These dreams," Dr. Freud had said, "can be understood only as a part of your neurosis." She liked the way he pronounced the word—"neurOHzis." And he told her of a paper he had written a few years earlier, after someone had asked his medical opinion about a case described in an old manuscript. It concerned a seventeenth-century painter who signed a pact with the Devil. "When I considered that bond with Satan as if it were the case history of a patient," Dr. Freud told her, "the problem of motivation arose at once. Why should one wish to sell oneself to the Devil? In the case of the painter, the fact that his father had recently died provided the answer. The man wished to take the Devil as a father substitute. The pact was, in actuality, a neurotic phantasy. Just so, we must learn what phantasy is being fulfilled for you by the dreams in which you become the witch Kella Hagaward."

Psychoanalysis, he explained, had found the true nature of demons: What in earlier times had been considered evil spirits, originating in the outer world, could now be seen as originating in the patient's inner life. And to find them, he believed, one must go far back, to childhood, even to infancy. "The child you once were," he said, "can tell us why your arm and leg will not move and why you are obsessed with that witch."

She had not minded looking back. She even began to dream of her childhood, and during the sessions with Dr. Freud she talked of the dreams and whatever they brought into her mind—how she loved her cousins, Duncan and Bruce, yet sometimes wished they were dead, how excited she had been when she got her first flute, and how she used to stand beside the big canopied bed and watch her mother, Sarah.

Sometimes Sarah Hayward had lain there as pale and motionless as the hand-embroidered sheets; sometimes she had thrashed about, sobbing in a hollow voice.

What the family referred to as Sarah's "states" were taken at first as evidence of her refinement—she was nervous and high-strung because she was delicate and sensitive. In fact Kelvin Hayward seemed rather proud of his wife's condition. Often he would say that this or that event had been "too much" for "the dear little woman," and one could tell he was pleased from the way his mouth curled inside its black, strawlike nest of beard and moustache.

But Sarah Hayward's states exceeded delicacy. She began to have strange fits of laughing or crying, to experience terrible pains in her jaw and eye sockets, to vomit frequently after meals, and to suffer muscle spasms in her legs, which she was sometimes unable to use at all. Doctors were summoned from New York and Boston and Philadelphia, and they all emerged from the sickroom with grave expressions and essentially the same diagnosis: hysteria.

They did not agree, however, on the treatment. Sarah Hayward was sent to spas to take the waters. She was sent to take a rest cure: kept in bed, aided in everything from turning over to eating and vigorously massaged. She was given "moral medication," which consisted of telling the doctor her life history. She was even sent to take an electrical cure in which she was treated with galvanic electric currents, on the grounds that her nerves and muscles were failing to produce properly the electrical signals that made them function.

Usually, no matter what the treatment had been, she would come back better. Then one could go to her dressing room and listen to her tell what they had done to her this time, as she dressed for various engagements, choosing from among the velvet cloaks and strings of little furs and the great wheels of her hats, trimmed with ribbons, flowers, feathers, and sometimes even with dead birds that regarded one with little glass eyes. But the symptoms would always return.

Sarah Hayward died at thirty-nine, presumably because of her "states," which never had been satisfactorily explained.

"Those states of your mother's," Dr. Freud said, "they too were a manifestation of an inner demon, which her doctors clearly did not understand. But the psychoanalytic mode of thought is able to deal with them. We do so by recognizing that from which they stem—the sexuality that permeates one's earliest years." As she listened to him, she gazed at the reproduction of a painting on the wall near the end of the couch: Oedipus interrogating the Sphinx. It hung directly above the useless left foot. Sometimes she fancied it pointed at her.

One afternoon as she talked, she recalled the frequent childhood dream in which she had gone into her parents' bedroom while Sarah was screaming in one of her states. Suddenly a flock of red birds came in through the window, flew into her mother's mouth, and choked her to death. Often after she woke from the dream, her father would take her up into bed with him.

"What occurs to you in connection with the birds?" Dr. Freud wanted to know.

The answers to that seemed to center around the flute.

One of her earliest memories was of being taken to the Metropolitan Opera House with both her parents—Sarah resplendent in a beaded gown, satin slippers, and momentary good health—and being transfixed by what she later realized was *Die Zauberflöte*. She got the idea, perhaps at that performance, that somehow the voices of many birds had been captured in the slender metal tube. Afterward, whenever she was in her mother's dressing room, she would look at the rows of hats on their stands and wonder whether the dead birds resting amid the flowers and ribbons might have been silenced to create the silvery voice of the flute.

By the time she was twelve she had become quite accomplished on the instrument. By fifteen she was so fine a player that the great pianist Josef Hofmann, on a visit to Rowan Hall, heard her play the Bach unaccompanied Sonata in A and pronounced her "very good." It was one achievement that her playmates all through childhood, her cousins, Bruce and Duncan, couldn't match.

Bruce was going to read law at Harvard, and Duncan was being groomed for a role in the Industries. When she discovered that her governess did not give her the same subjects the boys got from their tutor, she staged tantrums until her father finally acceded and Greek, Latin, and history were added to her French and music lessons. In return, she got the boys interested in music. Bruce even learned to play the piano and could accompany her in simpler pieces.

"So," Dr. Freud had said, "with the flute you felt you were as good as your male cousins?"—and in a way he was right.

When Bruce and Duncan went to Europe, she begged to go too; so many new movements in the arts were fermenting overseas. But her father couldn't be persuaded. "Where's the point, Cayla?" he would ask, his heavy black brows colliding in a frown. "You spend too much time with that instrument already. There's no need for you to play any better than you do. It's not going to make you a better wife and mother, is it?"

In some way, she realized, he expected her to "make up" for her mother—to become the exemplar of refinement, sensitivity, and sacrifice that, according to him, Sarah had been before her "states" took hold. On the day of the funeral, in fact, he took her into the library and, eyes as solemn as a baby's, said, "You're the only woman in the Hayward clan now. You must begin to use your woman's birthright—your natural goodness. You must be as beautiful of spirit as it has pleased God to make you of body. You must think less of competing with your cousins and more of what is seemly."

She loved her father and wanted to please him, but she wanted bitterly to study music in Paris. Then someone shot an archduke, in a place no one had heard of, and thoughts of Europe were impossible.

She considered trying to carve out a musical life for herself on her side of the Atlantic, but even without the disruptions of war it was hard to see what she might do. There were female singers, of course, and even a few pianists, but no one, male or female, went about giving recitals on an instrument like the flute. Conceivably an extraordinary talent might manage it; but Josef Hofmann had said only that she was "very good." And as far as she could determine, there were no female flutists in professional orchestras. She even thought of trying to buy her way into one of the Boston or New York orchestras that her family supported, but it was her father who would have had to do the buying, and his refusal was both instantaneous and angry.

Needless to say, his pleasure was great when she married a young man who worked at the Industries, and when she adopted the role of a patroness of the musical arts. Still she could not give up the flute entirely—it had enchanted her too completely. That was her curse.

When her daughter was born, she often took the flute to the nursery, fancying that Rachel liked to hear her play. And whenever the day was fine, she took the baby's carriage into the park that had been built to the east of Rowan Hall, fronting the ocean. It was lined with statues of Greek gods, and at each end was an ornamental pool whose waters cascaded from the mouth of a stone dolphin. Sometimes she took the flute with her and imitated the calls of the seabirds. Rachel would laugh and clap her tiny, perfect hands.

In the third summer of Rachel's life, on a day when the ocean was as blue as sapphires and the sun a ball of mother-of-pearl, she intended to take Rachel into the park. But that week she had started making some transcriptions for the flute—a harmless enough hobby—and was so involved in one of the Bach partitas for harpsichord that she let Rachel's nurse take the child out.

The windows of the music room overlooked the park, and she went to them to look down on the starched gray-and-whiteness that was the nurse and the tiny pink figure that marched about with delightful awkwardness. But then the music took hold, and she lost track of everything, as if in a trance.

When she went to the windows again, the gray-and-white figure was running jerkily toward one of the ponds.

The old woman on the red chaise longue, looking down the decades, made her thin hands into fists and placed them on her heart.

She heard a voice: "Gran, what are you saying?"

"The little pink dress was so wet . . . and water dripped from her little shoes . . . One morning when no one else was up, I took my flute to the ocean and threw it in. Let Poseidon have Euterpe's silver wand."

"Gran, Rachel did not drown! She's alive, and you know where."

The old woman shook her head dazedly, her eyes climbing away from the past. "Yes, that's right. Of course. I must have been thinking of a dream. About . . . Hester carrying me down a country road to a lake. I wanted to swim, but I couldn't move in the water, so she had to carry me. Then a boat appeared, a little one with a shroud. I wanted to tear the shroud off, but I couldn't. I couldn't."

"What did Dr. Freud say about that?"

The old woman blinked, confused. She had thought she was telling the dream to Dr. Freud, but it was a young man with green eyes. Slowly she pulled herself the rest of the distance into the present.

The young man repeated his question: "What did Dr. Freud say about your dream of the lake and the little boat?"

"Ah. He said that when a woman dreamed of trying to rescue someone from water, it symbolized . . . giving birth."

Stefan said, "I'm a little vague on the chronology here. Could you explain when you went to see Freud, in relation to your paralysis and your daughter's . . . falling in the pond?"

"Oh, I was fine for almost a year afterwards. Don't ask me how, but I was. The gracious hostess, as always. Why, the night before the paralysis struck, I was giving a musicale for thirty or so of Gary's friends—a young pianist, I can't recall his name, played Beethoven sonatas, all three from Opus 31. I thought it an odd choice. In the middle of the last one, the E-flat, I got very dizzy and had to leave. They found me fainted on the staircase, like a Sarah Bernhardt play, I expect. They rushed me up to bed, and the next morning my left arm and leg wouldn't move. Father was wild, of course. He refused to believe it at first. 'Not you, too, Cayla,' he kept saying. 'Not you, too.' "

"And a few weeks later they discovered the letter?"

"That's right."

"When were you sent to Dr. Freud, then?"

The answer came from the shadows: "The next year, in 1927."

Stefan said, "Did your analysis with Freud help you?"

Old Cayla frowned. "Ah, it did for a while. He was quite a kind man, you know. I liked to talk to him. And when it came time to go home, I was able to walk onto the boat."

"How do you think he helped you? I'd really like to hear his analysis of your problem, if you'll tell me."

"Oh my. I can't discuss such things in front of anyone. Certainly not my granddaughter."

"What's worrying you? Is it the sexual explicitness?"

"You know about that?"

"I think I can guess. For instance, I imagine he told you that the flute represented the male organ, which you envied."

"Ah. So you see why I can't discuss it."

"Just a minute." Cayla's voice was dangerously calm. She came toward the chaise. "I want to be sure I understand this. Gran, you don't want to discuss anything in front of me that pertains to sex? Yet all the years I lived here with you, you were perfectly willing to talk about my being the descendant of a witch and the next one to— You'd talk to a child about Black Masses and the Devil's goat-body, you'd recite her a letter about being tortured, but you won't use words like *penis* in front of a grown woman?'' Her voice leaped into the red zone. ''What's the matter with you? Why are you like this? Why can't you see how crazy and hurtful and—'' She stopped and stared at Stefan, who had gone to her and was gripping her arms.

''Hey,'' he said gently. ''Why don't you go and sit down and let me finish talking to your grandmother?''

She stared into his eyes until she seemed to find what she needed. Then she went to a chair and put her head in her hands.

Stefan turned to the old woman. ''She's right, Mrs. Randall. You should certainly be able to tell her what Freud said. I'm sure you realize that. And I'm sure you don't want to upset her, because I think you love her. Am I right?''

''Yes.'' Old Cayla's voice broke. ''I love her.''

''Then tell her, and me, about Freud's analysis.''

Old Cayla looked across the room at her granddaughter, then turned to the windows and the ocean. ''He said that I, that all infants, desire their mothers as . . . love objects. The girl infant, just like the boy, wants to . . . get her mother with child. But then she discovers that she has no ; . . . male organ, that she's been castrated. That discovery colors all of her life, and you blame your mother for the disaster. You can never forgive her. And it's true that I did resent Mother—why couldn't she be normal, like Bruce and Duncan's mother? And I used to dream that the red birds choked her to death and I was alone with Father. Dr. Freud said you turn to your father in the hope that he'll give you . . . what your mother has failed to give you. But when that doesn't happen, when you realize no one can give it to you . . . then you turn . . .'' In a harsher voice she said, ''Do you know what witches have the power to do? Witches can steal penises.''

Cayla stared at her grandmother. The fire snapped several times, and in the shadow Hester moved her feet, as if the sparks had threatened her.

Old Cayla went on softly. ''If you grow up to become truly feminine, he said, then the wish for a . . . male organ is replaced by the wish for . . . a baby.'' She sighed deeply. ''And if you have a baby and lose it . . . your feelings of loss and impotence may be so crushing that you can't bear them. So your mind will convert them . . .''

''Into something physical? Into a paralysis?''

85

The old woman nodded, and the room was silent. "When I got home," she went on, "Father said he'd give me anything I wanted. But, isn't it odd?—I couldn't think of a thing. I remember trying to imagine something I wanted, and I couldn't think of a thing in the world. . . . Oh my, I was tired. If Poseidon had thrown back my flute, tossed it up through those windows, I wouldn't have taken it." The surf boomed in the distance. "No, I wouldn't." She looked down at the red-velvet letter case still in her lap and put a hand on it. "I couldn't, because she wanted to come back to me."

"Who?" Stefan asked. "Kella Hagaward?"

"No, no. My little Rachel. She didn't want to be alone and cold anymore, and she knew I wouldn't let her drown again."

"Gran, that's enough. Stop it!" Cayla leaped up as if the chair had pushed her. "I know you didn't want to answer Dr. Veere's questions, but that's no reason to waste his time by telling him these wild tales." Stefan moved toward her, but she swung away. "Sigmund Freud told you you wanted to be a witch in order to steal penises? Because you'd been *castrated?* Do you think you can make people believe any nonsense you decide to invent? And Mother is not dead! It might be better if she was, but she's not, so stop pretending. Can't you face reality? She didn't drown, and she isn't the victim of a curse. Dr. Veere, I want you to know that my mother is in a psychiatric hospital. She's a paranoid schizophrenic. And Gran is a woman who can't face reality!"

Stefan finally caught her and held both her hands. "Please don't, Cayla."

The old woman was blinking rapidly. "I've lost my Rachel. Such a pretty child. So lovely . . . Her hands as pretty as if they were carved from pearls, and her tiny foot with six little toes like shells . . ." Her eyes narrowed until the sagging flesh of the lids hung like curtains, and she made a low gull-like sound.

Suddenly Hester was beside her, hissing at Cayla and Stefan, "You've upset the Lady and worn her out with all your awful questions. Go, now. Go!"

"I think maybe that's best," Stefan said. But first he went to the chaise and said, "Thank you for talking to me, Mrs. Randall."

* * *

They went back down the huge, ornate staircase.

"I take it she actually did go to see Freud?" he said.

"Yes, that much is true."

"Do you know how long her cure lasted?"

"I'm not sure. My relatives say she took to her bed permanently when Rachel was institutionalized. That's thirty years ago."

"So if she's eighty-seven now, it happened when she was in her late fifties. And when she went to Freud, she was . . . Wait a minute. You told me she was permanently paralyzed in her late *thirties*, like the other victims of the so-called curse."

They were on the landing above the main floor, with the portrait gallery. Cayla swung around to stare at him. "You're right, she was in her late fifties. You see how she distorts things to fit her fantasy world?" She shook her head. "I can't believe I just accepted it and never did the arithmetic."

"You were young, which means vulnerable. If something made a powerful impression on you, it wouldn't occur to you to check the numbers on it."

"It should have."

Stefan looked at the gallery. "Is she here?"

Cayla pointed silently to a painting of a woman in her early twenties, whose luxuriant black hair was threaded with pearls. Her dress was scarlet, her expression both intelligent and shy. "It's odd," Stefan said. "She has the same coloring as you, and she's also very beautiful, but you don't look anything like her."

"I'm *not* anything like her."

"No, of course not." Stefan took her arm. "Let's get out of here and find a place to have some dinner. We need to talk."

"About what? My emotional outbursts? It's bad enough to have had two in one day. I don't need to talk about them as well."

"I'm requesting a meeting, as your investigator. That's all."

Clutching the railing, staring down at the marble steps, she asked softly, "How does the Whiting woman know that a Hayward—my mother—has six toes on one foot?"

"I don't know," Stefan said. "I only know that I had a grandmother who, in her trances, sometimes spoke of a child with six toes. And seemed frightened."

Cayla's eyes widened and rose to his. "So that's why you wanted to investigate Polly Whiting."

"It was the reason. It's not the only one now." He took her arm again.

10

Outside, the moon was as white as a bone, and the clouds cut long, dark gashes beneath it.

When they went down the driveway, Cayla leaned forward in the seat, as if countering the pull of the house behind them. Finally its dark mass merged into the sky. For five minutes she said nothing except to give Stefan directions to an inn about twenty miles from Rowan Hall.

Then, in the crisp voice her staff knew well, she said she would get her private detectives to look for New York autograph dealers whose firms had been in existence in 1926, on the chance they might locate the firm of the expert who had examined the letter. "But even so," she added, "it's unlikely the man talked about the letter to someone who could then have passed it on to someone who could have told the Whiting woman."

"True," Stefan said. "But it's more likely than the idea that Sigmund Freud is the connecting link. Oh, I suppose it's possible that somewhere in his writing he mentions a case like Mrs. Randall's and a letter from an alleged witch—I'm familiar with his major works, but not with everything he wrote. I'll do some research, but don't count on any results."

"I won't. Any more than I'd expect to learn that he actually wrote about demonic possession, the way she claimed."

Stefan hesitated. "Cayla, what she told us about Freud . . ."

"Yes? What about it?"

"Nothing." A mile farther he said, "Let's assume that her

father and husband and uncles never told anyone about the letter. If so, the best possibility for a leak is Hester.''

''No, no.'' Cayla's voice was as hard and bright as chrome. ''Hester is fanatically devoted to Gran. You could see that. I can't conceive that she'd reveal something Gran told her not to.''

''In my line of work you learn there's hardly anything that can't be conceived of.'' When she didn't respond, he said, ''Let me think about it. Maybe there's something I can try at the other end, the Polly Whiting end.''

She made a noncommittal sound.

Casually Stefan said, ''If your grandmother's last name is Randall, that would make your mother Rachel Randall. So why are you Cayla Hayward?''

There was a silence. ''My mother wasn't married. Gran had my name legally made Hayward.''

The silence resumed. With each mile it made the small, enclosed space of the car a greater distance between them.

Finally Stefan said, ''I think we should talk about some of the things your grandmother told us.''

She smoothed her hair behind her ears. ''All right. Tell me about hysteria. Is it a legitimate disease?''

''You mean, is the person really ill or just making it up? Those aren't mutually exclusive, you know. Someone can be experiencing great pain and have nothing organically wrong at all. In fact that's one of the biggest problems in therapy—distinguishing the organic from the functional.'' When she said nothing, he went on. ''Officially, hysteria doesn't exist any longer. Since the fifties it's been called 'conversion reaction,' and it's rare. I've never seen a case, though I've heard of them. There seem to be fashions in certain neuroses, and hysteria just isn't in vogue anymore. Maybe it doesn't fit twentieth-century problems. It has a very long past, though. There are ancient Egyptian records that mention women who wouldn't get out of bed or had terrible pains in their jaws or eyes—the same symptoms your grandmother described in her mother.''

''You think she was telling the truth about that?''

''Do you have any reason to think she was lying?''

Cayla shrugged. ''Not really. I guess it's true that Sarah Hayward was ill a great deal. I've just never heard Gran speak of her in that kind of detail. In fact, I've never heard most of what she told you tonight. I'm afraid that wasn't the kind of story she used to like to tell me.''

Stefan glanced at her, but she was looking ahead, eyes on the two tracks the headlights were cutting along the country road. ''Actually,'' he said, ''hysteria is pretty fascinating. The way it's been perceived tells you a lot about the cultures that were trying to explain it. For instance, the ancients propagated the idea that it was a woman's disease. They believed it was caused by the way the womb wandered around inside the body. Sounds crazy, but it's a better explanation than the one they offered in the Middle Ages—demonic possession. During the witchcraft craze there was a virtual epidemic of what we'd now call hysteria. The so-called witches had convulsions, screaming fits, trances, partial anesthesia, attacks of vomiting, sexual delusions, and a lot more. Hysterics are very suggestible, so when one person manifested the symptoms, a lot of others always followed. And the hysterics weren't always the witches— sometimes they were the accusers. They'd claim their behavior was the result of being bewitched.''

''You're trying to take the demons out of it for me, aren't you?''

''I'm just giving you the facts, ma'am. Now, the nineteenth century was the other period when there was a virtual epidemic of hysteria, especially among women of the leisure class, like your great-grandmother.'' He waited a moment. ''Don't you wonder why?''

''All right. Why?''

''I think the Victorians forced it on their women. Remember how your grandmother described her father's attitude? He thought a woman should be delicate, refined, sensitive, etcetera, etcetera. So did most of the doctors. You could tell they didn't know what caused the hysterical symptoms—remember all the different kinds of cures they put your great-grandmother through?—but some of them believed the condition was caused by too much education and thinking. Women weren't supposed to be able to tolerate as much intellectual stimulation as men. Then there was a school that held to the old notion that hysteria was caused by the sexual and reproductive organs. I've read about a group that treated the patient surgically when they thought her sexual desires were excessive. They cauterized the clitoris.''

Cayla stared at him.

"So you get the picture of those poor Victorian women. Everything put into corsets—their bodies, their minds, their sexuality. No wonder they had fits and paralyses and all kinds of causeless ailments. Freud was the one, or at least the major one, who made the medical profession aware that hysteria was psychogenic in origin, that it was a way of dealing with repressed material. But his ideas about the nature of that material were disastrous, in my view."

"If hysteria is so rare now, why do you know so much about it?"

"It's in all the textbooks, of course. But I also did some research on my own."

"Why?"

"I've always been fascinated by what the mind alone can make the body do."

"Why?"

"Oh . . . it started because I was trying to understand someone I knew. Someone who raised me." Stefan shifted his grip on the wheel, flexing his long fingers. "My grandmother."

A few minutes later, in a softer voice, Cayla said, "The road to the inn is up on the left."

They had drinks in the corner leather chairs of a small library. The light from a fireplace turned Stefan's face ruddy and tried fitfully to throw its color onto Cayla's cheeks.

She slipped off her jacket. Beneath it was a sleeveless cashmere sweater that matched precisely the gray of her suit. Her bare arms were as thin and graceful as a ballerina's.

"You'd look wonderful in bright colors," Stefan said. "Do you ever wear them?"

"I don't care much for them."

"Has your grandmother's taste for reds ruined them for you?"

There was a pause. "I dress the way I think is appropriate for someone in business."

"OK," Stefan said easily.

Cayla lifted her Bloody Mary. "But my drink is red. Does that count?"

He grinned at her; she looked away. "Why do you always do that?" he said.

"Do what?"

"Look away."

She regarded him steadily and said, "I'd like to know whether my Gran is an hysteric."

"What does her doctor tell you?"

"She hasn't let one near her as long as I can remember."

"Who looks after her health, then?"

"Hester. She was a trained nurse when she came to Rowan Hall. So, is Gran an hysteric? Like her mother?"

"It was often the case that the daughter of an hysteric would become one herself. I told you, they're suggestible."

"That's not really an answer."

"Diagnoses take time. I'd need more information, more time with her. But on the basis of what I've seen and heard, I'd say it's entirely possible that she is."

"Creating a fantasy world—is that one of the symptoms of hysteria?"

"Very often. But that doesn't mean you can discredit everything she says." Stefan leaned to her across the arm of his chair. "Cayla, what your grandmother told us about her analysis with Freud was probably true."

She gave him a half smile, as if expecting him to say something that would complete it.

"What she described was straight Freudian orthodoxy. Infantile sexuality determines everything, dreams and free association are the means of revealing it, and the defining event in a woman's life is her childhood discovery that she's castrated. Surely you've heard of penis envy?"

The smile had retreated. "Yes, but I could never make myself believe it was meant literally."

"I'll show you Freud's actual words, if you like. There's a paper called 'Femininity' in which he says it all. He winds up claiming that the emotion of shame is a particularly feminine one, caused by genital deficiency. After all, he says, women haven't discovered or invented much of anything throughout history, except for the technique of weaving. And when they weave, they're unconsciously imitating the pubic hair that hides their genitals."

"You're not making this up?"

"I don't think I could. Of course Freud never wrote anything that tied witchcraft to penis envy, at least not to my knowledge, but it would be consistent with his other ideas if he explained your grandmother's obsession with Kella Hagaward by saying it represented her unconscious desire for the power to steal penises. I think it's true that witches were thought to be able to do such things.''

''A common charge against them,'' Cayla said slowly, ''was that they could make men impotent or steal their organs.''

Stefan raised both eyebrows but said nothing.

She looked away. ''You're telling me Gran was treated for paralysis by being told she was a castrated male? Freud explained to her, in the name of science, that she was genetically second-class?''

''Why are you shocked? Freud was revolutionary in some ways, but don't forget, he was a Victorian male. Just like your Gran's father.''

''But how could she have been cured, even temporarily, if Freud told her such nonsense? No, *worse* than nonsense.''

''I imagine most of what she did was to talk, and the mere act of talking can be beneficial. Besides, focusing on her childhood had to be better than brooding over the letter. It kept her closer to reality.''

Cayla gripped her drink with both hands. ''So, when I yelled at her for inventing tales about Freud, she was telling the truth. That makes me feel guilty.''

Stefan reached for her glass. He had to pry her fingers from it. He put the glass down but didn't release her hand.

''I don't like Rowan Hall,'' she said. ''And I don't like what happens to me when I go into it—what I become.''

''What is that?''

She shook her head. ''You have a way of drawing things out of people, haven't you? I think it's your eyes. I saw you do it with Gran.''

''And you don't want to be drawn out?''

''You already know more about me than anyone outside the clan.''

''It's not enough. I want to know everything.''

''Why?''

''I think you know why.''

Her eyes went to her hand, which he was still holding. His fingers were graceful and strong. On the middle one of the right hand was a topaz ring that caught the light. "No," she said, pulling away, "I don't want to talk about myself. I want to . . . Tell me what you would have made of Gran's paralysis if she'd gone to you instead of Freud."

"That's not fair. I haven't spent months with her the way he did."

"But you must have some ideas about her."

"Oh yes. I get ideas about people right away, I'm afraid." He stretched his legs and ran his hands through his hair. Its wiry curl sprang back immediately. "I'd say she did suffer a kind of castration, but it was intellectual. The Victorian era may have been over by the time she was growing up, but it seems her father kept it alive at Rowan Hall. I'd say she accepted his ideas of what a woman was and could do. I mean, she was a bright, talented girl who wanted to keep up with her male cousins, and could. But she was told *her* life had to consist of being a wife and mother. And even when she accepted that view and gave up the idea of a music career, she couldn't give up the music itself. Let's say she was absorbed in it when her daughter drowned. And when that happened, she'd have to feel—given the ideas she'd accepted—that her neglect of motherhood for music had destroyed her child. Let's say her guilt was so intolerable that it was easier to believe she was living out a witch's curse. That way, the event would be outside her control."

He frowned; triangles of fine lines appeared in the corners of his eyes. "Yet you say that Rachel, your mother, is alive, which means there was no drowned child. There's nothing but a big hole in my analysis."

"Yes," Cayla said. "But even so, it makes me feel . . . sorry for Gran. I haven't felt that in years and years. Not since I was . . ." She sat back, her head resting on the leather of the deep chair. "I shouldn't have yelled at her tonight. She's old and bedridden, even if she tied herself to the bed, in effect, and I'm . . . But when I was young, I fought against believing the stories she told *me*. Why couldn't she fight against the things they were telling *her*?"

"Apparently she didn't have your kind of strength."

"I know it can't have been easy to be a woman then, especially a Hayward woman, but . . . It's not just that she believes in the curse. It's that she's enthralled with it, almost in love . . . and that turns her into . . . it makes her so helpless . . . Oh, I don't want to talk about her anymore.''

"All right. Just one thing, though. She said you were married once. Does your ex-husband know about the Kella Hagaward letter?''

Cayla's eyes closed briefly. "I'm embarrassed to tell you that I don't remember whether I ever told him. I remember as little as possible about the marriage.''

"Then there is a chance he could be the link to Polly."

"I can't tell you how unlikely that is—someone who craves wealth and a poor farm woman? But I did have my detectives check for a possible connection. They couldn't find one.''

"You're sure those detectives are any good?''

"The best money can buy, I'm told.''

Stefan laughed. "Why did I even ask?''

He was looking at her profile, at the contrast between the fine angle of nose and chin and the fullness of mouth. He put one hand in her hair, his thumb stroking her temple. "Why don't we forget all of this for a while? Let's go in and have dinner and talk about relaxing subjects like religion and politics.''

She smiled, without moving.

He leaned closer to her, pushing back her hair a bit and touching the dark, irregular mark in her hairline. She pulled away.

"What's wrong?'' he said. "Did I hurt you?''

"No.'' With an odd bravado she added, "As a matter of fact, I didn't feel a thing.'' She stood up. "You're right. We should eat.''

She was as hungry for subjects other than Rowan Hall and Polly Whiting as for dinner.

She asked about Stefan's practice and his training, and how he countered the effects of listening to problems all day. When he said he had to make sure he got enough pleasure from the rest of his time—"which is what I'm doing right now"—she smiled, and when the smile stretched on between them, she didn't care.

He asked why she had started Biologiconn; she told him about her college friends—"DNA was the New World, and they had no real idea of what they'd find there, but they made me see it was essential to go.'' She felt too aware of him for safety, yet so safe that she forgot who he was and even talked of how much she liked to be in the labs—to go in at least once a day and talk with the scientists, and sometimes just to walk through the labs in the morning before anyone else was there, with the hoods and incubators and centrifuges gleaming and the whole place quiet, and somehow suffused with content.

Over dessert she heard herself say to him, "Are you . . . Have you ever been married?"

"If your detectives couldn't find that out, then they really are lousy."

She said lightly, "They reported that you were single and alone."

"And you wonder why a man of forty is in that situation? No, don't protest. You do wonder. I would. I'd be asking whether he was divorced or gay or a misogynist or what." He leaned back, looking into the candle flame that flickered between them in the center of the table. "Her name was Barbara. I loved her so much it hurt. That old cliché is true, I discovered. But of course what hurts is the fear that someday you might lose the incredible human being who's making you so happy. Then one day you do. It was a Wednesday—two years ago next month, as a matter of fact. The phone rings, and a strange voice tells you to come to the hospital because Ms. Barbara Susan Collins has been attacked and your name is in her wallet. You get there just in time to say good-bye. She was mugged. She tried to talk to the man and he stabbed her. It turns out he was a mental patient who'd been deinstitutionalized two weeks earlier. The city's full of them—disturbed people roaming the streets, looking for objects for their private rages."

She wanted to touch him, but kept her hands on the table.

"Oh, it's all right now," he said. "Finally. The worst part is the way it freezes things in your mind. All you can see is the way she was at the end. All the wonderful times together, all the laughing and loving, are crowded out by the sight of the end. For months you just keep staring at it and going crazy. And then, gradually, the other things come out of hiding and take over, and one day you're able to smile at your memories." He lifted his eyes from the flame. "And then, another day, you realize you really are all right because you have the capacity to care about someone else."

She didn't look away. "I'm sorry I made you talk about it."

"Don't be. I'm not. I'd like you to know."

"Thank you, then. But I don't understand how you can talk about it that way. So easily, I mean. So openly."

He traced the outline of one of her hands with a finger. "Maybe I see too many of the consequences of locking things up and letting them fester."

She sighed.

"It's nearly midnight," he said. "Let me drive you to your apartment."

"Midnight? I have to get up early."

"On Sunday?"

"I like to. I'm a morning person."

He laughed. "That's good."

"Why?"

"It just is. Let's go."

The car seemed a different place, no longer forcing intimacy on them but reflecting it. On the radio, a Mozart piano concerto moved on its tightrope between melancholy and exuberance.

Cayla leaned against the back of the seat, her eyes closed. She opened them several times to look at Stefan's profile, as if she had to be certain how its lines were drawn.

Neither of them spoke, and the absence of speech became its own kind of intimacy, turning the inches that separated their shoulders and thighs into a contact deeper than words.

When they reached the town where she lived, Stefan had to ask for directions. She sat up and pointed his way.

Silently they went up in the building elevator. He took her keys from her hand and unlocked the apartment door.

In the foyer was a concealed panel of switches. She touched one of them, and a soft glow with no obvious source illuminated the fireplace and the raisin-colored chairs. Another touch summoned the continuation of the concerto. She moved into the room, looking around as if it were new to her.

Stefan laid her keys on a pewter-and-glass table and put down her briefcase, which he had carried. He went to her and put his hands on her throat. Then he moved them up to her cheeks. "Your face is caught in my mind," he said. "I can't get it out. And I don't want to." He kissed one side of her mouth, then the other. She made a small sound, like a contented child.

His hands went back to her neck, but this time they slid down to her shoulders, underneath her suit jacket. He slipped the jacket off and let it fall on a chair. Slowly he ran his hands up and down the length of her bare arms.

She had not moved; she was looking at him almost hypnotically. He lifted his right hand and traced her lips with two fingers. Suddenly she caught his wrist in a strong grip, and with a sound that was anything but a child's she took his hand from her lips and placed her mouth on his, opening beneath it.

Whatever gentleness he had intended was forgotten in the fire that leaped from her. Her body molded itself to his, driving it to the opposite of her softness, and her tongue played over his mouth. Her head fell back, and she made small panting sounds while his hands moved along her sides, his fingers edging her breasts.

He was taking her down with him into one of the deep chairs when she suddenly staggered and pulled away. "No," she said. "No!"

He righted himself and said, against the racing of his breath, "What is it? What's wrong?"

"I can't do this. I can't. Please!"

She had gone to the fireplace. He came up behind her, but the moment he tried to touch her, she moved away. He made himself stand still, forcing back a desire that was all the greater for its absence of nearly two years.

When he finally looked at her, she had turned on more lights. In their glare he could see that the tight calm with which she had come into his office that afternoon was back, more rigid than ever.

"Cayla, what is it?" He went closer to her. She didn't pull back, but he could see the effort it took not to do so. Her eyes were wide, with the fixity of someone who is frightened. "You're not the kind of woman who plays games," he said. "I know you're not. So what is it?"

"It's no excuse to say that it's all my fault, but it is. And it's unforgivable."

"No. But it sure as hell is inexplicable."

She locked her arms across her chest. "I guest I just . . . lost control again. Three times in one day. I'm sorry, Stefan. Terribly sorry."

He knew there was no point in arguing with her and no hope

of touching her again that night. He clenched his fists deep in the pockets of his sweater and said, "I'm not sorry. Remember that."

He left as the Mozart was just finishing.

II

OUTSIDE INFLUENCES

11

"I'll tell you what I resent," said the senior senator from New York. He and his companions were seated at one of many round tables in the Georgetown home of a retired ambassador who was known for black-tie dinners attended by those with proximity to power.

The senator put down his forkful of quail. "I resent the way these religious people have taken over the issue. There's hardly one of us who hasn't had heavy mail from them about it. They're taking it over, but it's a valid issue, dammit! Something with that much potential for good or evil can't be left in the hands of private industry. Do you realize there are practically no controls at all over what they're doing in their labs?"

"And whose fault is that?" said his neighbor, a syndicated columnist. "Congress is the one that relaxed the regulations that were in place."

"Not because I didn't try to prevent it," the senator said. "Letting a technology like genetic engineering run free, letting *any* technology run free, is damn dangerous."

"I presume you speak from experience, Freddie?" said the foreign journalist across the table. Everyone smiled, for the great wealth of the senator's family had come from oil.

"Don't pick on Freddie," said a woman to whose name the words "Washington socialite" were always added in the press. "Freddie's always the first one to say his grandfather was a real pirate."

The senator was not amused. "Suppose this woman with the Tay-Sachs child delivers a healthy baby. Sure, it'll be wonderful, but do you realize the pressure that'll be on then, for every research lab in the country to do the same kind of thing for every other genetic defect? With the work going unregulated, because it's in private industry, anything could happen. And then there's this Coalition for Traditional Values, trying to make it an issue of God versus Satan—when it's really a question of the dangers inherent in a completely free market. We can't let them run with the ball on this one. At the very least we've got to see that the ball goes to somebody neutral—by which I mean somebody outside that damn Coalition."

"Poor Freddie," said the socialite. "It's enough to give an atheist heartburn."

The television audience for the program, said to be eight million, saw on their screens a line-drawn caricature—a beehive of hair above huge glasses, above a jutting chin—and then a logo reading THE VERA LEOPOLD SHOW.

The studio audience of several hundred applauded wildly as the hostess of the top-rated daytime talk show swept through curtains that seemed to be made of blue feathers, and held out her arms as if she wanted to embrace not just the audience she could see but the eight million as well. In her, the combination of outmoded hairdo, elaborate gowns over tight corsets, consuming curiosity, and grand-motherly warmth had somehow fused into one of the most popular personalities on television.

"How many of you believe in reincarnation?" she cried. "Let me see hands!" When about a quarter of them rose, she said, "Well, we'll see how you feel at the end of the show, shall we? Because that's the subject for this morning, and I have some guests who are going to make you think twice about living twice!"

For the first part of the program, which was telecast live, Vera Leopold talked with a group of experts about religious attitudes toward reincarnation, "although," as one of them said, "transmigration of souls, or metempsychosis, is a more accurate term."

The panel, whose members' names were all followed by at least a Ph.D., surveyed beliefs held around the world annd going far back in time. In ancient Greece, they said, the idea of reincarnation probably originated in the Orphic mysteries: The secret rites in which believers worshiped Dionysus included eating the raw flesh of an animal they thought was his reincarnation. There was no gore in the Australian aborigines' view. According to an anthropologist on the panel, they believe that the soul looks, in effect, for family ties and finds its new home with an infant born into its blood kin.

A Hebrew professor and an Indian scholar contrasted their traditions: the view in the Jewish cabala that the soul's impurities force it to undergo transmigration, and the Hindu belief that the soul exists eternally, with the happiness or misery of each of its new lives determined by its karma.

"I thought karma meant destiny," said Vera Leopold, who had a knack for voicing attitudes prevalent among her audience.

"No, no," the Indian scholar explained. "Karma is the sum total of the soul's past moral conduct."

"Oh dear," Vera said. "You mean there's no going to confession and being forgiven?"

The scholar smiled dutifully. "Christians do not believe in reincarnation. We on the other hand do not believe in confession."

After half an hour Vera said, "My goodness! Most people talk about reincarnation as if it's kind of glamorous—you know, in another life I must have been a princess or a white cat or something—but you're saying it's a matter of good and evil. People's souls keep traveling so they can make up for their sins, isn't that so?"

The panel agreed that in large part it was.

"And if it all goes back as far as you're saying it does, why, then it must be one of the oldest ideas in the world."

That too, the panel said, was so.

After the next commercial break Vera Leopold was seated on the other side of the set, alone. "And now," she said, "I want you to meet two people who are directly involved with the question of reincarnation—a lady we've been hearing a lot about, and her minister—Polly Whiting and the Reverend Walter Bailey!"

As applause rose, he came through the blue feather curtains, bringing Polly behind him. She had refused to allow the makeup man to touch her face so on the screen it was a pasty, unhealthy white. Her whole attitude, in fact, was one of unwillingness, and when Vera Leopold had summarized the story of her trances—"for those who've been in Timbuctoo"— she said, "Mrs. Whiting didn't want to come on the program, not at all. How did you persuade her, Reverend Bailey?"

He straightened the automatic slope of his shoulders and said nervously, "She thought it would look like she's taking money for what she does, and she just couldn't tolerate that. But then she came to me and said she'd decided that if any money was offered to her for anything connected with this business, she'd do it and give the money to our church. The Church of the Shepherd."

Applause rattled from the audience. Polly looked even more uncomfortable and clenched her hands on her knees.

Vera Leopold reached over to touch one of those hands. "Bravo, Mrs. Whiting." To Walter Bailey she said, "I understand that just yesterday you got some interesting news from Scotland. Will you tell us about it?"

"Of course. I didn't get the news personally, though—a professor at the university down home got it. He'd written to a colleague in Scotland, a professor of history, and it seems as if they've now located some records over there indicating that a woman named Kella Hagaward was burned as a witch in 1643, in a parish in Dumfriesshire."

"And that's exactly what Mrs. Whiting's trance-voice has been saying about herself!"

"Yes."

"It was reported in the press awhile back that the Hayward family had an ancestress by the name of Kella Hagaward, but they've never officially acknowledged that. You've never heard a word from them, have you?"

"No, we haven't."

Vera Leopold lowered her head and sent a knowing glance over the tops of her huge glasses straight into the camera. Then she turned back to Walter Bailey. "My spies tell me there's a book in the works," she said. "I hear the publisher is rushing to get it out in a month. What's it going to be called?"

"They say the title will be *I Polly, I Kella.* And I'd like to add that Polly won't be taking any money for the book, either. Her share will all go to the Church of the Shepherd. Otherwise she wouldn't go along with the book. She's . . . well, she's a good Christian, that's what Polly Whiting is."

"But good Christians don't believe in reincarnation!" Vera Leopold cried. "That's what my experts said—reincarnation isn't part of Christian doctrine."

"I know." Walter Bailey lifted his hands in a gesture of supplication. "But Our Lord never told us that reincarnation was impossible or *wrong*. He must have known that many of the people of His time believed in it, Jews and all, but He never spoke against it or forbade it. If He had, of course, I couldn't go against His teachings. But since He didn't . . ."

"Then do you believe, Reverend Bailey, that Mrs. Whiting's trance-voice is a case of reincarnation?"

"I don't know," he said apologetically. "But the only other explanation that makes sense would be to say that somehow Polly Whiting heard or learned about this Kella Hagaward and then forgot all about it, except that it stayed in her subconscious mind. But we can't think of any way at all that she could have come across that information. So . . ." He lifted his hands again.

"Tell me something," Vera Leopold said casually, although her chin was determined. "As a good Christian, what do you think of genetic engineering?"

Walter Bailey stretched his neck, as if the collar that proclaimed his calling was suddenly too tight. "Life is the Lord's business, and only the Lord's."

"But does He speak against genetic engineering? Does He forbid it?"

It was Polly Whiting who answered, her voice strong and her hands still locked into fists. "We can't set ourselves up against His will. Whatever way He sees fit to make us, that's the way we are. If a child is born lame or halt or blind, well, that's His will. Or if a child is born to live just a little while, just a few years, that's His will. We can't set ourselves up against it."

Again Vera Leopold touched one of Polly's hands. "You're very devout."

Staring straight ahead, Polly said, "I aim to be."

"You know that I'd like to hear, my dear? What I know my audience wants to hear too? We'd like to know what *you* think of this thing that's happening to you. How do *you* explain it?"

There was a silence, long by television standards, in which Polly's pale blue eyes began to water but were restrained by the weathered skin around them. "I give up trying to explain it. I can't help it, and I can't stop it. So I figure it's His will."

"Polly—do you mind if I call you Polly, by the way?" When the expected response didn't come, Vera Leopold continued smoothly. "What do you feel when you're in one of your trances? Can you describe it for us?"

Polly frowned; it was not a question she had been asked before. "I don't guess I feel anything. When I first go into the state, when the hypnosis starts, I just feel real relaxed and easy. And if the Reverend or whoever is doing it asks me to go backwards in my own life, like to one of my birthdays or something, why, I just slip into it, as easy as water. But when *she* comes, when she takes over, it's—I don't know—like I'm not there anymore. Like she blots me out."

"You mean you don't hear the voice that's coming from your own lips?"

Polly frowned again, shaking her head. "I kind of hear a couple words at the beginning, I guess, and then . . . nothing. Not till I come out of it."

"Have you ever heard a tape recording of a session?"

"She's only listened to two tapes," Walter Bailey said. "To the first one I made, and then to one of the sessions when they were testing her here in New York."

Vera Leopold nodded and told her audience, "Polly wouldn't agree to do a session on the show, and of course we can understand that. But in a minute we'll all listen to a tape recording of one of her sessions!"

After a break for commercials Vera started the recorder on the small table in front of them, and for several minutes they and millions of others listened as Walter Bailey's voice asked innocuous questions about the early years of Polly's marriage. She answered them slowly, as if living through the experiences.

When the voice of Kella Hagaward suddenly cut in, hoarsely crying out about the fire, there was a wave of reaction from the studio audience, and Vera Leopold, even though she had listened to the tape before, flinched visibly.

Polly stared at the small black box of the recorder, blinking erratically. As she listened, her hands began slowly to move up from her thighs and then to climb the front of her navy-blue dress.

On the tape, the voice that wasn't hers but had come from her said, "Fire on all my body. Eating me . . . fire eating me . . . they hurt me UNHUNHUNHUNHUNH hurt . . . they use the pin and the pilliwinks, they sent me to the fire because I

108

love the Master . . . yes, the Master! Sabaoth, Sabaoth! Give me the baptism of blood . . . UNHUNHUNHUNHUNH . . .''

In the TV studio, the voice that was Polly's own said, ''No!'' Hands clapped over her ears, she lurched to her feet and cried, ''No more! Stop it! Make it stop!''

For several moments the two voices from her throat rose in one cacophony. Then Walter Bailey snapped off the recorder, leaving only one voice: ''I won't listen! I can't! No more! I can't listen!''

An astounded Vera Leopold regained her composure and tried to help Walter Bailey calm his parishioner. But the effort was useless, and the director of the show cut away to a commercial.

By the time they returned to the air, Polly had been taken off the set, and Vera Leopold was left to close by asking how many in the audience believed in reincarnation now. A majority of the hands went up, but Vera's manner was distracted, for she was thinking that the show had made real news.

It had. That night clips of Polly's outburst were on the news shows, along with an announcement that she had decided she would no longer submit to hypnosis, by anyone, for any reason.

Stefan Veere saw the story at eleven o'clock. Exhausted after a day of six patients and a group-therapy session in the evening, he lay in bed and watched the news through tired eyes that were jerked open by the sight of Polly Whiting.

He sat up, shaking his head. Why would she do that? he wondered. Was she becoming frightened by something about the situation? Or was she, with the guile of the disturbed, clever enough to see that refusing further hypnosis would only strengthen her credibility by making her seem unwilling to be exploited?

In either case, he thought, her refusal destroyed the plan that had come to him the day before: If he could hypnotize her again, then he could ask her, under hypnosis, whether she had ever heard about the Kella Hagaward letter. In fact he could ask whether she had ever met any members of the Hayward family.

It was such an obvious thing to try. He was irritated that he hadn't thought of it sooner. He'd been debating whether to call

Cayla and discuss the idea with her but he could still feel her hands pushing him away, and had done nothing. Now there was nothing *to* do.

At the end of the story, he reached for the remote-control switch, but the anchorman's words stayed his hand in midair.

"In what some would call a related development," the man was saying, "Senator Moroni Gray of Utah tonight told an audience of western civic leaders that he intends to call a Senate hearing to investigate the issue of genetic engineering. Various scientific and religious groups, notably the Coalition for Traditional Values, have lately been pressuring Congress to do just that. Gray, who has no affiliation with any of these groups, said that the hearing will focus on the ethical questions raised by such recent practices as the gene therapy performed on a test-tube fetus by the Biologiconn division of Hayward Industries, and will consider whether Congress should curtail or even halt industry's use of genetic engineering."

Stefan switched off the set and lay back slowly. But it was a long time before he could get to sleep.

Up in the Bronx was another sleepless viewer, a young man who had just gone back to live with his parents after being dismissed from the psychiatric hospital where he'd been an attendant for several months. The job had been his third such within a year, and the resentments with which he could usually co-exist were seeking hegemony.

Long after the news had given way to the late movie, he was seeing, in his mind's eye, the film clips of Polly Whiting's outburst. He knew all about Polly. Since he had spotted the story in one of the tabloids several weeks earlier, he had followed the coverage studiously.

Finally he got up, punched the TV off, and went into the kitchen to get a beer. He was thinking of all the crazy people in the hospital he'd left—and of the woman he thought was craziest. Everyone believed her name was Brown, but by accident he had learned who she really was.

He was alone in the house, so there was no one to ask him why he was making the phone call.

12

Three days later, on Sunday, Stefan woke early, got his car out of the garage, and headed south out of the city.

Once he got past the industrial complexes at the northern end of the New Jersey Turnpike, he saw that the world had turned green; the grass and leaves that the city hemmed in with bricks and concrete, like prisoners in their cells, were claiming every vista along the road. He found a symphony concert on the radio. slipped out of his jacket, rolled the window down all the way, and thought of a patient who recently had confessed a frequent need to take long drives with music on full blast. The patient had been embarrassed. People often were, Stefan had noted, about the things that gave them personal pleasure. Yet those were the things from which a self was built.

By the time he got into Maryland, with the April sun so warm and the window all the way down, it almost seemed as if he were out to enjoy the drive.

Following the TV news announcement the previous Thursday he had, almost desultorily, done some research in the collected works of Sigmund Freud. As he expected, there was no reference to any case resembling Mrs. Randall's. He did, however, find a 1923 paper titled ''A Neurosis of Demonical Possession in the Seventeenth Century.'' The contents were just as Cayla's Gran had described them.

Then the next day, out of the blue, it occurred to him that Polly Whiting might conceivably be known in the spiritualist world. If she had ever consulted a psychic, that fact could mean, at the least, that she had a demonstrable history of belief in the supernatural. At best, it could mean someone in the psychic world knew something about her that no detective or reporter had uncovered— something that, at the very best and luckiest, might even be a lead to some connection with the Hayward family.

No reporter or detective would ever look because none had

the necessary background in, or access to, the psychic world. He was the only one he knew who could to it. But the place to look was the capital of the spiritualist world, Camp Red Cloud—the place he had run away from at fifteen, swearing never to return.

He had told himself that going would be pointless. It was too much of a long shot. He had asked himself how Polly Whiting could have had anything to do with psychics—she was a hardcore fundamentalist, and such people believed that mediums and their spiritualist churches were inspired by Satan. Fundamentalists thought calling up the dead was possible—but evil. He had tried to forget that there were exceptions, that in his boyhood he had occasionally heard the mediums speak of fundamentalists who were converted to spiritualism, or who at least attended some of the services.

He had told himself the only reason to go was a reason that no longer mattered: Cayla Hayward.

He had neither heard from her nor tried to contact her since she'd thrown him so off-balance. Once he cooled off, the therapist in him understood her reaction. The man couldn't be quite so equable. Having her as eager to make love as he—there was no mistaking that—and then pull away had been a demeaning experience, however much she might say it was her fault. If only she had called him in the next day or two . . . Probably fear kept her from doing so—the same fear that had caused the reaction in the first place. Still, he had thought of her dozens of times since. Only some of those thoughts were angry.

But on Saturday night he dreamed about her, and anger was not one of the dream's vivid sensations. When he woke on Sunday morning he sighed, knowing he was going to do it: go back to Camp Red Cloud.

He crossed the state line into Virginia about two o'clock. The air was almost summer-warm and smelled of jasmine and pine needles—the scents he recalled from boyhood.

By two-thirty he was driving through the small town near the camp. The courthouse square at the town's center had a new statue and different benches, and there were new stores and signs, but the feeling was the same—of a world with no horizons. He passed the corner where he had waited fearfully for the bus that took him away forever. The store that housed the bus station was new, but the people waiting in front looked the same. Perhaps, he thought, that was the essence of small-town life: The buildings changed, but the people did not.

As he approached the camp, six miles beyond the town, he saw that the sign was still the same: a white board with the faint outline of a man's head and CAMP RED CLOUD printed across it in red letters. Red Cloud was the Indian spirit-guide of the medium who had founded the place. As a youngster Stefan had asked his grandmother why guides to the spirit world were so often Indians. Once she told him it was because Indians had always believed in the spirits. But another time she chuckled deep in her throat and said it was because their names were easy to remember.

For the first time, Stefan wondered why the place was called a camp, for nothing about it suggested temporary quarters. The driveway was as long as the one that led to Rowan Hall, and at its end was the white bulk of the central auditorium, the Temple of All Spirits, built in the late 1930s with believers' donations. Most of the people who headed down the drive—they had numbered over fifty thousand a year in Stefan's time—hoped to commune with their dead.

For a moment he felt like one of them, for his grandmother's voice rose from the corners of his mind, calling his name. He shook his head to silence her, and drove into the circle around which the camp's main buildings were arranged. There were now three hotels, he saw, instead of one. The gift shop was much larger, and a handsome museum had been built. Behind the buildings stretched acres of parkland, presumably still studded with fountains, gazebos, and "retreats."

He parked in one of the lots. He had meant to go into the Temple of All Spirits but found himself walking toward the streets that fanned out from the main circle. The mediums had always lived on those streets.

There were some new houses, but many were familiar. He headed toward the one he had known best, his grandmother's white Colonial. After she died, one of her colleagues, Mavis Grant, had bought it. Stefan, who was twelve, stayed on to live with Mavis for a while, then he went to another medium, across the street.

As he stood looking at the house, the many years that had passed since he left it condensed into one emotion: shock, at seeing that it was a perfectly ordinary house.

He headed toward it, telling himself that if Mavis was still there, it would be as good a place as any to start asking questions about Polly Whiting.

On the front door, where his grandmother had once had a silver plaque engraved DAME DORCAS VEERE, was tacked a white card reading REVEREND MAVIS LESTER GRANT. He walked around to the side. The curtains were drawn on what Dorcas had always called "the séance parlor." He walked to the back entrance and pushed at the screen door; it gave. He went in.

The house was cool and quiet except for the faint sounds coming from behind the closed parlor doors: the singing of a hymn. Stefan looked down at his dark shirt and slacks and thought them fortuitous. Then he wondered whether he had really dressed that way by chance; perhaps his subconscious had been preparing for what he was going to do.

He didn't go to the parlor doors. There was another way into the room, which his body took without consulting him.

He slid into the room. It was dark except for the glow of a single red bulb. Once his sight adjusted, he made out four sitters in a semicircle, facing the curtained-off area known as "the cabinet," which was as sacred to spiritualism as an altar was to a church. Mavis Grant would be inside it, going into a trance. No doubt the sitters, if at all suspicious, had been invited to inspect the cabinet before the lights were turned out, to verify that it contained nothing but a chair. During Stefan's years at Red Cloud, skeptics had sometimes insisted on inspecting even their mediums, but nothing suspicious had ever been found in anyone's clothing.

The room was very quiet. The eye of red light turned faces and bodies into shadow-fragments. Stefan could just make out the folded arms of someone standing near the cabinet—the medium's attendant, or bodyguard, who was there to make sure no one tried to touch the ectoplasm that would begin to emanate from the medium's body. Once, his grandmother had told him, someone had grabbed at the ectoplasm when she was in a trance. It had snapped back into her body, she said, with the force of a catapult and had left a searing burn all along her right side. He had seen the scar many times.

In the midst of the darkness, low down, near the floor, appeared a tiny flickering sphere that could have been imagination. But it began to glow. It had motion rather than shape or color, like tongues of smoke lapping around one another. Gradually it began to acquire a face and a torso, but they seemed to have no substance and to undulate like an image in a heat-haze.

Was this, Stefan wondered, the way some people envisioned what took place in the labs at Biologiconn? In a red glow like hell-fire, something was brought pulsating out of nothing?

In the séance-rooms of spiritualism, he thought, the "creation of life" took place every day and had done so for decades. But there was no public outcry against it. There never had been.

Then he almost cried out himself, for something else was growing in the room. It was the scent of jasmine—the fragrance his grandmother had always worn, which had exuded from her most powerfully when she was in one of her trances.

She had entered his life in the middle of a night shortly after his father's death, looming out of his sleep and the darkness as if she came from his dreams.

He remembered little of his father and had been told even less. Henry Veere had led a peripatetic existence as an "occultist," whose business cards said ASTROLOGY, NUMEROLOGY, AND TAROT READINGS. The most Stefan could recall was being in a car and staring out the window while Henry whistled along with the radio, the sounds emerging tunelessly from the blueblack stubble that surrounded them. It had been strange to hear such a high, birdlike sound from a man so tall and heavyset and otherwise saturnine. Stefan's mother existed only in the memory of his father's imprecations: "That redhaired Irish bitch left you in your crib, damn her soul, and ran off with a teacher. A *teacher!*"

What Henry Veere died of Stefan never knew. One day he just wasn't there anymore, and some people, presumably colleagues in the psychic world, took Stefan in. He heard them arguing—"But Dorcas and Henry haven't spoken in twenty years, not since he ran off with her files"—but they must have contacted her. She later swore to Stefan, though, that she had learned of his existence in a dream.

Whatever the case, he went to his borrowed bed one night and awakened hours later to find a figure reared up beside him, with the beak and wings of a huge night bird. "Stefan Veere, Stefan dear," it was saying. "They've heard my prayers, they've sent me a grandson."

Gradually he saw that the wings were a black cape and that the bedside lamp was casting shadows on a long, sharp nose and black hair. Even so, he was pinned beneath the covers, between fear and fascination, a first impression that proved prophetic.

"Oh, Stefan dear," she crooned. "Now come, my little boy—yes, mine—we'll put all your things in your suitcase, and we'll go."

"Now?" he had managed to croak.

"Yes, yes, now. Quick!"

And they had gone at once, to Camp Red Cloud.

In the beginning he had simply accepted her, like a phenomenon of nature one could not question or change: a tall woman who favored black dresses and ropes of pearls and whose eyes were pools of dark water that could pull one to the brink and, sometimes, in.

He must have been about eight when he began to question her behavior. Why was she sometimes so warm and loving but at others so forbidding he hardly dared look at her? Why did she sometimes crush him to her breast so strongly that her pearls cut into his cheeks, and weep bitterly? How could she be doing something quite ordinary, like snapping beans for supper and asking him about his arithmetic, and suddenly stop, stare into a place more distant than space, and become impervious to everything, almost catatonic?

The first time he saw her in a trance, in the kitchen, he was afraid she was dead and shouted at her, touched her, and finally even pinched her. But she didn't come out of it for half an hour. In later trances, though, she often did speak. Sometimes Stefan would understand the words but not their meanings, and sometimes the words themselves would be strange. Once he wrote down a few of them, but when she returned to herself and saw the paper, she merely shrugged and said, "*Ktharlok li voorn?* I don't know what it means. When the spirits take over, they control me completely."

Years later, when his struggle to understand her had broadened into a fascination with the human mind and he started to take psychology courses in college, he had come across a passage that described Dorcas perfectly: a woman who could be harmless and chatty one minute and, the next, a powerful seeress, half sibyl and half witch. But the passage wasn't from a case history. It was a description of Carl Jung's mother.

Like Jung, he had found the question of the spirit world the most difficult to grapple with. Could Dorcas really do what she claimed to do in a trance: leave her body behind while she explored the hearts of mountains and the spirits of druids and elves? Or commune with a *quattrocento* Italian princess or an ancient Egyptian embalmer? And if she could, what gave her the power?

Shortly after his arrival at the Camp she took him to a service she conducted in the Temple of All Spirits. It was a "message service," she said, at which she would bring people communications from their loved ones on the other side. Stefan sat in one of the front rows, in a new sailor suit, and watched her run her pearls through her fingers like water and address the crowd with words that meant little to him but sounded as compelling as waves. At length, eyes closed and body rocking gently, she began to call out the spirit messages. Around and behind him Stefan heard the recipients gasp at their accuracy. "Wonderful, wonderful!" a man cried after she described the objects his father had kept on his dresser.

Dorcas cried back, "It's the power of the spirits! They can do anything, you understand?" Eyes glittering, she took a bright, sharp knife from behind the pulpit, walked down to the man and told him to plunge it into her abdomen. When he refused, she put it into his hand, grabbed his wrist, and shoved. A heavy grunt came from her, and gasps from the crowd. The knife went in several inches, against obvious resistance. Stefan's heart sailed into his mouth, pulling him to his feet as he waited to see her bleed and crumple. He ran to her, shouting, "Grandma, please don't be hurt!"

She stood quite still, eyes wide, hands clenched around the hilt of the knife. Then her eyes cleared. Looking down at him, she pulled out the bloodless metal blade and said, "Of course I'm not hurt. I was under the protection of the spirits."

She lifted him up in her arms as the crowd called out its relief and blessings, and the scent of jasmine was overpowering.

"Oh, my darling girl," said a woman's voice. "My sweetest little angel."

Stefan saw that the white evanescence visible in the dim light from the red bulb had become the figure of a child, which hovered near the knees of one of the sitters. "Do you still have my teddy bear on the window seat?" it asked.

"Of course I do. You know I do. I keep everything just the way you liked it."

"Do you, Daddy?"

"All your little dresses and shoes—just the way they were when you left. And the new yellow coat we got the day before . . ."

"But you don't have to do that, Daddy," said the child-figure. "I think you should give them away, so other kids could use them."

"No! Never!"

"Oh, Daddy, I'm sorry, but I'm getting awfully sleepy. I'm afraid I have to go now, but I'll come back another time. I do love you. Good-bye."

The man stifled a sob, and there were sympathetic murmurs from the other sitters.

"Good-bye, Daddy . . ." The voice faded, and the child-figure dissipated like smoke in a wind. For a moment a shimmering spot of it was left, and then that was gone too.

The lights would be coming on in a moment, Stefan thought. He moved silently back to the secret entrance. Minutes later he was closing the kitchen screen door behind him.

He waited until he saw the four sitters emerge and go down the front walk, followed five minutes later by the medium who had served as the attendant. Then he went back inside and sat at the round table in the kitchen.

Shortly the Reverend Mavis Grant came in, coughing and pulling a cigarette from a nearly empty pack. She was much heavier and grayer than he remembered her.

She yelped when she saw him, and dropped the cigarette.

He picked it up and laid it on the table. "Haven't you given these things up yet, Mavis?"

"Who are you?" she said. "Do I know you?"

"You used to, pretty well."

She pulled out another cigarette and came to sit at the table, staring at him while she struck a match. She inhaled deeply and coughed. "I met you down in Tampa, right?"

"No, here in this house. Remember the hamsters I kept on the back porch? And a chemistry outfit in the basement?"

"My God," she said. "It's Dorcas's grandson. Stefan." When he nodded, she leaned back, cocked her head, and eyed him through a veil of smoke. "You used to be as skinny as a broom handle. And your hair was a lot redder."

He smiled. "Yours was a lot browner."

"I never thought you'd dare set foot in Red Cloud again."

"That's all ancient history, Mavis."

"Yes? Seems to me I heard where you live in New York now."

"I do."

"I heard you went on TV up there and showed up that mind reader from Australia."

"True enough."

"So what are you back here for?"

"Don't you think I'm entitled to make a sentimental journey?" When she snorted he said, "OK. I'm looking for a little information." He hesitated. "Do you use fragrances now, in a séance? Perfume?"

She raised a penciled eyebrow. "That's what you came to find out?"

"No. But . . . do you use them?"

"Once in a while."

"Ah. That explains why I smelled jasmine in the house."

"Never use that one," she said. "Reminds me of Dorcas."

After a moment he said, "Yes. Well, let's get to the information I want. Don't worry, I'll pay for it." He took out his wallet, extracted a recent clipping about Polly Whiting, and laid it on the table. "I imagine you've been reading about this woman. I wonder whether you've ever seen her before, or heard anything about her, apart from the current publicity, that is."

Mavis looked at the picture and lifted her head sharply. For a moment surprise cleared her pale, cloudy eyes, and then they narrowed. She snorted again, this time without amusement. "You," she said, "have got a lot of bloody nerve."

13

Stefan sat in a windowed corner of the Camp Red Cloud cafeteria, looking out at the main buildings. The sun was setting, coating the roof of the Temple of All Spirits with copper and turning its windows into sheets of gold. Nature's illusions, he thought, were so innocent.

As he nursed a cup of coffee he pondered Mavis's reaction. She had said she knew nothing at all about Polly Whiting, and had ended the conversation quickly. Had she been lying?

He tried to decide by recalling the clues her gestures and tone had provided. It was the same thing he did in his office, where he had a standing order to remind himself that the patient could be lying. His natural tendency was to believe what was said, on the grounds that people paying for help with problems would be foolish to lie about the nature of those problems. But they often did. For some, that was part of the problem.

With Mavis, he decided, more data was needed. Then he smiled at his use of the word—with its scientific connotations—in a place like Camp Red Cloud. Of course spiritualists said that theirs was not only a religion but also a science. Most religions, he reminded himself, were unwilling to abandon such ideas as proof and evidence because most people had a psychological need for them. He smiled again, realizing he had just taken a new angle on the idea fundamental to his school of psychiatry: the importance of the cognitive faculty in human behavior.

Dialogue that seemed to confirm the point drifted from a neighboring table: "My husband doesn't believe in any of it, you know, so last week I asked the spirits to send a sign for him."

"Do you think you'll get it tonight?"

"Oh, I know you can't count on any *particular* thing happening at a sitting, but Fawn and Reverend Kilgore will do their best. I'm sure of that."

Stefan's eyebrows lifted. He knew those names. As he listened, he learned that Clara Fisher Kilgore would be holding a group trumpet séance in the temple in half an hour.

He was there in fifteen minutes, joining the group of people waiting to enter one of the small chapels that edged the periphery of the main auditorium. Some chatted with the knowing air of old hands, but a few were clearly newcomers.

When the crowd went in, Stefan followed them. A young woman stood inside the door, collecting receipts. "I just drove in," Stefan told her. "I didn't have time to go to the office and sign up."

120

The woman frowned. "Are you new to Red Cloud?"

Phrases Stefan hadn't heard in twenty-five years came to his lips. "I'm just passing through but I'm a member of the Church of Life Energy in Miami. I've sat in many trumpet circles down there, and I can't believe Reverend Kilgore wouldn't be glad to have me. I hear she's so wonderful."

The woman hesitated before she went to speak to the medium, but when she returned, she let Stefan into the room, a windowless rectangle that was heavily carpeted. On the wall hung two pictures, one of Jesus, one of Red Cloud.

The medium who faced the large semicircle of participants was smaller than Stefan remembered, her face as thin and sharp as a lizard's. But then, he thought, he was unrecognizable too—fortunately.

On a table beside her was the trumpet, actually a long tin megaphone. She folded her hands and explained that after she had gone into a trance, the spirits, brought by her guide, Fawn, would speak through the trumpet by forming a kind of voice box with the ectoplasm they would draw from her body. She asked the circle to pray with her and then to join her in singing several hymns. Many of them sang with their eyes closed and their bodies rocking gently.

When the lights went out, the darkness was as dense as black velvet. The group sat absolutely quiet, as they had been told to, although the separate strands of their breathing, and their desire, began to weave together into something almost palpable.

Suddenly the woman beside Stefan made a single, faint, whimpering sound. Where the trumpet had been, glowing bands of light had appeared in the black.

The silence stretched on.

The trumpet broke it, emitting a high, singsong voice. "Hello. Hello, Clara. Here I am. I heard you calling, and I came as soon as I could."

The medium's voice, sounding drugged, said, "Fawn. Dear little girl. How are you today? Are you well?"

"Of course. I'm always well, Clara. And happy. Very happy! I want everyone to be happy, like me."

"That's sweet, Fawn. You're a good girl."

There was a giggle. "Except when I'm naughty."

The silence resumed, even thicker and more expectant.

Into it, the child-voice piped from the shimmering trumpet, "Is there a Franklin here?"

Someone gasped. "Yes, yes. Franklin Cox."

"I have a lady who wants to talk with you. A tall lady with beautiful hair. Brown and long. Her name is Margaret."

"She's welcome! Yes! Oh my dear Lord, she is welcome."

The bands of light that the trumpet had become rose into the air, stopped several feet above the heads of the sitters, and hung there serenely. "Hello, Franklin," said a silvery voice. "Franklin, my dear, it's so good to be with you again. Are you well?"

"Yes, I am. Yes. How are you?"

"I'm at peace, Franklin. I have no pain. I'm happy, and you must be, too." The trumpet then swooped down onto the sitter's knees. "I'm close to you now, Franklin. As close as if you were sitting beside my bed and reading to me, the way you liked to do."

"Yes, I can feel your voice. I can *feel* it."

"I'll come to talk with you often, as often as I can . . ." The trumpet lifted, and the voice began to fade.

The man cried agonizingly, "Don't go, Mother!" Then he added, "I'm sorry. I know you stay as long as you can."

Silence descended again. Someone near Stefan took a deep, ragged breath. When he was a youngster, Stefan thought, the darkness of the séance-room had been a cloak, but now it seemed to strip away everything, reducing the sitters to the naked emotions in their voices and the catches in their breathing.

The trumpet moved once more, performing a series of graceful arcs before stopping again to hang in space just at eye level. "The spirits have a gift for someone in the room," said the child-voice. "A gift for someone named Sally."

"Oh!" a woman cried. "I'm Sally."

"Is your husband named John?" asked the voice. "John Martin?"

"Yes!" the woman cried. "John Martin Loomis!"

The trumpet sailed to the sound of her voice. "You asked the spirits for a sign to convince your husband," said the voice. "Last month you lost the bracelet his mother gave you before she died. Tonight the spirits are apporting it back to you." The trumpet began to swing from side to side and then to maneuver in dizzying archs. Something seemed to fall from it.

"Oh!" cried Sally's voice. "It's in my lap—I can *feel* it, the bracelet. Yes, it *is*. I can't believe it—it's too wonderful. Thank the spirits for me, Fawn. Thank them! Oh, I can even feel the engraving on the inside!"

When she got it into the light, Stefan knew, it would indeed be her dead mother-in-law's bracelet.

He stood up quietly, in the dark, and made his way out—not by the way he had come in.

Once he was back in the temple lobby, he did what he realized he should have done when he first arrived. He went to the main office.

There, from a stack on the table, he took a flyer that listed the Reverends and counselors currently serving Red Cloud. He recognized three names besides Mavis Grant's and Clara Kilgore's. Then he studied a bulletin board above the table, and jotted down all the events of that day and the next.

Half an hour later, he stopped Clara Kilgore as she emerged from the trumpet séance.

"You're the one," she said accusingly. "You broke the circle. When I came out of the trance, there was an empty chair. You're the one!"

"Yes."

"You threw the spirits off. All the vibrations were wrong, and Fawn could hardly—"

"Why don't you just drop it, Clara?"

She drew herself up. "I don't know what on earth you mean."

"I'm not from the Church of Life Energy in Miami. I'm Dorcas Veere's grandson. Stefan."

The pious anger drained from her face but left the shell of its expression behind. "I don't believe it."

"It's true. I was going to pretend to be one of the faithful, so I could ask you some questions, but I find my stomach can't take any more fraud."

Her eyes darkened. "You're Stefan Veere, all right. What did you come back for? To stir up more trouble?"

He shook his head. "Just to ask a question. About a woman named Polly Whiting." He decided belligerence might work with Clara and added, "You know who she is, so don't bother to deny it."

Cautiously she said, "Yes, I know."

"I need to know whether she's ever been here at Red Cloud."

The medium looked at him for what seemed like a full minute. Then she threw back her head and laughed.

"Is it that funny, Clara?"

"It sure is—the idea that I'd tell you anything. You think I forget things because I'm old?" She tucked her large purse more firmly under her arm. "Excuse me, but I've got better things to do with my time."

She walked off, an air of wounded piety trailing her like a cloak. She was so small, Stefan thought. But when he ran away she had seemed gigantic.

He leaned against the wall, wondering what her laughter had meant. Just an expression of her scorn? Or did it come from something she knew about Polly Whiting? The latter seemed more likely, especially when combined with his impression that Mavis Grant might have known something too.

There were still the three other mediums from the old days. He went back outside; the sun and its warmth were gone, so he stopped at his car to pick up his sport coat. He looked up at the sky, where twilight was laying down strips of gray and purple, and let himself think for a moment of the brilliant red of Cayla Hayward's mouth.

Then he sighed, ran his hands through the tight curl of his hair, and headed back to the streets where the mediums lived. One of the three in question, he seemed to recall, was "shut-eye" rather than "open."

When Stefan first heard those terms, he was so young he took them literally: He thought shut-eyes kept their eyes closed during séances, whereas open mediums didn't. Eventually he learned that the terms were metaphoric, that shut-eyes believed in their powers, but opens admitted—only to their colleagues, of course—that they were frauds. And which kind was Dame Dorcas Veere? He had never been able to decide.

Certainly she achieved her effects in the séance-room by fraud, although Stefan didn't think of it that way in the beginning. He simply had to do certain things for her—"It's kind of a game, Stefan dear," she said, "and I know you like games." He started by being a "spirit-child," materializing in the dark, skipping around the room, laughing, touching the sitters, sometimes kissing them. Before he came, Dorcas said, she had had to do the children herself, and it had been hard on her arthritis.

She taught him the secret of ectoplasm: chiffon or gauze. She bought him a long-sleeved jersey, long pants, sneakers, socks and gloves, all in black, and had him practice climbing up through the trapdoor in the floor of the séance-room. She would go into her trance, moaning and mumbling her strange mixture of English and tongues, and then her spirit-guide, a child named Jasmine, would take over. When Jasmine gave him a prearranged signal, Stefan would take a ball of chiffon from his pocket and unfold it gradually until it covered him. In the glow of a red bulb the effect was wonderfully eerie, for the black clothing was invisible, and the chiffon looked as ethereal as smoke.

Of course he had never seen the spirit-child effect he produced, but he often watched his grandmother when she "materialized" as one of the dead she was invoking. She was an expert at manipulating chiffon, better than any of the other mediums he worked with after her death. The chiffon, which was amazingly compressible, could be hidden in her cabinet attendant's purse until the lights went out, so that no skeptic or investigator would ever find it on Dorcas's clothing or body. The attendant then passed it to her in the dark. Dressed in black, Dorcas would stand at one side of the room, let a ball of chiffon unwind away from her, and by means of skillful hand and arm motions, make it rise and grow to cover her. The first time Stefan saw it happen he had been hard put to remember that the ghostly, compelling figure was his grandmother.

To end the materialization, she would pull the chiffon from her body very slowly and shape it back into a ball. The spirit would fade away to a wisp of ectoplasm and then dissolve into nothing.

Dorcas also taught Stefan to help her in trumpet séances, for which she was famous. The tin megaphone, with its luminous bands, looked short but was actually built in collapsible sections, so that she could pull out a section or two in the darkness, hold it with her hand while she spoke through it, and make the trumpet float, soar, or swing. With her free hand she could throw out the "apports," or spirit gifts, that seemed to fall from the trumpet. Stefan's role was to provide a special effect. Wearing a black face mask in addition to the rest of his outfit, he would take the trumpet from her, quickly collapse it to the length the sitters believed it was, and place it in someone's lap. Then his grandmother, who was a decent ventriloquist, would throw her voice into the trumpet while the sitter held it—thus hearing a spirit voice while being able to confirm that no human mouth, or wire or thread, was attached to the trumpet.

When he first learned the séance-room "games," Stefan was actually relieved: The strange private trances into which Dorcas fell must be just more games. But one afternoon he came home from school feeling sick and found her in the kitchen, body rigid, eyes staring, mouth emitting the strange languages. He stood over her shouting, "Please stop it, Grandma, I don't feel good," but nothing changed. Miserably he crawled into his bed. When, some time later, he found her bending over him, and asked why she had kept on playing the game when he was sick, she said forbiddingly, "It's not a game. When the spirits call me, I have no choice but to go." A moment later she was all warmth and concern, saying softly, "Oh my dear little Stefan, they sent you to me as a sign of forgiveness, so I must keep you well."

Was she open, then, or shut-eye? When he finally asked her outright, he still didn't get a satisfactory answer.

He had been rummaging in a closet for a box to hold gerbils, when he came across a large, slightly concave metal plate that was covered with several inches of plasticine and had straps attached to it. He took it to Dorcas. "Ah!" she cried. "There it is. I thought it was lost. I've been wanting to use it again." When he asked what it was, she grinned, winked, and showed him. She tied the contraption to her torso, put an apron over it, took out a paring knife, and pushed it slowly into her abdomen.

She laughed. "Good, eh? The plasticine makes it seem like the knife is going into flesh, and the metal plate stops it from touching me."

"But, Grandma," he said when he could find words, "you told me you weren't hurt because the spirits were protecting you. Only it's just another trick. I don't think there are any spirits at all!"

Suddenly she had his hands in a steel grip, and her eyes were sucking him into their black depths. "The spirits are real, never doubt it," she said, the knife still protruding grotesquely from her apron. "And never doubt their power. But people's faith can be very weak, so we have to help them believe sometimes, by arranging things that will convince them. It's in a good cause, isn't it?"

Mesmerized, he had nodded. "Some of it *is* real then?"

"Yes! You've seen the burn on my side—you think chiffon could do that to me?"

After she died, a month later, he kept to himself the strange mixture of his feelings—grief and relief, and the frustration of knowing he would never understand her.

Later, in college, he learned that a trance medium, if she was not merely pretending, could in fact experience states of changed consciousness, including auditory, visual and kinetic delusions and the feeling of being "taken over" by someone else. Clinically the phenomenon was known as dissociation—a part of the personality that was a source of distress separated and functioned outside the individual's control.

But alongside the remembered power of Dorcas Veere's presence, the explanation didn't always seem to be enough.

He sometimes wondered whether he would ever have found that explanation—whether he would have gotten out of Red Cloud at all—if it hadn't been for an incident that took place about three years after Dorcas's death, when he had become accustomed to living with other mediums and working for them to earn his keep.

A camp patron asked to film a séance in order to obtain photographic proof of a materialization. Everyone had been informed in advance that the shooting would be done with infrared lights and film, so that anything in the dark would stand out. And the camp's board of directors, mostly mediums, agreed. Either they didn't believe what they were told about infrared film, or they thought they could somehow get the better of it.

The finished film revealed, of course, that the seemingly evanescent spirits were really two of the camp's mediums. One of them was Clara Kilgore.

The affair had caused a terrible scandal in the psychic world, and some of its most devoted believers, including the one who had arranged the experiment, were disillusioned and denounced Camp Red Cloud. But the majority of the faithful simply refused to accept the evidence of the film. They insisted that someone had doctored the print in order to frame the mediums.

.Up until that time Stefan hadn't paid much attention to the sitters themselves; his efforts to understand his world had been concentrated on Dorcas and the other mediums. The chicanery they all practiced was part of the puzzle of their behavior, which, with a child's singlemindedness, he had barely connected to the larger world. But the scandal made him confront the real nature of what was going on at Red Cloud by forcing on him the realization that for the sitters there were no games. Everything was in deadly earnest for them, and the mediums were simply exploiting their willingness to believe.

He began to pay more attention when the mediums talked among themselves, making cracks about "the suckers" and jokes about the Bible. He realized they believed in nothing but the money they collected—some in such quantities that they had expensive cars and large homes in Florida.

One night he overheard several of them talking, using words he didn't understand, like *dildo*. When he finally grasped what they were saying—that the things they were willing to produce in the séance-room included sex "with the departed loved one"—he had been unable to get to sleep.

The next day, the realization he had seemed to be avoiding reared up in his mind: Even Dorcas, though she might have believed in her own powers, had cheated and fleeced people as long as he had known her. And he had helped her do it. His stomach grew permanently queasy with the knowledge.

One woman, a Mrs. Trent, became the center of his new perspective. She had been going regularly to Clara Kilgore to commune with her dead child. She was outraged at the scandal—not at Clara and her colleagues but at those who had conducted the experiment. They were evil, Mrs. Trent said, for they had tricked the mediums. Tall, young, not very pretty, she was particularly pathetic and disturbing to Stefan. How could she go on believing in the face of the film's evidence? How could Clara, how could all of them, go on feeding off people's weaknesses and their pain of bereavement?

One day as he was going into the temple, Mrs. Trent was coming out, so preoccupied that she walked right into him. She apologized vaguely, and then, as if the contact with him had unleashed emotions she couldn't contain, she flung her arms around him and said, "Oh, aren't the spirits wonderful? Isn't Reverend Kilgore the most wonderful woman in the world?"

The queasiness that had been trapped within him for weeks suddenly rose into his throat. He shook off Mrs. Trent's hold and cried out that everything was a fake and a fraud, that no one could make her dead baby speak to her, that he himself had often pretended to be people's dead children so he knew what he was talking about. He felt that if only he could make her understand, he would feel clean and good again.

She stared at first as if he held a gun. Then she began to scream, so that everyone nearby heard and the mediums came running. They calmed Mrs. Trent but absorbed her fury into their own and turned all of it on Stefan. Led by Clara Kilgore, they hauled him into the Temple of All Spirits while he kicked and struggled and shouted at them—"Cheats! Fakes! You cheat people and hurt them, you bunch of old frauds!" They had locked him in a room in the basement and left to hold a council to decide what to do with him, but he managed to get out. He ran into town, got some money from a school friend and waited on the bus corner, his heart thudding. . . .

It skipped a beat, in memory, as he approached the end of one of the streets where the mediums lived. He felt a strange need to turn and run again, which he made himself ignore.

Twenty-five years earlier the last house on the street had belonged to a medium named Lettice Barrow. Her name was still on the mailbox. He wondered whether she was still shut-eye. The shut-eyes he'd known had always seemed rather nice. Perhaps that was why the frauds kept them around—their sweetness and obvious sincerity must have been good for business.

Ten minutes later, Lettice Barrow, so old now that her face was like cracked glass, was giving him coffee and cake in her kitchen. "Dorcas's boy," she kept saying, fixing him with her pale blue eyes. "I still miss Dorcas, you know. She was about the only real friend I ever had here at Red Cloud."

She was chatting away about her winters in Florida when she suddenly stopped and asked, "Where did you go? After you ran away? I worried about you."

"I went with a carnival for a while. It was the only way I

could find to earn some money." He didn't add that its tricks and sideshows had seemed innocent after Red Cloud.

Lettice sighed. "I should have taken you in. After Dorcas died, you should have come with me. I could have helped you. But I was having a lot of trouble then. Sickness, I mean . . . If the spirits hadn't healed me, I would have died." She shook her head. "A carnival. Dorcas wouldn't have liked that."

"I made enough money to go to school. Now I'm doing fine."

"That's good, Stefan. That's real good." She picked a cake crumb off the tablecloth. "Dorcas loved you, you know."

He said nothing. He had learned in his years of practice that people could love the children whose lives they were blighting.

"Dorcas worried about you, too. She said the spirits warned her that you'd go through a time of doubt and rejecting them. And of course you did—I remember that." She nodded to herself. "But now you've come back, so the doubting must be over."

Gently he said, "Lettice, I only came to get some information. I was hoping you could help me." He took out the clipping of Polly Whiting and handed it to her. "I expect you know about this woman. She's been all over the papers and TV."

"That's true. She has."

"Have you ever seen her here at Red Cloud?"

Lettice gave him a long look, just as Clara Kilgore had. Then she put the clipping down and patted it with a wrinkled hand. "But don't you recognize her? You should, you of all people. We knew who she was right away, even if she calls herself Polly Whiting now. When she came here, she called herself Polly Trent."

14

On a TV screen the hero and heroine of a 1930s comedy fought and made up hilariously. Their antics didn't even make Stefan smile. He watched them without seeing.

When he left Lettice, knowing he had to stay another day, he drove the six miles back to town and checked into a motel. Staying at one of the Red Cloud hotels had seemed neither a pleasant nor a smart idea. Fortunately there was no problem about staying over because he always took Sunday and Monday off unless there were emergencies. The problem lay with strategy, not schedule: He hadn't thought of a way to learn more about Polly Whiting and her visits to Red Cloud.

Every time he tried to think constructively, his mind drifted in amazement back to the Mrs. Trent who had become such a symbol to him. Her image was as indistinct as a materialization. Even when he recalled the day he ran away, he saw her as little more than wild eyes and a shrieking mouth. She had been more a receptacle for his feelings than an entity on her own, he decided. Perhaps that was the way of symbols.

Obviously she hadn't recognized him either, though that wasn't hard to understand. The gawky boy who once accosted her at Camp Red Cloud could have no relation in her mind to the forty-year-old psychiatrist who was examining her in New York.

Lettice Barrow didn't know much about Polly Trent. Shortly after Stefan ran away, she said, the woman stopped coming to Red Cloud, and no one knew why. When her picture began appearing in connection with the story of a reincarnated witch, one of the older mediums thought she might have been from somewhere in Pennsylvania. "Oh yes," Lettice added, "they said she was real religious."

They might have said more among themselves, Stefan thought, but opens always guarded their tongues when talking to shut-eyes. No cracks about suckers or the Bible then. There was a good possibility that one of the opens, especially Clara Kilgore, might know more facts about Polly, but there seemed no possibility that any of them, especially Clara, would tell him what they knew.

And he wanted to know a lot. The detectives' report Cayla showed him made no mention either of the name Trent—it said Polly's maiden name was Kendall—or of a child who had died. Where had the name come from then? Had there been a previous marriage? Had there in fact been a child who died? Was there some connection with the Hayward family buried in the story of those years? Was there some significance to the fact that Polly had quit coming to Red Cloud in the same year she had married Bill Whiting—twenty-five years ago?

Stefan sat up, rubbed his eyes, and focused for a few moments on the TV screen, where a man in a tuxedo was talking earnestly to a poodle in a jeweled collar. Life was so elegant in those old films, he thought, looking around at the motel room, with its gold-flecked formica, turquoise vinyl chairs, and rug as busy as Grand Central. He visualized Cayla in the room and smiled. Had she ever been in a motel in her life? He remembered the huge staircase at Rowan Hall and the fireplaces and tables, all of marble, and the velvets and damasks that hung rich and red in a room where two old women had done their best to guarantee that Cayla would grow up to be as disturbed as they. He thought of the amazing extent to which they had failed.

But now there was a new trial for her. In the evening paper there was a story about a patient in a psychiatric hospital who believed she had born the Devil's child and who talked of a witch named Kella. She was thought to be Cayla Hayward's mother.

He sighed, lay back on the garish bedspread, and watched the man in the tuxedo.

The man was going down some stairs with a supercilious butler. He unlocked a door, and the two of them went into a wine cellar and began reading the labels on bottles as if they were rare books.

Stefan sat up. "The cellar," he said. "My God, I forgot about the files in the cellar." He stared at the screen, not seeing it, his eyes bright. Then he leaped off the bed and fished in his pants pocket for the notebook in which he had jotted the schedule of Camp Red Cloud events for the next day.

In the morning he bought a ski mask, dark gloves and black sneakers.

After lunch he drove back to Red Cloud and was heading to the temple, where he planned to disappear until it was time to put his plan into action, where he heard Lettice Barrow call his name. She was on her way to a message service in the temple, she said, and wasn't it a lovely day, and why was he still at the camp?

He told her he just wanted to look around a little more for old times' sake before he went back up north. She accepted that, but then wanted to stand and chat. In the sunlight she looked even older and frailer than she had the night before. Through her white hair, which was as thin as cotton candy, Stefan could see pink skin. He began to feel almost as exposed as her scalp, but he could not get away without being rude. Finally she stopped, fished in her handbag for a watch, cried, "Oh, I'm late," kissed him with withered lips, and went off to the temple.

He waited five minutes and went there too.

He made his way down the stairs at the back of the lobby. The day before, he had escaped from Clara Kilgore's trumpet séance by means of a trapdoor reached from the basement. All the chapels in the temple used to have such trapdoors, and he was assuming that because one still did, they all would. It took him a while to locate the one that led up into the chapel he wanted to enter, where, according to the camp schedule, the first materialization séance of the day would take place in half an hour.

He had to get into the séance because he had to steal a key. The key would open the secret file room where the mediums, at least the open ones, kept their records. Although no one had ever told him about it, he had overheard references to it and once he had followed Mavis Grant when she went into a storage room and unlocked a door concealed in one wall. He never got inside the room, so he wasn't sure what it contained, but he thought it was information on the sitters. If he was lucky, he would soon know for sure.

He found the storage room and the door in its wall; the file room was still there. He put on the ski mask, the gloves, and the black sneakers, and waited.

Twenty minutes later he eased himself up through the trapdoor into the red-lit darkness of a séance and took a position against one wall. The medium, whom he didn't know, was in the cabinet. The curtains were drawn, but she could be heard breathing heavily. He made out the attendant sitting on a chair beside the cabinet. She was one of the opens whose name he had recognized in the camp flyer, and she was his target.

From within the cabinet the medium began to speak as if she were being "controlled" by her spirit-guide, whose voice and words were those of a child. Mediums, Stefan learned in college, are often hysteric personalities—that is, they have a neurosis characterized by evasions and retreat mechanisms, by subterfuges and self-dramatization and by an arrested development of the personality, so that they themselves are immature, often childish. It was natural that they would choose children for their spirit alter egos.

While the child-voice came from the cabinet, he inched his way toward the attendant until he was directly behind her. In the murky red light he could just make out a large handbag at her feet. If luck was with him, she would have her keys in that bag, and they would include a key to the file room.

As he put out an arm, slowly, he had a strong, unpleasant sense of *déjà vu*. Sometimes Mavis had had him go through sitters' handbags in the dark, to take objects that could later be used as apports. Usually the sitters wouldn't realize their loss for several days, by which time they would no longer connect it with the séance. Mavis would then wait several weeks before she had the spirits return the object. If she couldn't get anything that way, she would try to hold a séance in a sitter's home, find some excuse to look around a bedroom or a den, and pilfer some personal object that could seem to fall from a trumpet a few weeks or months later.

Stefan's gloved hand was two inches from the handbag when the attendant's hand came snaking down. He froze. She picked up the bag, which bumped into his hand. He pulled back. She groped around near the floor for a moment, then seemed to decide she had been mistaken. She reached into the bag—for chiffon, Stefan thought.

He felt her get up and move slowly away—to pass the chiffon to the medium in the cabinet. As soon as she moved, he reached for the bag.

It was a large, soft pouch. He had planned to find the keys, take them out and leave the bag, but he discovered that in its shapeless depths his gloved hand could find no keys.

He managed to slip off the glove. It was still impossible to identify all the objects he was fumbling through, but one of them seemed to be a change purse. When he moved it, coins chinked.

He froze. He saw that the attendant was returning.

He slid the bag back into position beside her chair.

She sat down and reached to touch it. She must have been re-assured, for her hand lifted to her lap.

Very slowly Stefan pulled the bag back to him.

Very quickly he made his way to the trapdoor and out.

In the dim light of the basement he emptied the bag out on the floor. He pulled off the gloves and the ski mask, which was very warm, put them aside, and bent over the bag's contents.

There actually were a number of small purses, each of a different color. The woman must use them as file compartments, odd as that seemed. He began opening them—tissues in one, indigestion tablets in another, business cards, lipsticks, nail fixings. And, at last, keys.

He debated returning the bag then and there, but he would still have to make another trip later to return the keys, and he was nervous about using the trapdoor more than absolutely necessary. Who knew what plans the medium might have made for her cohorts to use it?

He would have to hurry even more, he thought, for now there was the danger of the attendant's discovering at any moment that her bag was missing.

He stuffed everything back but the key ring and went into the storage room.

Not one of the keys fit the padlock on the door in the wall.

He stared in disbelief and tried them all again. Same result.

He dumped the bag out once more and scrutinized everything. He lifted a balled-up, knotted handkerchief by one corner. It weighed a bit more than he expected.

He undid the knot and found a small key.

It fit the padlock. He thanked God he hadn't returned the purse.

The room was fairly large, lit by a bare bulb with a pull chain. Metal filing cabinets stood against all the walls, with no space between them. Above them were shelves holding boxes and loose notebooks.

Stefan took down one of the boxes. Inside was a jumble of rings, pins, watches and tie clips and an invoice for their purchase. Apports, he thought. In case the mediums couldn't get what they needed by stealing it.

He picked up one of the notebooks and opened it at random. "Lucille Voss" was printed across the top of a page, and below that was a list:

O Father Martin. Lung C. Called her Lulu.
O Mother Ottilee. Born Berlin.
X Husb. Carl. Good Cath. Car dealer.
X Son Pete. Dogs.
G= Pansy, Chief Whitewater, Dr. Brown.

G, Stefan thought, must refer to the spirit-guides the medium had assigned to Lucille Voss. *O* and *X,* he decided after looking at a few more pages, must mean *dead* and *living.* With those scraps of information, gathered during sittings and from eavesdropping on the participants beforehand, a good medium could give an impressive sitting. The spirits could tell Lucille Voss that her father had died of lung cancer, her mother was German, and her son Pete loved dogs.

He put down the notebook and leafed through several others. The handwriting in each was different, but the idea was the same. He realized now why the mediums always insisted that sitters book in advance for a service or séance: so they could get information from the files and then stun their clients with the accuracy of the spirits' knowledge.

If there was information on Polly in one of those notebooks, he thought, it could take him all day to find it. Still, he picked up one more. Its pages were written in purple ink.

Dorcas Veere had always used purple ink. And she dotted her *i*'s with tiny circles.

A whiff of jasmine reached his nostrils. He stared at the notebook longer than he could afford to, knowing no scent could cling to anything for so long but smelling it anyway. He stuck the notebook in his pocket.

He looked at one of the file cabinets. The card in the slot on the top drawer read WIS. Inside were file dividers with names arranged alphabetically—MADISON, MILWAUKEE, NEENAH, and, he saw with a smile, OH CLARE. Under each city name were file cards with notes on individual sitters: "Dtr. X, long red hair, calls her Totie." "Has azma." "Believes but always wants to test. Watch out." "Wears mother's wedding ring on keychain." Objects were clipped or taped to some of the cards—a driver's license, a credit card, a key—presumably stolen and waiting to reappear from a trumpet.

Stefan looked around at the rest of the cabinets. The labels indicated that most of the country was represented. If so, he was looking at record-keeping on a scale he hadn't imagined. If such files were kept by mediums all over the country, if they swapped the contents with each other, then sitters from almost anywhere could walk into Red Cloud, or any other psychic hangout, and receive astoundingly correct and detailed spirit messages from a medium who was a total stranger. They would sing the praises of spiritualism, and pull out their checkbooks.

Stefan took a breath. What he was feeling, he realized, was caused not by the cupidity and chicanery of the mediums, not even by the scope of their record-keeping, but by the blindness of those who let their lives be reduced to, and run by, those misspelled scribbles on file cards. *Mundus vult decipi,* as Ben Jonson or somebody had said. And sometimes, Stefan thought, mankind not only wanted to be deceived—it begged to be.

He reminded himself that time was breathing down his neck, and went to the file cabinet where Polly Whiting's records should be, if they existed.

There was no Polly Trent card in any PENN file.

He frowned, then moved to another cabinet and began to search.

There was no Polly Trent card in any W VA file.

He sighed, inhaling dust and disappointment.

There must have been sitters whose hometowns were not known, he thought. How would their records be filed? He looked for U for unknown and NA for no address. There were no such files.

He checked his watch and knew he couldn't afford to wait any longer; the séance could be finishing momentarily. He picked up the handbag, opened the door, and took a last look around. His eyes fell on a cabinet labeled RC. Red Cloud? he wondered. He hesitated, then went over to open it. He was right.

It was there: a card headed "Polly Trent." The notes were sparse:

O Son Lenny. 1½ yrs, Teddy bear. Spoon.
X Father John. Dissapproves of RC??
Strong believer but never talks about family. Only baby.
???Penn.???

The report from Cayla's detectives on Polly Whiting had mentioned no son who died. It said her father was a John Kendall, but John was too common a name to be a meaningful clue.

A small envelope was taped to the back of the card. Stefan pulled it off and opened it. It contained a tiny silver cereal spoon, rather gaudy, and a beautifully worked silver locket. He turned the locket over. On the back was engraved CHR.

He told himself it wasn't possible.

He inserted his thumbnail into the locket catch and opened it. There was no photo, only slivers of a material he couldn't identify.

He shook them into his palm and went to stand directly under the bare light bulb. The slivers were slightly curved, and none was over half an inch long. He counted them.

"My God," he said aloud. "Nail parings? From six toes?"

Behind him there was a gasp.

He spun around. Lettice Barrow was in the doorway. Her eyes, large with shock, weren't looking at him. He thought she was reacting to the room's existence and tried to decide how to explain it.

Before he could do so, she whispered, "Six toes? Like Dorcas's girls?"

His expression became a mirror of hers. "What do you mean?"

"Dorcas must have sent you. Yes! Her spirit must have guided you to come here asking about that Trent woman. Did she do it so you would learn about the girls, then?"

"What girls? What are you talking about?"

Lettice was looking at some inner vision, not at him. "That must be it. Yes. Dorcas guided you here, to me. And then she guided me to be suspicious of you and follow you down here and wait to see what you were up to—" Her eyes cleared. "What *are* you up to, Stefan? What is this place?"

"Just a storage room," he said lamely.

With a movement swifter than he had thought her capable of, she sprang to him and grabbed his closed hand. He let her pull the fingers open. She bent close to his palm. "Yes," she muttered, "from one of Dorcas's girls. So Dorcas did want you to learn about them." She lifted her head to look at him, her face pulling into a cracked-glass frown. "I don't understand. She always said it would be bad for you to know about the girls. It could bring trouble on you, she said. Has she changed her mind, then? Does she *want* to bring trouble on you? But she loved you."

Stefan disengaged his hand. He took the locket from his shirt pocket, replaced the nail parings and asked Lettice whether she had ever seen it before.

"No. Is it Dorcas's? I suppose it must be."

He didn't answer. If he told her the truth—that it bore the same initials as those of a very rich, paralyzed old woman and apparently had nothing to do with Dorcas—he would have to explain things he didn't understand himself.

"But why was the locket in here?" Lettice said. "What kind of a storage room is this?"

Foolish as she was, he didn't want to open her shut eyes lest the shock be too much. "It's just a room where a lot of records were kept," he said. "Grandma told me about it, and I thought I might find something of hers if I looked down here. I found a notebook as a matter of fact." He took the old woman's arm. "Tell me what you meant by 'Dorcas's girls,' Lettice."

"Oh, I'm not sure I should . . ." Her hands climbed around each other. "She always said it would be bad for you to know. . . ."

"She was my family, all I had. I've got a right to know."

"That's true. Yes. And if she guided you here . . ." Lettice sighed as if abandoning responsibility. "Well, she had two baby girls. Before your father Henry was born. Twins, they were. One of them died right away, and the other one . . . I'm not exactly sure how it went, you see. It all happened before I got to know Dorcas. I only know what she told me. I only know that something happened to the other twin. I don't think she died, but Dorcas would hardly ever talk about her."

"And those girls were born with six toes instead of five?"

Lettice nodded. "It's really quite wonderful, isn't it? Dorcas sent you a sign, she guided you here, so I could tell you about the girls, and I—''

''There wasn't any sign.'' Stefan's voice was harsher than he had intended, but the old woman's credulity was beginning to seem like flypaper—sticky and dangerous. ''Dorcas didn't send me. I came on my own.''

''Stefan, we do nothing on our own. The spirits are always with us, watching over—''

''Sssh!'' he said, gripping her arm. He heard voices; people were coming into the basement.

''I'm telling you,'' said one of them, ''my purse is gone, and none of the damn sitters took it, that's for sure. Somebody else had to be there. And there's only one way they could have got in.''

''All right, take it easy. We'll look,'' said a man's voice.

Stefan ran to the file cabinet in which he'd found the locket, scooped up the Polly Trent cards and the cereal spoon from the top where he'd left them and shoved them in his pocket. ''They mustn't find us in here,'' he whispered to Lettice. ''We were only in the storage room, understand?'' He pushed her out into it.

He grabbed the cabinet attendant's handbag, closed the file-room door, and snapped the padlock shut. He threw the bag into a corner of the storage room. ''So long, Lettice,'' he whispered.

But he was too late. The mediums were clustered in the hall outside the storage room. There were half a dozen of them, including two men, and one was holding the ski mask and gloves and shouting, ''Somebody's been down here, somebody who doesn't belong!''

Stefan's mind slammed him back twenty-five years, against another wall in that same basement, facing a group of mediums all dressed in black, like great crows, ready to come at his eyes.

When the present rushed back, they weren't wearing black dresses, but they were coming at him. He was ready to charge into and through them when he heard someone—Lettice—shouting, ''Dorcas Veere sent him! To learn about her twins! It's a sign from Dorcas, Dorcas is with us today in spirit!''

Amazed, Stefan saw the mediums stop. He realized that those fakers of spirit-voices were afraid of the possibility of a spirit-voice that might be genuine. He used the moment to bolt past them.

But they followed soon enough, clattering up the basement stairs, shouting to people in the temple lobby to stop him, panting behind him toward the parking lot, gathering numbers as they came.

Breath rasping, he slammed his car door and turned the ignition. When he was halfway down the long drive, he saw several cars coming after him.

He swerved out onto the main road. The tires protested loudly, and he felt, as before, that in fleeing Red Cloud, he was fleeing for his sanity.

15

Cayla Hayward leaned across her desk and took the list of names from the research director of Biologiconn.

She nodded as she read it. "It looks good, Leslie. If the public can just be made to understand our work, that's got to help counter the negative publicity and the letters. Our people should make as many outside appearances as we can spare them for. Just be sure you send the articulate ones."

Leslie Hatch, one of the microbiologists Cayla had met while they were both students at Westchester University, smiled. The two of them had often discussed the inability of many scientists to talk in terms laypeople could understand.

"What kind of reaction has there been to these appearances so far?" Cayla asked. "Is the public friendly or hostile?"

"Something of both," Leslie said. "I went out twice myself last week, to a college and to a civic symposium. There certainly was genuine interest and approval, but I won't pretend there weren't barbed questions, too, mostly on the issue of anyone's right to manipulate genetics. A few people got up and just quoted scripture at me, but the audiences didn't seem to appreciate that very much."

The two of them were in Cayla's office, which, like the building's lobby, was all chrome, glass and black leather. Behind Cayla, on the wall, was framed the original architect's sketch of the building. She moved a pile of folders on her desk an inch to the right and asked, "What kinds of questions did you get?"

"You know what everybody wants to know? Who the Tay-Sachs parents are. It really seems to get to people that we won't reveal their identities."

"It's getting to the parents, too, Leslie. I spoke with the father yesterday, and he thought the two of them should go public, maybe even ask to be heard at the Senate hearing when it's scheduled. They want to make a personal statement about their willingness to be involved and their belief in the project. Of course the lawyers and their doctors and I all think that would be unwise and unnecessary. They're going through enough private tension, waiting for the birth, without having to become public spokespeople."

"Did you convince them?"

"For now, at least." Cayla folded her hands on the desk. "I'd like to know whether there were questions that you found embarrassing to answer. About . . . my family, for instance."

She saw Leslie hesitate, but the relationship between them was too longstanding to require or tolerate evasion. "Yes, but I can handle them. So can the others. I tell them to say we're there to discuss science and the ethics of science, not to provide grist for the tabloids."

"Thanks." Cayla made herself look at Leslie. "I know you've heard about the story that came out yesterday. I think everybody has. I'd like to tell you, but don't discuss it with anybody else, please—the story is true."

"Oh, my," Leslie said after a moment. "You did tell me your mother was in a hospital, but I had no idea . . ."

"I keep thinking about our Tay-Sachs parents," Cayla said. "No one's ferreted out *their* identity, and God knows people have tried. So how did some reporter learn about . . . Rachel?"

"You don't have any idea how it happened?"

"The head of the hospital is sure no one there gave information to the press. It would have been too stupid. They depend on Hayward money. Maybe some other patient learned who she is and told a visitor." Cayla sighed. "It's not possible to make a situation leak-proof, I guess. But the timing is rotten. I wonder how many more hundreds of hostile letters we'll get because of it."

"I'm so sorry, Cayla. Everybody here in the labs thinks you—"

The desk intercom buzzed. Cayla depressed a switch. "Yes?"

"I have a Dr. Stefan Veere on the line. He says he has some important information and would like to bring it to you around five o'clock. I can't get him to be specific about what kind of information it is." There was a pause. "Cayla?"

"He wants to come here?"

"That's what he said. Do you want to talk to him?"

"No, I don't. No. Tell him I'll see him at five. Briefly."

She became aware that she had been staring into space when Leslie said, "Hey, are you OK?"

"Oh yes. Fine."

"I don't mean just this minute. I mean are you OK for the long haul? You've been looking tired lately."

Lightly Cayla said, "I just haven't been getting enough sleep."

"I wonder why. When's the last time you took time to relax?"

"I played tennis twice last week."

"Oh yes, I keep forgetting your definition of relaxing—exhausting yourself on the courts."

Cayla smiled. Leslie's eyes held hers for a moment. Then Leslie tucked the list of names into the pocket of a lab coat and rose. "I'd better get back to the gene machines. Take care now. We all think you've got more pressure on you than is fair."

Cayla stared after the departing figure. Then she rubbed her burning eyes. She took off her suit jacket, hung it on the back of her chair, pushed up the sleeves of her ivory crepe blouse, and pulled a pile of correspondence toward her.

She answered a dozen letters and then went to have lunch with the chief executive officer of Hayward Industries. He had taken the position after Kelvin's death, and although his name was Jones, he had absorbed the Hayward hatred of publicity. She told him that, like him, she had been asked to testify at the Senate hearing, and, along with Leslie Hatch, she would do so.

He sighed. "Yes, refusing would be even worse than going."

"Don't worry. There won't be any sensationalism. I intend to give them nothing but facts—as cold, hard, and brief as possible."

"But you know what they'll all be doing, don't you, the committee members and the damn TV audience? Half of them won't take in what you say because all they'll see is your looks. And the other half won't take it in because they'll be trying to decide whether you're a witch."

Back in her office, his bluntness still lodged against her temples because he was right but she could do nothing about it, Cayla worked through a provisional operating budget for the next fiscal year and interviewed two candidates for director of marketing.

Then it was five to five, and the image she had forced out of her mind all day, and much longer than that, had to be faced.

She was afraid of Stefan Veere. It was that simple. He made her feel that the life she had built since her divorce—the solid, satisfying life structured around Biologiconn—was somehow threatened. Polly Whiting made her feel that way, too, she realized, and then grimaced at the comparison, for everything about the Whiting woman distressed her, whereas everything about Stefan . . .

She found herself remembering what Leslie Hatch had said to her several years earlier: "I think that if you find a man attractive, you keep him at bay. I think you won't even have dinner with somebody unless you feel there's no chance of anything serious happening."

Perhaps Leslie was right. Perhaps she should just tell Stefan that she was afraid of becoming involved. But with his psychiatric skills, he would have arguments to make her position sound childish.

For a moment she saw, as if from the outside, that the way she felt was in fact childish and foolish—that if she had approached her career in such a manner, Biologiconn wouldn't have come into existence. The perspective was jarring, like seeing oneself as a cubist painting. She put her head in her hands.

The intercom buzzed. Her secretary said, "Dr. Veere is here."

She sat up, smoothed her hair, and put on her suit jacket. "Send him in." Suddenly she felt quite unprepared and tried to imagine what he might say and to plan her response. But the door opened too soon and she had no plan at all. She lifted her chin.

He stood in the doorway for a moment, unsmiling. "Hello."

"Hello." She said it cautiously.

He walked over to the desk and looked down at her. "I don't want to feel awkward, or make you feel that way, so let's not have any talk about apologies. On either side. OK with you?"

She thought that no matter how much time she had had to plan, she never would have imagined those words. "Yes," she said. "It's OK."

He sat in one of the black leather chairs opposite her and looked around the room. His expression was noncommittal, but she knew he was thinking the office was stark and severe, and she was disconcerted, not by what he thought but by the ease with which she knew it.

"I thought you'd be seeing patients at this hour."

He turned to her. "Normally I would, but I managed to reschedule most of my afternoon appointments to later in the week. What I have to tell you is too important." He was dressed more formally than she had seen him before, in a three-piece navy suit, a crisp white shirt, and a tie. "When you hear it, I think you'll agree that we should go talk to your grandmother again." He smiled. "That's why I'm dressed this way—so she'll think I look like a real doctor this time."

When she started to protest, he said, "I've got a lead on Polly Whiting's past. She once had a locket that I think belonged to your grandmother."

Cayla clutched the edge of the desk. "You found a connection?"

"I think so, but Mrs. Randall will have to confirm it." He took something wrapped in tissue paper from his inner jacket pocket and laid it on the desk.

She unfolded the paper and saw a silver locket. The design etched on its front was a lacework of leaves and flowers. She

145

turned it over and saw initials: CHR. She looked up at Stefan and, for the first time since they had met, was oblivious of the power of his presence; he was only someone to share amazement with.

"Look inside," he said.

She did. It took her several moments to identify what the six tiny objects were, and when she did, she allowed herself to feel hope, for the first time since the *Profiles* reporter had asked her about Kella Hagaward. "It's got to be Gran's. Where did you find it?"

As Stefan told her, part of her mind was intent on his story of the spiritualist camp where he had grown up, an exposure of its deceit, and some files locked in a basement room. But at the same time her awareness of the man behind the words was returning. Once the story was finished she said, "When I asked you to investigate for me, I didn't mean to send you back into your own . . . life."

"It's all right. Maybe I laid some ghosts to rest that way."

"I think you took on more than you bargained for."

"Does it matter?" His eyes were holding hers.

Her intercom buzzed. "Cayla, your Aunt Grace is calling. Do you want to talk to her?"

For once she was grateful for an interruption by the clan. It rescued her from Stefan's eyes. She picked up the phone.

Grace's voice came at her brusquely. "I just wanted to tell you, young Cayla, that Frank was all set to call for another clan meeting, but I think I've talked him out of it."

"That's good, Aunt Grace. How did you manage to do it?"

"I have my ways. But you may hear from him anyway. He's all steamed up."

"Because of the publicity about Rachel?"

"That's the cherry on the cake, all right. But there's also Isobel. She went to the Sphinx to try to get some capital. Some crony of hers died and left a lot of antique collections up for sale—dolls and thimbles and God knows what-all nonsense—and Isobel wants to buy them. But she needs two and a half million. She tried to get money from the Sphinx, and of course they said no. They told her they have to be especially cautious until the Senate hearing is over and they can see what effect it will have on the Industries. That got Isobel upset, and she got Frank upset, and then that piece came out, and there you are."

"Aren't you upset, too, Aunt Grace?"

"Sure, but I don't see how another clan meeting could help one damn bit. And you know how I hate going into New York. Especially when my best mare is going to foal any minute. So I just told Frank to leave you alone and not put any more pressure on you. Your head's on straight. You'll do OK."

"Why . . . thanks, Aunt Grace."

"You're the best of the lot, you know. Kelvin always said so. You just hang in there, my dear."

Cayla put down the receiver. She looked at Stefan and heard herself say, "They found out about my mother. I suppose you know."

"Yes. I saw the piece. I'm so sorry."

"From the very beginning, I was afraid the Whiting woman would drag out all my family skeletons. I was right."

Stefan said, "Let's go to Rowan Hall."

It was a half-hour drive. At first Cayla asked for more information about his trip to Camp Red Cloud. When he had told her everything and they had run out of speculations on how Polly Whiting might have come by the locket, the car filled with silence.

It was a carefully neutral silence. Stefan seemed inclined to say nothing at all of a personal nature, and his eyes, which in the office had given the only sign that their relationship was anything more than professional, were fixed on the road, leaving her the impersonality of his profile. Increasingly it seemed to her that she must say something, that in the face of the journeys he had made she must speak of her behavior at their last meeting. But each moment of silence made its successor even harder to break.

He was the one to break them. "The Aunt Grace you spoke with—are you close to her?"

"I'm not close to any of them. But Grace is . . . all right. She isn't really my aunt, though. She's the widow of one of my third cousins." She heard herself adding, "Grace and Kelvin are the ones who took me out of Rowan Hall, away from Gran."

"Ah," he said. "I wondered how that happened. You were rescued, in effect?"

"Yes. They used to come for dinner on the day after Christ-

147

mas, all of them. The table would be set in the main dining room, with a red lace cloth and special china. Gran would even have herself carried down to sit at the head of the table.'' She took a deep breath. The words seemed to know that her guard was down; they came out faster than she could consider or censor them. ''But that year, when I was twelve, I couldn't come to the table. Grace and Kelvin found out why and took me away with them.''

''Why couldn't you come to the table?'' Stefan asked quietly.

''Hester had locked me in my room for three days without any food. When she let me out for the family dinner, I was ill.''

''Why had she locked you in?''

''I wouldn't go with her to the hospital to see Rachel. I hated to go. I didn't like to do anything with Hester, but more and more Gran let her look after me. The worst part wasn't even what Hester did. It was that I didn't understand how Gran could let it happen, how she could . . . lose control of everything. If I wanted or needed something, she would tell Hester to take care of it. Half the time she didn't seem to care whether Hester did or not.'' She stopped. Her hands were clenched too tightly and her fingers hurt.

''What about the other half of the time?'' Stefan asked. ''Did your grandmother seem to care about you then?''

''Yes, that's what was so . . . . Sometimes I felt she would smother me—she'd hug me and kiss me and pull me up into the bed with her so she could tell me stories. . . . Sometimes they were nice ones. Sometimes. And they would watch me, she and Hester would, as if they were watching for something to happen, but I never knew what it was. I just had the feeling I wouldn't like it if it ever did happen.''

''Did you ever figure out what they wanted?''

''Yes, when I was older. It was pretty obvious, if you consider the things they did. Gran made me study singing, for instance, long after it was clear I had no aptitude for it. And she gave me a cat, a big black cat with amber eyes. As it turned out, I was allergic. That upset her, made her almost angry. And Hester—there was no question that she was angry. She took me down into the wine cellar and gave me a beating.'' Cayla relaxed her fingers again. ''As I say, it's all pretty obvious. But even to this day, I can't be sure whether Gran *wanted* me to be

. . . cursed, or whether she was just afraid it would happen. Maybe some of both."

"One of my biggest occupational hazards," Stefan said, "is that I'm always surprised by the phenomenon of mental health. I've never been more surprised than I am right now. How did you manage to survive and become what you are?"

It was a question she hadn't considered in those terms, but the answer came readily. "Gran had tutors and governesses for me, at least most of the time, and I always liked my lessons. Especially arithmetic. I remember feeling . . . I was going to say 'safe,' which seems odd, but it's true. That is what I felt. It was comforting and . . . safe to go into the schoolroom and learn about numbers. They were intriguing because you could make them do so many things, but no matter how you added or multiplied or divided them, they were still what they were. Solid. One of the tutors used to say, 'You can scream or pray or stomp up and down, but the numbers don't care.' I never forgot that. I—"

She looked up and saw Rowan Hall in the distance. They were approaching the entrance. "We're here," she said flatly.

"Afraid so." Stefan pulled the car to a stop.

She got out and spoke to John on the gatepost phone. As the huge gates swung open and the car passed through, she said, "This is the first time I've—I never talk about any of it."

"I know. You told me last time that you don't like talking about yourself."

As the bulk of Rowan Hall bore down on them, its gray stone tinged red and purple by the twilight, she felt she had revealed a great deal more to him than some stories from her childhood. When he stopped the car she said, without looking at him, "I suppose you know, Stefan. I'm afraid of you."

"No," he said. "I don't think that's what it is." She turned to him. His eyes and nose were in shadow, but the light lay full on his mouth. "I think you're afraid of something in yourself. I can understand why, and I can even live with it. For a while." He leaned forward and slid one hand inside the collars of her suit jacket and blouse, so his fingers circled her neck. His thumb slid along her lower lip. "But just for a while. I want you too much."

She put her hand on the wrist that was so close to her face and held it tightly.

Finally he said, "We'd better go show Mrs. Randall a locket."

A few minutes later Cayla knocked on the door of Gran's suite of rooms. After a delay it opened and Hester's sharp features appeared in the crack. "John sent up word you were here," she said. "What do you want?"

"I want to talk to my grandmother, Hester, so open the door."

The crack widened. "That man is with you again. You've come to upset the Lady, haven't you?"

"Open the door and let us in, Hester. I'm not going to argue with you." Cayla watched the old woman back away resentfully from the steel in her voice, and the door swung wide.

No lights had been turned on, and the twilight coming through the leaded windows cast a blue pallor on all the reds in the room, including old Cayla's dressing gown. As usual, she lay on her chaise by the window. Cayla looked at the woman in whom cruelty and kindness were blended in so strange a way. She went to her and touched one of her hands. "Hello, Gran."

The old woman turned to her and sighed. "Yes, they said you were coming." Her eyes seemed to look from beneath a veil of water.

"Dr. Veere and I have to ask you some more questions, Gran. I'm sorry, but it's necessary. We'll be as quick as we can and we'll try not to tire you."

Hester shuffled up in her odd rigid way. She was wearing one of her eternal long black dresses. "Why can't you leave her alone?"

"Please don't interrupt us," Cayla said evenly.

Hester made a clicking sound of disapproval, but she moved to one side and folded her hands.

Stefan said, "Hello again, Mrs. Randall." When she peered at him uncertainly, he added, "I'm the doctor who came with your granddaughter a little over a week ago. We spoke about Sigmund Freud."

"Ah, yes. Dr. Freud. I was talking about him recently. To you, was it? Yes. You look better this time. Properly dressed."

Stefan smiled. Cayla was watching him, and suddenly, seeing the slant of his mouth, she knew she would sleep with him that night and would be angry with herself afterward. The knowledge seemed to come from nowhere, and to be as impersonal as a fact out of the labs. She looked around at the red, hated room and felt that in some way it was responsible for her reaction. But for which part, the desire to sleep with him or the anger that would follow?

She saw that Stefan had picked up one of the brocade chairs. He put it beside the chaise and sat down. "Mrs. Randall, I'd like to ask you about something that I think belongs to you but that you haven't seen for many years." He reached into his jacket pocket, unwrapped the tissue paper, picked up the locket by its chain and held it so that old Cayla's gaze fell on it directly. "Do you recognize this?"

There was an intake of breath, but Cayla realized it had come from Hester.

"Maybe a little light would help," Stefan said. "Cayla?"

There was a Tiffany lamp of blue and red glass on an end table. She pulled the chain, and the locket seemed to brighten.

"I think you recognize it now," Stefan said. "You see the initials on the back?"

"Oh . . ." the old woman whispered.

Stefan was still holding it by the chain. It swayed gently, and the watery old eyes rolled with it from side to side.

Left to right. Right to left. Left to right.

As Cayla grasped what was happening and wondered whether Stefan was doing it deliberately, he turned to her, and she could see he hadn't planned it. He was as surprised as she. But he wanted to take advantage of it. His eyes asked for her approval.

She nodded.

He turned back to old Cayla, his voice soft and steady. "That's right, Mrs. Randall, watch the locket. Watch it swing. The motion is starting to make you feel sleepy. . . ."

Hester began to move in, but Cayla held out an arm to stop her.

"Sleepy," Stefan said. "Very, very sleepy . . ."

16

The old woman's eyelids closed by fractions of an inch, leaving her face nothing but bones and webs.

When Stefan got to the count of five, her head fell to one side. He laid the locket beside her on the chaise.

"Now please go back with me," he said, "back through the years to the time when you got this beautiful locket. Let the scene come into your mind. When it does you'll remember it perfectly. It'll be very clear, and you'll be able to answer all my questions about it. Just let your mind go back, back to the time when you got the locket. Now. Now you see it clearly. Tell me where you are."

There was a pause, but at length the old woman's voice, quite soft, said, "In the nursery at Rowan Hall."

"Are you alone?"

"No, no. Gary is with me." A faint smile crossed her face. "And Rachel. Rachel is in her crib."

"Her crib? How old is she then?"

"Only two months old. Yes. Two."

"Can you tell me what year it is?"

"Ummmm . . . 1930."

Stefan frowned. "Are you wearing the locket?"

"Yes. After Gary gives it to me. Puts it on me."

"It's a gift?"

"For my birthday."

"Is there anything inside the locket when he gives it to you?"

"No. But we get a scissors and take a snip of Rachel's hair and put that inside."

"I see. Fine. Do you show the locket to other people?"

"Yes, I do. To Hester, of course, and to Father at dinner that night."

"How about the people who work at Rowan Hall, the servants—do they see it?"

"Oh . . . I don't know. Maybe."

"Who are the servants? What are their names?"

Another pause. "There's John and Emma, of course. And Kate, who helps Emma in the kitchen, and her husband Peter."

"What's the second couple's last name?"

"Oh, I'm not sure. Something Swedish? Larson? Johnson?"

"All right. Who else is there?"

"The maids—Betty Lewis and Fiona Hamilton and Cora. Cora something, I don't know. And Ralph, who looks after the cars. He's Betty's husband."

"Anybody else?"

"Oh, yes—the gardeners. Lem and Joshua. They're brothers. Lem and Joshua Hunter. They have two helpers, but I don't know their names. That's all, I think."

"Very good. That's excellent. Now, will you think about the locket again, please? Think about the next time you do something with it, or pay special attention to it. Just let your mind slip ahead to a scene like that, and tell me about it when I ask you. Just let the scene come into your mind. OK. OK—now. Tell me what scene is in your mind. What do you see?"

Another smile, less faint. "Rachel and Hester and I."

"Where are you?"

"In my dressing room."

"What are you doing?"

"Hester is holding her. I have the scissors, a little silver scissors, and I'm trimming the nails on her toes. Such pretty little toes, like shells."

"How many toes are there?"

"Five on the right foot. But on the left . . . six."

"What does it all have to do with the locket?"

"Hester says why not put the nail trimmings in it, six of them, one for each toe."

"Why does she suggest that? Do you know?"

"She says anybody can have a baby's curl in a locket, but Rachel is special, and her toes are the sign. So the locket should hold evidence of that."

"Do you agree?"

"Yes. So we take out the lock of hair." The old woman sighed.

"Very good, Mrs. Randall. Excellent. Now let your mind move ahead to the next time something special happens with the locket. Just relax and let your mind move ahead. . . . Now. Now you're there. The scene is in your mind. What do you see?"

Agitation stirred the webbed old face. "It's gone. The locket is gone. I went to a party last night and wore my rubies, so I left the locket in my dressing-table drawer. But now it's not there."

"What do you do?"

"We turn out everything and hunt, Hester and I and Betty, the maid, but it's not anywhere. Someone must have taken it."

"Do you question everyone?"

"Gary does. But they all deny it."

"Do you know what year it is?"

A pause. "Nineteen thirty-two. Yes, because Rachel is two."

"Are there any new servants? People who weren't there in 1930 when you first got the locket?"

"Oh . . . I don't know. . . ."

"John and Emma and the Larsons or Johnsons, are all of them there?" She nodded. "Betty Lewis is there, you said, but how about the other two maids, Fiona Hamilton and Cora somebody? Are they there?" Another nod. "And the Hunter brothers and their two helpers? And Betty's husband, who looks after the cars?"

"Yes, Ralph. He's there. They all are there."

"Is anybody new there?"

"I don't think so. No. Nobody new."

"OK. Fine. Now you can look ahead a bit and tell me whether any of those servants leave within the next year or so?"

A longer pause. "One of the maids leaves. Cora? Yes. Cora. Her mother has passed over, and she had to go help her father."

"Do you know where she's going?"

"Somewhere south. That's all I know."

"And when does she leave? What year?"

The old woman sighed. "Shortly before Gary passes over. In 1933."

"Does anyone else leave?"

"Yes, Ralph does. He starts drinking a lot, so Father has to let him go. But Betty stays on. She's going to divorce him."

"All right, Mrs. Randall. That's wonderful. Now, just rest and relax and let your mind wander over the years 1930 to 1933, let's say. Let it wander freely, and tell me whether there's anyone in those years named Trent, whether you know anyone by that name. Just relax and let it come. . . . Is there anyone named Trent?"

"Oh, yes. Morris Trent."

"And who was he?"

"The concertmaster of the Philharmonic." She smiled. "He often played at my musicales."

"In those years? From 1930 to 1933?"

The smile faded. "No, before that. Before I gave them up."

"I see. And why did you give them up?"

"For . . . for Rachel." Pain crossed her face.

"What do you mean? How did Rachel make you give them up?"

"No more music . . . because of the pool . . ."

Stefan frowned, then glanced again at Cayla, who was leaning forward in her chair, hands clasped. She lifted her shoulders and eyebrows, puzzled. Then she nodded, as if to assure him that whatever he was considering had her approval.

He turned to the old woman. "Mrs. Randall, we've been talking about the time when Rachel was born and the years right after that, 1930 and so on. But now I'd like you to go back a little further in your mind, back to 1927. To the time when you came home from seeing Dr. Freud in Vienna. Relax and let your mind take you back there, to the time after you returned from Vienna. Dr. Freud has enabled you to walk again, and you're home with your husband and father. The scene is going to come into your mind very, very clearly. Now it's there. What do you see?"

Her face seemed to shiver. "The fire," she said after a moment. "I'm watching the fire."

"Where are you?"

"In my room. Looking into the fire and feeling . . . Oh, she's with me all the time. All around me."

"Who is?"

"Rachel. All around me. I want to talk to her so badly. If only I could talk to her . . ."

"Why can't you?"

"Because she . . . passed over."

Stefan hesitated. "How did that happen?"

"Drowned. In the pool. Oh, oh, oh, my . . ." The bony hands began to move, picking at the red dressing gown.

"It's all right, Mrs. Randall. Just relax now, and be comfortable. Yes, that's right. Rest and relax." The hands settled back. Stefan shot another glance at Cayla, then said, "Did you manage to talk to Rachel, Mrs. Randall? You said you wanted to talk to her so badly—did you find a way to do it?"

There was a long pause. "Yes."

"Tell me how it happened. Just let your mind visualize the place where you talked to her, and then tell me what you see."

After a moment the old woman said, "Brooklyn."

"You went to Brooklyn?"

"Yes. As a last resort."

"You had tried other places first?"

"Yes."

"Where?"

"Oh . . . Boston. New York. Many places in New York. But none of them . . ." She didn't go on.

Stefan asked, "What were you looking for?"

"I wanted Rachel to . . . sound like Rachel."

Stefan leaned forward. "Do you mean you wanted someone who could bring her from the spirit world?"

"Yes."

"A psychic?"

"Yes."

Stefan ran his hands through his hair and took a deep breath. "How did you become involved with psychics?"

A pause. "Hester told me people went to them sometimes. But I didn't think I . . . Then there was a dinner. Some of Gary's friends. One of the wives was going to a psychic."

"And she told you about it?"

"Yes. She said everybody was going. She said even famous people were interested in spiritism—Thomas Mann, Carl Jung, Conon Doyle, and . . . She was right. Once I knew about spiritism, I heard about it everywhere."

"So you went to consult a number of psychics?"

"Yes."

"Did your father and your husband know what you were doing?"

"Oh, no. No. They would never . . . Their minds were closed."

"Were the psychics able to bring Rachel's spirit to you?"

"Yes. But it wasn't right."

"Why not?"

"Not like her. Too . . . I don't know. Too grown up sometimes. Not Rachel."

"And then you found somebody in Brooklyn who made her sound . . . who brought her to you as you remembered her?"

"Yes. A wonderful woman."

"Tell me about her. Let your mind take you to that place in Brooklyn. See the scene. Tell me what it's like to be with her."

"We sit in her living room." The old woman smiled. "On a red couch. She puts her hand on my arm, and I feel so . . . She understands. Then we go into the other room, and in the darkness she comes, Rachel comes . . . her little laugh just the way it always was, and she calls me 'Mumma'. . . . And sometimes I can see her, so pale and pretty and smiling. . . ."

"Do you go often?"

"I want to go every day, but . . . Only three times a week because it tires the medium so much. She's a wonderful woman. And when she tells me—Oh, such wonderful news!" Pleasure, almost exaltation, was gripping the old face.

"What did she tell you?" Stefan asked. There was no answer. "What does she tell you that makes you so happy?"

"She's pregnant!"

"Why is that so wonderful?"

"She's carrying my Rachel. She says the spirits are letting Rachel come back because I need her so badly, and when she's born, I'll have her. We arrange everything. She promises me the child will be mine!"

For a long moment Stefan didn't move. Cayla was staring at him, but he seemed unaware of her, and of everything else. Finally, his voice as careful as a tightrope, he asked the old woman, "What was her name?"

"Why, I called her Rachel, of course. Because she was Rachel born again."

"Yes, I understand that. But what was the name of the medium, the child's mother?"

"Dorcas Veere."

Stefan sighed.

Cayla's eyes were too large for her face. As if he could see without turning to her, Stefan held up a hand, warning her not to speak. "So Dorcas Veere had a child who was the reincarnation of your Rachel. Did she just . . . give the child to you?"

"Yes. She was a wonderful woman."

"You didn't have to pay her something?"

"She wouldn't let me. But I donated some money to her building fund. She was trying to build a church, so I gave her money for that. I was happy to do it."

"How much did you give her?"

"Ten thousand dollars, it was. I told Gary I was giving it to one of my charities."

Stefan's hands lifted and curled into fists, but he took a breath and brought them down slowly to rest on his knees. "Mrs. Randall, I want you to think about the time when Rachel was born, when you got her. Relax and let the scene come into your mind. Just let it come. That's right. Now tell me what you see."

A pause. "The hotel suite. All blue silk and white velvet."

"A hotel? Where?"

"Paris."

Stefan frowned and thought for a moment. "Are you alone?"

"No. Hester is with me."

"Where is your husband?"

"At home."

"Why isn't he there?"

"I don't want him. He can't be there."

"Why not?"

"He has to think I'm expecting. That's the plan."

"I see. Who worked out the plan, you or Dorcas Veere?"

"We did it together."

"Tell me about the plan, will you?"

"Oh . . . I told Gary and Father I was expecting, and I insisted on spending the term in Europe. They were against that, of course, but they were too busy to fight me, because of the mess on Wall Street."

"I see. This was in 1929, then, in October or November?"

"Yes. November."

"So you and Hester went alone. What did you do?"

"Visited relatives for a while. Scotland and England."

"Why?"

"To show them I was expecting. So they could write Gary and Father and tell how I looked."

"How could you show them you were expecting, if you weren't?"

She sighed. "I wore pillows. Little red pillows. Hester made them, in sizes that got bigger."

"OK. Fine. So you visited relatives, and then you went to a hotel in Paris. Why did you do that?"

"I waited there, to hear from Dorcas."

"And finally you did hear?"

"Yes. A telegram. Just one word, our signal. *Rediviva*. As soon as I got it, I wired Gary that he was a father again and said we'd come home in a few weeks."

"And then?"

"I sailed to New York. . . ." She shook her head from side to side. "Terrible trip. I was sick."

"So you went to Dorcas Veere and collected your— You got Rachel?"

"Yes. Yes. Two weeks old, the darling child . . ."

"Did you take her back to Paris?"

"No. We stayed at a little hotel in Brooklyn until the next ship arrived from Paris." She gave a smile so happy and young that it contrasted cruelly with the face it transformed. "I have my Rachel again! I wrap her in blankets as pink and soft as the dawn. . . . She's so much like Rachel. She *is* Rachel, yes, she is, perfect in every way, and I keep touching her, her perfect little nose, as small as a collar button, and her fingers, so tiny . . . and when I take off the booties, her toes are like shells. . . ." The smile dissolved. "But on the left foot . . . six of them!"

Stefan sat back slowly in the brocade chair, his eyes darkening. He looked at Cayla, whose hands had lifted to her face and were clinging there.

"So," he said, his eyes still on Cayla, "there were two Rachels. And the child with the six toenails you clipped for the locket was the child who came from Dorcas Veere."

The old woman said, "She's not perfect, like Rachel was.

159

Her toes . . . She can't be Rachel, then. . . . But she has to be. I'll make her be. . . .'' Her hands were in motion again, clutching the lace of her dressing gown. "Oh, oh, oh," she said, almost whimpering.

Hester, who had not moved during the whole proceeding, took a step forward. Stefan held out a hand to stop her.

"It's all right, Mrs. Randall," he said. "Just relax and be comfortable. Let yourself relax now. You're going to come back to this time and place. I'm going to count to five. You'll wake up when you hear 'Five,' and you'll be fine. You'll wake up gradually, feeling more and more peaceful and comfortable with each number you hear, and when I get to five, you'll be back in this time and place. You'll feel very comfortable, and you'll remember everything you've said." When he reached five, he added, "Open your eyes slowly now, so they can adjust to the light. Slowly. That's right."

The dark eyes opened and blinked half a dozen times. Into them came the slow realization of what had been confessed. "Oh . . ." the old woman said.

"It's all right, Mrs. Randall," Stefan said. "Everything is quite all right. Don't worry."

The eyes settled on Stefan, searching his face. "What's your name again?" she said.

He answered quietly. "Dr. Stefan Veere."

"Veere?" she whispered. "Do you . . . ? No, no. It couldn't be."

Stefan was silent.

The old woman turned her head to the windows, which had grown dark. The moon hung in one of them, a ball as white as her hair.

Cayla got slowly to her feet. She glanced at Hester, and her nostrils flared. She walked to the chaise. Arms locked across her breasts, her fingers digging into the brown cloth of her jacket, she said, "Gran, look at me." When the old woman finally did, she said, "Why didn't you ever tell us that Mother was . . . I suppose the word is *adopted?*"

"Bought," Stefan murmured, so low that no one heard it.

"They wouldn't have let me take her. Father and Gary never would have allowed it."

"But they've been dead for decades! You could have told— Gran, you certainly could have told me."

"Why should I have?"

Cayla's crossed arms lifted with her deep breath. "If I wasn't a Hayward by blood, don't you think I'd have liked to know it?"

"What difference would it have made?"

"You can't seriously be asking me that question. After all the times you've told me about the Hayward family curse? And how I was going to be—" She stopped. In a soft voice she added, "You can't seriously be asking me what difference it would have made."

"None. None," said old Cayla fretfully. "Because I passed the curse on to Rachel, and she'll pass it on to you, you'll see, and—"

"Gran! What's the matter with you? If mother was adopted, how could she be a victim of the curse? Of course she couldn't be, in any case, but— How could a Hayward curse be passed on to someone with no Hayward blood?"

The old woman lifted herself on one elbow. "That's the very proof of its power. If someone who's taken *into* the family can be cursed, then it's the Hayward name and influence that are the curse, and it's stronger than blood."

Circles of color as bright as Cayla's mouth leaped onto her cheeks, and her voice rose high and red, too. "Can't you hear yourself, Gran? Can't you hear that what you're saying makes no sense? I know you've spent your whole life with crazy ideas, but this is— Can't you hear how irrational you're being?"

Still propped on an elbow, her head lifted by straining neck muscles, the old woman said, "And can't you *see?* Don't you look like a Hayward? Don't you have Satan's mark on you? Can't you see that's the proof of the curse, that it brings you under its power, just the way it brought Rachel?"

The only motion in the room was the draining of color from Cayla's face. The two women stared at one another as if separated by a chasm that each would find dangerous to cross.

Finally old Cayla fell back against the chaise. "I've destroyed my Rachel twice, don't you see? First I let her drown. Then I lured her back in another body, so she could be cursed. . . ." She began to sob—dry sounds, like paper tearing.

Hester was beside her in a moment, taking her in her arms and hissing, "Leave us alone!"

17

The butler placed a silver tray with coffee, sandwiches, and creamy linen napkins on a small inlaid table. "Will you be wanting anything else, Miss Cayla?"

Her eyes were so far away it took half a minute for his identity to register. "No, thank you, John."

He had almost reached the door when Stefan said, "Just a minute. I'd like to ask you some questions, if you don't mind."

The man turned around—slowly, for he was in his eighties and hadn't done anything quickly for a decade. "Do you want me to speak with this gentleman, Miss Cayla?"

"Yes, John. Please sit down."

He took a chair near the door. They were in the library, a large, handsomely proportioned room on the main floor. Three walls were occupied by enclosed bookcases of leaded glass and the fourth by heavy oak paneling and a large marble fireplace where a fire had been laid. Once the ceiling had been painted in gold leaf, which had hung in tatters for years.

Stefan poured coffee into one of the Meissen china cups. He had taken off his tie and opened his collar, offsetting the formality of his dark suit and vest. He walked to the butler, "John, Mrs. Randall was telling us tonight about a silver locket she had in the 1930s, which was lost or stolen. If you remember anything about it, Ms. Hayward and I would like you to tell us what you know."

The butler worked his hands, as if stirring his memory. "Yes, I recall that a locket was missing one day. Mr. Gary called everyone together and spoke to us about it. He said he would ask no questions if the person who had taken it would just put it back by morning. But no one did." He thought for a moment, studying his hands. "I'm afraid that's all I recall."

"We'd like to check the names of the servants who were

here at the time. For instance, there was a couple helping you and your wife—Kate and Peter. Do you happen to remember their last name?''

"Peter?" the butler said. "Red hair, Peter had. He was a bit lazy, I'm afraid. Wanted to read the racing form instead of keeping up the silver. He didn't last more than several years."

"Yes, but his name? Was it something Scandinavian?"

"I don't know about that, now. Seems to me it was more Irish."

"OK. How about the two undergardeners? Do you remember their names?"

The man frowned, kneading his thighs. "One of them was Freddy, I think. But the other . . . he's just slipped from my mind. It's hard, the way so many things just slip from your mind."

"Don't worry about it, please. Would you remember what happened to Ralph Lewis, who looked after the cars?"

"Yes, him I know about. He wound up in jail, in Pittsburgh. Or maybe it was Philadelphia. He wrote to me when he got out, asking for the loan of some money, but when I learned why he'd been arrested—for stealing—I didn't care to help him. Not at all."

"Do you know what he had stolen?"

"Some jewelry, I think. Imagine! Him, who had worked in a fine house like Rowan Hall."

"While he was still here could he have stolen Mrs. Randall's silver locket?"

Surprise made a crack in the man's impassive face. "I never once thought of that. But it's true—he could have."

"Do you have any idea where Ralph Lewis is now? Or his wife, Betty?"

"No, none at all. I never heard from him again, and Betty— was that her name?—she left during the war to work in a factory and didn't come back."

"OK, John. I guess that's it, then. Thanks very much. If you remember anything at all about the locket, please come back and tell us. Of if something comes to you after we've gone, please get in touch with Ms. Hayward and let her know."

The old man nodded and rose slowly. On his way out he stopped at a table to straighten an ormolu clock that wasn't askew.

Stefan finished his coffee and walked back to the table for a refill and a sandwich. "You're not eating?" he asked Cayla.

"No." She was sitting very straight in a rose damask chair. The firelight moved erratically over her face, giving it a play of expression where there was actually none.

"OK, then," Stefan said. "John gave us a lead. Ralph Lewis, the chauffeur or whatever, is a known thief, who winds up somewhere in Pennsylvania. Polly Whiting grew up in Pennsylvania. That's promising, I'd say. I don't know exactly what to do with it, but I suppose your detectives will be able to— Oh, damn. I forgot to ask John about that maid Cora. Well, I'll do it before I leave." He tasted the sandwich. "It's good. Please eat something, Cayla."

"I just can't. Not for a while."

Lightly he said, "Every time we come here, I seem to wind up urging you to eat."

"Every time we come, I learn things that ruin my appetite." She looked at him, tried to smile and gave up. "I still can't take it all in. That Mother wasn't really a Hayward."

Stefan said, with a curious emphasis, "I know you haven't taken it all in."

She seemed not to hear him. "All those years when I would feel I never wanted to see Gran again, two things would keep me coming back here. One was that there had been some good times, at least in the beginning, when I loved her and wanted to grow up and take care of her because she was sick. And then she was a Hayward—we were the same blood. But we're not. So why should I have any more to do with her? Why should I care whether the Kella Hagaward letter is made public and the press finds out that she believes in it and thinks she's a—" Cayla shifted in her chair and looked at the fire. "What do I owe her, now? *Nothing.*" Her teeth clenched around the word.

"What did you think you owed her before?" Stefan asked mildly.

"I don't know. Loyalty, I guess. And a kind of neutrality—a holding back of my anger, because she's pathetic, when you consider what her life has been. . . . And pity. Yes, pity."

"Does what you learned tonight really change those things?"

"Yes. It makes me twice as angry at her." She sighed. "And it makes her twice as pathetic." She turned to Stefan.

"Why didn't you tell her that Dorcas Veere was your grand-mother?"

"I thought it would be a great shock to her, which I didn't want to risk."

"Yes. I see. But hasn't she had quite a shock anyway?"

Stefan sat across the fire from her. "Believe me, Cayla, if she hadn't wanted to tell those things, she wouldn't have told them under hypnosis. It's my guess she's been wanting to clear her conscience for years, maybe decades, and didn't know how to do it. Until I gave her the opportunity." He took another bite of his sandwich. "Actually that's not true. I didn't *give* her the opportunity—she created it. I had no intention of hypnotizing her when I went in there. But the way she reacted when the locket started swinging, it was almost as if she was begging me to put her under. I wonder whether Freud used to hypnotize her—she didn't respond like someone experiencing it for the first time."

There was a silence. Cayla studied his face. "You're not as shocked by all this as I am."

"No. At least not in one way."

"Why is that?"

"Because I know something I didn't tell you." Stefan put down the crust of his sandwich and used one of the soft, thick napkins. "When I found the locket, an old medium was there." He told the story he had heard from Lettice Barrow. "The more I thought about it, it just seemed too damn coinci-dental that your mother should have six toes on her left foot and my grandmother should have had twin girls with the same de-formity. I thought there had to be a link, but I didn't say any-thing because if I was wrong . . . I just concentrated on the Polly Whiting connection."

"That's still the thing to do, of course. I mustn't be dis-tracted by how I . . . by what I've learned about Gran and Mother."

He studied her over the rim of his cup. "In one way, though, I'm more shocked than you are."

"What do you mean?"

"I think I see more of the ramifications than you do."

Her eyebrows lifted quizzically, then sank under the impact of a new thought. "What on earth made you ask Gran whether she had gone to consult a psychic? To me that came out of the blue.''

"When she referred to the deaths of her husband and her baby, she said they had 'passed over.' That's the way spiritualists always speak of the dead. They're not the only ones who do, of course, but still, it gave me the idea.''

Cayla sighed and turned away. In the silver coffeepot on the table beside her, her face looked back at her strangely, the mouth and nose pulled into alien roundness by the curved bowl of the pot. "I want it to be a lie," she said. "Just one of Gran's stories.''

"She didn't invent the name Dorcas Veere or the fact that Dorcas was a psychic.''

"Who really did live in Brooklyn?''

"I don't know about that part. But Camp Red Cloud wasn't built until the mid-thirties, so obviously she lived somewhere else before she went there. I wonder . . .'' Stefan stopped. But then his eyes cleared and he went on. "Apart from the fact that Mrs. Randall was genuinely under hypnosis, she had too many details right. Like the fact that spiritism was in vogue at the time, like the business of the church building fund—''

"What about it?'' Cayla turned back to him.

"It's so typical of mediums to have one. It's a great way to get people to give money, and keep on giving it.'' He smiled wryly. "Sometimes they even get around to spending some of the fund on a church.'' His face changed, and he brought his fist down on the arm of his chair so hard that the old damask coughed out a little cloud of dust. "Damn her! I knew she was a fraud, at least some of the time, but to sell her own child! I just didn't think she was capable of something that ugly.'' Anger not only erased the customary civility from his face but made his features look different, almost harsh.

"Stefan, don't!''

He came out of himself. "Don't what?''

"Look like that.''

After a moment he said gently, "I wish you wouldn't be so afraid of strong emotions. Neither someone else's, nor your own.''

Into her eyes, drawn by his, came the memory of the night they would have slept together if she hadn't stopped them. But then he looked away and said abruptly, "So, was it the deformity of the left foot that made Dorcas Veere want to get rid of her twins? No, that couldn't be the reason, because she concocted the scheme to give her baby to your grandmother early in her pregnancy, long before she could have known about the deformity. Even before she knew she was carrying twins. When they were born, she must have realized she could give only one of them—sorry, make that 'sell' only one—to Mrs. Randall. And then, according to old Lettice Barrow, the other twin died shortly. Maybe Dorcas started to feel guilty about what she had done. Maybe that's why she always seemed so agitated when she talked about the child with six toes. If only I could remember more of what she used to say. . . . It was in her trances, and she said so many crazy things in those trances that I didn't always pay much attention. . . .'' He stopped, his eyes far away.

Then he said firmly, "Yes. I'll try it. Why not?" He looked at Cayla. "I'm going to see whether I can recall more of what she said about that child. I'm going to hypnotize myself."

"Can you do that?"

"Sure. I do it sometimes when I can't relax or have a headache. Of course what I want to do now is a little more complicated. Just give me a minute." He sat in thought, hands cupped over his knees. Then he got up and moved to a softer chair, one with wide arms and a deep seat, which he turned toward the fire. He took off his jacket, unbuttoned his vest, and sat down.

"What shall I . . . ? Is there anything I should do?" Cayla said.

"Just stay where you are, sitting off to one side of me, and listen like hell. I'll do it out loud, so you know what's going on."

He closed his eyes.

Cayla watched his body settle into the deep chair. Then his head fell against the back, his hands curled over the edges of the overstuffed arms, and his legs stretched in front of him.

She had the sudden desire to go over to the chair and let her body sink slowly down on his and stay there until neither of them could bear to be motionless any longer.

The reaction was so out of context that it appalled her, yet she couldn't dispel it. Throughout the evening's revelations, even the most astonishing of them, the awareness of Stefan's physical presence had flickered at the edges of her mind, rising each time she stamped it out, making her feel vulnerable.

His chest rose and fell with several deep breaths. Then he began to speak.

"I'm going to relax even more. All the muscles are going to relax deeply, especially around my eyes, and all the muscles of my face . . ." As he kept repeating the idea, Cayla watched it take place. The tiny lines that often clustered in the corners of his eyes seemed to let go and disappear, and his mouth grew slack, so that his words came out more slowly. "Now relax the whole body," he said. "All of it. Gradually every part will relax. My neck and my shoulders and my arms . . . and the relaxation will move down through my torso, through my thighs, all along my legs . . ."

Cayla's eyes followed his words, moving down, until she forced them to rise and concentrate on his hands. The fire glowed in the topaz ring on his right hand and lit the pale hairs along his fingers.

He repeated his litany until he seemed satisfied with its result. Then he said, "Now concentrate on the sensation in the right hand. There's going to be a sense of lightness there, of great lightness, and it's going to spread to the arm, all up the arm. . . . The lightness will become even stronger, until it's so extreme that my hand will rise . . . slowly . . . then my forearm . . . then my upper arm . . . until my finger touches my nose. . . ."

As Cayla watched his body obeying his voice—no, she thought, it was obeying his mind—her own thoughts obeyed too and lost their awareness of everything except his words.

"By the time my finger touches my nose, I'll be deeply relaxed . . . in such a state of mental clarity that I'll vividly remember being about ten years old, in the kitchen of the Red Cloud house, watching Dorcas in a trance and listening to everything she says . . . and I can then lower my arm. . . ."

His arm sank slowly back down to the chair and settled. His fingers looked waxlike in their stillness.

His face stirred, and then an expression crossed it that made Cayla's eyes widen because it seemed to reflect what she had felt so often as a child: a mixture of caution and dread.

"Jasmine," he said softly. "The kitchen . . . warm and

dark. Always a little dark. Even in the morning. A round table. And coffee . . . she always has coffee on the stove. . . ."

"Oh, no," he said. "She's doing it again. I only went away for a little while . . . down to the cellar, that's right, for the hamsters. And when I came up, she was in the chair, yes, one of the wooden chairs . . . and something was burning on the stove. Her hands are on the table, flat on the oilcloth, and her eyes . . ." He shook his head in agitation, and when he spoke again, his words came more slowly than ever. "Her eyes are not . . . here. They're looking someplace I can never see. I don't touch her. It never does any good. I just take the burning pot off the stove . . . the old range with the yellow tea-kettle. . . . I'd like to go back to the cellar, but I can't stop looking at her. Wondering why she does it and where she goes. And what she means . . ."

He frowned and seemed to be listening intently. " *'Nolu vidama,'* she says. Over and over. *'Nolu vidama.'* Or something like that. And *'Cresta li grondell.'* . . . She says she's leaving her body in the chair, in the kitchen, while she goes into the woods. . . . I don't understand the words, not any of them, but she takes a lot of deep breaths. . . . Her pearls move up and down on her black dress, and she moans. . . ." His face twisted again. "She says she's . . . on the ceiling? Yes, on the ceiling, looking down at herself. She says her body is covered with ashes and blood. She keeps talking about her pennants. . . . No! I thought that was the word, but it didn't make sense because I was thinking of football pennants. Now I see. It must be atonement she means, that kind of penance. . . . She keeps saying the spirits want her to do penance . . . and she says something about six toes. . . . Yes, she talks about them and cries. 'Oh, the six little toes, the babies' toes,' that's what she says."

There was a silence. Cayla didn't know whether he had finished or not. His face was still and his breathing regular. Then he frowned again, as if straining to hear. "She swears at herself. Calls herself 'stupid.' She says she never would have gotten in trouble . . . some kind of trouble . . . on her own, but the spirits made it happen . . . She's angry at the spirits, I think, but then she says she loves them, too, and belongs to them. It's confusing. . . . She says she's been doing penance for years, for her . . . lost one? Yes, lost one. She says she gave away the money, and the spirits must have forgiven her because finally they sent her a grandson. . . . And she's taking care of him . . . because she loves him. . . .''

He stopped. Apart from the whisperings in the grate, silence was thick in the room. Cayla wanted badly to reach over and touch him. She felt no sensuality, only the desire to let him know she understood the boy he had been and what that boy had felt. Just as he understood her.

Always, with people outside her clan, she talked as if her life began after age twelve, after leaving Rowan Hall, because the differences between her childhood and others' was a distance she couldn't cross. She looked at the first man—the first person—to learn about those years, and knew he understood what they meant to her. The sense that such a private and crucial part of her life could be shared and comprehended was so new and strange that it almost made her light-headed.

She realized that Stefan was speaking again, quietly. ''The right arm, focus on the right arm. It's going to feel normal in weight again, not light any longer. I'll count to three, and on three I'll open my eyes. I'll be fully conscious, and I'll remember everything.''

When his eyes opened, he blinked several times and then stared straight ahead. ''Jasmine,'' he said in his normal voice. ''Are you wearing a jasmine scent?''

''No.''

''Of course not. It's a trick my mind plays on me, that's all it is. My mind and my olfactory nerves.''

''I don't understand,'' Cayla said carefully.

Slowly he sat up, rubbed his eyes and ran his hands through his hair, which looked more red than brown in the firelight. ''At least we know now that Mrs. Randall was telling the truth.''

''Yes.''

''I guess my grandmother did feel guilty about selling one of her twins. Somehow that seems to matter to me.''

''Of course it does.''

''Funny, the way I've carried her voice in my subconscious all these years and have never really known what she was saying. But I never forgot her face when she talked about the babies' six toes. Except I thought the word was *baby's*, singular.''

He sighed heavily. "Do you think she did something . . . awful to the other little girl? I thought I might be able to recall her saying something about it, but nothing comes. . . . Maybe the other twin died in childbirth. Maybe that's why she never talked about her." He sighed again. "I guess it sounds as if the twins were illegitimate, doesn't it?"

"Yes."

He got up. "I could use some coffee." He poured it, took a swallow and said, "Dorcas died when I was twelve. Ran her car into one of the big sycamore trees that line the driveway to Red Cloud. I always wondered whether she was in a trance when it happened." He rocked the coffee in his cup and stared down at it. "In school I realized she must have been a borderline schizophrenic. I presume you know that there's evidence suggesting a genetic base for schizophrenia. It seems to run in families. So she—Dame Dorcas Veere, my grandmother—she could be the reason, or at least the predisposing influence, that made your mother what she is. It had nothing to do with the Haywards, after all. It came from outside—from the Veeres."

"And of course it's just a coincidence," Cayla said slowly, "that I look like a Hayward."

"Of course."

Her eyes clung to his face. "There are lots of cases of unrelated persons who resemble each other. Aren't there?"

"Sure. Movie star lookalikes—you read about them all the time. Coincidences like that do happen."

"And it's just another coincidence that you and I should meet? That it should turn out our grandmothers knew each other? That they were—" She stopped. She felt the skin around her eyes crawl, as if someone were pulling her hair to the back of her head. "My God. If your father was Dorcas Veere's son, and Rachel, my mother, was her daughter, then you and I are . . ."

"That's right. I didn't think you'd made that connection yet."

"No." She heard the word emerge as a whisper.

He moved toward her chair. "It was the first thing I thought of. And the most upsetting."

She looked up at him. His eyes were dark. In the open neck of his shirt she thought she could see a pulse beating. She said, "I was so busy trying to accept the fact that Mother wasn't a

Hayward, I didn't focus on who she really was." She felt her eyes widen again. "Mother is your *aunt*."

"Yes."

She didn't take her eyes from Stefan, but they suddenly gave her a double vision: He was still the man she wanted to touch and be touched by, to sleep with. And he was her blood relation. The two images seemed to cancel each other out and leave her numb.

She wished she had no knowledge at all of genetics. She put her head in her hands.

When Stefan spoke, his voice was odd, as if he were quoting something. "Dorcas always said it would be bad for you to know about the girls."

"What's that?" Cayla asked, without lifting her head.

"Something the old medium told me. She said my grand-mother believed that if I learned about the twins, the knowl-edge could mean trouble for me. I guess she was right."

Suddenly Cayla felt his hands gripping her arms. He pulled her close to him, so close that they were separated only by inches and his eyes were huge.

Through those inches, which neither of them seemed able to cross, she could feel every line of his body.

After a long time he released her. He took his vest from the back of a chair and put it on. "I'd better go." He got his jacket. "Would you like me to drive you to your apartment?"

"I think I'll stay here for a while."

He nodded. From his jacket he took the locket. "Would you like me to leave this with you?"

She seemed unable to think. "I don't know."

"If you don't mind, I'll keep it for a while, then." He hefted it in his hand. "As far as I'm concerned, I'm still investigating Polly Whiting for you. Is that OK?"

"Yes." The word came out so faintly that she repeated it.

"Good. You'll have your detective start trying to trace the chauffeur, Ralph Lewis? And of course look for any connec-tion between Polly and the name Trent?"

"Yes." That time the word was too loud.

"I'll see if I can think of any way to look into the Trent angle, too."

She forced her mind to attention. "And I'll be getting ready for the Senate hearing."

172

They left the room and went back to the central hall. The walk seemed endless and silent except for the mocking sounds of their heels on the polished floor.

Finally Stefan pulled open the heavy oak entry doors. "I'll be in touch," he said.

"Yes."

She stood in the doorway, watching. When he was halfway across the porte cochere, she called after him. He turned round. "I haven't even thanked you," she said.

"For what? Bringing so much peace and good news into your life?"

Without moving, she watched him continue down the steps, get into his car, and start down the drive.

She sighed and was ready to go back inside when something came from behind her, something that felt like an arm, and closed around her neck.

III

CHOICES

18

At nine-forty on Thursday morning Senator Moroni Gray gaveled open the U.S. Senate Select Subcommittee to Investigate the Commercial Use of Genetic Engineering.

From his seat at the center of the raised, U-shaped dais Gray surveyed the hearing room. The spectator section was full, the witness chair waited expectantly, and on the dais beside him were the six other senators who compromised his subcommittee of the Commerce Committee, as well as eight television cameras. Not only would there be good coverage on the network news shows, but public television was covering the entire proceedings live.

The TV people were always placed on the minority side of the dais so that the majority members could be filmed to better vantage. Moroni Gray's party, after many years of sharing space with the cameras, was now in the majority, and the cameras were concentrating on him.

"We who live in these latter decades of the twentieth century," he said, "are witnessing the most awesome technological advances in the entire history of the human race. Nuclear power, space shuttles, computers that fit in a briefcase—why, when I was a boy in a little town in southern Utah, none of those things were even a gleam in somebody's eyes. Let alone in the eyes of our forefathers when they founded this great democracy of ours. But now there's something that's way more awe-inspiring than any of those things. It makes the idea of computers and space shuttles seem almost kind of modest. After all, they're just *machines*. But now we've got the capacity to engineer the very stuff of life, and if that doesn't inspire awe . . ."

From the minority seats, Freddie Canfield of New York sent one of the coolly impatient looks that were his trademark. At fifty, Canfield was not only the wealthiest man in the Senate but also the best-looking and, as if in permanent apology for that fact, one of the hardest-working. Gray smiled benignly at him, signaling "Don't try to rush me" and thinking that however much Canfield might like to believe the hearing was his, it wasn't. True, Canfield had urged him to call it. He had argued that the chairman of one of the Health and Human Services subcommittees was considering an investigation of gene-splicing, in response to the onslaught of mail and phone calls by fundamentalist religious groups, but was too identified with them to do a decent job. Nonetheless, it was he, Moroni Gray, who had made the decision to move quickly and preempt the subject matter, and it was he who would run the hearing. At his own pace.

He spoke for twenty-five minutes, outlining the areas the committee would investigate, sometimes glancing at his notes but largely improvising. A prepared text always made him feel as if his mind were in a girdle. He liked, in his grandchildren's phrase, to "stay loose," a term that might also have applied to the way in which his perennial blue suit covered his ample frame and his gray hair cascaded over his collar.

He spoke of the proliferation of genetic-engineering companies, over two hundred at the last count, noted that much of the research on which their work was based had been done at universities and funded by the government, and vowed, "As the elected representatives of the American people, we're here to make sure the awesome discoveries of science are not abused by the marketplace."

He recited a long list of the products of genetic engineering, beginning with innocuous items like industrial enzymes and a crossbreed of a tomato and a potato—"which surely does astound this old Utah farmboy"—and progressing into the human realm. "And now there is fetal engineering," he said in his peroration. "Why, at one of our largest drug companies, Hayward Industries, in their Biologiconn division, they fertilized an egg in a test tube, they let it grow into an embryo, they performed a kind of genetic surgery on it, I guess you'd say, and when they were done, they put it into a woman's body."

His eyes lifted to the ceiling and then sank back under the weight of thick gray brows. "When that kind of thing can happen, then I for one am awestruck. We are all awestruck. I bet

178

even the scientists who do the work are awestruck. We'll certainly find out, because we're certainly going to ask them.''

The first witness was one of the country's top geneticists, whose testimony featured a clear statement of just what genetic engineering was: "Perhaps we should call it by its more scientific name, recombinant DNA, to remind us that it is a technology for working with DNA, deoxyribonucleic acid, which is the storehouse of all genetic information. DNA is a microscopic computer, if you like, which programs the nature of life, and does so in a remarkably efficient way. For instance, here's a statistic somebody figured out: A single thread of DNA from just one human cell can contain as much information as a thousand books—each one six hundred pages long. Now, in all living things DNA is the same. That is, it's made up of the same four chemical bases. It's their *order* that accounts for differences. But, chemically, we all belong to the same family. That's what makes it possible to do what we've learned to do in the last decade: how to cut pieces out of one DNA molecule and reinsert them into another—in other words, how to recombine genes. How to combine genetic material from two different organisms. Then, to make that combination start reproducing itself, we use a middleman—a bacterium, which is a simple form of life that doesn't do much of anything except read the messages in its DNA, manufacture whatever proteins the DNA tells it to and reproduce itself. That's how industry has been producing insulin and vaccines and most of its genetic-engineering products: by getting bacteria to manufacture them.''

When the questioning of the witness began, the third senator to speak was Parker Bell of Arkansas. A young man who was serving his first term in the Senate, he had so far been very unassuming, almost invisible. He tugged at his collar—he was plump, and so neatly and tightly tailored he might have been turned out by cookie cutter—and asked whether the professor would state his worries about genetic engineering.

"I believe I explained them all in my opening statement.''

"I know, sir, but would you mind just summarizing them?''

"If you like. I'm not concerned about safety in the labs, but I do worry about the possibility of the military's wanting to wage biological warfare and producing something dangerous under that label. I also worry about the ethical questions that arise when you talk about repairing genetic defects. Of course I want us to lessen human suffering, but I think when we start to change people, we open up a real Pandora's box. And I worry a good deal about the issue of who decides what kind of changes we make. Who has the authority to say what's an improvement and what isn't?''

"Don't you think that authority belongs to God?" Bell asked.

"No, Senator, I don't."

"Are you a religious man, sir?"

"I must admit that I'm not."

"An atheist?"

"The correct description for me would be an agnostic, Senator. But I don't see what that fact has to do with this hearing or my testimony."

"Don't you, sir?" Parker Bell adjusted his collar. "Don't you think the American public has a right to know that the people who do this kind of work, who tamper with life, are not God-fearing men?"

"Many of them are religious, Senator. It happens that I and some others are not. I hope you're not implying that ethical considerations are the exclusive province of religion?"

"All I'm trying to do is find out how people who deny the Lord can justify tampering with His work."

"Mr. Chairman, point of order!" came Fred Canfield's voice. When Gray asked what point he referred to, he said, in a diffident manner, "It is not the mandate of this hearing to grill people on whether or not they believe in God."

"Mr. Chairman," Bell said, "I think there's a simple question on the minds of the American people, and we should assure them we're going to be asking it. I think the people realize that what's happening here with genetic engineering is that science is trespassing on God's territory. And we're going to ask whether maybe science shouldn't be turned out of that territory, because it may be setting itself up against God's wishes."

"As far as I know," Canfield said dryly, looking over the tops of his glasses, "neither this committee nor even the full United States Senate is qualified to decide what God's wishes are."

There was a murmur of amusement from the public gallery, which he ignored. "If my colleague from Arkansas will just allow me the floor for one minute more," he said, "there are plenty of reasons to investigate the genetic-engineering industry without having to get into the Lord's business. For instance, the question of what the profit motive is doing to the scientific integrity of the university researchers who are also paid consultants to the genetic-engineering companies."

"We can't lock God out of this hearing," Bell said doggedly.

"I don't want to lock Him out, or anybody else," Canfield retorted. "But I think it's pretty presumptuous to suggest that we could make decisions for Him."

"Gentlemen!" Moroni Gray used his gavel and one of his moderately threatening frowns. "Let's remember that we're here to talk to our expert witness, who can only be with us today and tomorrow." He checked the old pocket watch that was propped on the table in front of him.

But one of the majority members, a well-known moderate, asked whether the senior senator from New York had meant to suggest that God's name should never be invoked in the deliberations of the United States Senate.

For a moment Freddie Canfield's eyes looked like the business ends of two pistols. However, he smiled, ran his hands through dark hair that was turning not gray but elegantly silver, and said of course he hadn't meant to suggest any such thing. He merely hoped the hearing would not turn into a theological discussion, which would be inappropriate.

"But after all," said Packman, on the minority side like Canfield, "we're conducting business here for the nation, and it's one nation *under God*."

"Amen," said Parker Bell.

Moroni Gray shot quick glances to the left and right, at the rest of the committee. He caught two nods of agreement, one set of nostrils flaring in disapproval, and one expressionless face. "Gentlemen," he said, "I suggest we continue with the questioning of our distinguished witness." He paused and then added, "Whom we shall hear and consider with God's blessing, I hope."

The look that crossed his face would have been easily recognized by many members of the Church of Jesus Christ of Latter-Day Saints, which he had served faithfully for all of his sixty-seven years and for one of whose angels he had been named.

Polly Whiting watched his face, which covered the screens of four of the television sets in the major-appliance department at Sears.

That morning she had told Bill she had some shopping to do in town, and he hadn't questioned her. He was too busy working on the tractor, which was acting up again. She had driven off in the pickup, stirring up little tornadoes of dust all the way down to the main road. By the time she pulled into the Sears parking lot, her face was flushed, and she went up the escalator to major appliances two steps at a time.

The Whitings had a television set of their own, in the front parlor, but the images were often blurred and snowy, and always in black and white. In any case, Polly had told Bill she had no desire to watch the Senate hearing. "It don't have anything to do with me," she had said, and Bill's answer had been a shrug and "Whatever you say, Poll." Still, he had given her the idea without knowing it: When she was on the Vera Leopold television show, he said, he had driven in to Sears, so he could see it all in color.

Although Bill hadn't fussed about the newspapers and the television, or even the woman who had come to talk to her for two days in order to write the book, he had said, more than once, "You got to calm yourself down, Poll, and get back to normal."

She stood in the aisle at Sears and watched, large hands shoved into the loose cuffs of her sweater and blue eyes moving among the four identical images of the hearing. She nodded at Parker Bell's words and the chairman's wish for God's blessing; she frowned when Freddie Canfield spoke, she leaned forward in an effort to understand the geneticist.

Whenever the name Hayward was mentioned, she took a deep breath, and her eyes glowed.

She stayed for nearly two hours, until one of the appliance salesmen began to fuss. She turned to him slowly, rubbed the back of her neck as if it hurt, shifted her shoulders, and left without a word.

Stefan watched as a reporter on one of the late news shows commented on "the performance of the Arkansas senator whose colleagues had thought he was so quiet" and then concluded, "Many observers expect the most volatile days of the hearing to be those featuring the testimony of drug-industry officials, especially Cayla Hayward of the Biologiconn division of Hayward Industries."

He switched off the set and lay staring into the dark of his bedroom. Through the open windows came street noises, muffled only slightly by their four-story rise, and a breeze carrying a hint of April freshness from the greenery in Central Park.

As he had done so many times since he had left her the night before, he thought of the chasm that had suddenly opened between him and Cayla and wondered what she felt on her side of it.

No doubt she had thought of the nearly unanimous opinion of geneticists: With second or third cousins, there was no cause for concern, but first cousins should not have children.

Or perhaps she hadn't been thinking at all—just feeling a deep, gut revulsion at the thought of sharing her bed with a man who shared her blood.

Freud said incest was the primal taboo; was he right about that, at least?

Stefan sighed and locked his hands behind his head. If he couldn't interpret Cayla's feelings, he was doing little better with his own: a complex and contradictory mixture that had lain at the back of his skull all day like an incipient headache.

Despite his premonition that the locket might hold news that involved him personally, the actuality had been a shock. Something internal and subterranean had shifted, leaving him as disoriented as if the horizon were at an angle. Each time it occurred to him that Rachel Randall was his aunt, the realization was newly jarring.

He sat up, almost angrily, and switched on the light. His bedside clock read eleven-fifty. He got up, wandered into the living room, and stood in its center, looking at the furnishings he had lived with for years, now transformed by darkness and shadow into slightly alien shapes. His mind seemed a bit alien, too, feeding him odd thoughts—such as the notion that maybe he should try to see Rachel Randall, in his professional capacity, without telling Cayla. But when he asked himself what purpose that would serve, he had no good answer.

He moved to a chair, turned on a lamp, and took from the

drawer in the end table an envelope containing the objects he had brought with him from Camp Red Cloud: the Polly Trent file card, the tiny cereal spoon, the locket and the notebook belonging to his grandmother. He had glanced through it before, but the contents looked meaningless: The pages of notes in purple ink had nothing to do, as far as he could tell, with Polly Trent.

He leaned back in the chair. For a while he sat holding the notebook against his chest with both hands, thinking nothing, simply staring at his past and asking whether it had doomed his future—and receiving no answer.

Finally he sat up and opened the notebook. He went through the pages again, looking for anything that might conceivably refer to old Cayla, telling himself he wouldn't find it, and being proved right. However, he did see the name Cora in one of the entries and was reminded that he never had gone back to old John, the Hayward butler, to ask about a servant of that name.

He looked at the entry more carefully. It was headed just "Cora," no initial. "Mother Gladys," it read, with the *O* next to it that seemed to be the symbol for *dead.* "Father Herman" was alive but caused her "trouble." A cousin had died in the war. There was a living friend named Esther and a—

Stefan sat bolt upright. Esther. Was it possible that Dorcas had made a slight mistake and the friend's name was really Hester?

He realized he had forgotten all about old Cayla's companion. The night before she had melted into the shadows and then out of his mind, but she had attended the old woman for over sixty years and could very well know something old Cayla didn't.

He wanted to rectify his error immediately and go to Rowan Hall, but of course that was out of the question. Instead he went to the telephone, looked at it for a long time and finally decided that he could not call Cayla at that hour. Not under the circumstances.

He tried her apartment the next morning at seven forty-five but there was no answer. And when he finally got an answer at Biologiconn, at eight-thirty, her secretary said she had not come in the day before, as expected.

When he called again, at ten, the secretary said Cayla still hadn't come in and then, succumbing to the firmness and concern in his voice, confessed that no one had heard from her or knew where she was.

19

By five o'clock on Saturday evening Stefan was heading out of the city, on his way to Rowan Hall.

He had been unable to get away on Friday. His schedule included appointments he had postponed from midweek in order to make his trip to Connecticut. One simply couldn't cancel patients. They were in trouble, and for some of them, the hour with him was a lifeline that got them through the week. So he had seen people until nine o'clock Friday night and started again early Saturday morning.

He had called Cayla's office several more times on Friday, until he and her secretary were almost friends by the end of the day. No, the woman told him, Cayla never departed from her schedule without notifying someone. The present situation was quite unprecedented. Yes, she told him, Cayla's car, the sports car she sometimes drove herself, was in the Biologiconn parking lot, but she sometimes left it there while using her limousine and chauffeur, so people hadn't paid much attention to it, and no one was sure how long it had been there. Yes, she told him, someone from Biologiconn had even gone to Cayla's apartment, but she wasn't there, nor was there any sign of trouble. No, they hadn't contacted the authorities, but they planned to do so on Monday if they didn't hear from her by then.

The secretary said she had called Rowan Hall and had been told that Cayla had left on Wednesday night around nine and hadn't been back. Stefan persuaded the woman to give him the number, which was unlisted, and had an unsatisfactory conversation with John, the butler: "Why, Dr. Veere, didn't you two leave together? Miss Cayla didn't have her own car, and she didn't take one from the garage, so how else could she have left?''

How else, indeed?

Perhaps she was still there, refusing to talk to anyone but her grandmother while she grappled with the shocks the old woman had administered. And if she wasn't there, if someone had kidnapped her to keep her from testifying at the Senate hearing . . . but such possibilities were not to be considered.

Her disappearance had one positive consequence, though. It had made him see clearly, immediately, and exactly how he felt about their being first cousins: He didn't give a damn. The disorientation and concern of that discovery vanished the moment he learned that he could no longer reach her—that a world in which she existed was also a place in which he couldn't find her.

She had to be at Rowan Hall, he thought grimly, taking the exit off the parkway. And then, when they were together again and the world was right, they could talk to Hester about the locket and the maid named Cora.

He had not told John he was coming and had trouble finding the phone in the gatepost; it was cleverly concealed, and he hadn't watched carefully when Cayla used it. He realized how worried he was when he found himself wanting to kick the post in frustration, but finally a panel slid open, and there was the phone. It seemed to take another ten minutes to get John to grasp who he was—"Your name is Fear? I don't know anyone named Fear"—and finally to open the gates.

As he went up the drive the silhouette of the house looked for a moment like a coven of huge figures huddled beneath their pointed hats. There were almost no lights on, and when he parked and walked up to the porte cochere, the flood of illumination he expected did not occur. He made his way to the door and banged the knocker.

"It is you, then," said John when he finally opened up. "I wasn't sure."

"I'm afraid I need to see Mrs. Randall again." On the assumption that he could, he had again dressed more formally than usual, in a gray suit.

"Oh, I don't know how you can see her," John said impassively. "She's had a couple of bad days lately. No one but Hester's been allowed up there."

The back of Stefan's neck tightened, but he kept his voice from giving any sign. "That's all right. I'll just talk to Hester for a minute, then, if I may."

"Talk to Hester?" the old man said, as if it were an alien notion.

"Yes. Would you call her, please?" When John hesitated, Stefan said, "Never mind. I'll just go up and see her myself."

"No, no," the old man cried. "You can't do that."

"Then you'd better take me." Stefan put the snap of order-giving into his voice.

The old man's obedience to that tone seemed automatic. He led Stefan past the massive staircase, down a long hall and into a small elevator that creaked upward so slowly there was no sensation of movement. When it finally reached the second floor, John went along the hall a few yards and knocked on a door. Nothing happened, and the snail-pace of the night's events made Stefan's heart race in compensation.

At length the door opened a few inches. "Someone here to see you," John said.

"What do you mean?" rasped Hester's voice. "Who?"

"He's here. Right here. That doctor."

The crack in the door widened, like a disbelieving eye. "What do you want?"

"I'd like to come in and talk to you for a bit." Meaningfully Stefan added. "About Cayla."

Hester stood still, all motion confined to her eyelids, which blinked like an erratic pulse. She was frightened, Stefan knew. But why? Of him? Or of his learning something she didn't want him to know? "I want to come in and talk to you," he repeated firmly.

After another slow crawl of time, she backed into the room, allowing him to enter.

He presumed he was in her own suite, which looked smaller than old Cayla's and did not front on the ocean. The dimly lit room was musty and seemed full to bursting, not so much with furniture as with shelves of curios, wall hangings, prints and paintings, bookcases spilling their contents. Figurines of birds and animals—many of them cats—perched on every spare inch of space. The room was a violent contrast to Hester's gauntness and the repressive severity of her clothing.

Keeping his voice firm but not threatening, Stefan asked whether the two of them could sit down and talk.

"About what?" she said. "Why should I talk to you?"

"It would be a good idea, Hester. There are things we have to discuss." He regarded her steadily, willing her to consent.

After a moment she shuffled over to a carved wooden chair. Stefan sat on a blue velvet loveseat piled with beaded pillows. The table beside it was crowded with objects, among them a carved Egyptian ibis and a stack of very old books. He caught sight of one title—*The Psychic Way.*

In three of the walls were doors that, he presumed, led to adjoining rooms. "Are you next to Mrs. Randall here?" he asked.

"Yes." Her voice was flat with caution.

"Have you had these rooms since you first came to Rowan Hall?"

"Yes."

"That was over sixty years ago, if I remember."

"Yes." There was no hint in her face that it had ever been attractive. The bones all seemed to lie on awkward planes, and the skin that stretched over them now lacked even the softness of wrinkles. It was as withered and tight as a mummy's.

Stefan asked, "Were you ever married, Hester?"

She blinked and smoothed the long black skirt over her knees. "No."

"Did you work other places before you came here?"

"Yes."

"Where?"

"Hospitals."

"Oh? Which ones?"

"The last one was in Brooklyn."

"You've devoted your life to taking care of people then?"

"Yes," she said, with visible satisfaction.

Without pausing or changing the tone of his voice, he asked, "When did you last see young Cayla?"

Her eyelids beat a rapid pulse. "When she came here with you."

"What do you mean?" he asked, testing her.

"You know. The other night. Wednesday."

She was properly oriented, then, as to time and place. He went on. "Have you heard from her since Wednesday night?"

"She hardly ever comes here. She's turned her back on this house." Resentment had reared up in Hester's voice, so high and jagged that although Stefan's professional training kept his face from revealing the fact, he suddenly felt that old John had been right to ask whether his name was Fear.

Still speaking calmly, he asked. "Do you wish she would come here more often?"

She didn't answer. Above the sharp nose, her eyes hooded with caution.

"Why do you think she comes so seldom?" Still no answer.

By that time Stefan had a strong feeling about a way he might reach her. Whether its source was his childhood memories or his years as a psychiatrist, he couldn't say—perhaps some of both. He kept talking, his voice even, of Cayla's childhood—"If you liked to take care of people, it must have suited you to have a young girl in the house"—and slowly moving his hand toward the table beside him, from which he picked up a cameo no bigger than a coin.

With both hands in front of him, he held the cameo between two fingers, closed the other fist over it, and made it disappear. Still talking—"I suppose you took care of Rachel, too, when she lived here with you"—he made the cameo reappear, and then vanish two more times. He saw that Hester's eyes had fixed on his hands and were staring with a kind of nervous amazement.

He reached to the table again and picked up an ornamental spoon. Resting one hand on the table, he made a fist, inserted the spoon with the bowl and part of the stem protruding, stared at it intently, and whispered, "Bend. Bend. Bend."

In a few moments it did.

He glanced at Hester. The look on her face told him his hunch had been right.

He put the spoon down, reached into his suit pocket, and, with another of the simple sleights-of-hand he had picked up during his year with the carnival, made the CHR locket appear in the palm of one hand.

Hester whispered, "Do you have it, then? Do you have the power?" Fear and fascination struggled in her eyes and immobilized one another, leaving a gray, glassy surface.

Stefan thought that he could not go through with it. To exploit her weakness and gullibility would be to repeat the very crimes he had run away from at Red Cloud and to betray the goals he had set for his life since then. "Those were just elementary magic tricks," he said to her wearily. "Anyone could do them."

"Do you have the power?" She was still whispering. "Is that how you made the Lady talk to you? Your eyes . . ."

She looked the way Lettice Barrow had when she cried, "Dorcas sent you here!" The way Polly Trent had looked when he tried to tell her the truth.

He crossed his fist over the locket so tightly that it cut into his palm. "Where is young Cayla?"

When Hester didn't answer, he leaped to his feet and repeated it, almost yelling, "Where is young Cayla? Where is she?"

Her eyes slid a fraction to one side and then jerked back.

Stefan swung in the direction of her look. He saw bookcases, a shelf of figurines, and one of the room's three doors. In a moment he was at the door, pulling and jiggling the large brass knob. It wouldn't turn. "Cayla!" he yelled. "Cayla! Are you in there?"

He slammed his shoulder against the panel, but the door was solid wood, and nothing gave. He turned around and forced his voice down to something resembling calm firmness. "Please open this door, Hester."

She shook her head.

"Ah, you see, Hester, the fact that you won't do it makes me certain young Cayla is in there. So you can be sure I'm going to stop at nothing to get in. Nothing, Hester, whether that means calling the police or breaking down the door with an ax." He was watching her intently. She had the trapped look of someone who knew she had to act but also knew she couldn't. "Of course," he went on, "the first thing I would do would be to speak to Mrs. Randall. She would make you open the door, wouldn't she?"

For a terrible moment he thought he had taken the wrong gamble and old Cayla was in on Hester's scheme. But then she glanced at another of the three doors, presumably the one leading to her mistress's suite, and the glance was fearful.

"Yes," he said, "I would tell Mrs. Randall you've done

something to Cayla. Because you have done something, haven't you? Just the way you did before, when she was only twelve years old and you locked her in her room at Christmastime and made her sick.''

She gasped. ''You have the power to know that?''

Stefan felt almost ill. Why didn't she simply conclude that he had learned about the Christmas incident from Cayla? But he knew why: She didn't *want* simple, natural explanations for things. Probably she was no longer capable of accepting them, after what he now suspected was a lifetime of desiring their opposite. ''Yes,'' he said harshly. ''I have the power to know everything.''

She blinked several times. Then, still staring at him, she slid one of her hands into a pocket and came out with a key.

''That's right,'' he said. ''You have to open the room, and you know it.''

It was a bedroom, as musty and choked with objects as the room it adjoined. The bed had a heavy, faded purple canopy and a mottled blue spread, and Cayla lay in its center, in the clothes she had been wearing Wednesday night. Her hands, like her feet, were bound together and then tied to one of the bedposts. Above the scarf that covered her mouth, her eyes were huge, and the irises seemed to tremble.

When her mouth was free, she said, ''Oh, God, Stefan, you came. Thank you, thank you.''

When her hands were free, she gripped his arm and said, ''If I slept, I had the nightmare. If I stayed awake, I had . . . her.''

''It's all right now,'' he said.

''What day is it?''

''Night,'' he said. ''Saturday night. You've been here about seventy-two hours.''

While he was untying her legs, she crossed her arms over her breasts, shivered, and said, ''She told me I had to be locked up so I couldn't bring you here again to upset Gran and ruin everything.''

While he helped her sit up and put her feet on the floor, she said, ''I don't know where she got the strength for this. She's nothing but skin over bones. I fought as hard as I could, but her arms were like steel cables.''

"Sometimes the mind can give the body incredible strength."

She reached to the small table beside the bed. On it, directly in her line of vision, was a black ceramic figure of a cat. She picked it up, stared at it, and threw it into a corner of the room, where it landed with a hollow sound but did not break.

Stefan sat beside her, took one of her hands in his, and started to rub the wrist.

"What made you come?" she said. "I almost gave up hoping."

"I realized we'd never asked Hester about the locket. I tried to call you. When your office didn't know where you were, I suspected that somebody at Rowan Hall would."

She looked at him but soon turned away and said, "I feel dirty. I *am* dirty. My clothes, my hair . . ."

"Did she feed you? Let you go to the bathroom?"

"Yes, but she kept my hands and legs tied. I couldn't get away. . . ." She shivered again.

Then she glanced up and said, "Oh my God. Look."

He did. It was Hester. He had left her in the other room, muttering to herself, but now she was standing over them, the fear and awe that had immobilized her displaced by rage. A long knife was in her hand, and a matching glitter in her eyes.

"You ruined everything," she hissed at Stefan. "You made the Lady say Rachel isn't a Hayward. But she is! She belongs to Kella! She has to!"

Once, Stefan recalled, but it seemed to come from another world, he hadn't wanted to exploit Hester's gullibility. Now he had only moments to figure out how to do it, because it was the only way to immobilize her again.

Gripping Cayla's hand, he told her to stay quiet. Then he stretched his arms in front of him like a sleepwalker and gazed into the distance. "From the woods, O Ktharlok, from the heart of the woods where you lie asleep until we call your sacred name . . . speak to your servant on earth. Command him, tell him your wishes."

Hester stopped. Her eyes had frozen over, but the knife still threatened.

"Yes, Master," he said. "You wish the woman to put down the knife she has taken up in her short-sightedness, and then to

192

ell your earthly servant what he wishes to know. From the heart of the great woods, where your spirit lies, you command that she lay down the knife and speak to your servant who has the power . . .''

The knife wavered, then stiffened again.

Stefan kept repeating the phrases, his voice low and strong. Although his gaze had to seem fixed on the distance, he stole glances at the silent struggle before him: the thin lips, and the hand on the knife, clenched with anger because he had challenged a crucial illusion, the eyes blinking and darting with the will to believe they were in the presence of some other-worldly force.

He said, even more strongly, "She must obey your command to lay down the knife!"

But she raised it higher and sucked in a deep breath. Then she began to sway from side to side, slowly, until she leaned far to the left and stayed there for an interminable time, like a sawn tree hanging in the air before falling.

She crumpled to her knees, still holding the knife. Finally that, too, fell onto the patterned carpet, and her eyes closed.

Mundus vult decipi, Stefan thought—one way or the other. He picked up the knife and with his other hand grabbed her forearm. Through the black cloth of her sleeve, the muscles felt as thin and slack as ropes.

He heard Cayla say in a low voice, "It looks as if you could get her to talk now."

"I don't think you have the strength for an interrogation right now," he said.

"Didn't you say the mind can sometimes will the body into whatever strength it needs? If Hester could do it, so can I."

And when Stefan looked at her, he saw that indeed her eyes were returning to their normal, perceptive brilliance. She stood up. Her knees started to buckle, but she clenched her hands and said, "I'm OK." And in a moment she was walking slowly out the bedroom door, saying, "I'll be back. Just give me a minute."

She was so slim and delicate, Stefan thought. She was one of the strongest people he had ever known.

He got Hester to her feet and led her to a chair in the other room. She whispered, "The Lady. Who will look after the Lady now?"

She sank down, the hump of her back accentuated by the rest of her body, from which all tonus and will seemed to have gone.

20

Sunk in the chair, she stared at the hands curled over her knees and at the tips of her shoes, which lay below the hem of her skirt like the flat heads of two snakes.

She knew she had done her best to protect the Lady, but that had not been enough to counteract the young doctor's power. From the beginning she had been wary of him, and had suspected his aura was strange and powerful.

She couldn't see the aura, of course, the way someone with the gift would have been able to do.

She knew she had no gift. But she had tried long and hard to develop it ever since the night she had been called in to help her sister and some friends hold what they called a séance. It was the first time she had ever been invited to join them; her sister always said, "Oh, you're too shy, Hester, you'd never mix in," but she knew where the truth lay: in her face. That night, however, they wanted more people to make the vibrations stronger.

They had used a ouija board, and it was astounding to watch the little wooden planchette move by itself and to receive messages from a spirit entity.

The spirits were friendlier than most people.

Except for people in the hospital, of course; they were constantly clamoring for her—"Nurse, please fix my pillows just the way you did last night"; "Nurse, please give me another backrub; no one gives it as good as you do." It had been good to have them depend on her. She probably would have stayed there if the doctors hadn't been so unappreciative; they acted as if one barely existed, though one was doing everything for them. Almost worshiping them. Yet they could barely deign to say a word of thanks. Like the surgeon, so handsome, who had repaid all her devotion by scoffing at spiritism just because he knew she was interested in it and wouldn't dare to reply.

It had been a relief to leave and come to Rowan Hall. The Lady had been so different from the doctors, and so like the patients.

"Hester. Hester!"

They were speaking to her, young Cayla and the doctor who had the power. Her eyes lifted from her shoes to the two of them. Cayla, sitting on the loveseat, rubbing her wrists, had changed into some other clothes—a pair of blue jeans and a yellow sweater from years ago. They must have been in her old bedroom. She had begged for clean clothes each time the scarf was untied from her mouth, but getting them would have been an unnecessary risk. Besides, clothes were quite unimportant.

"Hester," said the young doctor, standing only a few feet away, "I have some questions to ask you, and as you heard the Master command, you must answer them."

His aura was terribly strong. It must be, even though it couldn't be seen, because one got almost dizzy looking into his eyes. So green, they were, and cold, as cold as ether. But burning, too.

Shall I say his amber eyes did burn on me and drive out my will? Kella Hagaward had written that, in the letter.

But the amber light was not coming from the young doctor's eyes. It came from the locket he had produced from nowhere again. The locket he had used to make the Lady tell her secrets. The locket she herself would have to talk about now.

He didn't ask about it, though. Just held it and said, "I never heard your full name, Hester. What is it?"

If only it was Hayward. "Carlson."

"So, Hester Carlson, why did you come to work for Mrs. Randall?"

Blink. "I heard there was a job. I wanted to leave the hospital."

"And you came after the first Rachel drowned?"

"Yes."

"Did you ever meet the woman from whom Mrs. Randall got the new baby, the second Rachel?"

Hands clamped more tightly on the kneecaps . . . It was hard to accept the idea that the secret of Rachel was out. For so long it had been theirs alone, hers and the Lady's. It was part of their lives, of the soft stream of confidences and memories that ran between them like a skein of wool being forever rolled into a ball and then unrolled again, and it never mattered which hands did the holding and which shaped the ball.

The young doctor repeated his question. "Did you ever meet her, Hester? Did you ever go with Mrs. Randall to see Dame Dorcas?"

"Yes."

"Did you join in the séances that called up the dead Rachel?"

"Sometimes. She was wonderful, Dame Dorcas was."

The green eyes flared. "Did you ever go there alone?"

"No."

The doctor stopped and seemed to be thinking. He looked away, at a shelf where the cats crouched in permanent, ceramic poses. How sleek their bodies were, and who knew how many spirits had looked out from their eyes over the centuries?

Another question came. "Were you Rachel's nursemaid?"

"I took care of her, yes. After what happened before, that woman letting the first baby drown, the Lady wouldn't have a regular nursemaid in the house."

"I see. Were you fond of Rachel?"

How could he ask such a question? But perhaps his Master had told him to do it, in order to test her in some way. "I love Rachel." The truth of that was so strong it hurt. "I loved Rachel from the first moment I saw her!"

And even more when they discovered that the precious little body bore a sign, the six toes. It had been clear then that the child was special, like no other. Although of course they didn't know at first what the sign meant. No. Not in those early days . . . to Paris and back . . . the pink blanket . . . "No. Not at first."

"What was that?" the doctor asked. "You say you *didn't* love Rachel at first?"

His words tore at the throat. "Of course I did! I told you I did! Ask the Lady—she knows! I loved Rachel even more than she did, at first. She was upset by the sign, by the toes, but I knew it meant there was something special about Rachel. I didn't know how special, though."

"What did you think the sign meant?"

"That Kella had marked her in some way. What else could it be? Kella had written as plain as plain could be, in her letter, that all her husband's family should feel her power. 'I pray to my lord to make to suffer Thomas Hagaward's daughters who have caused me this agony. And if I have such power as they would make me confess, then let there be in every Hagaward family down to the end of time one who is just like me, so that I may have their company and be not alone in what I endure.' That's what Kella wrote, plain as plain."

"You know it by heart?"

"I do."

"The whole letter?"

"Yes." The green eyes flared. "Well, why shouldn't I know it? Because the Lady's letting me read it showed that she trusted me completely, that I was more than her nurse!" The Lady had begged her husband to take the letter from the safe where it was kept, and when he left the room, the two of them had read it, and the Lady had said, "From now on, I want you to share everything with me, Hester."

The doctor sat down, so close that his eyes made one blink. "Tell me about the locket." He was still holding it.

"No, not the locket . . ."

"Why not?"

"I don't know what happened to it. I don't. I've never been sure. Never."

"But you have some ideas."

Lips dry. Lick them.

"Did you give the locket to someone, Hester?"

"No, I could never do that. It was the Lady's. It had the sign in it, the sign of Rachel. . . ."

"Yes, the parings from her toenails, which you yourself suggested should be put inside it. Isn't that so?"

"Yes."

"Did you ever *show* the locket to someone? When Mrs. Randall wasn't there? Perhaps to one of the other servants?"

"They all knew about it. All of them."

"Did you tell them?"

"Maybe. Yes. Maybe I talked about it at dinner."

"You all ate together, and one night you told them about the locket?"

"Yes."

"What did you say?"

"Just . . . that Mr. Gary had given it to the Lady for her birthday. That's all."

"No, Hester, I don't think it is all."

"Yes. It is." Make sure the skirt is tucked over the legs . . .

"Did you show the locket to somebody later on? Maybe to Ralph Lewis, the chauffeur? Or to his wife, or to one of the other maids?"

"No, no. I wouldn't show anything to them. I didn't like Betty Lewis. Gave herself airs."

"What about the maid who was named Cora? No, don't look away. Look at me, Hester. Tell me whether you liked Cora."

Pause. "Cora was nice."

"Good. I'd like to hear about her. How old was she? Where did she come from? What was her last name?"

Green eyes would not let one go. Blink. Blink. "Cora was five years younger. We had the same birthday, May twenty-second. That's how we got to be friendly."

"Why did you like her?"

"She . . . she believed."

"Believed?" Fire in the green eyes. "Do you mean she believed in the spirits?"

"Yes. She had . . . She studied with a medium I knew. When I still worked in the hospitals. Who would teach you how to develop your powers. If you had any."

"Did Cora have any?"

"Not really. She was . . . sort of like me."

"The two of you tried to hold séances, didn't you?"

"You *know* what we did?"

"Of course. You got together, right in this room here, and turned off all the lights and tried to commune with your spirit guides, to see whether your loved ones in spirit would try to reach you from the other side. Isn't that so?"

"Yes."

"And Cora's last name was Trent, wasn't it?"

"Yes."

Young Cayla jerked in her chair, eyes snapping open.

"Why didn't you tell us Cora's last name when I was asking Mrs. Randall about her?"

"I . . . Too many questions. Questions! I didn't like you to know things. But now I can't. . . ."

"That's right, you can't stop me from knowing. Cora Trent left when her mother died, to go help her father. What was his name?"

"I don't remember."

"Wasn't it Herman?"

"Maybe. I don't know."

"What was the name of the town she went to?"

"I don't know. No, please don't look at me that way. I really don't know! A farm, she said, down in southern Pennsylvania. Right on the edge of West Virginia, that's all I remember."

"Did she tell you anything about her father?"

"She . . . she didn't like him very much. She said that. But she said her brother insisted she go. I remember that."

"Do you remember her brother's name?"

Blink. "Something with a J. John, I think. Yes, John."

"Did Cora write to you after she left?"

"Hah!" Memory so strong it made the hands dig along the thighs. "Not even a postcard. And she promised me . . . She wasn't a friend, after all. None of them were. Not the doctors. Not even my sister . . . Nobody was a friend, except the Lady."

"Let's go back to the Kella Hagaward letter, Hester. Did you ever recite it to anybody?"

The room shifted, like a treehouse in a high wind. One had to blink to steady it. Blinkblinkblink. And then to speak. Quickly. "I recited it to Rachel sometimes. Wouldn't you like to hear about Rachel? The darling little Rachel? Ah, she was a lovely child. Lovely. Brown hair she had, as fine and soft as feathers. I'd wash it and brush it and make it curl up in nice little shapes. And I played games with her. Pat-a-cake, pat-a-cake, baker's man . . . This little piggy went to market, this littly piggy went to town . . . But of course you count that one out on the toes, so I had to add an extra little piggy. 'This little piggy went dancing in the woods,' that's what I would say. And she would laugh. Oh, we spent so many hours together. Playing and telling stories and reading . . . I read all the fairy tales to her— 'Rapunzel' and 'The Little Match Girl' and 'The Miller's Daughter' and the princess who had to weave shirts out of nettles for her brothers who were turned into wild swans, and the goosegirl who married the king. Wonderful stories. And poems, too. She loved poems . . . 'O sweet and far from cliff

and scar/The horns of Elfland faintly blowing.' And the egg-
shell poem:

> *Oh, never leave your egg-shells unbroken in the cup;*
> *Think of us poor sailor-men and always smash them up,*
> *For witches come and find them and sail away to sea,*
> *And make a lot of misery for mariners like me.''*

There was time to steal a look at them, the doctor and young
Cayla, but they were sitting quietly, both of them with their
eyes wide, his green and hers as black as they had ever been,
and he did not have a question ready to spring out. But if one
stopped for any time at all . . .

"Oh, she was a lovely child. And smart! She started saying
words at nine months. And it wasn't long at all before she was
saying 'Hessie.' That's what she always called me—Hessie.
She could say her letters and numbers before she was five, and
talk a blue streak with no babytalk, either. It was clear she was
going to be one of the special Hayward women, one of Kella's.
I told her so even before she was old enough to understand, but
it wasn't long before she *did* understand, her being so smart. I
told her all about Kella and the Hayward women who were so
beautiful and talented and how it was an honor—nothing to be
sad about, or frightened of. And she understood. I'd go into her
room sometimes and find her there on the bed, swinging her
foot and staring at it and singing to herself. . . . Because she
loved to sing, you know, right from the beginning. Loved
every kind of music, in fact. The Lady didn't like that—she
knew it meant Rachel was coming under the curse, and of
course I understood how she felt—but what could anyone do,
when all the signs were there? Nothing. And she had such a
lovely voice. I'm sure she could have been a great singer. Because they always suffer in some way, great singers do. All
great artists suffer. That's what I always told her, and she knew
it, too. Why, she would find books about it and bring them to
me, books about people who had suffered—like Mozart and
Beethoven and Van Gogh. She liked to read about Van Gogh.''

"Hester, don't you see what you—'' That was young Cayla,
face as white as paper, eyes two burnt holes, but the doctor put
out his hand and made her be quiet.

"Go on, Hester," he said. "This is exactly what the Master wanted you to tell me."

Yes? Yes, it was true.

The doctor said, "Go on about Rachel. Did she study singing?"

"Oh, the Lady didn't want her to at first, but she begged and begged, and she could tear at your heart when she begged! So she got her way, and pretty soon she was telling me she knew she had one of the great voices of the century, like Lily Pons, even if the teacher didn't realize it. She said the teacher was jealous and wanted to hold her back, and she told her mother. So the Lady took her to a man who had coached a lot of important singers—I can't remember his name—and he told the Lady that Rachel had a pleasant voice but nothing more. That was his word, 'pleasant.' Poor Rachel! She said it proved they were all against her but she was going to show them and keep on singing anyway. And she did, for a while. But then she started acting really strange. Sometimes she was just like a child, giggling and wanting to play our old games, and her nearly seventeen. But mostly she would be so lifeless and faraway that it was like a stranger had come into my life. And sometimes she would throw things—pull the flowers out of the vases and smash them. Once she took some crystal pieces that had been in the Hayward family for over two hundred years, and she ran up to the third floor and leaned over the staircase and threw them all the way down to the main floor. The maids were picking up slivers for weeks afterward. But the worst thing was . . . She started to talk as if we were trying to hurt her. Oh, it was terrible. Broke your heart. Finally the Lady had to let them take her to the hospital. I cried for a month, I just couldn't stop. And the Lady . . . The doctors hemmed and hawed and finally told her they weren't sure what was wrong with Rachel. Maybe it was schizophrenia, they said, or maybe hysteria. Well, after she heard that . . . One night the Lady went to bed, just as usual, but the next morning she couldn't move her left arm and leg. The paralysis had come back, exactly the way it was before, and it never went away again."

Silence. Great silence in the room. Rub the eyes, which hurt from staring so long at the bronze figures on the étagère. The bronze orchestra players that Rachel had liked so much. And when the eyes lifted, there sat Rachel's daughter like a stone.

201

"Go on, Hester."

"Yes. Well. The Lady never walked again. Not even when they let Rachel out. They did, you know, after about a year, and when she came home, she was fine, just as if nothing had happened. She said she wanted to go back to her singing, only this time to go study in Europe. The Lady was terrified of that, but how could she say no? When she wanted to do the same thing herself at Rachel's age? So she compromised. She said Rachel could go study in New York, and live there, in a nice little apartment near Carnegie Hall, and if it worked out, after a while maybe she could go to Europe. But that was a mistake, of course, a terrible mistake. Because we lost her. She didn't come home to see us and she didn't answer her telephone and her teachers hadn't seen her for days. Nobody could find her. The Lady had to hire detectives, but for six months they couldn't find a trace of her. Six months! She was smart, you see—she told me afterward how she had hidden and changed her name and bleached her pretty hair. California, that's where she was. With a young man. A singer, he was, too, and he wanted to go to Hollywood. So she ran off with him. But then he left her—just abandoned her. She said he was jealous of her voice, but I don't know if . . . I thought it probably was because she was pregnant. Yes, pregnant. At nineteen. Of course the Lady was beside herself, but what could we do? Nothing. We just had her brought home and took care of her, and when the baby came . . . I wanted her to name the child for Kella, and she did. She always listened to me. But then she started saying people were trying to steal the child. She said we were trying to take the child away from her."

And there sat the child, right there in the room, in the house but pulling away from everything it stood for. That was in every line of her body, every look in her eyes. Always had been. Young Cayla had no feeling at all for the family she had the great good fortune to be born into. A tragic family, of course, but a glorious one, for not only was it blessed with wealth and physical beauty, it was touched by the mystery of things that were unnatural. . . . Things beyond nature. Far beyond! And how many people had the luck to be lifted beyond themselves, out of themselves, by contact with forces from another time and place? Young Cayla had tried all her life to deny them, but she—

She was talking, young Cayla was, in her voice like ice. "You treated Mother just the way you tried to treat me! Don't you see what you did? Don't you see that all your nonsense and your constant talk about Kella helped drive Mother into the hospital?"

Red. Red boiling up in front of the eyes. "Don't you say that to me, young miss! Kella doesn't need anyone's help. She has the power to do what she wants without any help! I had nothing to do with it. Who am I to deal in such things? I have no power. I didn't even understand what was happening at first, not for a long time. I thought Rachel was sick, like the doctors said. When they put her back in that hospital, that awful place, and I was the one to go see her because the Lady couldn't go, I would weep all the way back to Rowan Hall. She had gotten so far away, Rachel had. No more smiles for me, sometimes not even a word for me . . . And if she did talk, she would tell about the voices she kept hearing and how people were controlling her thoughts. She would pull at her hair something awful, trying to get them out. . . . I *should* have known what was happening, because of the sign, the six toes, but I didn't. I just believed she was sick, you see, like the doctors said. Doctors! What could they know about it?"

"You mean she *wasn't* sick?"

Who was asking that question. Whose voice? Oh yes, the green eyes, the cold, burning green eyes. He was a doctor himself. Who came and ruined everything, like doctors always did. But he had the power, he could talk to those in spirit. That was how he had got into the bedroom, where young Cayla was tied. Tied . . . They had tied Rachel in that hospital. . . . "It was Kella! That's what I finally understood. When they put Rachel back, for the third time, I wanted to know what they were doing to her. So the Lady told the doctors to tell me, and they had to, because the Haywards supported the hospital. All new to me, it was. I never heard of anything like that when I was still working in hospitals. They said they injected her with doses of insulin, making the doses stronger until they put her into deep coma, and they did it five or six times a week until she'd spend fifty hours in coma. No wonder she would look so pale and drained when I saw her sometimes. Fifty hours in coma! It made my mouth dry as sand just to hear about it. But there was something even worse. They said the insulin didn't really help, so they were giving her shock therapy, with electricity. Well, when I heard that, I demanded to *see* it. I had to know what they were doing to her, and the Lady told them they had to let me watch. So they did. They brought in my sweet girl and laid her on a padded table, close to their awful machine. She looked so confused, and kind of wild, too, but she knew who I was. She said, "Is that you, Hessie? Are they after you, too?' Then they put a restraint sheet over her thighs, and one of the nurses held her arms and shoulders. Another one forced her mouth open and pushed in a tongue depressor and held her chin tight with the other hand. And they smeared some kind of paste on both sides of her forehead and brought the wires up so they touched her skin, and then the doctor put his finger on the button and she, she, she . . . Her jaw snapped down in spite of the nurse holding her chin, and she rose up off the table as hard and curved as a bow, like someone was pulling her tight, getting ready to shoot an arrow out from her heart, and she stayed like that so long . . . Oh, oh, oh, oh . . .''

A voice. A voice saying, "Are you all right? Hester, are you all right?"

"Convulsion . . . convulsion . . . And when it was over she was as dazed as a drunk. Her jaw hanging crooked, and saliva . . . She looked right at me and never blinked or knew me. Her jaw had been dislocated. They said that happened sometimes. I had seen a lot of things when I worked in the hospitals, terrible things that you train yourself not to . . . But I never saw anything like that. They just pressed one button, and her body went like a bow. They did it to her for more than a year. Three times a week, they said. Dear Lord, what they did to my darling girl . . .''

The young doctor. Very close, clutching the arm. "Take it easy, Hester. It's all right."

"No! No! It's not all right! They torture her, you see, because of who she is. That's what I finally understood, after I'd been there and watched it. You made the Lady say Rachel isn't a Hayward, but it's not true. She *is*. She belongs to Kella, you see, just the way I told her. Kella's power is stronger than blood, and Kella finally claimed what belonged to her. All the times Rachel acted so strange—that was Kella, taking over. Coming back. That's what I didn't understand for so long. I knew my Rachel was special, but I didn't realize Kella had hosen her as the vehicle of her return. *That's* what the six toes meant! And of course Kella had to suffer again, the way she did before. But they couldn't do that. They couldn't put her to the humbscrews and the fire, so they used their insulin coma and heir electric shocks, torturing her.''

Eyes that didn't believe. Black eyes. Her own daughter! 'Yes, young miss, it's true. Your mother is Kella, come back! know! Because I loved her. More than *you* did, even more han the Lady. . . . I loved her and took care of her! And now he's Kella, come back!''

21

There was silence.

Hester's words hung in it, as heavy a presence as that of the room's many objects. The faster the words came from her, the more rigid her position: fingers gripping the sides of the chair, the cords in her neck as tight as metal, and her whole face straining with the effort of trying to will her belief into the minds of her two listeners.

Cayla looked as if she was going to be sick. She put the palms of her hands together and lifted them, thumbs under her chin and fingers against her nose. Her eyes closed.

"You don't believe me," Hester said petulantly.

Stefan put his hands on her shoulders. "Come on, Hester, sit back now. Just sit back and relax." She resisted his guidance but finally sank into the chair as if the hump on her back were a weight that unbalanced her.

"You don't believe me," she repeated, her voice sinking, too—no rasp left in it, and no energy.

Stefan stood up. "It's nearly over. Just a few more things the spirits want you to tell me. It won't be much longer now, and then you can have as much rest as you'd like. I know you'd like to rest."

"Oh, yes. Yes." Her hands clenched. "But now I've . . . I'm . . . Who will look after the Lady?" Suddenly the gray eyes were swimming.

"Don't worry about Mrs. Randall. She'll be fine." Stefan took her hands, pulled them apart and placed them in her lap. "You told Cora Trent about Rachel's sign, the six toes on her left foot, didn't you?"

"She liked to hear . . . Nothing wrong with that. Nothing! Why do you do this to us . . . ? Why do you upset the Lady . . . ?" She began to rock back and forth.

Stefan took out the locket again and held it in front of her eyes. "You showed this locket to Cora Trent one day, didn't you? Because she was your friend?"

"Yes. . . . Why do you make me . . . Why do you upset the . . . Oh, the Lady, the Lady . . ." She rocked more quickly.

"Did Cora Trent steal the locket?"

"I don't know! I don't know, I don't know anything except what I've done to the Lady. . . ." The face that had been so withered was no longer dry, but instead of lifting to wipe her eyes, her hands locked over her kneecaps, and the tears ran unchecked.

"Did you show the Kella Hagaward letter to Cora Trent?"

"No, no, I wouldn't do anything against the Lady's wishes . . . but now I've . . . I'll have to leave her, you'll take me away. . . ."

"Did you recite the Kella Hagaward letter to Cora Trent?" The rocking and the crying became more violent.

"Answer me! Did you recite the Kella Hagaward letter to Cora?"

"I don't know! Maybe I did! I don't remember! She was no friend. The only friend is my Lady . . . my Lady. . . . You'll take me away from her. . . ."

Suddenly she stopped rocking, threw back her head so far that the tears reversed their downward tracks and began to emit a low, animal howl that signaled the permanent end of speech, and perhaps of more than speech.

Stefan looked at her wordlessly for a moment. Then he stepped back and turned to Cayla, who was shaking her head in small movements and holding her cheeks as if they hurt. "We do have to call someone," he said. "A hospital, maybe the one where your mother is. Or the police—after all, she's guilty of kidnapping and attempted murder."

Cayla lowered her hands and sighed.

Two and a half hours later she held her hands out to the fire in the library.

John had brought coffee and sandwiches for her and Stefan, just as he had the last time they were together in the room, except that this time he had kept muttering all the while, "Young Miss Cayla upstairs the whole time, and Hester gone crazy, who would have thought it? Young Miss Cayla up in Hester's room all the time, and Hester gone crazy."

Stefan had said, when he left, "Was he always so ineffectual?"

"I don't remember, I'm afraid. But anyone willing to stay on here would hardly be ambitious and authoritative, would he?"

"I still can't believe you grew up in this house. I think the place should be condemned. I think you should take your grandmother out of it and put her in some private hospital."

"I could never make her leave. But I'll get her a nurse. Nurses plural, maybe. Shouldn't she have someone around the clock?"

"Let me worry about that," Stefan said. "I'll make some calls in the morning and have someone sent out. You should be having a sandwich, you know. Good Lord, can you believe I'm doing it again—telling you to eat?"

She smiled, for the first time that night, and did as he suggested. They ate in silence, not quite looking at each other, and when they were finished, Cayla got up and went to hold her hands out to the fire, and they went back to talking about what happened because it was a safer and easier subject than that of their relationship, to which neither of them had yet referred.

She said, "Do you think Hester knew what she was doing?"

"You mean tonight, or all through the years?"

"Both."

"Oh, she knew, all right—in some way, at some point in her life. But does she know now, in the sense of realizing how aberrant and destructive her actions are? Almost certainly not."

"So she's not responsible for them?"

"I told you that was one of the hardest questions in psychiatry—to decide when and how something stops being volitional." Stefan leaned back in his chair and stared up at the ceiling, where the tatters of gold leaf hung. "I said nothing ever shocked me anymore, but this really is extraordinary. For decades they sat here in virtual isolation, she and your grandmother, brewing up their own unique mix of spiritualism and Satanism and God knows what else."

"Haywardism," Cayla said softly.

He looked at her. She had put her right hand around her left wrist and begun to rub it. "Do your wrists still hurt?" he asked.

"Not really. It's just . . . nice to be able to move my hands." In a moment she added, "If I had called the police, everything would have had to go on the public record. The last thing I want is more publicity. I can't bear people to know about . . . any of it."

"Of course."

"Oh, Lord," she said suddenly and swung around to face Stefan. "The Senate hearing. I never asked you— Did it start on Thursday? How was it? What happened?"

"I didn't see the full coverage, but it appears that so far it's a battle between Canfield of New York and Bell of Arkansas, who surprised everybody by suddenly acquiring a voice, and a rather loud fundamentalist one."

"The office will have a tape or a transcript for me. Whom did you talk to at the office, by the way? How were they?"

"Your secretary. She was very precise, but not so calm when it came to your absence."

"I can't believe I haven't called her yet. I will in a minute." But Cayla turned back to the fire and held her hands out to it again. "I feel so detached from that world. From the fact that I have to testify at a Senate hearing—even from the lab. I'd never have thought Biologiconn could get that far away from me."

"Kidnappings and knife threats have a way of focusing your mind on survival."

"Yes, but . . . It hasn't even really penetrated that we may have found a link between Rowan Hall and Polly Whiting."

Stefan ticked off the points on one hand. "A woman who believed in spiritualism, who may well have heard the Kella Hagaward letter, and whose name is the same one Polly used at Red Cloud."

"It adds up, doesn't it?" Cayla said slowly. She turned from the fire. "How did you know Cora's last name was Trent? How did you know her father's name? How did you know she and Hester held séances?"

Stefan told her about Dorcas's notebook. "I wondered whether the name of Cora's friend could possibly be Hester instead of Esther. I thought it was just possible that she was *this* Hester. But I didn't expect to hit paydirt the way I did."

"If they were such good friends, why didn't Hester hear from Cora after she left Rowan Hall?"

"We'll probably never know. But the fact that both she and Polly were in the Red Cloud files—Cora in my grandmother's notebook and Polly in the drawers of cards—that's another connecting link."

"I'll call the detectives in the morning and have them stop looking for the ex-chauffeur and start on Cora Trent."

The fire snapped. Cayla started, and then rubbed her wrist again. "I know it should make a difference to me that Hester is ill," she said. "But I can't seem to make that matter. She's . . . I still think she's . . ."

"Horrible?"

"Yes. Worse than Gran, according to the things she said."

"Yes."

"Talking about how much she loved Rachel . . . Mother . . . describing herself as the loving guardian . . . And all the time she was doing things that must have encouraged, must have positively nurtured any schizophrenic tendencies Mother might have inherited from your—" She stopped abruptly, pulled her hands away from the fire as if they had touched it directly, and locked them behind her.

"Yes," Stefan said quietly.

"I suppose it offends a psychotherapist to hear someone say a mentally ill person is horrible."

"Mental illness is an explanation. It's not absolution. To lose the ability to recognize and deal with reality is not only the most horrible thing that can happen to a person but it is potentially one of the most dangerous. A mental patient can do things you can't forgive, no matter how much you might come to understand them."

After a moment Cayla said, "I'm sorry. I forgot that the man who killed your . . . Barbara was a mental patient."

Stefan didn't answer, merely watched her as she gazed into

209

the fire. The jeans and yellow sweater revealed the slender so⟩
ness of her body.

At length he said, "I'm sure they'll take good care of Hest⟩
at the hospital. Dr. Patrick seemed very competent. And ve⟩
devoted, to come out here at ten-thirty on a Saturday night.⟩

"We finance the hospital. And he knows how upset we a⟩
were that the press found out about Rachel . . . abo⟩
Mother." She sighed again. "I wonder whether Mother wi⟩
recognize Hester."

"I expect they'll be kept in separate parts of the hospital.⟩

"Oh. Of course."

The ormolu clock at the other end of the room began to stri⟩
the hour in a silvery voice.

When the twelfth note had sounded, Cayla said, "It's late.⟩

Stefan got to his feet. "Shall I drive you to your apartment?⟩

"No," she said quickly. "No." She turned around to fac⟩
him. For the first time since he had found her on Hester's be⟩
and untied her, she looked at him directly, without the prote⟩
tive screen of the concerns of the past hours. Their eyes hel⟩

"I don't like to leave you," he said softly.

"No." It was part question, part confirmation.

"I mean, leave you alone, here in this house."

"I've probably never been safer, with Hester gone."

"But after everything you've been through tonight—"

"It's my own fault, you know. That's what I have to face.⟩
I hadn't been so anxious to avoid this place and everything co⟩
nected with it, if I hadn't come here as little as possible, wi⟩
my eyes shut when I did come, then I would have known mor⟩
about what's been going on. And if I'd known, I could hav⟩
stopped it. I could have, you know. I could have sent Hest⟩
away years ago, and gotten better care for Gran and—"

She stopped because he had gone to her and gripped her arm⟩
with both hands.

"Don't," he said. "Don't berate yourself like that."

Then they both froze, aware that his impulsive movemen⟩
had brought their bodies to within inches of each other and to⟩
point of contact. Her glance fell downward, to the white shi⟩
beneath his gray suit jacket, and then lifted again, slowly, t⟩
the hollow at the base of his throat, visible because he ha⟩
taken off his tie, and finally to his mouth and eyes.

They were moving even closer, his mouth and eyes, whe⟩

she said, too loudly, "Does it matter to you that we're first cousins?"

"I don't give a damn about it. Do you?"

When she didn't answer, he released her arms and moved back. In a moment, as if nothing had happened, he said, "OK, if I can't persuade you to leave this house with me, I'd better get going myself. Are you sure you're all right?"

"Yes," she whispered. "I just . . . I just need time to think."

"I understand."

"Do you? It seems too much to ask, on top of everything else."

"Just try to get some rest," he said. "And don't sleep in your old room with all those childhood ghosts. Why don't you sleep in here, by the fire? Or does this room have a lot of associations, too?"

"Not really."

But when he had left, she looked around the room and knew that it did have associations. It still held his presence.

22

"My friends, our fight against the influence of Satan is never-ending, for he whispers in the ears of God's enemies and makes their voice loud. We hear that voice on all sides. It claims our schools should not teach the great story of the creation. It claims our schools *should* teach works of depravity and atheistic communism. It claims our courts were right to legalize the murder of the unborn. And now it is claiming that science should be permitted to tamper with the work of our Lord—with life itself."

It was Sunday morning, and the voice of the speaker—who had completed his most recent tour of the Southeast—was being raised in the decidedly modest space of his home church in Georgia. But his audience was not small. Every pew was filled, there were rows of chairs in the back and the aisles, and the microphones of the radio network of the Coalition for Traditional Values poked above the pulpit like nightsticks raised against enemy attack.

"My friends," the speaker said, "we can take some small credit, I think. Because the legislators of this great nation, this nation whose values we must defend, are now holding public debate on the issue of this tampering with creation—or genetic engineering, as those who practice it prefer to call it. But we must keep our efforts strong, my friends, so that we may prevail."

"Amen," cried several voices.

"The scientists say what they do is good because they're curing a child's genetic defect. But that denies the child's redemption by Christ! The Bible teaches that only Christ can make men whole. The lame and the halt and the blind are to be raised up and restored in Heaven by Christ, not repaired in some laboratory on earth!"

"Amen!"

"In the weeks ahead those who falsely worship science will raise their voices loud and strong—and our voices must be stronger than theirs!"

"Amen! Praise the Lord!"

"So, my friends, let us once more prepare to do His bidding, to make our voices heard in the very capital of this great nation of ours, whose values we defend in His name and for His eternal glory. Let us march to that capital, as many of us as are able. Let us march to show those who dwell in the seat of power that the will of God cannot be denied! And let us carry with us the words of Luke, chapter one, verse thirty-seven, 'For with God nothing shall be impossible.' "

"Amen! Praise Him and all His holy works!"

"Now, my friends, let us bow our heads and pray for His wisdom and guidance in our continuing fight."

The churchful of heads obeyed, like rows of flowers cut with a single stroke.

Stefan was heading west on the turnpike, trying to find some music on his car radio. But he kept getting broadcasts of church services. He checked the clock; Connecticut, like so much of the country at ten-forty on Sunday morning, was obviously at worship. Finally he got a station that said it was playing golden oldies, although he had never heard the songs before. You realized you were forty, he thought, when there was a whole generation of "oldies" you hadn't grown up with.

He had spent the night in a motel near Rowan Hall, telling himself he wanted to be nearby when he phoned Cayla in the morning to make sure she was all right. That was true, of course. He had phoned her, and she was all right, although he could tell that the cloak of impersonality and efficiency was in place again. The cloak, he thought, was her means of surviving difficulties. And to her, perhaps that last word was superfluous.

But he had had another reason for staying overnight in Connecticut. He had told Dr. Patrick he might stop by the hospital, on the family's behalf, to see where and how Hester had settled in. He hadn't discussed it with Cayla. There was no need to involve her.

Anyway, it wasn't really Hester he wanted to see.

No purpose would be served by going to see Rachel Randall; he knew that. But now he knew where she was and would be passing by on his way home . . .

He shook his head impatiently. He simply wanted to see the woman who was Dorcas's daughter and his own aunt. Was any other reason needed?

Dr. Patrick was not there but had left word that Dr. Veere was to be accorded every courtesy.

A woman in her thirties, with a firm handshake and a manner to match, came out to greet him. "Lorraine Scott," she said. "I'm the senior psychiatrist on duty today, but I only joined the staff last Monday, so I'm not really an expert on the place, I'm afraid."

Stefan smiled. "As long as you know where the patients are."

He knew the hospital only by reputation, which was a very good one. As Dr. Scott led him down tiled corridors, the feel and the smell of the place reminded him of the state psychiatric hospital in which he had done his training, but the look was different. The walls weren't institutional green, the nursing stations didn't look like prison control centers, and the windows, although reinforced with wire, gave on a landscape of green velvet and trees. There was also a pond ringed with azaleas ready to spring into color. Hayward money, Stefan thought, had done as much as could be done for such a place.

Hester was asleep, sedated, in a narrow bed with metal sides, in a room whose spare, bright furnishings provided the greatest possible contrast to her quarters at Rowan Hall. In fact everything about her looked different. Above the white hospital gown her face was free of the mistrust and hostility that had sharpened her gaunt features into knives. At her age, of course, that serenity could be achieved only by drugs.

For the record Stafan asked Dr. Scott in some detail about the treatment Hester would be getting. Then he said, "You have another patient here from the Hayward family—Rachel Randall."

Dr. Scott looked quizzical. "Dr. Patrick said you're a friend of the Hayward family. Presumably they told you about Rachel?"

"Of course."

"I'm not sure there's any 'of course' about it. One of the first things I was told was that her true identity is not supposed to be known—she's 'Rachel Brown' here, both in person and on all her records. There was that unfortunate publicity about her a few weeks ago—I was in Philadelphia, but I saw it in the papers there—and everyone is still pretty uptight about it."

"I understand," Stefan said. "Did they ever find out how the tabloids got hold of the story?"

"Dr. Patrick says they suspect a former employee, but there's no way of proving it."

"I'd like to see her."

"Rachel Randall? You want to *see* her?"

"Yes. I mean that literally—just look, not examine her or even talk to her. Is there some problem about it?"

"Well, no, I suppose not. Since you come from the Haywards. Actually I haven't met her yet myself. Let me just find out which wing she's in."

She was not in her room. They found her in a dayroom, which was large and pleasant, with a TV at each end, furniture arranged in seating groups, and flowers on some of the end tables. There were about a dozen patients, a few talking to one another but the rest silent, with the intense, autistic quiet that could be the most terrible of all the sounds in a psychiatric hospital. Only one patient looked up when Stefan and Dr. Scott came in. She cocked her head, grimaced at them, and then went back inside herself.

After Dr. Scott checked at the nursing station, she said, "Apparently that's Rachel over there with her back to us, staring out the window." They moved closer to her.

Her shoulders looked thin, and a heavy braid hung down the back of her red terry robe. She was not as tall, Stefan thought, as her mother Dorcas had been. As her daughter Cayla was.

From behind them, on the other side of the room, a patient gave an enormous groan and then was silent.

"Hello, Rachel," the doctor said. "I'm Dr. Lorraine Scott. I'm new here, and I've been wanting to come by and meet you."

Rachel turned around.

Stefan thought he heard Dr. Scott suck in her breath, but his gaze didn't leave Rachel. He didn't know quite what he had expected—perhaps some dark reflection of Dorcas's eyes or some echo of the sharpness in her nose or cheekbones. But there was nothing, only a hint in the slant of the mouth. Perhaps Rachel had looked more like her mother once, but the disease had superimposed its own mask.

Her hands flew to her temples. Her fingers splayed out and stayed in the air for at least ten seconds, they slid down her cheeks and locked over her mouth.

"Yes, it is," Dr. Scott said softly, almost to herself.

Stefan started to turn to her, but Rachel spoke.

"Hello? Hello. Hello. Hello." Once more her hands lifted to her temples in the same gesture. "Full. So full. Can't hold any more. Doctor, I must be taken out of this place at once, before they poison the food to keep me from singing." Her eyes, as dark as Cayla's, swung to Stefan. "I must be taken out of this place and returned to the fire in the square, so my song can be heard in the kingdoms of heaven and hell. I consider that their interference with my song constitutes an act of treason and treachery." She took a step toward Stefan and looked at him beseechingly. "Have you come to take me out of this place?"

Never in his professional life had he wanted so badly to help someone, and been so sure there was no help. He felt knocked backward in time—to that day in his adolescence when, in the course of his insatiable reading about psychology and the mind, he had learned that there was no known anatomical difference between the brain of a mental patient and that of a normal person. He had been shocked, and realized he had been assuming that aberrant behavior like Dorcas's came from something he would one day learn to see under a microscope, like malignant cells. But if that was not so, he had thought, then what was the value, or the rightness, of treating mental patients by physical means? What were treatments like electric shock aimed *at,* if the person's brain was physically no different from his own?

Later, of course, he learned there was considerable evidence of *physiological* change in the brains of the mentally ill. In any case, as he soon discovered, doctors prescribed many medications, including even aspirin, without knowing exactly how they achieved their healing effects. Lack of that knowledge did not prevent the healing.

But as he stared at Rachel Randall, he felt once more his adolescent sense of shock over the state of knowledge in psychiatry—which sometimes seemed little better than witch doctoring because it treated the psychoses even though it barely understood their etiology. Among the causes once postulated for schizophrenia were an accumulation of poisons from infected teeth, a chemical found in patients' urine, a substance in their sweat, an inability to metabolize copper . . . and such explanations had come to little more than the primitive notion that madness was caused by evil spirits.

The sad creature standing before him—his aunt—had undergone electroconvulsive therapy and insulin comas and no doubt all the other physical treatments, like dialysis and drug therapy, as they came in and out of vogue—all except lobotomy. At least she had been spared that.

And what had they achieved? She was still locked in her private prison, unable to grasp what a child could learn easily: that the world her thoughts created was not the real world.

Without realizing, he reached for one of her hands. She did not resist, and he looked into her eyes, trying to force his vision along their twisted corridors to reach the brain and its thoughts. . . .

Green, the eyes are green. Green is always against me. Everything green is against me, the grass and trees that refuse to let e pass over them. . . . But red is with me. He has red hair. ike Vivaldi. The red priest of Venice. Will he take me away to ing? My song is the cabaletta that has transcended the pheres. My song is the causal connecting link that precipitates he joining of heaven and hell. Maybe he came, with green in he eyes, from THEM. No, no, the voices would not come to me n the shape of green eyes. The voices will wait, they'll stay si- ent until I'm alone, and then they will shriek WITCH! WITCH VHO LAY WITH LUCIFER, WHO GAVE HIM THE DAUGH- ER WITH BLACK HAIR! WITCH! BITCHWITCH! LET THE IRE COME CRACKLING TO HER AS SHE SINGS IN THE QUARE. . . . Full. So full. Can't hold any more. It's grow- ng. They put things into the head when I sleep. It's getting too ull, it can't hold any more. . . . In view of the tessitura lying o high, in view of the appoggiatura, in view of the passaggio hat is negotiated so smoothly, one must consider that my vocal ords are never to be examined or touched. Any interference vith them is an act of treason and treachery. The red priest has eard me sing, he knows I am the canticle of all that rises from he earth and condensates into the song of the earth. He will ake me out, to the fire in the square, where I must sing. Yes. es. Yes. Yes, yes, no, no, no, NO. GREEN IS AGAINST ME. ILL GREEN IS ALWAYS AGAINST ME. THEY LOOK COOL IND GREEN, BUT ONLY TO SLIP POISON INTO MY 3ODY, INTO MY THROAT. NEVER LET GREEN TOUCH THE BODY OR THE THROAT!

Rachel jerked her hand away.

Stefan said to Dr. Scott, "All right. I guess we may as well go."

After a moment she nodded. But her eyes were narrowed and her manner preoccupied.

When they were back in the tiled corridor, she said, "That was a very odd experience."

"It certainly was."

She stopped. "Do you mean you know her too?"

He stopped too. "What do you mean by 'know her'?"

"Just that. She was a patient in Philadelphia when I was doing my residency there. But we didn't know who she was hen. She was just a Jane Doe. The police had found her wan- ering on the streets, and we never could get a coherent history from her. Most of the time she was delusional, and when she had periods of lucidity, she would simply withdraw. To think she turned out to be part of the Hayward family! I wonder how they found her."

"I don't think it could be the same woman."

"But there's no question! The only difference is her hair. It was short then. Otherwise she's just the same, including that automatic mannerism, hands flying up and sliding back down, which I remember very well."

"I'm absolutely positive," Stefan said slowly, "that Rachel Randall has been here, in this hospital, for thirty years."

He knew he was staring, like Dr. Scott. But he doubted she could be having the same suspicion he was.

23

Cayla ended a meeting with her lawyers in the small conference room and walked briskly down the hall to her office.

Her secretary smiled broadly—they had all smiled broadly since she had "reappeared" the week before—and said, "The man from the agency is here. I told him to wait inside."

"Good." Cayla walked even more briskly into the office and shook the hand of the senior operative at one of the best detective agencies in the Northeast. "You got here quickly," she said

"You told me you wanted the news right away, in person. I figure you're paying to get what you want."

"That's why you're handling my business." Cayla went to her desk, signaled him to take a chair opposite, and pushed her hands through her hair. She wore a linen jumper the color of espresso and a matching silk shirt. Her only jewelry was a pearl ring. "Tell me everything you've learned and how you learned it."

"Right. Well, according to the information you gave me, a

roman named Cora Trent left Rowan Hall in 1933 and went to farm in southern Pennsylvania, on the edge of West Virginia. That's the same area where Polly Whiting's family, the Kendalls, were living at that time. So we went back there again. Only this time we spread out and went beyond the town near their farm. We looked in every little village or hamlet within a thirty-mile radius. And sure enough, in a little place called Spoonerville there was a Herman Trent family back in the 1930s. The local paper didn't have issues any farther back than the forties—they'd had a fire that year—but there were records in the town hall. And one of them showed that the Trent household had two kids: John and Cora.''

''Ah,'' Cayla said with satisfaction.

''The hard part was locating somebody who'd known the family. We spent five days combing the area, but apparently old man Trent sold his farm during the war and moved away. Finally we got lucky. Somebody had an old aunt in a nursing home, and she turned out to have known Cora Trent pretty well. Her mind wandered some, but she told us she and Cora Trent had gone to high school with an Esther Cole, who married John Kendall and became Polly Whiting's mother. So we—''

''My God,'' Cayla said softly. ''Esther. Her good friend *was* named Esther after all, not Hester. We forgot the name of Polly Whiting's mother.''

''Beg pardon, Ms. Hayward? I forgot something?''

''No, no. Dr. Veere and I. We were so focused on . . . oh, never mind. So Cora went to high school with Polly Whiting's mother?''

''Yup. In fact the old woman said Esther and Cora Trent had been best friends. She said when Cora came back from working up north—from your grandmother's place, that would be—she used to spend a lot of time with Esther Kendall. She went over to their farm whenever she could get away from her own father.''

''Did she remember Cora's talking about Rowan Hall? About things that happened there? Did she by any chance, please God, remember seeing the locket in Cora's possession?''

The detective shook his head. ''Negative to most of that, I'm afraid. She did recall that Cora said she'd worked at a big house

219

on the ocean, for a very rich family. And she said Cora believed in 'a lot of nonsense about the spirit world,' but that was about it.''

"Damn," Cayla said softly.

"Yup. On the other hand, she was very clear about Cora spending a lot of time on the Kendall farm. She said Cora was real fond of Esther Kendall's daughter.''

"Polly Whiting!"

"Yup. Cora used to look after her when the parents were busy. Had her for a month or two once, the old lady thought, when the parents were sick or something. Cora used to say the child was sensitive to the spirit world, or words to that effect.''

"Cora Trent actually had Polly living with her at one time?''

"That's what the old lady in the nursing home remembered. So, that's the good news. The bad news, like I told you on the phone, is that Cora Trent is dead. Over twenty years ago, out in Washington State, according to the old lady. They lost touch for a long time, and then Cora started sending her Christmas cards from Seattle. We haven't gone after the death certificate yet. Shall we?''

Cayla sighed. "I suppose so. For the record. Was she married? Did she have children? They might know about the locket.''

"Never got married, the old lady said. But we can check.''

Cayla placed her hands flat on the desk. "It's not everything I hoped for, but it's good. Quite good. Thanks very much.''

"My pleasure," the detective said. He laid an envelope on the desk. "Everything's written out here. Dates, places, all that. Transcript of my conversation with the old woman.''

As he was leaving, Cayla said, "Did you ever find any evidence that Polly Whiting had a son who died before he was two?''

"Nope. But there's a gap in her life, a couple of years before she got married. We're still looking.''

When he was gone, Cayla flexed her fingers. She lifted her hands, turned them over, and started to smile. She felt foolish, sitting there grinning at her own palms, but she couldn't help it. A connection with Polly had been found, if not solidified.

A woman had worked at Rowan Hall at the time the locket disappeared. She would have known that the child of the house had a deformity. She had been friendly with Hester and shared er belief in the supernatural, so she probably heard Hester explain the deformity as some kind of sign that the child was cursed. It was equally likely that Hester told her about the Kella Jagaward letter—even recited it to her. And then that woman had returned to her hometown and her good friend, whose daughter Polly she was fond of and looked after. So no doubt she told her all about the letter from a dead witch and the "cursed" baby with six toes. And as a keepsake of their shared interest she could have given Polly the locket.

Cora could have told her about Camp Red Cloud. Then, when Polly the adult went there—probably afraid to use her real name because her religion frowned on spiritualism—it would be natural for her to use Cora's name instead of her own.

Cayla's eyes went to the phone. She wanted badly to pick it up, to call Stefan and tell him. Just to hear what he would say. How he would sound. But could she go on calling him, involving him in her life when she didn't know whether he could share it?

She picked up the envelope the detective had left. It weighed little in her hand, but if the contents were made public, they would crush the Whiting woman. The newspapers would love the exposé. The tabloids would revel in it. It would be all over television. She smiled again, feeling a dark, sweet jolt of satisfaction.

Then, as clearly as if they were in the room, Cayla saw the clan's faces, horrified at the idea of telling the story of the locket. It could lead easily to the story of Rachel's adoption, and then to more pieces in the tabloids about her illness and her delusions. And as a result other stories could be rattled out of the closet: Gran's belief in a family curse, Hester's craziness and cruelty, the childhood of young Cayla Hayward . . .

The envelope slid from her hand, and there, in the starkly efficient office, she felt the claws and amber eyes of the nightmare bulging at the edge of her vision.

She leaped to her feet. The nightmare had never before invaded the office, or any part of her life connected with Biologiconn. It had confined itself to the dark, and to sleep. But the week before, when she had been tied to Hester's bed, it had come while she was awake, creeping into that stale, crowded room. And now it had crept into the one place where she had

never felt threatened, where she could let herself becom
deeply involved, without reservations.

What was frightening wasn't the nightmare itself, but th
fact that an adult who tried to live by the exercise of her intelli
gence could be prey to something so irrational. That her hea
could be set racing and her skin turned cold and wet by a mer
dream.

She sank back into her desk chair and picked up the envelop
again, wondering how she had ever imagined that a link be
tween Polly Whiting and the Hayward family could be expose
without also exposing the family's ugly secrets and harming th
Industries.

The answer came: She had been acting blindly, thinkin;
only of destroying the woman who had brought back the night
mares, who made her feel as threatened in the world of he
work as she had once been at Rowan Hall.

Blindness, she thought, had characterized her response t
Stefan, too. Her silk blouse slid against her skin like goose
flesh.

The problem wasn't that they were blood relatives, unset
tling though that discovery had been. The problem was tha
from the beginning she had behaved like a schoolgirl who be
lieved love occurred by lighting bolt. She had let herself fee
too close to him—as if, she thought wryly, they were kindre
spirits. She had been ready to sleep with Stefan—and to commi
herself to more than that—on the very night she learned he wa:
her first cousin. Learning it was a sign that she had been led by
her feelings and should pull back and think long and hard be
fore she did anything.

She reached for the phone, then punched the intercom butto
instead. "Janet," she said to her secretary, "I'm going to leave
early, to do some last-minute preparation for the Senate hearing
tomorrow. Tell Leslie Hatch to meet me at the airport at six
thirty in the morning. Also, call the detective agency and as
them to deliver a copy of the report they just gave me to Dr.
Stefan Veere."

Senator Moroni Gray looked out over the room in which his
hearing was now in the middle of its third week. There was no
more space even to stand.

Outside the building were two clashing phenomena: a lighthearted, beatific spring day with Senate pages stretching on the lawn, kites soaring above the Washington Monument, and spectacular displays of cherry blossoms, azaleas, and daffodils everywhere one looked; and a militantly righteous crowd of protesters, many of whom had found seats inside the room.

Although some in the crowd had carried signs of a purely political and economic nature—DRUG COMPANIES EXPLOIT THE SICK, AND THE POOR and NO GENE-SPLICING FOR PROFIT—the majority of the protesters were from the Coalition for Traditional Values, who had chosen to appear that week because of the witnesses who were scheduled. Their signs had read ONLY GOD SHOULD "PLAY GOD" and GENE-SPLICING IS A SATANIC BUSINESS. One placard had said EVEN THE ATHEISTIC HUMANIST IS WORRIED, apparently referring to the scientist who had testified the week before: Although he had declared that God was a superstition, he was uncomfortable with the idea that human DNA could become corporate property. Another sign read WHEN SATAN SPEAKS, DOES HAYWARD INDUSTRIES LISTEN?

The press coverage, Gray knew, would again be excellent that night. Indeed, so far it had been all he could hope for.

He glanced at the pocket watch propped before him and then along the tables to his left and right, where the other committee members were either shuffling papers or speaking to aides, except for Parker Bell of Arkansas whose head was bowed, as was his custom at the start of each day. Gray cleared his throat loudly, a sound the microphones turned into storm warnings, and gaveled the hearing open once more.

The day before, the chief executive officer of a drug firm had testified. He had been questioned closely about the ties between his company and several universities and on the nature of the research in progress. As with all the previous witnesses, Parker Bell, supported to some extent by Senators Packman and O'Toole, had tried to determine the speaker's religious beliefs and to relate them, or the lack of them, to the scientific work in question. "Point of order" had been cried so many times that Gray had begun to hear the phrase in his dreams.

When the chairs at the witness table were filled he peered at them, frowned, and then said to the distinguished-looking man close to the microphone, "Sir, you are Dr. Leslie Hatch, head of research at Biologiconn?"

The man leaned into the microphone. "No, Senator, I not."

One of Gray's aides was tapping him on the shoulder, but didn't turn around. "You're not Dr. Hatch? I was told D Hatch was here and ready to go."

"I am," said another voice.

"*You're* Dr. Leslie Hatch?" Gray said.

"Yes, Senator. The gentleman next to me is one of the la yers for my company, Biologiconn."

"But you're—" Gray stopped himself, pushed his hair ba over his collar and continued in an avuncular tone. "I know t president of your company is a lady, but nobody told me y were going to be a lady, too."

"I hope I am one already, Senator," Leslie Hatch's voi was very polite, but there was a murmur of amusement fro some of the audience.

Gray's hand closed on his gavel, but he didn't use it ar went on affably. "I can see you're a lady, and one just a lovely as this beautiful spring day, and to tell you the truth, I' glad. I think these hearings could use a little feminine pulchr tude." He smiled.

Leslie Hatch did not. "I hope you were told that I have statement I'd like to read, Senator."

"Yes, yes," Gray said. "Please go right ahead with it."

"Thank you." She glanced at the seven members of th committee, all looking at her attentively, picked up her pape and began. The TV cameras trained on her, knowing goo copy when they saw it: a trim figure in a yellow linen suit, face framed by shiny blond hair, and a background, describe in a low, pleasant voice, that involved degrees granted wit honors and training gained in one of the country's finest lab:

"Biologiconn has become one of the leading genetic-engi neering companies," she continued, "thanks to Cayla Hay ward, who has managed the company with great skill and wit an understanding of the scientific issues that I think is unusu in a businessman or -woman. Of course she can speak for her self, as you'll hear when she takes this chair. But there's been good deal of nonsense about her in the press, so I thought yo should hear from those who work with her—and believe me, speak for all of Biologiconn—that she is a truly fine executiv and human being."

In her seat to the right of and slightly behind Leslie, Cayla felt that every eye in the room, both human and camera, was on her. She hadn't known Leslie would say such things. It was imperative that she not move because if she did, she would cry. It would be exactly like the time at the university when she had closeted herself in the library to read about the history of Hayward Industries and had found herself dripping tears on the books. But this was worse, because it would be on television, in front of the whole country.

She locked her hands tightly under the witness table and managed to keep looking calmly at the side of Leslie's head. But she heard little of what else Leslie was saying. Presumably it was what had been planned: that although Biologiconn, like any other company, couldn't reveal details of the projects it was working on, she would describe the project that had garnered so much attention. In fact Leslie was doing that, giving her usual lucid presentation of the technology, stressing the challenges involved and the safeguards that had been in operation.

It was Parker Bell's voice, when Leslie had finished and the questioning was under way, that snapped Cayla's mind back to full attention. "Dr. Hatch," Bell said, "I'm wondering how you reconcile the work you do with your purely womanly concerns."

"And what would those be, Senator?"

"Now, now, Doctor. I think you understand me, I surely do. I'm referring to your being a wife and a mother. Now, supposing you were pregnant and you knew your child had some kine of genetic defect. Would you let them do to *you* what they're doing to the mother with this Tay-Sachs child? This woman who won't even come forward and tell us who she is?"

There was considerable stirring in the audience. "In the first place, Senator," Leslie said coolly, "nothing is being *done* to the Tay-Sachs mother, in the sense you intend to convey. As I've already explained, everything is happening with her full knowledge and consent. Perhaps you've forgotten that one of the parents actually works in the field of genetic engineering, so they certainly knew exactly what they were doing. In the second place, you have the sequence wrong. It isn't the case that the woman discovered she was pregnant. She and her husband deliberately permitted the *in vitro* fertilization of her ovum with his sperm."

Parker Bell lifted his eyes to the room's high ceiling. "I think you're deliberately misunderstanding me, Miss Hatch, I—"

"*Dr.* Hatch," snapped Fred Canfield into his microphone.

Senator Gray reached for his gavel, but Bell said, "Yes, excuse me, ma'am, I know it's Dr. Hatch, but I still think you're misunderstanding me. I'd just like to know if you'd let a child you yourself were carrying be put through this procedure. Be changed from what the Lord intended it to be."

"Point of order!" cried Canfied. "Dr. Hatch is testifying as a scientist, not as a mother."

"I'm not aware of any point of order in that," Gray said. "And I think it would be a service to this committee, and to the country, to hear someone who's a scientist *and* a woman answer the question."

Over the tops of his glasses, Canfield sent a look of furious impatience.

"I don't mind answering," Leslie Hatch said. "If I knew I was likely to have a genetically defective child with a man I loved, I certainly would want to use whatever help recombinant DNA technology could give me. But I must be fair and say I don't think the situation will arise."

"I'm sure we all hope it doesn't," Bell said. "I'm sure we all wish for you to have healthy children."

"Thank you, Senator, but that isn't what I meant. I meant that the situation won't come up because I don't plan to have any children at all."

After a moment of silence, a segment of the audience gave a collective, disapproving "Oh."

Senator Gray gaveled, but Bell went on, his throat working inside the tight confines of his collar. "Do you believe in abortion, too, Dr. Hatch?"

"Point of order!" cried Fred Canfield, and four of the senators on the committee were only moments behind him. As the audience's murmur grew, Gray gaveled furiously and, when he had restored order, announced that the hearing would adjourn until the next morning.

Senate security guards led Leslie and Cayla out of the room as they had led them in. In the hall one of the protesters shouted

226

at them, "You tamper with God's creations! You're Satanists, that's what you are!"

It wasn't until an hour later, when she was in her hotel room, that Cayla had time to focus on the message one of the guards had given her: Would she please call Dr. Stefan Veere in New York, as soon as possible?

Because it was still early in the day, the protesters who had been able to get into the hearing rejoined their colleagues outside the building. Some press people moved among them, hoping for more usable reactions than the committee had provided.

One man said he had been "shocked" by Dr. Hatch's words and was sure she did advocate abortion, even though she hadn't answered the question. He felt "real sorry for that couple who could have a baby with the terrible Jewish disease" and understood why they would want a healthy child. "But God had a reason for giving them a sick child, even if they can't see it, and to try to change what God wants—well, maybe it's not murdering the unborn, but I don't see how it's all that much different than abortion. Both of them defy God's will, don't they?"

The mother of a severely retarded Down's syndrome child said, "God gave us Tommy like he is so we'd have a special love for him. Why, he's wonderful, and that's the way God wanted him to be, not to have his brain fixed up by some kind of deviltry."

A reporter from one of the large Southern dailies was just about to leave when he saw the tall woman in navy who stood behind the Down's syndrome mother, listening intently with an odd, fixed stare. He watched her curiously before he realized who she was. He maneuvered his way over to her and grabbed her arm. She swung around to face him, her free arm lifted as if to ward off a blow.

"Ms. Whiting," he said hastily, and identified himself and his publication.

"Yes?" The word hissed with tension.

"I'm surprised to see you here, Ms. Whiting. You were so definite about wanting nothing more to do with all of this. Can you explain why you came today?"

She lowered her arm slowly. Her pale blue eyes bored into the reporter's without seeing. "I just felt like I had to come.

Like somebody wants to be here. Wants to see. And that somebody is making me come.''

"I understand. Did that somebody see what she wanted?"

"I . . . don't know."

"Could she be waiting for Cayla Hayward to testify?"

Polly's eyes came back from whatever private place they had
been and looked at the reporter's face for the first time.
"Maybe," she said slowly. "Maybe so."

"Ms. Whiting, did you actually get inside the hearing today?"

Polly shook her head.

"Why don't you let me help you get in tomorrow? If you
meet me right here at nine o'clock, I'll see you get in and get a
good seat. Will you let me help you that way?"

"Yes," Polly said. "Yes." She clutched his arm suddenly
"If a child dies when he's just a baby, that's God's will, isn't
it? And nobody should interfere with God's will."

"Er, yes," the reporter said. "That's just what it is."

She turned and moved away from him, her gait both frantic
and aimless. He ran after her and offered to help her to wher-
ever she was staying. But she shook his hand off angrily. He
wondered whether she would in fact return the next day.

24

At seven that evening Stefan was in the reception area of the
hospital. Everything had been arranged and there was nothing
to do but wait for Cayla.

He stood by one of the tall windows, staring at the grounds
that were still dappled with late sun and then at the pond, a
bronze plate with a rich patina. His mood swung with his
glance—between the calm of the pond and the nervous shifting
of the sun patterns.

Finally a car appeared at the end of the drive. Even from that distance it spoke of noiseless elegance and chauffeurs. He went out to meet it. The driver got out, but Cayla opened the door herself. She wore a gauzy dress of a green as dark as bottle glass. Stefan noticed for the first time how long and shapely her legs were.

"Hello," he said. "No problems getting here?"

"No." She came toward him cautiously, like a child who expects a surprise but isn't positive she will like it. "It was all very easy."

"If I hadn't thought it would be, I'd have postponed this. But it's taken me a week to arrange, and I guess I'm impatient."

"You're being so mysterious. Something that involves Mother and that we should see together?"

"Yes, because it can happen only once. But if I tell you what it is, you'll have preconceptions, and I'd rather you didn't. Thanks for trusting me enough to just get on the plane and come."

"After all you've done for me, I would have to come no matter what you said or didn't say."

Stefan smiled. "I didn't know blind obedience was your style."

"Obedience, no. But I can be blind."

The driver asked, "You want me to wait in town, Ms. Hayward?"

"I'm not sure, Carl, I don't know how long I'll—"

"He doesn't need to wait at all," Stefan said. "When we're finished, I'll drive you home, or to the airport, whatever you want."

Cayla started to object, but his eyes held hers. Finally she nodded and told Carl to leave.

As they walked into the building, she said, "When I got the message to call you, I thought it would be about the detectives' report. You did get it?"

"Oh, yes. It's obviously what you were hoping for, a link to your family. But with Cora Trent dead, you're not going to be able to prove some of the connections. People could say it's all just—"

"People aren't going to say anything. I don't dare make the story public."

Stefan stopped and stared at her. "But I thought that was the whole point of looking for a connection to Polly."

"It was. I just hadn't thought of how many other things could come to light. I'd have to talk about Hester and Gran and . . . Do you think I want the whole world knowing about my family and my mother? I wish nobody knew, not even you. No, don't say anything. Let's see whatever it is you have to show me. And then leave."

Stefan lifted his hand, as if to touch her cheek, but instead he ran it through his wiry, auburn hair and told her to wait a minute. He walked over to speak to the man at the reception desk.

Soon an aide appeared and led them through heavy doors and down a hall to one of the small visiting rooms.

When the aide left, Stefan said, "They'll be bringing your mother in a minute. Don't you want to sit down?"

"I'd rather stand." She stood behind one of the tweed chairs, hands digging into its back. Her eyes, fixed on the door, seemed to preclude conversation.

When the door finally opened, a voice out in the hall said, "Go ahead. Yes, yes, it's all right, go on in."

In a moment Rachel came into the room. The door closed behind her. She wore a red-and-white striped dress that made her seem even smaller and thinner than she was. She shoved her hands into its pockets, making her shoulders slump even more, and looked at Cayla. Without changing, her glance went to Stefan. Both her visitors might have been strangers, equally uninteresting. She tossed her head, swinging the thick gray braid, and walked into one corner of the room, from which she turned around to face them.

"Hello," Cayla said.

Rachel regarded her emptily and at length. Then she took her hands from her pockets and said, "Hello."

"It's Cayla, Mother."

"I know. I know that. The many things that I know. Why don't you kiss me?"

Cayla went to her and leaned down to kiss her cheek.

"Mmmmm," Rachel said. Then she exhaled deeply. "Don't come near me. Your dress is green. Green is against me. The things that are always against me."

Cayla looked at Stefan helplessly.

"Just sit down for a minute," he said. "Rachel, wouldn't you like to sit down too?"

Rachel took one hand from her pocket. It clutched a cigarette. "Do you have a match? Does anybody in this room have a match, or do I have to rub your heads together to get a fire?" She cackled, a sound chilling in its lack of humor.

Stefan took a lighter from the pocket of his brown corduroy jacket, snapped it on, and held it out. She looked over her shoulder, leaned forward to catch the flame, and pulled back quickly, inhaling. She drew deeply until there was a quarter inch of ash.

Cayla pointed to one of the end tables. "There's an ashtray over there, Mother."

"I know. I know that. I know many things. The many things that I know."

There was silence. The light coming through the wired window had begun to cool. Rachel smoked more quietly, staring at the cigarette after each puff. When it was finished, she put it out in the ashtray and went back to the corner. She folded her arms. "I'll sing now," she said, "but if you try to stop me. The tessitura lies very high. They want to keep me from it." She had a sweet soprano voice, but there were no words, just a progression of notes without any recognizable melody.

"Mother," Cayla asked, "what song is that?"

It stopped abruptly.

The door opened.

"Go in," said a voice in the hall, just as before. "It's all right. Go on in." Cayla turned to Stefan and lifted both eyebrows, but he shook his head. He moved to where she sat and put a hand on her shoulder.

Once more Rachel came into the room: small and thin, her face a sad, aging mask, her shoulders pulling slightly downward.

But this time she had short hair and wore a blue dress.

"My God," Cayla whispered.

The woman looked at her without expression, then at Stefan in the same way, and then across the room. When she saw herself standing there, in the corner, she seemed to stop breathing.

There was no movement from the corner, either. But the two pairs of eyes locked on each other with a fierce grip. They were of the same gray and were set identically into the flesh and bone around them.

"Stefan, who . . ." Cayla whispered, but her words died before he could signal them to do so.

Rachel's right hand lifted to her mouth. The other right hand had lifted, too. Slowly the two women began to move toward one another. They were of a height, and their motions and posture were so eerily similar that it looked as though each of them approached a mirror.

When they were barely a foot apart, they stopped. Rachel lifted her hands to her temples. The other pair of hands flew up in the same gesture, and then there were four sets of fingers stretched out, like a quartet of wings. They hovered and then slid together down the two cheeks and closed over the two mouths.

Above the hands, the two pairs of gray eyes bored into each other as if they were reaching into tunnels, whose depths they at last seemed to find. The two women stayed that way for five minutes, motionless, except that the locking of their eyes made the room seem to pulsate with its intensity.

Then Rachel started to back away. Her eyes, grown hostile as arrows, darted about the room. Suddenly she lunged forward, her arms stretched out like bayonets, and pushed her mirror image into a chair.

The other woman sank down without a sound. "Hah!" Rachel cried. She too sat down, but on the floor, where she glared up at her own face as if it had become an alien's.

Cayla leaned forward, ready to move, but Stefan's hand pressed more firmly on her shoulder, and she sat back.

Rachel's hands lifted, as if they might be moving to her temples, but instead her glance dropped to the floor, and the hands pounced. They ripped off the other woman's shoe, hesitated, then clawed at the stocking beneath until they had torn it open and revealed the toes.

There were six of them.

"Aaaah," Rachel said, and when the face above her echoed the sound, she took off her left slipper and placed her own foot next to the one she had exposed.

After that the room was silent for a long while.

Finally Rachel looked up, peacefully, as if for once it did not cause her pain to look outside her own mind, at reality.

232

The other woman's face lost its masklike quality, too. She smiled down.

Rachel got to her feet. She put out a hand and helped her twin to rise. The two of them walked to a couch on the other side of the room and sat down.

Their hands found one another, and so did their eyes, and they seemed complete.

Stefan thought of their mother, Dorcas Veere. Under the spell of the wordless joining he was witnessing, it seemed easy to believe that she had indeed guided him back to Camp Red Cloud, to find the clue to the twins' existence and bring them together. . . .

The questions that had been on his mind all week returned, but there still were no answers. There never would be. Had Dorcas lied to Lettice Barrow about one of the twins dying, or had Lettice simply been confused? Had both of the twins been "sold"—one to Cayla Hayward Randall and the other to someone else, who abandoned her? Or was it Dorcas who had abandoned her, leaving her to become eventually the homeless Jane Doe?

The most important question could be answered, though. Was it really bad for him to have learned about the twins?

He looked down at Cayla but could see only the side of her cheek.

He knelt beside her and whispered, "These two women tie us together. Are we going to let them tear us apart as well?"

She reached for his hand, blindly, because she was crying.

By the time they left the hospital, night had come. A light wind ruffled Cayla's hair and rearranged the folds of her skirt. She locked her hands on her forearms.

"Are you cold?" Stefan asked.

"No, I just feel . . . I don't know. Like Alice through the looking glass, maybe. As if everything is different."

"I think it is," Stefan said quietly. He took off his jacket and put it over her shoulders.

"Not just the fact that Mother's twin sister turned out to be alive, but . . . everything."

"Shall I take you home?" Stefan said.

She looked at him. In the moonlight his eyes were black. "Yes," she said.

In the car she gave directions and then was silent until, halfway there, she said, "You were right not to have told me beforehand. I'm not sure I would have come. The idea that there was someone else exactly like Mother . . ."

"I know."

She leaned her head against the seat. "Did you expect them to be the way they were?"

"Dr. Scott told me the Jane Doe patient was identical to your mother. And of course I knew that extraordinary things have happened with identical twins reared apart, and I knew each of them had been told she was going to see her twin sister. But did I really expect what we saw? No." His grip on the wheel tightened. "Maybe all I mean is that I didn't expect to be so touched by it."

A few miles later he added. "They could be important to medicine, not just to each other. I did some reading this week, and I found they're very rare, those two women who . . . belong to us."

Cayla's voice was unsteady. "I know you said one can't predict anything, and tomorrow both of them may be different, but . . . I don't remember ever seeing Mother look so peaceful before. In fact she always seemed dead inside, except for her fears and angers." She pulled his jacket around her more tightly. "I suppose she sang to me when I was little. I often think of singing when I think of her." Five minutes later she added, "Until tonight I never fully understood how cut off she's been. How alone."

"She isn't anymore."

At her apartment Stefan took her keys and unlocked the door. Once inside, she touched the concealed panel of switches, and a faint glow filled the room. She put down her purse, slipped his jacket from her shoulders, laid it on a chair, and turned to face him. "I can't explain it," she said, "but somehow I feel as if they've made it all right for us, the two of them."

"Yes." He went to her and touched her cheek. "They showed us it's better not to be alone."

Her eyes glittered. "Don't make me cry again."

"Never, if I can help it." He pushed up the sleeves of his

234

e shirt. "Let me make us a fire." In a leather chest with ver hardware there were logs and paper and matches. He rked for several minutes and then sat back, against the uch. Cayla slid down beside him, and they watched the fire ke its quick way into the logs, curling its pale smoke around m, licking redly at their edges and entering them.

They turned to each other in the same moment. Their hands ted in the same motion, to trace the lines of each other's face. en Stefan's mouth moved into the palm of Cayla's hand, and e angled her head to kiss his neck. When the fire cracked be- nd them, they lifted their faces again, and slowly, as if it was pleasurable to prolong the distance between them as to cross they let their lips touch and give against one another.

When they finally drew apart, it was with the same breath, d in that, as in everything else they did—rising to take off eir clothes, sinking back to the thick rug, discovering each her with lips, tongues and hands—their movements seemed be reflecting each other, as if the strange mirror-meeting ey had witnessed earlier, of two beings who shared one phys- al identity, had laid not only its sanction upon upon them but so its silence and its spell.

When their bodies were ready to join, he rose above her to ok at her. She opened her eyes to him, and then all of herself. e moved down slowly into her, and then against her stomach d breasts. The sensation took control of them in the same oment and manner: Instead of a thrusting and circling where eir bodies met, there was a hurricane eye of stillness that sent t waves of agonizing sweetness, each swell causing the next be deeper and stronger. Their eyes, wide with surprise be- use they were creating such intense pleasure by barely mov- g, finally closed in a completion that seemed endless.

Long after it was over they stayed locked together. When ey did separate, they looked at each other and smiled because e glutted satisfaction that each felt was visible in the other's ves.

She curled beside him, and they watched the firelight casting d and gold patterns on their bodies. "I knew you'd look won- erful in colors," Stefan said, and kissed her breast.

At length she sat up, staring into the fire, and he reached out stroke her cheek. Then he sat up too, pushed her hair back from her temple with his thumb, and said, "What's that birthmark?"

"No," she said softly. "It's the Devil's mark."

He started to smile, but something glistened on her chee the fireglow. "What is it?" he said. "What's the matter?"

"I've had the mark all my life. When I was little, Gran Hester said . . . They told me that I . . ." Suddenly she looking at him from the center of a storm of tears, and he co tell from its violence that it had been held in check for a l time, perhaps for many years.

He held her and managed to reach his slacks and fish a ha kerchief out of the pocket, and waited. Finally she got up, w to put cold water on her face and came back wearing a wh terry-cloth robe. "I don't know what's the matter," she sa sitting crosslegged before the fire. "I think I'm fine, but a s ond later I'm crying about it again."

"Tell me about it. About what Hester and your grandmot told you."

Her voice was watery. "You remember that in Kella Ha ward's letter she talks about the Pricker? It was also in some Gran's books, and then I went to the library in town and read on witchcraft, secretly. All the books said it, that the Devil his mark on his witches. It was the proof they belonged him—a mark that was often in the shape of an animal and k no feeling and wouldn't bleed. They could blindfold the wi and stick pins into the mark, and if she showed no sign of p and there was no bleeding, she was guilty. She *was* a wit And I had . . ." She hiccuped with tears. "My mark looked me like a spider, and there was hardly any feeling in it. Hes used to stick pins into it, and it wouldn't bleed."

"Christ," Stefan said. More quietly he added, "Damn soul."

"That was the one thing that made me wonder whether wl they said was true, after all, and I would be a victim of Kell curse. When I left Rowan Hall I tried to forget about it I never could, not completely. Finally, when I was fifteen forced myself to ask a doctor about it."

She gave another hiccup, which turned into a short laugh. told him I was writing a paper on the history of witchcraft a needed the medical explanation of why the witches felt no pa in those Devil's marks. He said the most likely explanation w

236

hysteria—what you talked about that night after you first saw Gran. He said if a witch really believed the Devil had marked her, she could unconsciously make a mark be insensitive and not bleed. But that explanation terrified me because it meant that I . . . After about six months I worked up the courage to talk to another doctor. I used an assumed name—I guess I was afraid he would see the mark and refuse to treat me. But he was very nice. He told me it was just a birthmark. And he laughed, I remember, and said he had once had a patient with quite a large birthmark in the shape of a rat. I asked him why mine had almost no feeling in it, and he said there was a lot of epidermal thickening—a type of keratosis. Then I asked him about the witches, and he said yes, it could have been hysteria, but if they were innocent it could also have been an insensitive birthmark, or several other things. He said one of them tended to run in families.'' She shivered.

Stefan reached out and pulled her into the circle of his arm, her back against his chest. "When I think of what you went through in that house, the hell that . . .''

"But even after I knew the truth, even after a *doctor* had told me, I could still touch the mark and feel frightened.'' Her hands clenched. "When I knew better, I could still be scared!''

"And that was the worst part,'' Stefan said, pushing aside the hair at her temple and kissing the mark.

"Yes,'' she whispered. "Because it was so irrational.''

"What's irrational about a response to a childhood event that was traumatizing?''

"But I'm not a child anymore! I've put all that behind me!''

He put his arms over hers and held her hands. "My darling who had the strength to survive her upbringing, I think you paid a high price for that survival. I think you used science and logic to save your life, quite literally, and thank God you did. But in the process you may have thrown out the baby with the bath water. I think the way you feel about the past frightens you, so you try to seal it off and force it out of existence, so it acquires even more power to frighten you.''

"I'm thirty-five,'' she said. "Too old for childhood fears.''

"But you never got rid of them in the normal way. You locked them away as shameful. And now . . . Look, why shouldn't that mark call up memories of fear, when it's associated with a terrifying time in your life? If you could see the fear

237

as a logical consequence of your experience instead of as some kind of threat, it would lose a lot of its power.''

She sighed. ''You're telling me to just let go. To feel . . . whatever I'm feeling.''

''That's right.''

''But I thought you believed *thinking* properly was all that mattered. That's the only reason I felt I could go to you, in the beginning, because you believed in the importance of the mind.''

''I do. But that doesn't mean it's irrational to have feelings. I think you think it is, though. I've had patients who agreed with you and tried to cut off their emotions—usually as a kind of defense against the craziness of the world and the people around them. And I've seen *most* people assume, implicitly or otherwise, that their minds and feelings are at war. But why should they be?—unless of course you refuse to think about what you're doing. Then you do put your mind and your emotions in conflict. But if your eyes are open and you *know* what you're doing and why it's the right thing . . .''

She sighed again. ''I once told you I was afraid of you, and you said I was afraid of something in myself. What did you mean?''

''With all due lack of modesty, my darling, I meant you were afraid of how strongly you were responding to me.''

''I think you were right,'' she said softly. She was cradled between his bare legs, and one hand moved along his thigh.

He made a soft sound of pleasure. ''Was that really the only reason you came to see me—because you knew I believed in the importance of the mind?''

Her hand moved over his thigh again. ''No. But the other reason wasn't . . . rational. Just a desire to do what I'm doing now.''

''You'll never convince me it's irrational.'' He kissed the back of her neck. ''I think sex with someone you have reason to love is the ultimate state of mind.'' He smiled, his eyelids heavy, and lifted her around to face him. ''Look what you've done to me, with just a few touches of your hand. But I know why I want it to be *your* hand. And body . . .''

He opened the white robe and ran his tongue over and around the nipple of one breast until she gasped and swung her leg around to lock over his. He lifted his lips to hers, but instead o closing over them, they spoke of the sensations she was causing in him. Then his mouth moved all over her body, first telling her how it aroused him and then using it to make her cry out her own pleasure, so that finally neither of them knew which was the greater source of the fire between them, their bodies or their words.

Finally Cayla rolled away from him, onto her side.

Stefan raised his arm, as if that act took the last of his energy, and looked at his watch. "It's midnight. Do you testify tomorrow?"

"If they finish with Leslie Hatch." She smiled. "I haven't thought about the hearing since I got to the hospital. Washington seems years ago. Light-years."

"I could leave now," Stefan said, "or wait till morning and drive you to the airport on my way back to New York."

"Stay," she said. "Forever."

"Do you realize we never had dinner?" He smiled. "I'm doing it again—telling you to eat."

"I forgot about that, too. I'll go make us something now.' She pulled the white robe around her.

Stefan put on his shirt and shorts and banked the fire. They went into the kitchen, where he sat at the butcher-block island and reached for her only half a dozen times, until she threatened him with one of the copper pans hanging from a ceiling track. When he grabbed her wrist, desire flared up so quickly that she was kissing him, pressing against him, with the copper pan still in her hand.

Suddenly she pulled away. "I can't help it," she said. "It disturbs me, in some way I can hardly explain, to be feeling this way—so strongly, so quickly. It seems to . . . violate something."

Stefan sighed and sank on a stool. "If I were in my office, instead of half naked in your kitchen, sitting on my hands to keep them off you, I'd ask you to tell me exactly what you're feeling right now."

She put down the copper pan and took the sash of her robe in both hands. "I feel . . . naked." She smiled ruefully. "I don't mean my body. I mean I feel . . . vulnerable." She tied the sash firmly.

"I see." Stefan rested one bare foot on a rung of the stool. "As if you're in some kind of danger?"

She blinked. "Yes. That's right."

"But you feel strongly about Biologiconn, too, don't you?" When she nodded, he said, "Do you feel vulnerable there?"

"No. Not in this way."

"But this is more personal." He smiled. "Much more. And when it's personal, feeling something strongly equals being in danger? Out of control?"

She put one hand to her throat. "Is that what I meant?"

"And being out of control equals being like your Gran and the rest of the accursed Hayward ladies? Maybe even like your mother?"

The other hand climbed to her throat. "Helpless," she whispered, "and obsessed . . ." For a long time she simply looked at him, so pale that her eyes and brows were ink lines on white paper. "Are you right? Can you be right?"

"Darling, if I am, it's an idea you developed in self-defense, and no one could blame you for it. Only it does happen to be a wrong idea, one of those underlying errors that can keep someone from being as happy as possible. But it's not some genetic defect you were born with—it's an idea you could change, if you decided to." He reached for her hands, pulled her to him and smiled. "Why am I giving a lecture when what I want is a demonstration?" His hands went inside her robe, and he said, "Just tell yourself that you know what you're doing and if you want your money's worth out of me, the only way is to lose control."

She started to laugh, but his mouth closed off the sound, and soon her hands were inside his shirt and he had opened his legs to wrap them around her, and then she moved up to sit astride him, and the stool rocked, so that they both had to lean against the island, and when she lowered herself onto him, she made sounds like an animal's, and he groaned, and one of them knocked a copper pan off the island, and they both cried out while the pan clattered dizzily on the terrazzo floor.

They lay gasping against each other. When they finally untangled themselves, Stefan was wincing. "I think my back is broken. Don't you have any sense of control at all?"

After she had made eggs and toast, they sat at the island eating and looking at each other. When she leaned over to lick jam from the side of his mouth, he said, "I don't give a damn about your mind, you know. Just your tongue," and soon they were

240

kissing each other, deeply and probingly, while the food got too cold to eat.

Around two o'clock Stefan looked at his watch and said, "My God, we have to get some sleep. I have patients in the morning, and you have to face the nation."

They showered together and went into her bedroom, in which all the colors were austere, shades of champagne and taupe, and all the textures sleek and rich—satin, silk, lacquer, and a carpet like velvet. They slid naked between sheets as soft as handkerchiefs. Stefan lay on his back, and Cayla, on her side, pressed against him.

"You feel so right," he said.

She smiled into the darkness, and in moments they were asleep.

25

Even though the sky was the harsh, naked-bulb yellow that presaged a storm, protesters began to gather outside the Senate office building around nine in the morning. Their numbers had increased since the day before, and some new opinions appeared on the signs they waved in the air, which was heavy with the promise of rain.

Some fifty women, from groups that feared the previous day's testimony would turn the hearing into an attack on abortion, had come to register their objections. They carried signs with legends like A WOMAN'S RIGHT TO HER BODY INCLUDES HER GENES and shouted at the people representing the Coalition for Traditional Values, who brandished the signs expressing their sentiments: FETUS-FIXERS, FETUS-KILLERS—WHAT'S THE DIFFERENCE

But attracting the most attention was a huge papier-mâché figure dressed in a red so bright it seemed fluorescent. One hand held a pitchfork, the other lofted a huge laboratory beaker that wobbled in the rising wind, and the banner around its chest read HAYWARD.

The figure was the first thing Cayla saw as the limousine with her party approached the building.

She felt Leslie Hatch sigh, saw the lawyer raise his eyebrows, and heard the chief executive officer of Hayward Industries, who had flown down with them, mutter something about a sideshow. None of them looked at her, so she said to the car at large, "It's no more than I expected. It's all right."

But it wasn't. The figure in red, with its crude grin, burned on her eyes long after they had been escorted into the building and up to the hearing room.

Even without that image, her eyes burned from lack of sleep. And when she thought of why, every nerve in her body recalled Stefan's presence. She had never felt so vulnerable to the emotions that leaped to the surface and had been doing so since Leslie Hatch's unexpected tribute the day before. In retrospect, that event and everything that followed seemed a series of internal unlockings, each one intensifying the next, so that by the time she was alone with Stefan there had been no way to deny the violence of what she felt for him.

Or was it so violent precisely because she had been trying to deny it? That, she thought, was what he would say.

She watched the senators assembling behind their tables, consulting aides and lawyers and leafing through papers. As she opened her briefcase and took out her own papers, she waited for the cool sense of control to slip over her as it always did. Instead, she looked at the green felt that covered the witness table and thought of the dress she had worn to the hospital the day before, of Rachel's dislike for it, and of Stefan's eyes as he tried to coax her to wear it to the hearing instead of the tailored suit she had chosen, which was the champagne color of the bedspread on which he had nearly made her late for the plane. . . . The kaleidoscope of the previous twenty-four hours surged up again, and even as she fought it back, she heard Stefan's voice say, *Feeling something strongly equals being in danger? Being out of control?*

Then Senator Gray's voice preempted her attention as he called the hearing to order.

There were more questions for Leslie, but the committee had obviously made some kind of behind-the-scenes agreement not to elicit her views on motherhood and abortion. Fred Canfield did most of the questioning, about her dealings with Biologi-conn's university consultants. He was apparently trying to establish that the industry's emphasis on applied research threatened the universities' traditional focus on pure research. But Leslie insisted that the professors she worked with were quite able to wear two hats and were not in danger of wearing either in the wrong place.

Canfield was frustrated when he finished, Parker Bell was restive and the audience in the hearing room was unhappy, for most of them had expected some kind of fireworks.

The only storm that broke, however, was the one outside. By the time Cayla began to read her statement, shortly before eleven, rain was cascading down the building, foaming into the streets and hissing an obligato to the proceedings.

"The purpose of my testifying here is not exactly clear to me," Cayla read. "If the committee, and the country, wants to know what genetic engineering is, it has been well explained by many previous witnesses, including Dr. Leslie Hatch, and excellent presentations are also available in the popular press. There is nothing I could add that would make the technology clearer to either the senators or the country. If you want to know whether the fact that this work is being done for profit is compatible with its being done ethically, I can only say, with-out wishing to minimize the consideration, that of course it is."

As she went on, she began to feel normal. The words were recapturing something of the cool dispassion with which she had prepared them. "Genetic engineering is a technology that produces products," she read, "just as the technology of the transistor produces our present communications industry. Vir-tually all the products used in this country are made by the pri-vate sector, for profit, not by the government. That system has made us the freest and most prosperous country on earth, and if that result isn't an ethical one, I cannot imagine what is."

She looked up at the dais where the committee sat, aware of its political spectrum and the differing ways her last remarks would strike the members. In another context Parker Bell would have been smiling at her. Why, she wondered, were so many who believed that enterprise should be free so ready to force their views on society in other areas? At the opposite end of the spectrum, and the dais, was Fred Canfield, impatience on his handsome face because he did not want the freedom he advocated in so many other realms extended to the economic one.

She took a drink of water from the tray at her elbow and went on. "If it is the committee's purpose to decide whether government should more tightly regulate, or even abolish, the genetic-engineering industry, I would simply remind you of the initial fears and guidelines that accompanied the inception of the industry, and of the fact that the latter were greatly relaxed because the former proved to be groundless. I don't know of anyone more aware of the implications genetic engineering has for the future, or more concerned to use the technology properly, or more cognizant of the social and moral issues it deals with, than the scientists working in the field. Their science is biology, after all, the science of *life*, and no layman or clergyman or senator could be more conscientious and dedicated than the biologists it is my privilege to know and, in many cases, to work with. Without intending disrespect to the committee, I believe that a meeting of legislators is not the proper forum to discuss the social and moral issues entailed in the use of recombinant DNA technology. I believe that scientists must explain its use but that the ultimate decisions rest with the individual."

From the audience behind her Cayla heard a noise she couldn't identify, followed by much rustling and coughing. She waited for a moment. Her views were now on record, as briefly as she could state them, and she didn't intend to be lured into debates about them or trapped into answering personal questions. She glanced at the dais again and went on. "The only other things I might tell the committee would pertain to the staff and operations of Biologiconn. So let me describe those for you." She turned a page of her text and began to read the material she had had prepared for her: a breakdown of the number of Ph.D.'s, their combined years of laboratory training, the number and types of papers and books they had contributed to the scientific literature, the honors and awards they had won, and, finally, a list of the recombinant DNA projects on which they had worked successfully. The lawyer hadn't been thrilled with what she was doing, but she wanted it that way: no defenses or apologies, just the crisp, clear presentation of the massed brainpower of Biologiconn and the things it had achieved.

Although there was an air of restiveness in the room, she paid no attention and paused only once, for another drink of water.

She was reading about the production of animal vaccines when thunder cracked as loudly as a whip laid against the door of the room. There were gasps and jerks from both the audience and the committee dais. The thunder rolled away slowly, like a cannon pulled over cobblestones, and as it was fading, a cry came from somewhere—UUUUUUUNNNNH—as if one of the animals pulling it had been goaded beyond endurance.

A moment of collective, amazed silence was followed by an excited chattering, and then by the banging of Gray's gavel.

"There will be order!" he called. "There will be order, or I will have the audience cleared from this room!"

Gradually, with the Senate guards looking on sternly, the noise died. When the silence was total, Gray leaned into his microphone again and said, "Miz Hayward, I do apologize for that interruption. Will you continue, please?"

Her heart was beating in her neck and wrists, and she almost said no, she wouldn't continue, but she told herself that what she feared couldn't possibly be happening. She picked up the paper that had slipped from her hand and reassembled her composure. "As I was saying, Biologiconn, like its competitors, has produced various animal vaccines by means of recombinant DNA technology. In particular we've been successful with a vaccine against hoof and mouth disease, one of the most serious livestock diseases that—"

"Master! Oh my Master!" cried a hoarse voice, in a Scottish accent. "Oh my Lord of Darkness, see how your power lives on!"

The spectator section twisted in on itself, every head turning to the middle, where the source of the voice rose up, tall and awkward, clutching a purse. Her pale blue eyes were shining but looking at nothing. "See how your power has come down all the generations! See how the name Kella is still sacred to your works!"

Gray's mouth was open, his hand lifeless on the gavel. Parker Bell rose in his seat, his plump face nearly as white as his collar. Aides to the senators, who had been crouched behind them in whispered colloquies, raised their heads like startled animals and froze, as the harsh, dark voice came again from the plain, middle-aged woman.

"Yea, my Master, Beelzebub who rules from the dark world, you gave me the power and I passed it on, down to all the women who love you as I do and bear your mark upon their persons! Down to all the women who do your bidding and your work!"

Black laughter burst incongruously from the face on which there was no expression or sign of feeling. "They do the work of Satan by usurping the work of God!"

The sound of the laughter broke several Senate guards from their paralysis of amazement and sent them running toward it. Moroni Gray's face came back to life, as did his gavel. "Get that woman out of here," he commanded. "Get her out of this hearing!"

Within moments the guards had reached her. She flailed her arms and began to hiss, almost as loudly as the rain. It took four guards to lift her out.

Even after she was gone her voice could be heard from the hall: "Yea, my Lord of the darkness, see how I have passed your power down, see how the woman does your work and spites God!"

The TV cameras, which had been riveted on her, came back to Cayla, pulling with them every eye in the room. She sat at the center of that collective stare, choking back a living nightmare. The Whiting creature, like some ungainly Fury, had followed her everywhere, even here, to play out the final, humiliating act of revelation. She thought her face must be as red as the cloak worn by the papier-mâché Satan, but in fact it was deadly white.

Parker Bell sat back down in his chair, pulled the handkerchief from his breast pocket, and mopped his face. The other senators began to look around at one another. Several of them exchanged incredulous glances. Moroni Gray consulted with the colleagues to his immediate left and right and with one of his aides. Then he leaned into his microphone again. "I reckon," he began, "that most folks know who that woman was, and I must say, Miz Hayward, we, the whole committee and myself, we regret the unfortunate incident. We're just as surprised and upset as you are. I reckon strange things do hap-

246

pen sometimes in the chambers of the United States Senate, and this surely was one of the strangest."

"It was a sign!" called someone in the audience. "A sign from the Hayward witch!"

"Amen," several voices called.

"Quiet!" others demanded.

Gray gaveled furiously. "If there is one more sound from the public, if there is so much as a cough or a sneeze, I warn you that I will have this hearing room cleared immediately!"

He glared into the quiet and then went on. "Like I said, this incident was unfortunate, and I do assure you, Miz Hayward, that there won't be any repetition of it."

"If you can't guarantee that," Cayla said tightly, "I will not continue to be a witness before this committee."

The chief executive officer of Hayward Industries, sitting near Cayla, leaned into her microphone and said, "That goes for me, too, Mr. Chairman."

"Of course, of course," Gray said. "I guarantee you that woman won't be admitted into this hearing room again." He fished in the jacket pockets of his rumpled blue suit. "Miz Hayward, I don't believe you had finished your statement. Do you want to go on?"

"No"' she said coldly. "There were only a few more facts and figures to give you, and I'm not sure how interested the committee and the country are in facts."

Gray colored, but Canfield and the senator sitting next to him, Packman, both nodded imperceptibly. "All right, then," Gray said, "I know the committee has questions to ask you. And I believe it's the turn of Senator . . ." He consulted his papers and paused. "The senator from Arkansas. Mr. Bell."

Barely making a sound, the audience managed to convey, from different sections, both dismay and eagerness.

Bell aligned some papers in front of him, pulled his microphone closer, and said, "Miss Hayward, before I start, isn't it true, just as a matter of historical fact, that one of your female ancestors was burned as a witch?"

His words seemed to touch a match to her face. Three of his colleagues started to object, but she forced herself to cut through their words. "Many Americans have ancestors who were persecuted in that barbaric way."

Bell looked at her stolidly. "I take it that means yes."

Gray cut in, trying to defuse the situation with humor. "Let's all remember," he said, chuckling, "that there's a statute of limitations on ancestors, even witches, so nobody can hold Miz Hayward's against her."

No one laughed. Parker Bell never reacted to Gray's sallies, the rest of the committee was edgy, and the audience had been intimidated.

"Senator Bell," Gray said after a few moments, "we're waiting."

"Yes, sir." Elbows resting on the table, Bell folded his hands in front of his chin and lifted his eyes to the chandelier and beyond. Cayla braced herself, determined to walk out if he said another word pertaining to witches, but what he lowered his gaze to ask surprised her. "Miss Hayward, you think gene-splicing is a great scientific achievement, don't you?"

"Yes, of course."

"Maybe the most important one of the twentieth century?"

"Maybe."

"Do you believe a great scientific achievement should fall into just anybody's hands?"

Cayla frowned. "I don't believe I understand the question."

"Sorry, I thought it was pretty clear. I mean, shouldn't we be careful who uses these great new technologies that are developed?"

"I'm not sure whom you mean by 'we.' "

"The American people."

"I think the history of American business would show them that new industries are generally started by pretty responsible people."

"As a matter of fact, Miss Hayward, I agree with you on that. And I bet you're thinking of your own family, the men who built Hayward Industries. They were real pioneers of American business."

Cayla didn't respond. She couldn't tell where he was leading, and to be puzzled by him seemed even worse than to know.

"I guess," he said, "that those men, those ancestors of yours, never expected one of the divisions of their company to be run by a woman. I wonder what they'd say. How do *you* think they'd feel, Miss Hayward?"

She waited until she was sure her voice would be level.

"Senator, are you suggesting that my being a woman has any relevance to the matters this committee is supposed to be considering?"

"Well, Miss Hayward, I don't know. After all, we're talking about a technology that gives us the power to change human beings, if we want to use it that way. And here you are in charge of this truly awesome power, and you're a young woman—meaning no disrespect, but a young woman from a family where it seems the women have a lot of problems, including some pretty serious mental problems, I gather, which is a good example of the dangers of letting—"

"Point of order!" Fred Canfield snapped into his microphone. "Mr. Chairman, this kind of thing can't be tolerated!"

"Mr. Chairman," Bell protested, "I have the floor!"

"Mr. Chairman, we can't allow a witness to be subjected to such questions!" said Senator Packman, next to Canfield.

"Mr. Chairman, I really must protest!" said one of the majority senators.

But the more his colleagues tried to stop him, the louder Bell shouted. "We must learn what kind of people are following Satan's commands and doing his work! And *I* have the floor!"

Cayla felt someone grip her arm, but she shook off the hand—it was Leslie Hatch's—and cried, "How dare you tell everybody about my mother, that she's *crazy?* How dare you let everyone know what my family is like? I've been hiding those things all my life! How dare you—"

She stopped as abruptly as if her air supply had been cut off, because the meaning of her own words had just registered. She could only pray that most people hadn't heard them, with all the other shouting that was going on, but they kept ringing in her mind. If Parker Bell had talked about her family's history and her mother's illness as if all of it was filthy and evil, she had just done the same thing.

She stared inward, gripped by the insight. But the noise in the hearing room pulled her back.

Gray was gaveling madly, shouting that they were all out of order, and a voice overriding that and everything else: "The prestige of the Senate can't be lent to this sort of talk!"

The other voices quieted as committee and audience alike realized that the words had come not from Freddie Canfield but from a quiet man on the majority side, who had asked few questions to date. "This is the United States Senate!" he said. "What the hell are we doing talking about witches and Satan?"

Parker Bell tugged at his collar. "Is the honorable senator from the state of Arizona telling us there is no Satan? No evil?"

"I'm just trying to remind us that this is a Senate hearing."

"And I remind you," Bell said, his face gleaming with sweat but his eyes cold with certainty, "that we are one nation under God and that the Senate opens its sessions with a prayer to Him! If you say there is no Satan, then you're saying there is no God."

"Don't you dare!" cried the senator from Arizona. "I believe in God! I'm a member of the board of my church!"

"God exists, so Satan exists, so we must fight him!"

"Mr. Chairman!" cried Freddie Canfield, "are you going to rule Mr. Bell out of order, or are you not?"

Everyone looked to Moroni Gray, knowing the conflict that had underlain the hearing since its first day finally had to be resolved.

Gray's glance went slowly around the room and along the dais. He cocked his head back so that his hair hung like a mane and there was about him the air of someone named after an angel. Then his eyes came down, level with the audience and the TV cameras. "I cannot be the man," he said, "who declares that the United States Senate is a place where Satan—and God—cannot be mentioned. Continue, Mr. Bell."

There was a stirring in the audience that he did not attempt to gavel down. Cayla felt the lawyer take her elbow, heard his whispered advice that she refuse to continue, but she shook off his hand and reached for her microphone.

"Mr. Chairman," she said, in a voice that silenced the room. "I should like, after all, to finish my opening statement before there is any further questioning. In view of what's happened here, I believe I'm entitled not only to that consideration but to a postponement of at least a day or two."

The permission came quickly. Most of the committee seemed relieved, even Gray, who gave her more time than she had asked for by adjourning the hearing until the next Monday.

That night she went to Rowan Hall.

She took her own small car. As it headed up the long driveway toward the monolith that bulked in front of the moon, she wanted to get out and run in the opposite direction. She noted her response to that feeling, the one she had every time: shame.

She went up the marble staircase, past the portrait gallery, thinking of the words that had flayed away her veneer of calm in the hearing that morning—*a family where it seems the women have a lot of problems, including some pretty serious mental problems.*

The long red room fronting on the ocean contained a touch of crisp white: the uniform of one of the nurses who had been with Gran since the night Hester was taken away. "Leave me alone with her for a while," Cayla said.

She went to the chaise and looked down at the sleeping figure. Gran's hands were tucked into the sleeves of one of her red robes, and the webbed skin of her face seemed to lie over its bones more delicately than ever. Those bones were so fine, Cayla thought, and once the mind they housed had been fine, too—active, educated, artistic. She stared down at the face as if she could burn her way through the closed eyelids and into the brain, to learn why it had changed so terribly, shriveling a promising life into immobility.

The eyes opened, startling her, and startling Gran, too, for she gave a little cry and then, when she saw who it was, said fretfully, "Where is Hester? Why did you send Hester away?"

"Because she's ill. I told you that."

"I don't believe you. She's not ill. You're just . . . She always tried to help you accept your destiny. But you never wanted to do that. You wanted to escape the curse, so you had to get rid of Hester."

The words were not surprising, but Cayla let herself feel the hopeless anger they induced, rather than trying wearily to deflect it. She saw, as if by direct perception, the connection between the old woman's states of mind and her shriveled life.

If her fear of becoming like Gran, she thought, had made her run in the opposite direction, trying to deny her own emotional life, it was still the right direction to have run. Indisputably the right one.

She shook her head, aware that she was staring down at the old woman intently. "No, Gran," she said, "I don't accept the destiny you see for me. I never have. But I've never accepted you, either. I've tried to run away from you, and to hide you—you and Hester and Mother and all the Hayward women you believe are cursed. And Kella Hagaward herself. I told myself I was hiding you to protect the family, but that's only part of it. I was ashamed of you and afraid of you. So I was hiding you from myself. Today in Washington, though, I saw that if you try to hide something, the world finds out about it in a way much worse than any you could have imagined or chosen. It happened in such a dreadful way because of the way *I* felt. Because of my shame and fear, and my wish to hide everything.''

''What do you want? Why did you come?''

''To tell you that the hiding is over, even though I don't expect you to understand. Or to care.''

''Leave me alone. Let me be.''

''Soon. When I have the key to your safe.''

''No,'' the old woman whimpered. ''No.''

''Yes, Gran. Yes. Give it to me.''

26

Stefan entered the hearing room on Monday just as the proceedings were starting.

He took the seat that had been kept for him, near the door so he could get in and out easily. His eyes went immediately to the witness table, and softened.

Cayla's manner was in calm contrast to the dress she wore. She had shopped for it on Saturday afternoon, taking a break from the work of preparing her statement, and he had been startled when she took it out of the box, for it was made of tissue-thin material, it had huge pleated sleeves and a full skirt, and it was a brilliant red. ''When people watch me testify,'' she had said. ''I want it to be as easy for them to see me as a witch as to think of me as the president of Biologiconn. So it has to be red, just as red as their papier-mâché Satan.''

Stefan smiled, thinking of the elegant, eager body beneath the dress, and of the mind that animated it, which had conceived such a courageous response to the hearing and the events that took place the last time it convened.

Moroni Gray was convening it again. His gavel came down heavily, as if it felt the weight of the huge crowd of demonstrators outside, which now included a number of feminists—one of their signs declared WITCHCRAFT IS A MYTH INVENTED BY MEN—and of all those who had fought their way in. The line had begun forming at seven A.M. and had been seventy feet long before the doors opened.

The other senators and their aides looked as somber as Gray. The committee had been pursued by the press over the weekend, but none of them, including Parker Bell, had given interviews. Female reporters had tried to get Gray to answer questions on the Mormon view of women, but he had evaded them with "No comment."

"I remind the audience in this room," Gray was saying, "that even though this hearing is held for the benefit of the public, no interruptions of the proceedings will be tolerated." He shuffled the papers in front of him for a moment. "Miz Cayla Hayward, president of the Biologiconn division of Hayward Industries, has requested to finish her opening statement before Senator Parker Bell resumes his questioning. So . . ." He inclined his head to her. "Miz Hayward?"

She did not say, "Thank you, Mr. Chairman." She picked up the first page of her statement and tossed back her head so that the light from a chandelier struck sparks from her blue-black hair. The audience rustled and shifted in anticipation.

She began with no preamble at all. "The reputation of my family and my company has been prejudiced before this committee, and before the whole country, by extended news coverage of the most sensational kind. Normally one pays little or no attention to sensational stories, but normally they do not engender the kind of response that has been visible in the streets outside this building, nor do they lead to the kind of interruption that took place last Wednesday inside this room. I have decided, therefore, not to finish my original opening statement but instead to provide an answer to both the sensational stories in the press and the charges that have been made in this hearing room."

Around and behind him Stefan could feel attention so keen

253

that it seemed to crackle. On the dais there was complete concentration.

"The woman who interrupted us last week claims, or it is claimed about her, that while in a hypnotic trance, she becomes the vehicle for a long-dead Hayward ancestor who was burned as a witch in 1643. It is true that there was such a person. It is not true that she, or anyone else, can return from the dead to speak through a living person, or to speak by any other means. I find it embarrassing that such a thing has to be said in the chambers of the United States Senate, but apparently it does."

There was a protesting murmur from segments of the audience. Cayla ignored it. "I don't say that the woman who interrupted these proceedings was deliberately perpetrating a hoax, but the supernatural had nothing to do with her action. This hearing is not the place to explain and discredit her, but as soon as I have finished here, I will meet with the press to do so. I have asked Dr. Stefan Veere, a psychiatrist who is well qualified to deal with so-called psychic phenomena, to join me." She turned to Stefan, indicating him to her listeners, and one corner of her vivid mouth lifted briefly, so that only he could see it.

Moroni Gray turned over his gavel and cleared his throat. "Excuse me, Miz Hayward, but this hearing should not and cannot be used for announcing private press conferences."

"Mr. Chairman, I will take careful note of the things for which this hearing should not and cannot be used."

Gray looked at her as coldly and politely as she had spoken. For a moment he seemed about to use his gavel, but he said nothing, and she went on.

"If the purpose of this hearing is to discover truth, then I have some truth to put before you. It begins with a document that has been in my family's possession for hundreds of years, although it was rediscovered only during the 1920s and has never been made public. It is a letter, written in Scotland in 1643, by the Hayward ancestor who was burned as a witch."

This time there was no protest in the audience's murmur, and on the dais several senators leaned forward.

"I plan to make this letter available for examination by scholars, who I think will find it of considerable historical interest. I also propose to donate it to the Library of Congress. And I propose to read it to this committee now."

She paused to take a drink of water, and Stefan watched the dais. The expressions there were all similar—curiosity mixed with uncertainty. Gray turned to the aides and lawyers sitting behind him, and then back to the microphone. "Miz Hayward, I reckon I don't understand. We're all hoping to forget the unfortunate interruption that took place last week, but you seem to be making it the basis of your whole statement. Just exactly what does this letter have to do with the purpose of this hearing? With genetic engineering?"

"Mr. Chairman, it's irrelevant that the author of the letter—that is, her existence—became the basis for sensational stories about my family. But it's very much to the point that the voice produced under hypnosis, and attributed to her, helped inspire the opposition to genetic engineering that is responsible for this hearing."

Gray's eyebrows slammed together. "I remind you, young la—I remind you that this hearing was called because we are concerned about the use and misuse of a powerful new technology, not because of some press stories about a witch!"

"And I remind the chairman that Senator Bell asked me about the woman whose letter I propose to read and that he then—because of her—maligned the female members of my family and called into question my own suitability to head a genetic-engineering company."

Stefan felt the audience take a breath as sharp as his own. Gray glared at Cayla, who looked back calmly, and then transferred his gaze to Bell, whose expression merely solidified, the mouth and eyes granitic with rectitude.

A man crouched behind Gray, an aide or lawyer, whispered to him urgently. At length Gray turned back to his microphone and said, without expression, "Continue with your statement, Miz Hayward."

She picked up her pages again. "I'll be reading a transcript of the letter. No changes have been made, other than modernizations of the spelling. The actual document is written on vellum, in a dark ink, and the date is given at the bottom—'1643 yeare.' The writing is awkward, close to illegible in places. The author's name is Kella Hagaward. Many members of my family have carried a changed version of that name, and it is of course mine as well."

She lifted her head, took a deep breath and began, reading

with a cool, emotionless clarity that let the words speak with their own intensity, across the centuries.

My dear sister,
I shall die soon, and there being no help for it, I say good-bye to you with this letter which you must keep secret. For if any one find that the jailer has let it be carried to you, he will surely be tortured and killed, even as I.

I beg you, do not travel to watch them burn me for a witch, for you would weep to see what has become of your sister. They shaved off all my hair and pricked me everywhere with the brass pin. They bound my hands together and put the thumbscrews on me, until the blood came leaping from my nails and everywhere. Only now can I start to use my hands again, and if their writing be hard to decipher, you have the reason.

When I am gone they will take my house and goods to pay for the trial and the things they have done to me, but if you could go there first and if the house be still as I left it, you would find in the cupboard some packets of herbs and some plants hanging over the hearth to dry. Many hours did I spend in gathering and sorting them and may-haps you will have use for them. Some of their uses I never told to anyone but you, not even my husband when he lived. Never did I find the way to keep a fetus from leaving the womb early, as happened to me both times and as I have seen many others to do, and have never been able to help the women. Mayhaps you will find the way.

Oh to think I will never again go gathering in the woods and bogs, singing to myself as I was wont to do, and never again sit before my house at day's end with my cat and play upon my flute! I do greatly miss its bird-voice which sang to me so many an eve.

And you, dear sister, I miss above all else, though of late we have seen each other too seldom. I think often of when we were bairns and would sing together and how your laughter always made mine come too, even in the kirk sometimes, so that we choked with holding it back. Never shall I laugh again, only weep for dying in the fire at eight-and-thirty years with no husband or bairn or sister near me.

I will tell you what has happened to me. My nieces, the daughters of Thomas Hagaward, told that I bewitched them and others told it also, so that the parson came out from Dumfries to make me confess. But in the midst of his praying he gave a great cry and died. Then all was lost. They came and took me away to this prison and exhorted me to confess freely that I am a witch. "Never," I told them, "for I am not a witch but a Christian woman who has a good conscience." "All witches do claim innocence," they said, "but we have ways to find them out."

They stood me naked before the court, and the Pricker who came from Edinburgh did prick me all over with his pins to find the Devil's mark, so that blood ran over all my body. But still I told them I was innocent. Then came the Witchfinder-General, to question me for a day and a night but never letting me to lie down or even to sit, so that near the end I began to shake as if with the palsy.

He came often to my cell to sit for many hours on end, talking of God's mercy and telling me to confess. And then Thomas Hagaward's daughters did say they had followed me secretly into the woods and there seen me at the Sabbat. Afterwards the Witchfinder-General came more often than before, exhorting me to tell of my carnal traffic with Satan. Thrice he has made me stand in my cell without moving or sleeping for I know not how long, but it did seem like all eternity. He has caused two needles to be thrust under each nail of my toes, even up to the heads. He has had fire from a pot laid to the soles of my feet while he sat watching my face. Himself he has bound my hands and stood behind me and dipped the nipples of my breasts into burning oil.

Then came even worse torment. They put me to the ladder, with weights tied to my feet, and drew me up as high as the pulley itself. Thus did I hang until my joints and limbs were stretched out dreadfully, and then they let me down with a jerk almost to the ground, by which terrible shake my arms and legs were all disjointed and I screamed so long that no sound came from my throat for two days after, only blood. Five times did they do this, and yet, dear sister, I know not how, I did manage not to confess.

I pray to my lord for power to make the Witchfinder-General suffer like to what I have endured till now, and shall endure on the morrow. For he sat by me for many hours to tell what more he will have done to me if I do not speak the oath I have taken to Satan and give the names of my accomplices in evil and tell how I have danced at the Sabbat and played my flute and sung bawdy songs and eaten mutton and given the kiss of infamy to Beelzebub with whom I also consummated my union. Dear sister, it is the iron boots he will put me to, causing them to be tightened even till the marrow spouts from my legs and they are crushed as flat as oat cakes, never to hold me up again. He swears it will happen, as it has been done to many before me.

The jailer himself, seeing the state I am in and fearing I can bear no more, has begged me to confess. "For they have the proof of the Devil's mark against you," he says, "and will never let you go."

Shall I then confess? I would that you were here to give me your comfort and counsel. Shall I talk of the Sabbats in the woods and the sweet music that did come from my flute and the great hairy goat-body that I did gladly take into my own? Shall I say his amber eyes did burn on me and drive out my will? Or shall I claim to the end that I am a good Christian woman who can bear as much suffering as her lord did bear? Whatever thing I say, the fire will be the end.

I call on him in whose name I shall die to grant me one wish. I pray to my lord to make to suffer Thomas Hagaward's daughters who have caused me this agony. And if I have such power as they would make me confess, then let there be in every Hagaward family down to the end of time one who is just like me, so that I may have their company and be not alone in what I endure.

Sister, keep near to your heart the memory of Kella Hagaward, for you know the truth of what she is and what lord she does serve. I hold you now in my thoughts and shall think of you at the end, which I pray to come soon.

Complete silence had prevailed while Cayla read. It continued for more than a minute after she finished. Finally she lifted her hands to tuck her hair behind her ears, and as the sleeves of her dress billowed out like flames, the audience sighed and shifted and someone on the dais cleared his throat. In spite of Stefan's prior knowledge of the letter, he found that he too needed to make some movement or sound.

She waited until the room was quiet again before she picked up another page of her text and went on.

"Few people have seen Kella Hagaward's letter, but of those who have, some believe it proves her guilt. For not only does she admit they found the Devil's mark on her, she makes no passionate affirmation of belief in God, as one would expect from an innocent person. To the contrary, she writes of how she often used to laugh in church; she seems to have firsthand knowledge of witches' Sabbat; and she shows none of the Christian virtue of forgiveness. In fact, she is bitterly vengeful. And, although she could easily have made her nieces suffer by accusing them of being witches, too, she chooses instead to invoke Satanic power and curse her husband's whole family in perpetuity. It is not hard to believe that Kella Hagaward was indeed a witch, whose curse has come down through the centuries, carrying a combination of Satanic power and suffering. One can believe that certain female members of my family who have been beautiful and talented but have suffered or died young are victims of that curse—or its beneficiaries, depending on one's perspective."

Cayla paused for a moment. "I have seen people in my family choose that belief. But it has brought them no peace of mind, no sense of confidence, no happiness and ultimately no hope. Because they are believing in something outside human understanding and control—which means, necessarily, that they are at its mercy."

She lifted her eyes to the dais and then turned for just a moment to Stefan, who hoped the faint smile he sent her carried something of the admiration he felt.

She went on. "But of course there is another way to see Kella Hagaward: as an innocent victim of the witch-craze. The

Witchfinder-General may have been a man who used the cover of religion to indulge his sadistic sexual fantasies and who enjoyed spelling out in erotic detail the confession he wanted. Surely a man who dips a woman's breasts in burning oil has some motive other than the love of his God. It is even possible that he raped her before she died, for accused female witches often were raped by the good Christians who were their jailers and torturers.''

She saw Parker Bell lift his chin in protest, and heard murmurs behind her. She went on.

''Kella Hagaward may have been persecuted because she was different—she was solitary and intelligent—or simply because she was a woman. Twice as many women as men were accused during the witch-craze, and the book instrumental in launching that craze, called *The Witches' Hammer* and written by two Dominican friars, claimed that women were more wicked than men—more carnal, more deceiving and more likely to abandon their faith. So it is quite possible to see Kella Hagaward as an innocent woman who knew what confession was wanted of her, who considered giving it only in order to avoid inhuman pain, and whose curse was just a bitter wish for a power she knew she did not have.''

Several women in the audience started to clap, but Gray lifted his gavel threateningly and they stopped. Cayla want on. ''One can take the letter either way, but one has to take the consequences of the choice. One can believe in a curse and a power that have come down through the centuries. But then one can do nothing to stop either its suffering or its power, because it is a thing beyond the mind and therefore beyond control. On the other hand, one can believe that Kella Hagaward was a victim of discrimination and persecution and that it's only coincidence—or more discrimination—that a number of female members of my family suffered certain problems and tragedies. After all, in any family that keeps records going back for centuries, there are bound to be similarities in the illnesses and deaths of some of its members. The question is, What do you make of such coincidences? Do you invoke the supernatural to explain them, or do you retain your belief in the power of your own mind? Superstition and the supernatural cannot change the world, or alleviate its suffering. Only the power of the mind can do that.''

Cayla looked up at the dais and the television cameras. "I'd like to remind all of us that Kella Hagaward's story is not ancient history. Only three years before the United States was founded, the Associated Presbytery of Scotland was still formally affirming its belief in witchcraft. And although the holocaust in our own century has overshadowed those of earlier times, and understandably so, we should not forget that the witch-craze was a holocaust, too—a reign of unreason, like the Nazis', but one that lasted for over *three centuries* and whose victims, estimated to be at least several hundred thousand but thought by some scholars to be as many as two or three *million,* were all individually tortured beyond endurance, as Kella Hagaward was, before they were put to death."

While she read the words, Cayla felt the stillness in the hearing room. She glanced over at Stefan. As arranged, he had moved to the door. His face was as grave as if he had not listened to her statement over the weekend but was hearing it for the first time. He nodded at her, and for a moment she saw only the lean strength of his body and the disciplined ease of its posture. His eyes seemed to flare across the room, and then he went out.

She glanced at the dais. Gray was staring down at his folded hands, his thick gray brows visible but not his eyes. Several of the other senators seemed in conflict, as if they thought what she was saying was both inappropriate and important. Parker Bell was looking at her. Suddenly his thoughts were transparent, and she knew that when he questioned her, he would accuse her of attacking the church. Well, so she was.

She picked up the last pages of her text. "You may think I'm one of those who don't believe in family curses. But you're wrong. In fact I believe I'm the victim of one."

The audience shifted and whispered like leaves in the wind, and the committee, to a man, stared at her.

"The curses I speak of work down through the generations, and until now they have largely been outside of our understanding and control."

Freddie Canfield was frowning at her over his glasses, and Parker Bell's gaze lacked an ingredient it took her a moment to identify: certainty.

"Let me tell you about one of those curses: the mental illness known as schizophrenia. Over the years researchers have hypothesized many causes for schizophrenia, but today there is strong and growing evidence that it may be transmitted genetically. In fact, so far every type of genetic study supports the theory of genetic transmission. But the most fruitful tests involve twins. Twin studies have been done at least ten times in the past several decades, with amazing results: The *fraternal* twin of a schizophrenic is only as likely to develop the disease as any other sibling. But with *identical* twins, it is five times more likely that both will have schizophrenia. In fact they both will have it an average of sixty percent of the time, thus providing clear evidence of a genetic influence.''

She paused for a moment to sense the stillness all around her. ''But even those tests could not completely rule out environment as a contributing factor. The best test of all would be to find identical twins separated from birth or close to it and brought up completely apart—at least one of whom has schizophrenia. Such twins are so rare that over the past several decades only sixteen pairs of them have been found. But even in that small sampling, the statistics held: Sixty-two and a half percent of the co-twins also had schizophrenia.''

Someone in the audience behind Cayla murmured, ''Extraordinary.''

She saw the door to the hearing room open. She got a glimpse of a pink dress. ''Now,'' she said, ''a seventeenth such pair of twins has been found. I'd like you to meet them.''

Everything had gone calmly so far, even the reading of the letter, but as Cayla watched the women coming toward her, guided by Stefan and the nurse who had stayed with them in the room where it had been arranged for them to wait, she saw that they were holding hands, and she was unable to speak. They blurred before her eyes, so that there were four of them, four slight figures with old-young faces and graying hair and pink shirtwaist dresses.

They reached the witness table, and Cayla forced her voice to return. ''I'd like to introduce to you Rachel and Jane. They have been separated since birth and raised without awareness of each other's existence. Both of them are victims of schizophrenia.''

The audience murmured so loudly that Gray used his gavel. Jane covered her ears, and Rachel put an arm around her.

Cayla went on. ''You will wonder why I have had them

262

brought here and whether it may be a cruel thing to do. But I want it to be cruel—not for them but for the rest of us. I want us all to look at them and realize that in Kella Hagaward's time, and for many centuries before and after, their illness would have been diagnosed as possession by the Devil. They would have been kept in chains in a lunatic asylum, and on Sundays the public could go to look at them—for a fee, of course, as is usually the case at a zoo.''

She turned and saw the audience staring. There was pity in the faces, and embarrassment. Was there also some aversion? She looked at the twins. They were holding hands again, faces as blank as two masks. She touched Rachel's hand and said, ''Won't you and Jane sit down?'' Stefan and the nurse helped seat them in the chairs at Cayla's right that had been left empty for that purpose.

She went on. ''Not until the end of the eighteenth century did a few courageous people begin to reject the idea of demonic possession and suggest that the behavior of the mentally ill might be explained by the concept of disease. And only in this century have we had the knowledge and the technology to begin to discover causes and talk about the possibility of cures. For many of the disorders, chemistry has been the new frontier, and I am proud that Hayward Industries has developed a number of the drugs most helpful in treating mental illness. I am even more proud that Hayward Industries, through its Biologiconn division, is also working on the newest frontier, genetic engineering. The possibility of a genetic cure for schizophrenia is very far in the future, but we are now correcting the defective gene that causes the tragedy of Tay-Sachs disease. One day we may correct the tragedy of schizophrenia, too.''

Rachel's arm rested on the table, Cayla put one hand on it. ''As I've told you, and as you can see, these ladies are identical twins. What you cannot see . . .'' She stopped, a great soreness welling in her throat and crowding out her voice. She told herself that she had reached the critical moment; she *must* be able to speak. ''What you cannot know is that they are . . .'' She swallowed painfully. ''They are my mother and my aunt.''

There was a murmuring in the audience and on the dais that went on for a blessedly long time, so that she could drink water, though it hurt, and, when the silence returned, go on. ''There are complicated family reasons for their having been reared apart, which I won't discuss. I will only tell you that, as the seventeenth pair of twins raised separately, both of whom have schizophrenia, they will send the correlation statistic even higher than it was, and they will contribute greatly to the research in this area. So although their lives have been ruined by schizophrenia—'' The next words blurred on the page—''they will not have been wasted.''

She couldn't see to finish her text, but she didn't need to. She rose and stood behind Rachel and Jane, an arm around each of them, her red sleeves falling over their shoulders. ''To anyone who would choose to claim that their illness is proof of some supernatural curse on the Hayward family, let me tell you that neither of them has any Hayward blood in her. My mother was *adopted* into the Hayward family, and if all the genetic studies prove to be correct, she brought her disease *into* the family with her. I have no Hayward blood either. And although I do not have the disease myself, I have the capacity for transmitting the genetic influence to any children I may have. So I am indeed, as I told you, the victim of a family curse.''

She lifted her head. ''And of course if my partner also happened to have such an influence in his genes, it could be dangerous for us to have children.'' She paused. ''But if I'm not a Hayward by birth, I do have the Hayward name, and the backing of Hayward Industries, and therefore the capacity to use recombinant DNA technology to break the *real* curses—the diseases that turn people's bodies and minds against them and, until now, have left them no hope, not even for their children. Leave us free to become their hope. Yes, the technology we use carries with it a terrible responsibility, but the true terror would be to halt its use or restrict it severely. Nothing can be done for my mother and my aunt, but for the thousands in the future—no, the millions—who can be helped . . . leave us free to become their hope.''

Gradually she became aware of the room again—of the committee staring at her and the audience absolutely quiet around her and of Stefan, who had moved the microphone closer when she stood up, looking at her with an expression she wanted never to forget.

Rachel and Jane, who had been motionless all the while she was speaking, moved slightly beneath her hands, and she released her grip on them.

"Shall I take them now?" Stefan asked.

"Yes. Please."

He and the nurse started to lead them out. The room was still silent, except for a whisper of movement as people turned to watch them go.

Halfway to the door they stopped. Rachel's hand released Jane's, and she turned and walked back to Cayla, who was still standing behind the witness table, hands clenched under her chin. Rachel looked around vaguely, as if she wanted to take in the whole room. Then she said, "This is my daughter."

She put a hand on Cayla's arm, leaned up and kissed her. Then she turned and walked back to Jane.

They went out.

The room seemed to release its breath, and Cayla, whose legs had lost their ability to support her, sank into her chair.

27

"I got to go into town for a while," Polly Whiting said.

Bill Whiting put down the spade he was sharpening with a file. "What for, Poll?"

"Get some things. We're near out of flour and lard."

"OK. Sure. You going to be long?"

"Don't worry, I'll be back to fix lunch."

Bill watched her stride off to the pickup truck and climb in. Ever since he and Reverend Bailey had brought her home from Washington, he worried she might disappear again. The hospital up there had wanted to keep her for a while. "It would be for her own good," the doctor said. Reverend Bailey had thought they should go along with the doctor, but Bill would have none of that. She just needed to get back to the farm and lead her regular life. As he told the doctor, she wasn't sick. All those reporters sniffing around had gotten her worked up, that was all.

She hadn't talked about what happened in Washington except to say, on the way back home on the bus, "It rained real hard up there that day." He hadn't asked her any questions; it was over, so why go on about it?

But he hoped to God she was all right. Having your wife on TV and in the papers wasn't all it was cracked up to be. He watched her pull out of the driveway. Picking up the spade again, he made a few passes over it with the file. But in a few moments he had put the file down and was staring into space because he was pretty sure there was plenty of flour and lard in the pantry.

She went to Sears.

For half an hour she walked around the street floor aimlessly. Then she squared her shoulders and took the escalator to major appliances. All the TV sets were on, and on most of them a caricature was just fading from the screen, to be replaced by a curtain of blue feathers, through which, in a moment, stepped Vera Leopold.

The program and its guest had been mentioned in the paper the night before. Polly was sure Bill hadn't seen it—he liked only the sports and farm pages—so there was no need to tell him what she was going to do. She waited stolidly through Vera's opening remarks and some commercials, and then leaned forward.

"Last week," Vera said, "after that much-talked-about session of the Gray hearing, Cayla Hayward explained to reporters how Polly Whiting could have learned all about the contents of the witch-letter written by her ancestor. I know you know all about that letter, because every paper in the country has printed it! Ms. Hayward gave her explanation, a psychiatrist joined her, and today he is my guest. A man who has been called on more than once to expose psychic phenomena, will you welcome please Dr. Stefan Veere!"

Polly crossed her arms and gripped her elbows as he appeared. For a while he and Vera talked about the growing numbers of people who believed in some kind of psychic power or events and why they did so. "For many people," he said, "it's easier to let some kind of magic explain things than it is for them to face up to the job of trying to understand them—and sometimes to the pain of accepting them. The death of a loved one, for instance—how much easier to believe you can go to séances and still talk to him or her."

Polly inhaled sharply.

"But," he went on, "psychic phenomena like that are all hoaxes. None of them have ever stood up to scientific testing. As a matter of fact, for many years a well-known magician has offered ten thousand dollars to anyone who could produce an authentic psychic manifestation under properly observed and controlled conditions, and the man still has all his money. Yet these beliefs go on and on, no matter how often they get debunked, and turn up every season on TV as the latest wonder."

"Why do they?" Vera Leopold asked.

"Because most people are not very good observers to begin with. On top of that, they know little about sleight-of-hand and deception, so they're easy to fool. And on top of *that,* a lot of people just plain want to believe. It's always been that way. You probably think of the Renaissance, for instance, as a great period of reason and science, and of course it was. But belief in the occult flourished then. Or look at how the modern spiritualist movement began, in the mid-nineteenth century—right in the middle of the Industrial Revolution, by the way—when a family in an upstate New York farmhouse started hearing a lot of mysterious rappings. It seems that the two young daughters, Katie and Margaret Fox, were able to decipher them and communicate with the ghost of a peddler who'd been murdered on the property. Only it turned out the girls were doing it all themselves—producing so-called spirit raps by cracking the joints of their knees and toes. Adolescent girls are particularly prone to that kind of mischievous activity, by the way. One of the Fox sisters confessed everything publicly when she was an old woman, but a lot of people simply refuse to believe the confession. The spiritualist craze went on, and today the Fox cottage is a spiritualist shrine."

Inside her worn shoes Polly wriggled the toes of her left foot. Soon Vera Leopold moved to the primary reason for her quest's appearance. "Not let me see if I've got this explanation about Polly Whiting straight," she said. "According to you and Ms. Hayward, Polly's mother had a good friend who worked for the Haywards up in their family mansion. And that woman was friendly with one of the other Hayward servants, who knew all about the witch-letter."

"Yes. In fact she had memorized it."

"So then the woman who was the friend of Polly Whiting's

mother went back to her hometown, where she saw a lot of Polly as a little girl and could have told her all about the letter."

"That's right."

"But you can't *know* that it happened. The woman is dead."

"It's true she can't ever testify, but in this context it's quite enough to show that Ms. Whiting had access to the material that was supposed to have come to her supernaturally."

"And she never said anything in her trances that wasn't in the letter?"

"Or couldn't easily be inferred from it."

"How about the Scottish accent?"

"Don't you think most people hear a Scottish accent at some point in their lives? On TV, if not in real life? I'm just thinking, for instance, that one of the clerks at my local grocery has a very heavy burr, and so does my accountant's wife."

Vera Leopold frowned and adjusted her huge glasses with one finger. "Yet you said you don't think Polly Whiting was deliberately trying to hoax anybody."

"No, I don't. I was one of those who hypnotized her when she came to New York to be tested, and she exhibited genuine age regression in regard to her own life. I think the Kella Hagaward material came forth without her conscious will or awareness."

"But why would it do that?"

"I don't actually know, Ms. Leopold, because I'm—"

"Vera, please! Call me Vera."

"All right. The fact is that I'm not Polly Whiting's psychiatrist and if I were, I could hardly be discussing her with you, Vera, or with anybody else. All I can do is call your attention to some facts that are public knowledge. For one, Ms. Whiting belongs to a fun damentalist religious group. Two, those groups are opposed to 'tampering with life.' And finally, it's widely known that Hay ward Industries is involved in genetic engineering."

"Are you saying Polly Whiting produced her Haywar witch-voice in order to attack genetic engineering?"

Watching, Polly shook her head slowly from side to side.

"I don't say that was her motive. I don't *know* what he motive was. And I really can't speculate about it, beyond wha I've already said."

Vera Leopold patted her beehive hairdo. "Well, whatever was, how could it all happen unconsciously? Isn't that wha you said, that it was all unconscious?"

"The human mind is incredibly complex, and we're only beginning to understand some of its workings. There are many we simply don't understand at all. Hypnosis, for example—nobody really knows how it works, or why. We only know that it does. And it can make extraordinary things happen. Recently I read about a man who, under hypnosis, could speak phrases in a pre-Christian Italian dialect that he swore he had never learned. But then investigation showed that he once had seen a grammar book of that language, lying open in a library. So obviously he had memorized the words subconsciously, without knowing he knew them until they emerged under hypnosis."

Vera Leopold pursed her lips. "I don't know," she said. "This whole Polly Whiting business—if you have to explain it by saying her mother's friend *could* have heard the witch-letter and then *could* have talked about it to Polly when she was a child, and then Polly forgot she knew it, but somehow, thirty or forty years later, it just happened to come out when she was hypnotized, without her realizing where she got it, and it came out in a perfect Scottish accent that she must have heard somewhere . . . Well, I mean, it's all so complicated and farfetched that I bet a lot of people would say the reincarnation explanation is easier to accept."

There was applause from the studio audience. Polly lifted her hands as if she were going to clap, too, but she only locked her fingers.

Stefan smiled. "I told you a lot of people find it easier to believe in magic and the supernatural." He leaned forward, and the camera moved in tight on his face. "Look, coincidences do happen. Thomas Jefferson and John Adams both died fifty years to the day after the country was founded, on the Fourth of July. A meteorite crashed in a Connecticut town twice in seven years—in locations only a mile apart. A number of ships and airplanes disappeared in an area around Bermuda. The issue is what you make of such things. Do you *accept* the fact that they happen, or do you look to the supernatural and the occult for explanations? That's the point Ms. Hayward made in her Senate testimony. You can choose to believe either way. But if you choose the occult, you're its prisoner, because you've surrendered your mind's power to deal with the world."

Although the program went on, Polly was no longer listening. She turned away, her eyes as blank as blue glass, and walked slowly to the escalator.

She wandered around Sears for a while. In the women's clothing department she stood before a full-length mirror, staring at the plain, awkward creature who looked back, shoulders slumping and hands plunged deep into the pockets of a print dress. When a saleslady tried to speak to her, she turned and walked away.

On the way home she forgot to buy flour and lard, but Bill didn't say anything about it.

That night in bed, when he was half asleep, she suddenly said, "She's not coming anymore, Bill. I can tell. She's going to leave me alone. She's gone."

"That's good, Poll. Real good."

"It was God punishing me. All along that's what it was."

"Punishing you?" he said groggily. "What for?"

But she didn't answer. Long after he was snoring, she lay staring into the dark, her hands clenched.

"How could you do it, Cayla?" Aunt Isobel asked. "How *could* you?"

Isobel sat in the living room of the Park Avenue mansion twisting her string of pearls as if to punish them. Most of the rest of the clan was there, too, in similar states of agitation.

"How could you exhibit your own mother in front of the whole country that way?" Aunt Dru asked.

"Such a shock to hear about it all on TV," said Aunt Sylvia.

"Be fair now," said Aunt Grace. "She did warn us there'd be some family revelations at the hearing, and then she sent that letter explaining all about the adoption and the twins."

"But think of the publicity!" Isobel said. "Mother and Father must be spinning in their graves."

Cayla, who was once again sitting on the claw-footed burgundy velvet sofa in the center of the room, leaned against its plump, hard back and regarded her relatives. "Did you ever consider that if we hadn't all been so terrified of publicity, the whole situation might never have occurred? Everybody was trying to keep secrets. Gran kept it secret that Mother was adopted, which kept anyone from learning she had a twin sister. The letter was kept secret for decades because Gran's husband and father were afraid it would embarrass the Industries. But if it *hadn't* been a secret, everyone would have known whe

Polly Whiting got her information, and no one would have paid much attention to her and the curse nonsense. Then there's Mother's illness. We were all keeping it a secret, as if it were something filthy and shameful. That's the way Senator Bell talked about it in the hearing, but wasn't he just echoing the way we felt about it ourselves? In effect, he took his cue from us."

"But you just don't *do* that—get your name in the papers," Isobel persisted.

Grace snorted. "Oh, back off, Isobel. Cayla did what she had to do, and as far as I'm concerned, it took guts."

"Yes," said Uncle Frank, speaking for the first time, "but how will it affect the Industries? What's the Gray committee going to recommend?"

"I'm quite certain they won't call for a moratorium on the use of recombinant DNA. Our Washington people say the most likely recommendation will be something on the order of 'we must all be watchful.' Of course there'll still be concern about how the technology is used, and I suppose we haven't heard the last of the fundamentalist objections to it. Or to a lot of other things. But maybe the scientific community was jolted a bit. Maybe they'll realize they have to do a better job of telling the public what science is and does."

"That's all well and good," Dru said, "but what if that baby is born with the Tay-Sachs disease after all? Or what if it turns out to be some kind of monster? *Then* there'll be trouble."

"There's absolutely no reason to expect the latter, and very little more to expect the former."

"But how can you be so sure?"

Cayla sighed. "As I was saying, the public needs to know more about science."

There was silence.

"Where have you been since the hearing?" Sylvia snapped. I tried a hundred times to reach you."

"I was with a friend."

"Male?" said one of Sylvia's daughters.

Cayla smiled. "Definitely." When the clan raised its collective eyebrows, she added, "I guess you may as well know, because he's going to be part of my life. It's Stefan Veere."

"Well!" said Isobel, and the word went around the room like a slow echo.

Finally Grace said, "But he's the one whose grandmother was . . . You said in your letter . . ."

Dru cut in. "He's your first cousin. You won't be able to marry him, you know."

"I don't see why not. We shouldn't have children, but there's no reason we couldn't be married if we wanted it. Actually we haven't discussed it. Marriage isn't the first thing people think of today. Or even the last."

"Well!" Isobel said again. After a pause she added, "Whatever you do, I just hope it doesn't get into the newspapers."

Cayla was still smiling as she walked uptown toward Stefan's office.

When she got there, his secretary-receptionist had left for the day but the door to the inner office was closed, so she knew he must be with his last patient.

She sat in one of the dark-green suede chairs and looked at the magazines on an end table. One of them, dated the week before, had her picture on the cover, with a legend in the corner GENE-SPLICING'S FIERY DEFENDER. The adjective still seemed inappropriate to her. What mattered was not fire, or the lack of it, but the logic of the argument. When she said that to Stefan he had laughed and said, "Did you ever think that maybe logic could be fiery?"

She knew what he thought. If he was right, if somewhere deep in her psyche she had equated strong feeling with being out of control, the equation was so longstanding that it felt like part of her identity. Probably she would never change, not in fundamental way. Where he could be open with such ease, she probably would always have to fight an inner obstacle course and she would often lose.

Unless she was not allowing for the influence of Stefan Veere on her life.

The door to his office opened, and her spirit leaped as if she were the child she had never been permitted to be.

But it was a woman who emerged, a woman in her thirties who had obviously been crying. She gave Cayla a look that expected to find a kindred spirit's but stopped instead, as if puzzled to see such an expression in a psychiatrist's waiting room. Then she secured her purse under her arm and went out slowly.

There was silence for five minutes, which to Cayla were the

272

longest of the day. Finally he called, "Are you out there?" When she said, "Of course," he told her to come in.

He was at his desk, putting away a folder. She went to him, framed his face in her hands, and kissed him, but his lips were almost impersonal, and she knew he was still deep in the world of his work. "Hard day?" she said.

"Yes. The last four patients without a break." He stretched his arms high and then pushed back the sleeve of the yellow shirt he wore under a brown sweater-vest.

She took the chair across the desk. "Would you like to go home and rest for a while?"

"No. I'd like to sit here and look at you."

He did just that, leaning back in the chair with his arms behind his head, his eyes on hers and his mouth promising a smile but not yet ready to give it.

"The patient who just left," Cayla said, "she looked so wretched. Are they all that unhappy?"

"Today most of them were."

"Did you help them?"

"Well, not all of them. But I did get one man to see that the reason his highly successful life seems so empty is because he isn't doing what he really wants—which is something he's always regarded as unimportant. When the realization came, he burst into tears." Stefan hesitated. "One of the others was a woman who is desperate to have a child and has just found out she can't."

"Ah," Cayla said softly.

They looked at each other for a moment. "We really should talk about it," he said.

"I suppose we should." She reached over to put a hand on one of his. "I never really thought of having children. I never expected to find a man who would make me think of them. I don't know that I would have wanted them, but now, to be forced into that decision by genetics—that's terribly ironic. And cruel. I don't like it. I want us to be free to make the choice."

He covered her hand with his. "But we can't. So does it mean we should leave each other?"

"That's another choice I'm not free to make, now."

But then, because she had spoken from somewhere deep inside herself, from the heart of her feelings, she had to pull back. She freed her hand and said, "This morning I finally got

273

to see a tape of the Vera Leopold show. She didn't want to give up the notion of Kella's reincarnation, did she?"

"Nor did a lot of the audience. And she made sure to remind them that the book about Polly will be out shortly. *Mundus vult decipi.*"

"You were very effective, of course. No, I shouldn't say 'of course.' That sounds as if I take your virtues for granted." He smiled, faintly. "The explanation you suggested for Polly's behavior—is that what you really think? That she did it out of some religious need to attack genetic engineering?"

"I think it's very likely, but I doubt it's the whole story."

"What else?"

"Oh, she could have a strong subconscious need to dramatize herself. Or a need for attention and approval, which she couldn't let herself know. She's a very unattractive woman, and she could have a great, unrequited desire to be the center of things. God knows she succeeded at that—she got the whole country talking about her. Then there's the obvious candidate, sex. If Polly is one of those deeply religious people who think sex is ugly and evil—and if she enjoys sex herself, which would give her a profound inner conflict—the attitude or the conflict could manifest itself in the form of descriptions of carnal traffic with Satan. Or, don't forget why she was at Camp Red Cloud— she had a child who died. But since there's no record of any child who died after she married Bill Whiting, it probably was illegitimate, born before her marriage. That could have been a great trauma. Maybe she buried her suffering and shame deeper and deeper, and years later, under the pressure of her religious ideas, they connected with the memory of the locket, which we assume Cora Trent gave her. Don't forget that the locket contained a baby's nail parings. And don't forget that under hypnosis she talked about a six-toed child."

"How could I?" Cayla said. "Hearing her say it made me leave the room—and got me rescued by you."

Stefan smiled again. This time it was full-bodied.

He got up, came around the desk, and pulled her to her feet and close to him. His lips were no longer impersonal.

After a while she murmured, "Is it always going to be like this?"

"I think so. Why don't we find out?"

EPILOGUE

The journalist, who worked free-lance, had recently returned from several months in the States and was so happy to be back in Edinburgh, renewing his acquaintance with various lady friends, pubs and restaurants, that it was several weeks before he got around to doing the checking he had planned.

Though the American press, or at least one element of it, had given the story a lot of play, he found virtually no mention of it in the Scottish papers—just a back-pages paragraph here and there. That was all to the good. If he worked up a nice magazine piece, it would be fresh to the editors who usually bought from him.

His first task was to talk to the man, a professor, who had located some records confirming the fact that an actual Kella Hagaward was burned as a witch in Dumfriesshire in 1643. The professor turned out to be a soft-spoken, white-haired old chap whose specialty was the seventeenth century. And it turned out that the records he had found, in a book written in 1679, did more than confirm the burning.

It cost the journalist three and a half hours in an office piled so high with books that it gave him vertigo, listening to the old chap talk on and on about the century in which he had spent most of his life—"A terrible pestilence appeared in Dumfries in 1598, you know, which spread over the whole countryside and lasted for a decade." But the time was well spent, for he left with a copy of everything relevant to his purpose. He had had to copy it all out in longhand, though, because the old boy wouldn't permit the book to go into a copying machine.

That night the journalist studied what he had copied. Grisly, the whole business was. There was even a list of the expenses incurred. The district had condemned many witches and therefore needed items such as "A dozen loads of coal, to burn them, 4 pounds, 3 shillings."

It was unclear whether the reference to Kella had been written by someone who had attended her trial or was based on secondhand reports, but it certainly confirmed the contents of the letter she had written:

> Kella Hagaward, a comely widow of eight-and-thirty years, was accused of bewitching the milk-cows of the brother of her husband, of making her nieces to fall into strange fits and at times be unable to move their limbs, of causing the death of one Parson Mitchell, and of sundry other evil deeds. Being a woman of great hardness of spirit, she suffered the Turkas and the Pilliwinks and even the Pulley and was examined by the Witchfinder-General himself, all without making a confession. But at length she did confess of trafficking with Satan and many times attending his Sabbats, there committing acts of great blasphemy. She was put to the fire, but without the mercy of strangulation, on 19 August, 1643.

The journalist shuddered. Pilliwinks, the old historian had explained, were thumbscrews, and the turkas was like a pair of pincers, with which they pulled off people's nails. He made himself a stiff drink, brooded for a while on the infinite human capacity for cruelty, and then took out the file he had brought from the States. It contained clippings with the Kella Hagaward letter and even transcripts from the Society of Parapsychologists of all the Polly Whiting trance-sessions that had been taped. Those had taken some fancy talking to obtain.

He laid everything out in front of him and let his eyes and mind wander over it all.

In ten minutes he stopped, his face immobile. He separated out several of the papers and went over them very carefully. When he was finished, he lifted his head and stared into space. Then he checked the papers one more time.

It was true. In the Kella Hagaward letter, the pilliwinks were not referred to by that name, and the turkas wasn't mentioned at all. But in Polly Whiting's sessions the voice of Kella Hagaward had used both words.

How could the Whiting woman have known words that were

not in the Hagaward letter if that letter was the source of what she said under hypnosis?

She must have seen the words somewhere, sometime, in a book about witchcraft. Of course.

But for her to have picked out just those two words, which were now validated by the historical record . . .

Oh, it had to be a coincidence.

But wasn't it just too much of a coincidence?

ABOUT THE AUTHOR

The winner of an Edgar Allan Poe Award for her first novel, THE WATCHER, in 1981, Kay Nolte Smith has a multifaceted background, having worked as an actress, an advertising copywriter, a journalist—with articles appearing in VOGUE and OPERA NEWS, among other publications—a theater and film critic for Ayn Rand's magazine, THE OBJECTIVIST, a teacher, and a theater producer. Her second novel, CATCHING FIRE, was published in 1982, and her short stories have been anthologized and published abroad. Between novels she steals time to work on her translations from the French of plays by Edmond Rostand. She lives near the New Jersey college where her husband, Phillip J. Smith, teaches.

KEEPING YOU ON THE EDGE OF YOUR SEAT...

Spellbinding suspense from Ballantine Books